Virginia Andrews is a worldwide bestselling author. Her much-loved novels include *Melody, Heart Song, Music in the Night* and *Olivia*. Virginia Andrews' novels have sold more than eighty million copies and have been translated into twenty-two foreign languages.

# VIRGINIA ANDREWS®

# UNFINISHED SYMPHONY

POCKET
BOOKS

LONDON • SYDNEY • NEW YORK • TORONTO

First published in Great Britain by Simon & Schuster UK Ltd, 1998
This edition published by Pocket Books, 2004
An imprint of Simon & Schuster UK Ltd
A Viacom Company

Copyright © by the Virginia C. Andrews Trust
and The Vanda General Partnership, 1997

1 3 5 7 9 10 8 6 4 2

Simon & Schuster UK Ltd
Africa House
64–78 Kingsway
London WC2B 6AH

www.simonsays.co.uk

Simon & Schuster Australia
Sydney

A CIP catalogue record for this book is available from the British Library

ISBN 978-1-8473-9302-9

This book is a work of fiction. Names, characters, places and incidents are
either a product of the author's imagination or are used fictitiously. Any
resemblance to actual people living or dead, events or locales is entirely
coincidental.

Printed and bound in Denmark by
Nørhaven Paperback A/S

# Prologue

&

The New York City skyline took my breath away. As Holly and I approached the sparkling city, I reflected on the rush of events that had brought me all this way. Too excited to rest yet too tired to talk with Holly, I decided to write Alice Morgan and thank her for sending the picture that had catapulted me into this odyssey, this journey to find my past.

*Dear Alice,*

*Thank you, thank you, thank you for sending me that clothing catalogue with the picture of the model who looked just like my mother. Kenneth and I agreed with you, and Kenneth contacted the catalogue company and they gave him the name of the model, Gina Simon, and her address. And you'll never guess where I'm headed right this very minute as I write this letter. Los Angeles! Hollywood! Well, actually, I'm in New York City now (or driving through it at least—we just passed the Empire State Building!). Kenneth's friend Holly offered to drive* me to New York, and then Holly's sister Dorothy and her husband, Peter, have volunteered to let me stay with them in Beverly Hills. Can you believe it?

I'm a little scared to be traveling so far on a dream, though. What if this Gina Simon just turns out to be a woman who looks a lot like Mommy? Or maybe even worse, what if she is my mother? What does that mean? Then who is buried in her grave in Provincetown? And why hasn't she let me know that she's okay, that she really didn't die in that car crash? Maybe she got sick and lost her memory. If Mommy has amnesia she might need me now more than ever. I just have to go. I have to have the answers to all these questions.

You would think that with all the excitement of finding a clue about my mother I would be happier. But leaving Provincetown almost broke my heart. I know when I last wrote you I told you that I was lonely, and that Grandma Olivia was giving me a hard time, and that certainly hasn't changed, but Cary and I have grown so close that it was painful to leave him. And to watch little May cry as she waved good-bye was just awful. They really have become like family to me. And Cary, of course, has become much more. I'll have to tell you all about it when we talk.

Well, Alice, I hope to have news for you soon, and I hope you are enjoying life back in Sewell. I really do miss West Virginia. And you of course! Say hi to everyone at school and keep your fingers crossed!

Love,
Melody

# 1
## ஐ

# A Glimpse into the Future

Holly's crystal shop looked small inside because every available space was utilized. The air reeked of incense and there was some kind of Far Eastern music playing. Large crystals, all shiny and jagged, stood on antique tables at the center of the shop and tall oak bookshelves lined the side walls. I turned my gaze to the books alongside me and noticed that the shelves were filled with titles describing meditation practices, astrology, faith healing, the afterlife and paraphysical wonders, whatever they were.

Along the back wall was a long glass case crowded with birth stones, as well as amethyst, blue topaz, citrine, garnet and other minerals set in earrings. On the shelves behind the glass case were boxes of incense, teas, Tarot cards and herbal medicines. The ceiling was covered with charts of the constellations, along with posters explaining the powers of various stones. Above the cash register, framed in flowers, was a photograph of a man Holly said was the Buddhist guru who had taught her about meditation. A curtain of multicolored

3

beads hung in the doorway that led to the rooms in back of the shop.

We'd only been in the shop a few moments when a young man in a wheelchair, whom I knew had to be Billy Maxwell, parted the curtain and appeared. He had silky ebony hair that reached his shoulders and framed his face, a face that had an angelic glow because of his rich, almost alabaster complexion. As soon as he saw us, his light green eyes brightened and a gentle smile appeared on his face. Perhaps because of his disability and dependence upon his arms and shoulders, his upper body was firm, muscular, obvious even in his loose, light blue shirt. He wore a pair of dark jeans, white socks and sneakers. There was a large, round gem in a gold casing dangling on a gold chain around his neck and his right ear was pierced and filled with a turquoise stone earring.

"Hi, Billy," Holly said as he wheeled himself closer, his eyes fixed on me.

"Hi. You got here earlier than I expected. How was your trip?" he asked her, while still concentrating on me.

"Good. This is Melody."

"Pleased to meet you," Billy said, extending his hand. He had long, soft fingers and a palm that was warm against mine.

"Hi," I said. There seemed to be such peacefulness in his face, a calmness that helped me feel at home.

"So you're on a big journey," he said, sitting back.

"Yes," I answered, unable to hide my nervousness.

"The Chinese say a journey of a thousand miles begins with a single step and you've taken that single step. That's usually the hardest," he added. "Now the momentum will take over and carry you to where you have to go."

I nodded and then glanced at Holly, not sure what I should say or do. She laughed.

"You'll get some good advice here, Melody. Billy's the best tour guide in our galaxy."

4

Billy smiled but kept his eyes on me. It was strange, having him look at me so intently, but I didn't feel intimidated or self-conscious. I felt his sincerity, his concern and it was as if he and I had known each other for years instead of minutes.

"What's been happening here?" Holly asked before we started across the shop.

"Well, Mrs. Hadron's daughter gave birth prematurely early this morning, but the baby is doing well. She stopped by to thank us for the smoky quartz—it really helped her daughter get through the crisis. And Mr. Brul was here this morning to tell you that the variscite helped him recall a past life. He had vivid details to share."

"Past life?" I asked.

"Yes. He saw himself in England, mid-nineteenth century. He said he was a bookkeeper, which made sense to him. He's an accountant now."

"You mean you believe we all have former lives?" I asked, looking from him to Holly and then back to him.

"Yes," Billy said smiling. "I have no doubt."

"Well, for now we'll have to concentrate on her present life," Holly said. "This way, honey."

"I'm sorry I can't help with your bags," Billy apologized.

"We'll be fine," Holly replied. "See you in a few minutes."

"Welcome again, Melody, and don't worry. There is good energy surrounding you." His eyes grew small. "Things will work out for you," he said with confidence. It was as if he really could look into the future.

"Thank you," I said.

The door chimes rang as two elderly women entered the shop. While Billy attended to them, Holly led me through the curtain of beads to the living quarters at the rear of the shop.

"Our rooms are right back here," she explained. I followed her through the doorway to a short hallway.

There was a small living room on the right with a sofa, a smaller settee, two easy chairs, a glass table and two standing lamps.

"This is Billy's bedroom," she said nodding at the first door on the left. "It makes it easier for him to be closest to the shop. I have the next room and you can take this room across the hall," she said opening the door.

It was a very small room with one window that opened on the rear of the building. There wasn't much to look at: just a driveway that provided access to garbage trucks and a small, fenced in area for someone's dog. The dog was in its doghouse at the moment, with just its large black paws visible. The window had light brown cotton curtains and a window shade with a quarter moon and a star painted on it. There was a large ball-shaped mauve candle on the nightstand. The dark pine bed had a light brown comforter and matching pillows. It looked comfortable. Actually, the room was cozy with its tan carpet, its dark pink walls, lamp, rocking chair, table and matching dark pine dresser. A set of chimes dangled in the corner above the chair, barely moving at the moment.

"This room gets a lot of use," Holly explained. "Many people who belong to our network of friends pass through New York going one way or another and stop over for a short visit. I know it's small but . . ."

"It's fine, Holly. Thank you."

"Why don't you just settle in. The bathroom's at the end of the hallway. Freshen up. I'll do the same and call my sister. Then we'll have some dinner. Billy does all the cooking, you know."

"Really?"

"And he's quite the gourmet."

"I forgot what you told me about why he's in a wheelchair. Did you say he was shot?"

"Mugged, about five years ago not that far from here. He ran and the mugger shot at him and shattered Billy's spinal cord."

6

"How horrible, but I'm glad you told me. I didn't want to say anything wrong."

"Don't worry about that. Billy is quite at peace with himself and his condition. Because of his spirituality, he pities more people than pity him. I can't think of a moment when he was depressed these past few years. Anyone who comes in here feeling the least bit sorry for himself usually leaves feeling ashamed of his own self-pity after they talk to Billy. And he's a wonderful poet, published in many literary magazines. We'll get him to read you something later."

Holly put her arm around my shoulders and squeezed.

"Just like Billy said, everything's going to turn out fine, Melody."

I nodded. The discoveries, the quick decision to make the journey and the ride to New York, as well as how overwhelming the city was, suddenly filled me with a deep fatigue. I felt my body sink, my legs soften, my eyelids turn to lead.

"Take a rest," Holly wisely advised. As soon as she left me I lay down and dropped my head to the pillow.

A tinkle, like the sound of glasses being jiggled in a dishwasher tray, woke me. For a few seconds, I didn't know where I was. The sun had gone down and the room was filled with shadows. Someone had come in while I was asleep and turned on the small lamp by the rocking chair. I sat up to grind the sleep out of my eyes. The window was slightly open and the breeze that passed through made the chimes hanging from the ceiling tap, which solved the mystery of the sound.

I heard a gentle knock at the door.

"Yes?"

Holly, dressed in one of her bright yellow dresses with a yellow and green headband, her silver crystal earrings dangling down to her shoulders, poked her head through the open door.

"You've been sleeping quite a while. Getting hungry?"

7

"Yes," I said.

"Good. I spoke to my sister Dorothy and everything is set. As soon as we know when your flight arrives, I'll call her and she and her driver will meet you at the airport. My friend is working on the ticket now and promises to call within the hour. Billy's been preparing a feast. Freshen up and come out when you're ready," she said.

"Thank you, Holly."

"You're welcome sweetheart. Oh," she said before closing the door again, "I spoke to Kenneth. He sends his regards and his best wishes," she added, but I picked up a change in her tone.

"Was something wrong?"

"He just sounded a little down. Maybe he misses us. Misses you, especially," she offered.

"He's probably working twenty hours a day."

"Twenty? More like twenty-two," she said with a small laugh. Then she closed the door and I got up and opened my suitcase to pick out something to wear. After I had washed up, fixed my hair, and changed, I went out to the kitchen. The aroma of the food was tantalizing and made my stomach churn. Billy, bent over a table obviously built lower to accommodate him in his wheelchair, turned as I entered. Holly was in the shop with a customer.

"Hi. How are you doing?" Billy asked.

"I feel better after my nap. Looks like I slept longer than I thought I would. Can I help?"

"Everything's done," he said nodding at the table he had set. "Holly will close the shop in about ten minutes and we'll have dinner. Oh, let me light the candles," he said. "I like to dim the room when we eat. It heightens the sense of taste when you diminish the power of the other senses. Did you know that?"

"No."

"It's true," he said, laughing at my skepticism. "Didn't you ever notice that food tastes better in the dark? Assuming it's good food, that is." He lit each candle and then returned to his work table.

8

"How long have you been cooking?"

"Since I became a vegetarian. It's just a lot easier to cook for yourself and besides, preparing good food is an art and very self-satisfying. Most people today think it's an ordeal, but that's because they don't take pride in what they do. They don't look for the essence, the inner rewards. Life for them is full of burdens. They're never at ease and they rarely enjoy their own accomplishments. Their days are full of stress and negative energy."

He turned back to me.

"I don't mean to bore you with a lecture. Holly says once I get started, I'm like a clock that won't wind down."

"No, really, I don't mind," I said. "Why are you a vegetarian?"

Billy paused in his food preparation and turned his chair so he could face me.

"I follow many Buddhist traditions and consider all animal life sacred, but other religious groups practice vegetarianism as well. In the Roman Catholic Church, for example, it has been practiced monastically by Trappists since 1666 and among Protestants by Seventh-Day Adventists. I believe that the killing of animals is unnecessary and cruel and can conceivably lead to disregard for human life. It's also a healthier way to live, as long as you don't neglect your protein."

He smiled.

"Now you think I'm some sort of kook, right?"

"No," I said, "but I know a lot of people in Cape Cod who would be unhappy if people stopped eating fish."

"Oh, well, for that I make an exception," he said with a wink. "I'll eat net-caught fish on occasion, as long as I know there are no chemicals added."

"Something smells very good," I admitted.

"Tonight's menu," Billy announced, sitting up straighter in his chair. "We shall begin with chilled okra-yogurt soup, then an orange, walnut and romaine salad, followed by rice, carrot, mushroom and pecan burgers

9

on toasted seven-grain bread. For dessert, I have prepared a carob cake with carob ricotta icing. Something special in celebration of your arrival," he added.

My silence brought laughter to his lips.

"Don't know what you're in for, huh?" he said.

"It sounds . . . interesting," I said, and he laughed harder.

"What's going on in here?" Holly asked as she entered the room.

"I just described the menu to Melody and she was speechless. Then she said it was interesting. How's that for diplomacy?"

"Oh. Don't worry, Melody. You're in for a delightful surprise," Holly promised.

"Did you close up?" Billy asked. She nodded.

"Then let the feast begin," he declared, slapping his hands together.

Once again I asked to help, but Billy insisted I was the guest of honor. It amazed me how quickly he could move about the kitchen, spinning himself on the wheels of his chair. Holly turned the lights down and took her seat.

The soup was delicious and refreshing. The salad was very good, but I was most surprised by the vegetable burgers because they did resemble meat in their texture and even their flavor.

"How do you do this?" I asked, munching away.

"He has magic hands," Holly said.

Billy asked questions about Cape Cod, my life there and my life before in Sewell, West Virginia. He was a good listener, absorbing every detail. Occasionally, he and Holly exchanged a look that told me they had discussed me and my situation at length.

"You have to realize," he said when I completed my explanation as to why I was on this trip, "that places change people. We react to our environment, to the other people around us, to the climate and especially to the sort of energy force that is there. Even if this woman is your mother, she might be more of a stranger to you now than you would expect."

"I hope not," I said mournfully.

"Just be prepared," Billy advised.

"I don't know how to prepare for something like that."

"Maybe I can help you," he said, his eyes intense.

The telephone rang and Holly spoke to her travel agent friend. When she hung up, she told me my flight was set for the day after tomorrow.

"It will bring you into Los Angeles about eleven A.M. Pacific time. I'll call Dorothy and give her the flight number and time," she added, returning to the phone. My heart began to pound now that my plans were becoming a reality. When I looked at Billy, I saw he was smiling softly at me, his eyes full of comfort. It helped me relax again.

This time when Holly hung up, she shook her head.

"Dorothy will take you to some Beverly Hills restaurant for lunch, where you will eat a piece of celery and a cupful of pasta for a hundred dollars, I'm sure," she said. "Think of my sister as someone who has to be humored. La La Land is just Disneyland for the rich and famous."

"Oh, now let her make her own conclusions, Holly," Billy said charitably. "Who knows? She may enjoy that world."

"Not this down-to-earth girl. You listen to me, Melody. Get in and get out. Find out what you have to find out and if it isn't what you expected or what you want, put yourself on the next plane out and come back here if you like before you return to Cape Cod," Holly said. "Also, ignore ninety percent of what my sister tells you and be skeptical about the other ten percent."

The phone rang again. Holly spoke to someone for a few moments and then, when she hung up, she announced she had to leave for a while.

"I have to do an astrological reading for someone. It's way past due. I hate to leave you your first night here, but . . ."

"She'll be fine," Billy said.

"Will you read her one of your poems?"

11

"If she would like," he replied, turning to me.

"Oh yes, please," I said. "But I insist that you let me help clean up."

"No problem. I'm a gourmet cook and all gourmet cooks let people help clean up."

He and Holly laughed and I smiled widely. I had been in New York only a few hours, but I felt more at home here than I had at the homes of my so-called relatives and family. Maybe Billy was right; maybe there was such a thing as positive energy and maybe he would give me enough to help me get through the dark valleys and tunnels that loomed ahead. The question was, would I find any light at the end?

After I straightened up the kitchen and put dishes and cooking implements away, I stopped by the living room where Billy sat gazing at a notebook in his lap.

"Come on in," he said. "I was sitting here thinking about what I had written that would be most appropriate for your circumstances and it's taken me all the way back to my rebirth."

"Rebirth?"

He nodded and flicked some strands of hair from his eyes. He had that soft, angelic smile on his lips again. I had never met anyone who seemed so at peace with himself. It reminded me of the deep calm before a storm, when the whole world seemed to be holding its breath. Cary called it Mother Nature's deception, claiming she tricked us into believing all was well just before she sent the furies down around us.

"Yes, rebirth, for I was dead to so much before my . . . my death," he said. "I was like most people, blind and deaf, confused by the clatter and noise, chasing material things, living on the lowest level and never hearing the song."

"The song?"

"The spiritual song, the voice deep within us all, the voice that links us to each other, to every living and even

12

non-living thing. Even the man who shot me is part of this overall spiritual essence, and in that sense, we're part of each other, forever."

"Did they catch him?"

"No, but that doesn't matter. He shot himself when he shot me. We're eternally tied together by that act."

"You mean you could forgive him for it?" I asked, astounded.

"Of course. There's nothing to forgive. The negative energy that was in him is what must be driven away. He was captured, a prisoner of that, just as I was captured and for a while made prisoner by the bullet that shattered my spine."

"How can you be so positive?" I asked with curious astonishment.

"I was lying on my hospital bed, feeling terribly sorry for myself, cataloguing all the things I would no longer be able to do, regretting how much I was dependent on other people, in truth, wishing I would die," he explained, "when suddenly Holly stopped at my bed accompanied by her guru, an elderly man from India who had eyes like crystals themselves. It was part of their charity work to visit the infirm and give sick people hope. Right from the start, I felt something about him, some inner strength that he was able to share with me, instill in me. He taught me how to meditate and opened the doors to my new self. I dedicated my first poem to him. He has since gone back to India. That's a picture of him in the shop.

"After that Holly came to me and offered me a job in her shop and I agreed. I've been here ever since.

"Let's see," he said, flipping the pages. "Ah, yes. This was when I first began to write poems. I wasn't working here long. I had read some poetry in this Village newspaper and thought I would like to try putting my thoughts down, too. Want to hear it?"

"Very much, please."

He stared at the pages for a long, silent moment and then in a very soft, low voice, read.

*"I had come to the end of daylight
and faced the doorway of darkness.
But when I touched my face,
I realized my eyes were closed and my skin was
   cold.
All that I thought I loved and needed was gone
and I was naked, shivering in misery.
They were measuring me for a coffin.
Suddenly, I heard a voice calling from within
   myself.
I turned my eyes around to look back,
to look down, to look deep
and I saw a single candle.
It drew me closer until I could reach out
and put my fingers in the flame.
Slowly, meticulously, I burned away my dead
   body
and when it was gone, I was no longer naked."*

He looked up slowly.

"It's beautiful," I said, "but I'm not sure I understand."

"I had to crawl out of my old, now crippled body, burn it away because it literally imprisoned me. Once I found the inner light, true spirituality, I was able to go beyond the physical body and reach a higher place. Someday, you will too. Everything you love and think you need looks lost. You're on a search because you feel naked, without meaning or hope; but you'll see that you have everything you need inside yourself and you didn't have to take a single step in any direction."

I said nothing. We gazed at each other in the silence and then he smiled.

"You've got that look in your eyes again. You think I'm a kook again."

"No," I said, laughing. "Actually, I hope what you say is true."

"It is, but these are discoveries everyone has to make for himself or herself. I can only show you the way, point you in a direction."

"Is that why Holly called you the best guide in the galaxy?"

"Yes," he said with a laugh. "All right, enough lessons for one evening. Want to go for a walk?"

"A walk?"

He laughed at my surprise.

"Well, you'll walk and push me along," he said.

"Oh. Sure," I said, hoping I hadn't insulted him with my astonishment.

"It's pretty warm out. You don't need a jacket." Without any hesitation, he turned his chair around and wheeled himself out of the living room, through the kitchen and out into the shop. I almost had to run to keep up. We paused outside the door for him to lock it and then he asked me to push him up the street. At the corner, we crossed and went down another street, past the shops, a few restaurants and a small theater. The sidewalks were crowded with well-dressed people, and I enjoyed seeing their glamorous hustle-and-bustle lifestyle.

When we reached the N.Y.U. campus, Billy had me pause to listen to some speakers. Some were making political speeches, others were ranting about the coming of the end of the world. At one corner a man played a guitar and sang folk songs to a small group that had gathered around him. He had his hat before him and people were putting in change and dollars.

Farther down, a group of young men sang spiritual songs a cappella. They were very good and they, too, had a basket out for contributions.

"What do you think?" Billy asked me as we moved down the sidewalk, past homeless people asking for handouts, a man arguing with a tree, and a black boy who looked like he couldn't be more than twelve playing the bongo drums.

"Now I understand why Holly calls New York a carnival of life."

Billy laughed and asked me to wheel him toward a bench where there were no people and little noise. I sat and we watched the traffic, the groups of tourists and city

1 5

dwellers making their way to and from their destinations.

"It was on this corner," he suddenly said.

"What was?"

"Where it happened. I was running in that direction," he nodded to the left. "It was about two in the morning. I was a student here, you know."

"Oh. Doesn't it bother you to come here?"

"No. It intrigues me. I can give you this advice, Melody Logan," he said in a deeper, darker voice that made my spine tingle. "Seize the moment, confront the face of that which frightens you and search until you find a way out. Don't let anything shut you up inside yourself. Wherever you go, whatever you see, when you are most afraid, think of this corner, of those shadows, of me sitting here and staring back through time at myself, at the gunman, at the sound of the pistol, at myself folding on that sidewalk and then, suddenly rising up out of myself and standing taller than before."

He reached out and took my hand and I felt as if his courage and spiritual strength moved into me. I smiled.

"Thank you, Billy."

"Thank yourself, cherish yourself and don't let anyone make you feel small."

He sat back and suddenly looked exhausted, as if he had spent all his energy on me.

"Maybe we should go back now," I suggested. He nodded.

Holly still hadn't returned by the time we arrived.

"Can I help you with anything?" I asked.

"I'll be fine," he said, smiling. "Thank you."

Billy wheeled himself down the corridor, first to the bathroom and then to his room. I prepared for bed myself. As he went by to go to his room, he paused at my door.

"Good night, Melody."

"Good night, Billy," I called. He wheeled into his room and I marveled at how cheerful he was and how well he had driven the shadows of loneliness from his door.

I wasn't in my room five minutes before those shadows began closing in on me. Here I was in a strange place, away from anyone I loved or who loved me, feeling like a wanderer who had lost all sense of direction and no longer knew her way home.

From what well of faith did Billy Maxwell draw so much strength?

I lay there in the dark thinking about Cary, hearing his laughter, recalling flashes of his smile, his beguiling eyes, even his smirk. Thinking about him made me feel better. I closed my eyes and concentrated on the memory of the sound of the ocean, visualized the sight of the tide rushing in to wash the shore.

And soon, the shadows of loneliness sunk back. Sleep, like the tide, washed over me.

I was drifting out.

When I woke the next morning, I was embarrassed by how late I had slept. I practically jumped out of the bed, washed and dressed. Holly and Billy had already opened the shop and were dealing with customers.

"I'm sorry I slept so late," I declared when the customers left.

"That's all right, honey," Holly said. "You must have been exhausted. Billy told me you two went for a walk," she added.

"I guess all the excitement of being in New York tired me out."

"I'll get her some breakfast," Billy called out as he headed for the kitchen.

"I hate being so much trouble."

"You're no trouble. After you have some breakfast, we'll go get your airline tickets," Holly said. "Then, I'd like to show you some of New York. What would you like to see the most?"

"I don't know." My mind reeled with the possibilities, the things and places I had only read about and Alice

17

and I had spoken about back in Sewell when the two of us planned a future trip together. What had once been a childhood fantasy was now a reality for me.

"I guess I'd like to see the Empire State Building and Broadway and the Statue of Liberty and the Museum of Natural History and . . ."

"There's only one day," Holly said, laughing.

"I'll show her most of that," Billy called from the kitchen. "Got some fruit, a bowl of multi-grain cereal, juice and coffee in here waiting on you, Melody."

"You'll show me?" I asked, not hiding my astonishment well. He and Holly looked at each other and then laughed.

"Billy gets around as well as anyone," Holly said. "He has a van with a lift and a specially engineered steering wheel."

"Gift from my parents," he said, and I thought, how strange that he had never mentioned them before.

"I can't take you away from the shop. I . . ."

"What do you mean? I'm due a vacation anyway, aren't I, Holly?"

"More than one," Holly replied. "Better eat breakfast so you can get started," Holly said. "Go on," she urged. "Stop being a worrywart."

I laughed and went in to have my breakfast. Afterward, Holly and I drove over to the travel agency where her friend worked and I picked up my airline tickets. Having them in my hand with the itinerary spelled out before me made me suddenly frightened. Would I really get on that plane tomorrow and fly across the country to stay with people I didn't know and search one of the country's biggest cities for a mother who might not want to see me?

Billy had his van in front of the shop when we returned. He showed me how the lift worked and then took his place in the driver's seat. Holly waved good-bye as we drove off for my tour of New York, Billy looking as excited about it as I was.

"It's always fun to see familiar things through virgin eyes," he explained. "It helps one appreciate what one has more."

Seeing the Empire State Building in the distance was one thing, but to ride right up to it and look up was another.

"You want to go up?" Billy asked.

"Can we?"

"Of course. I'll pull into that parking garage there and we'll take the elevator. It's a beautiful day for it. We'll probably see into Canada."

"We will?"

"No," he said laughing.

"You probably think I'm a country bumpkin," I said, grimacing.

"Absolutely not, and what if you were? It would be refreshing and honest," he replied. Billy could turn anything negative into a positive, I thought. How could anyone be so perfect?

Billy moved about the city as if it were just a small town no bigger than Sewell. The hordes of people, a veritable sea of bodies and faces moving up and down the sidewalks, the legions of cars, the noise and commotion seemed not to exist. He wheeled himself along barely noticing any of it, while my eyes raced back and forth, up and down, taking in everything.

The elevator ride to the observation deck of the Empire State Building was the most exciting I had ever taken, and when we stepped out and over to the railing, I thought we were literally on top of the world. I squealed with amazement. Billy laughed and gave me some change for the telescope through which I could see the Hudson River and clear across to New Jersey.

Afterward, we drove up to Broadway and past all the theater marquees, the great electric signs and through Times Square, a place I had seen only on television and read about in books. My heart pounded with excitement. I couldn't wait to write to Alice. Billy decided we should have lunch in the world famous Chinatown, where he could get his favorite—vegetable lo mein. While we were there, he bought me a beautiful hand-painted fan.

After lunch, we went out to the Statue of Liberty. The sky was still mostly blue and there was a warm breeze from New York Harbor. When we returned to shore, I realized Billy was more tired than he pretended and I told him it was time to go back to the shop, claiming I was tired myself. I wasn't. New York had a way of injecting its energy into me. The panorama of people, things to see and do was mesmerizing and helped me forget all my worries and troubles.

Back at the shop, the three of us sat and had some tea while I ranted on and on about the things we had done and seen. Afterward, Billy went into his room to meditate and Holly and I took care of the customers. I was fascinated with how much people were intrigued by her crystals and gems, how much they wanted to believe in the powers. All sorts of people came in to buy and inquire about the items: old as well as young, men and women alike. Some were frequent customers and many testified to the claims Holly made about her stones.

When Billy emerged from his room, he looked revived. Once again I offered to help him with dinner, but again he told me I was the guest and he enjoyed the preparations. After she closed the shop, Holly and I sat in the living room and relaxed while Billy made dinner. I told her about the poem he had read and the things he had said.

"He's a wonderful person. I'm happy he became my partner."

"He said his parents gave him the van, but he didn't mention any more about his family to me. Where are they?"

Holly grimaced.

"They live upstate and they are quite happy he's not there, too. They don't accept his way of life now. His father calls him a hippie."

"Oh, how sad."

"Billy isn't happy about it, but he's resigned and he accepts it."

"Does he have any brothers and sisters?"

"An older brother, an attorney. He sees him whenever he comes to New York; or, I should say, once in a while when he comes to New York. I don't think he calls every time. He wanted Billy to go home and live with their parents, but Billy won't be treated like some handicapped person, as you've probably already noticed."

"He's amazing," I said. "Inspirational."

Holly nodded. Then she turned a bit serious.

"I've been working on your charts, Melody," she said. "Now that I know more about you and the events, and I can pinpoint things, I can get a clearer picture."

"And?"

"I don't think you're going to find what you want," she said gently. "Maybe you should turn around and return to the life you have, the people you know you can count on."

It was like a clap of thunder above my head. I sucked in my breath and smiled.

"You know I can't," I said softly and she nodded. "But after being with Billy and learning from him, I'm not as afraid as I was."

"That's good."

"I'm very grateful to you for what you've done for me. I don't know if I would have had the courage to do this if it weren't for you, Holly. Thank you."

She didn't smile.

"I hope I've done the right thing," she said.

I could only wonder what it was she saw in the stars that made her even doubt it.

It's better, I thought, not to ask.

# 2

# Innocence Lost

Billy wheeled himself out to watch Holly and I get into her car the next morning. After I loaded in my luggage, I paused to say good-bye and he took my hand into his and looked deeply into my eyes.

"Often, most of the time, I should say, we feel like ships passing each other in the night," he said. "We spend so little quality time with each other, barely getting to know each other, but I don't feel that way about you, Melody. You have been kind and trusting enough to open your heart to me. Thank you for sharing."

"Sharing? Sharing what?" I asked with a smile. "My problems?"

"Your problems are part of who you really are, but you didn't just share your problems. I got to see your excitement. I was able to feel your energy and it's strengthened me."

I looked at him with astonishment. How could I strengthen anyone at the moment: me, trembling on the sidewalk, terrified of the journey ahead of me.

22

He leaned forward and removed the gold chain and unique locket he wore around his neck. Then he handed it to me.

"I'd like you to have this," he said. "This is a lapis lazuli. It helps release tension and anxiety, but more important, it will enhance your ability to communicate with your higher self. It has helped me a great deal."

"Then I shouldn't take it," I said.

"No, it's all right. I want you to have it. Please," he insisted.

I saw he wouldn't be satisfied until I accepted his gift, so I took it and put it on. He smiled.

"Thank you, Billy." I leaned down to kiss him on the cheek, which automatically turned crimson. Then I hurried to the car.

"Mind the galaxy while I'm away," Holly called back to him. He laughed and waved as we drove away. I looked back and waved again until we rounded a corner and he disappeared from sight.

"It's funny. I haven't been here two full days, but I feel like I've known Billy for years and years," I said.

Holly nodded.

"That's the effect Billy has on everyone. I'm glad you had a chance to spend some time with him before you left for California," she added.

California! Just the way she said it and the way I thought about it made it seem like another planet. I sat with my knees together, my hands nervously twisting on my lap as we wove our way out of the city and toward the airport. Think of something pleasant, something calming, I told myself.

On the way to the airport, Holly described her sister in more detail, but admitted they hadn't seen each other for nearly a year.

"I won't go out there, and even when she comes here, I feel like I'm embarrassing her. She's seven years older, so there's nearly a generation between us, but deep down she's really very kindhearted."

"It's very nice of her to do all this for me, a complete

stranger," I said, wondering just how deep was deep down.

"Dorothy loves being magnanimous. It makes her feel even more like a queen," Holly said, laughing. "I have something for you to give her." She reached into her pocketbook to produce a small jewelry box wrapped in paper decorated with the ram, the sign for Aries, Dorothy's sign. "It's a bracelet filled with amethyst. The gems for the Aries are amethyst and diamond, but she has enough diamonds. You'll see."

"I'll make sure she gets it right away," I promised, tucking the tiny box away in my purse.

"Thanks. Well," she said as the airplane hangars came into view, "we're almost there."

My heart thumped like a parade drum at the sight of all the cars, the limousines and buses, people scurrying everywhere and skycaps loading luggage. Horns blasted, policemen shouted at drivers and waved at pedestrians to make them walk faster. Airplanes thundered over-head. How would I ever find my way through this maze of activity? Everyone else looked like he knew where he was going and was going there fast. I felt like I was floating through a dream and could be bumped toward one direction or another.

"Now don't worry," Holly said, seeing the expression on my face. "As soon as we pull up, the skycap will take your bags and give you your baggage receipts. Then he'll tell you what gate to go to for boarding. The directions are posted clearly inside the airport," she assured me. "And if you have any questions, there will be someone from the airlines nearby."

I took a deep breath. I was here; I was actually going. She pulled to the curb and we stepped out. The skycap took my bags and stapled the receipts to my ticket.

"Gate forty-one," he mumbled.

"Gate forty-one?"

I tried to get him to repeat it, but he was already helping someone else. I turned to Holly.

"I can't stay parked here any longer. They just give you

enough time to drop someone off. You'll see a television monitor inside with your flight number and gate number, along with the time your plane takes off."

"Thanks for everything, Holly."

"You call and I'll call you," she said. She held my hands and stood looking at me. Then she shook her head. "Your mother must have been some blind woman to leave a daughter like you behind," she said. She hugged me and I held on to her, held her as if she were a buoy keeping me afloat in this ocean of people and noise and activity.

She turned and got back into her car, flashing a final smile my way. I watched her drive off, waving and looking after her until she was gone. Now I was really all alone, without a friend in the world. Two elderly people brushed past me roughly, neither realizing they had almost knocked me over with their suitcases. I was standing in the wrong place. I clutched my purse and headed inside before someone else trampled me.

It wasn't much different inside. People were rushing by, pulling luggage on wheels, calling to each other. At the desk, a man was arguing vehemently with the attendant while the people behind him all wore looks of annoyance and frustration. How they could all use Billy Maxwell's calming words and meditation, I thought, shaking my head.

"What's so funny?" a young man in a dark gray suit asked. He had curly blonde hair and impish-looking hazel eyes with a dimple in his right cheek that appeared when he pressed his lips together. He carried a black briefcase and an umbrella.

"What? Oh. I was just watching those people and seeing the steam coming out of their ears."

"Steam?" He turned and looked at the line. "Oh." He smiled pleasantly. "You're a seasoned traveler, huh?"

"Who? Me? No sir. This is my first trip on an airplane, ever!" I exclaimed.

"Really? Well, you don't look it. Where are you going? Wouldn't be Los Angeles by any chance, would it?"

25

"Yes," I replied. "I've got to go to gate forty-one."

"That's easy. I'm heading that way, too." He nodded to his left. He took a few steps and paused when I didn't follow. "I don't bite," he quipped.

"I didn't think you did." I said nervously, and started after him.

"I'm Jerome Fonsworth," he said. "Unfortunately, I have to travel a lot so I *am* a seasoned traveler." He grimaced. "Hotel rooms, taxis and airports, that's my life. What a life," he concluded with a smirk.

"Why do you travel so much?" Like everyone else, he walked at a quick pace. I nearly had to jog to keep up.

"I'm in banking and I have to go from Boston to New York or to Chicago or Denver often. Sometimes I go to Atlanta and sometimes I go to Los Angeles. Today, it's Los Angeles. Ever hear of that movie, *If It's Tuesday, This Must Be Belgium?*"

I shook my head.

"Well, anyway, that's me. Busy, busy, busy. Sometimes, I feel like a bee," he muttered, swinging his briefcase as he walked. He stopped suddenly and turned to me.

"Look at me," he said. "Do I look like a man in his late twenties or a man in his late thirties, early forties? Don't lie."

"I don't lie," I said, "especially to strangers."

He laughed.

"I like that." He paused and tilted his head to consider. "You know, that makes sense. You have to know someone to care enough to lie to him. I don't lie much to strangers either." He thought and nodded. "Well?"

"You don't look like a man in his forties," I said.

"But I look like a man in his thirties?" He waited, his eyes tightening.

"Early or mid-thirties," I admitted.

"That's because my hair's starting to thin out at the top of my forehead and that comes from stress. I'm really only twenty-eight." He started to turn and stopped. "What did you say your name was?"

26

"I didn't tell you my name, but it's Melody, Melody Logan."

"Melody? Don't tell me you sing and you're on your way to Los Angeles to become a star," he said disdainfully as he continued walking.

"No, I'm not going there to become a star," I replied, but I didn't think he really heard me.

"Right up here," he said, indicating an escalator. "You've got to check your purse, so if you have a gun in it, you'd better take it out now."

"A gun!"

"Just kidding," he said.

When we reached the entryway, I watched him put his briefcase on the table and realized they were looking at an X-ray screen. I put my purse on the moving table and walked through the metal door. A ringing sound started and the attendant stepped up to me.

"Have any change or keys in your pockets?"

"No, ma'am," I said.

"It's probably that necklace. Put it in the basket," she ordered.

Jerome Fonsworth stood watching and smiled at me. Slowly, I took off the necklace Billy had given me and put it in the basket. Then I walked through the gate again, this time without the ringing sound.

"Okay," she said, offering me the basket to take out my necklace. I did so quickly and put it on. Then I grabbed my purse and joined Jerome.

"I should have told you that would happen. I always have to take off this watch." He checked it as he slipped a shiny gold watch back on his wrist. "You're going on American, flight one-oh-two also?"

"Yes."

"We have almost an hour. Want a cup of coffee or something?" he said, nodding toward the cafeteria.

"I might have a cup of tea."

"Stomach's woozy?" he kidded.

"As a matter of fact, it is," I said. I didn't see why I should be ashamed of being nervous. I bet he had been nervous the first time he had traveled like this, I thought. He heard the defensive tone in my voice.

"It's all right. The reason mine isn't woozy is because it's turned into a tin can from all the fast food I eat on the road and all the plane food I eat. Come on," he said and led me into the cafeteria. He ordered a coffee and a doughnut and a cup of tea for me.

"Thank you," I said when he insisted on paying for it.

"It's no big deal. I'm a bank executive in my father's bank. Money grows on trees," he said and indicated a table near the front of the cafeteria. We sat and he handed me my tea.

"Do you really hate your job as much as you claim?" I asked.

"Hate it? No, I've gotten so I don't feel anything about it. I go through the paces, do what I have to do, and then go home," he said. He didn't look at me when he spoke. His eyes continually wandered. Like everyone else around me, he seemed to be a bundle of wild energy. I thought he might just go poof and rise to the ceiling in a small cloud.

"Where is home?"

"Boston. I told you that," he said. "You weren't listening, Melody Logan." He waved his long right forefinger at me. "See, I remembered your full name. Pay attention to everything and everyone when you travel," he advised. He bit into his doughnut and then offered it to me.

"No thank you."

"You'll calm down once you're in the air," he assured me. "Actually, flying's the best way to travel. You put on earphones, sit back and fall asleep. Most of the time, I've got to work on the plane because I'm behind in my paperwork. I hate paperwork."

"What exactly do you do?"

"I work on commercial loans," he said. "It's not as glamorous as what people do in Hollywood. So why are you going there? Vacation?" He continued to look around after he asked me questions, as if he didn't care what I would answer or he was looking for someone else.

"No, I'm going to meet my mother."

"Oh." He turned back. "Your parents divorced and you live with your father?"

"Not exactly," I said.

"You don't have to tell me your private business. I'm just being nosy to pass the time. Your name's Melody, but you don't sing?" he asked. He looked to his right, chewing his doughnut quickly, actually gobbling it.

"I play the fiddle."

"Fiddle?" He turned back to me and laughed. "Not the violin?"

"It's different. I was brought up in West Virginia where playing the fiddle is very popular."

"Oh. I thought there was something unusual about your accent. Fiddle huh? Well, I suppose that's nice." He swallowed the last morsel of his doughnut and licked his fingers. "I'm hungrier than I thought. I think I'll get another doughnut."

"Oh, let me get it this time. You bought my tea," I offered.

He laughed.

"A woman of independent means. I like that. Sure. Get me a plain . . . no, make it a chocolate doughnut this time," he said. I reached into my purse, opened my wallet and took out two dollars.

"Is this enough?"

"Yes," he said, shaking his head. "It's more than your tea cost so it's not exactly a fair exchange," he warned.

"That's something a banker would say," I replied and he laughed harder.

"Thanks."

I went to the counter and picked out the doughnut. His eyes were still full of laughter when I returned.

"I'm not used to women buying things for me. The girls I know belong to the leech society," he said, taking the doughnut. "Come on, share this one with me, okay?"

"All right," I said and took the half he broke off. We ate in silence.

"I was in Los Angeles two months ago for a convention," he said when he'd finished his half.

"Did you like it?"

"Los Angeles? I stayed at the Beverly Hilton. That's the way to see Los Angeles . . . chauffeurs, the best restaurants. Matter of fact, that's the way to see any place. Where's your mother live?"

I rattled off the address because I had committed it to memory soon after Kenneth Childs had given it to me in Provincetown.

"West Hollywood. Could be nice," he said. "How come you've never been there before?"

"She hasn't been there that long," I replied. He saw from my face that there was much more to the story, but he didn't look like he wanted to pry anymore. He nodded and then looked around again.

"I just remembered I gotta make a phone call. Would you watch my briefcase? I'll be right back," he said and jumped up before I could reply. He hurried down the terminal. The way he was burning up energy, he probably would look like forty or fifty soon, I thought.

I sat back and watched the crowds of people moving along, the children clinging to their parents' hands and the couples who also held hands or walked side by side. Where were all these people going? I wondered. Were any of them first time airplane travelers like me?

Suddenly, Jerome appeared again, looking all out of breath.

"I got a new crisis," he said, "here in New York."

"Oh, I'm sorry."

"I've got to return to the city." He picked up his briefcase and then he paused. "The trouble is I had to get these papers to Los Angeles today. Listen, could you do me a great favor? I would be willing to pay you."

"What is it?" I asked.

"There will be a man at the airport waiting at the gate when you arrive. He'll be holding a sign that reads

30

'Fonsworth.' Just give him this briefcase. I'll be calling and telling him to expect you. Okay?"

"Just give him the briefcase?"

"That's it," he said. "Okay? Here," he added taking a fifty-dollar bill out of his wallet.

"Oh, you don't have to give me any money for something so simple," I said.

"I insist."

"I won't do it if you insist on giving me money. If we can't do little favors for each other . . ."

He smiled.

"You know, I had a feeling it was my lucky day when I saw you standing there and smiling like that. Thanks. And if we ever run into each other again, I'll be sure to buy you another cup of tea."

He pushed the briefcase toward me.

"A man will be standing with a sign . . . 'Fonsworth.' He won't be hard to find," he declared and then he walked off, disappearing in the crowds of people who had just come off airplanes.

I finished my tea and got up. The briefcase was a little heavier than I had anticipated, but it wasn't too heavy. I walked down the terminal until I reached gate forty-one. There were many people there already. I asked the attendant what I had to do next.

"You'll get your boarding pass at the desk," she instructed and I got into line. Ten minutes later, I reached the desk and handed the attendant my ticket. She gave me my boarding pass and I sat and waited with everyone until the flight attendant announced our plane would begin boarding.

My heart began to beat madly again. When I heard my seat number, I joined the line and made my way to the airplane. The attendant at the door smiled warmly at me and directed me to the right.

"You have the aisle seat," she said. I found it quickly. There was an elderly man in a light brown suit sitting by the window already, his eyes closed. He opened them when I sat beside him.

"Hello there," he said.

"Hello." I put the briefcase under the seat in front of me and buckled my seat belt, just as I had been instructed. Then I smiled at him again.

"Going home?"

"No. I'm going to Los Angeles for the first time," I said. "How about you?"

"Going home. I visited my brother in Brooklyn. He's too old to travel anymore so I come to him. Used to be, we took turns. It's not easy to get old, but you know what they say, it beats the alternative," he added and laughed, his thick-lensed glasses bouncing on the bridge of his nose.

"How old is your brother?"

"Ninety-four, two years older than me," he replied.

"You're ninety-two years old?" I asked, astonished.

"Years young. If you think of yourself as being old, you're old," he said plainly. He did have remarkable young-looking light gray eyes, more hair than I thought a man of that age would have and a face that, although crossed with deep wrinkles in his forehead and temples, was not that weathered. He was slim, but he certainly didn't look fragile and weak.

"I'll have to ask you to tell me your secret," I said, smiling.

"You mean the secret to keep bouncing?" He leaned toward me. "Do what you have to do, but let someone else do the worrying," he replied and then he laughed again. "It's all up here." He pointed to his temple. "Mind over matter. So, are you in college?"

"Not yet," I said and told him a little about myself. He had a hearing aid, which I thought had to work very well. He seemed to hear everything I said.

I didn't realize how long I had been talking until the pilot announced we were the next plane to be approved for takeoff. I sat back, holding my breath.

"Is this your first time in an airplane?"

"Yes sir, it is," I said.

"Remember what I told you," my elderly friend said

32

with that twinkle in his eyes. "Let someone else do the worrying."

He closed his eyes and sat back, looking very relaxed. I was lucky to be sitting next to him because he had a calming effect on me. How could I be nervous when a man in his nineties was so brave?

Once we were airborne, he told me all about his life. He could remember the Spanish-American War, as well as the First and Second World Wars, of course. It was mind-boggling thinking about all the changes he had seen. He and his brother had worked with their father in the garment industry when they were only ten and twelve years old. He had had many different jobs in his life and finally had become an insurance salesman, married and moved to California where, he said, he made some money in real estate. His wife had died nearly fourteen years ago. I heard about his children and his grandchildren. He talked so much I didn't realize how much time had passed. We had our lunch and then he took a nap and I read a magazine. I fell asleep for a while myself and when I woke up, I heard the pilot say we were close to Los Angeles.

"Remember," my elderly friend said, his hand over mine, "stress and worry, that's what puts age in you. Now, time, time's just a reminder that we ain't here forever."

"Thank you," I said.

After that, it all happened so fast, the plane landing, getting my things together, saying good-bye to my new friend and leaving the airplane. My heart was thumping so hard and quickly, I was afraid I'd faint before I set eyes on Holly's sister. I didn't have to look long. She was right there at the gate doorway, unmistakable, an elegant beauty in a wide-brim white hat, a lace coat over her milk-white silk dress. She wore matching silk gloves and large diamond earrings. Her hair was a sleek cap of pale shining gold, pulled back from her face to show a sculptured profile and unlined face.

Holly had warned me that her sister Dorothy was

supporting a number of plastic surgeons in Beverly Hills. Holly called it Dorothy's Wrinkle Panic. The mere sight of a line would send her into a frenzy and put her on the phone with her cosmetic surgeon. Her nose had been trimmed, her eyelids and skin tightened so often, her face resembled a mask, but she did have Holly's youthful hazel eyes. Her lips were fuller. Later, I would learn that, too, was because of something else her plastic surgeon had done.

Beside her stood her uniformed chauffeur, a handsome young man with turquoise eyes and hair the color of fresh straw, trimmed close at the sides with a sweeping wave over the top. He had a cleft chin, and a sharp, strong-looking jawbone and high cheekbones. At the moment, his firm mouth was curled up slightly in the right corner, a laugh in his eyes as he contemplated me, wide-eyed and terrified walking into the terminal.

Dorothy was a tall woman, at least four or five inches taller than Holly. Her chauffeur was easily six feet two or three, I thought. He was trim, movie star sleek with that perfect Hollywood tan I saw on the faces of stars in fan magazines. The caramel tint emphasized his aqua eyes.

Dorothy waved. Beside them stood two uniformed policemen studying everyone who came from the plane. I waved back and hurried along.

"Melody?"

"Yes," I said.

"I just knew it was you. Didn't I, Spike?" she said as I approached.

"You had a good description," he said, widening his handsome smile.

"Oh dear me, look at you. You're so sweet," she said. "Isn't she just the freshest little thing you've ever seen, Spike?"

"Yes, ma'am," he said gawking at me, a silent laugh on his lips.

"Welcome to Los Angeles," Dorothy declared. "My sister has told me all about you, but of course, I want to get to know you for myself. I'm sure half the things she

34

told me are either exaggerations or figments of that wild imagination of hers. Spike, take her briefcase. Briefcase?" she asked herself, raising her eyebrows as soon as she said it. "Why would you be carrying something so . . . ugly? Couldn't my sister provide you with a suitable bag? Something more feminine?"

"It's not mine. I'm doing someone a favor," I said and gazed past them, looking for the man with the sign.

"Favor?" Dorothy looked at Spike. He shrugged.

"I met someone at the airport in New York, a banker. He was on his way here when he had an emergency and had to go back to the city. He asked me to take this to Los Angeles and give it to a man who held up a sign with his name, Fonsworth," I said still looking past them. "But I don't see him."

"What nerve," Dorothy said. "Especially to burden a young girl coming here for the first time." She looked at Spike again, whose smile had evaporated and been replaced with a frown that put furrows in his forehead. His eyes went to the policemen behind me and then he reached quickly for the briefcase, practically pulling it out of my hands. I thought he was being rather rude and I was about to protest. After all, it was my responsibility. He stepped away quickly.

"Did you have a nice flight, dear? Sometimes it's bumpy and they always manage to serve you your food just when it's bumpy. I don't fly unless I can fly first class anymore, not that it's less bumpy, but at least you know you'll be a little more comfortable. So, you must tell me all about yourself and your adventure and of course, tell me all about my sister. I hope you don't believe half the things she claims to be able to do. We'll have lunch," she added before I could utter a syllable. "After Spike gets your luggage."

She took a deep breath. Spike remained a few steps in front of us.

"I really want to get that briefcase to the man," I said. "I promised and I feel responsible."

"Of course, dear. Spike?"

35

He turned as we reached the long corridor.

"The gentleman she's looking for must be down at the baggage carousel, don't you think?" Dorothy said.

He paused, looked past us, and then started to open the briefcase, but it was locked.

"I don't think you should do that," I protested.

"I'll be right back," he told Dorothy as he headed into the men's room.

"Why doesn't he let me take care of the briefcase?" I asked.

"I swear, I have no idea," she said. "He's an actor, of course, and like all of them, he's moody and unpredictable. Everyone in L.A. these days is either trying to get into the entertainment industry or selling real estate. Enough about Spike. Please tell me about you. Where did you meet my sister?"

I told her about Provincetown and Kenneth, Holly's arrival at the beach and how we became friends.

"She still drives that ridiculous circus car?"

"Yes," I said, laughing and thinking about the bright psychedelic colors.

"She had her ears pierced when she was only eight, you know. She had a friend do it and she had to be taken to the doctor before infection set in. My father was furious."

Before Dorothy could continue, Spike reappeared, but without the briefcase.

"Where's Mr. Fonsworth's briefcase?" I demanded instantly.

"In the garbage bin. Let's get moving," he said to Dorothy.

"What? Why did he do that?" I cried.

"Quiet," he said gruffly.

"Now just a minute," I began, determined to make him explain. He surprised me by seizing my arm at the elbow and pulling me forward. Before I could protest, he turned to Dorothy.

"Drugs," he said.

"Oh dear."

36

"What?"

"That briefcase was lined with something called cocaine. Ever hear of it?" he said sarcastically. "That's probably why the police were waiting at the gate. They got a tipoff; he found out and planted the case with her," he told Dorothy and then looked at me. "If they would have stopped you, you would have been in great trouble. Maybe we all would have," he added.

"But . . ." I looked at Dorothy, whose eyes were almost as wide as mine. "He was a nice young man, a banker. Surely, this is a mistake," I cried.

Spike shook his head.

"He must have spotted her a mile away," he told Dorothy.

I pulled my arm out of his grip and swallowed over the huge, aching lump in my throat.

"That's not true. He had an emergency, and how would he know I would do such a thing anyway?" I asked.

"If you refused, he would have looked for someone else or given up for today. You just transported a lot of cocaine across the country and you might even have brought it to Mrs. Livingston's home," he added firmly.

I felt myself wilt, the tears burning as I looked at Dorothy. She wagged her head at Spike, flashing him a cool, chastising look.

"Oh don't be so harsh on her, Spike. She didn't know." She patted me on the shoulder. "It's nothing, dear. These things happen in today's mad world, but we won't worry about it now. Let's just get her luggage and go, Spike. I'm absolutely famished. We'll go directly to The Vine on Beverly Drive. Wait until you taste their baked goat cheese salad, Melody, and their grilled eggplant sandwich."

Thinking about the trouble I might have gotten myself into just as I had started out on this journey made my throat close. I took a deep breath of relief and shot a glance at Spike, feeling ashamed that I had gotten so angry at him when he was just doing what he thought he had to do to protect all of us. He was silent as we continued down the terminal toward the baggage area, where I spotted a man in a light blue jacket and dungarees holding a small sign with the word "Fonsworth" written on it.

"Don't look at him," Spike ordered.

We hurried by him to the baggage carousel. However, I couldn't help but glance back at him once in a while. As the crowd thinned, he turned and rapidly left the terminal.

"I'm sorry," I told Dorothy. "I had no idea what that man had given me."

"It's all right, dear. Please, I hate unpleasant things. When something nasty happens, I just buy myself something new to wear and make myself feel good again." Her eyes drank me in from head to toe. "That's what we'll do for you later, buy you something nice to wear. I'm sure you don't have the right things. You need something more fashionable if you're going to traipse around Beverly Hills."

"Oh, I can't ask you to do anything like that."

"Of course you can't, but I still can do it," she said with a laugh.

I spotted one of my bags and Spike scooped it up.

"I almost forgot," I said, digging into my purse. "Holly sent you this."

I handed her the small package wrapped with the sign of Aries. Dorothy rolled her eyes.

"Oh no, what magic charm did she deliver this time?"

Without opening it, she dropped it into her own purse. I thought how much Holly would be disappointed, but before I could say anything, my second bag appeared and I pointed it out to Spike. We showed my receipts to the attendant at the door and Spike carried my bags out to the limousine. It was a long, sleek black Mercedes with plush leather seats, a bar and a small television set in the rear. Spike opened the door for us and we got in. The leather smelled brand new.

"I'm really sorry about what happened in there," I

38

said again. The more I thought about it, the more ashamed I felt for endangering people who were being so kind to me.

"I don't hear you," Dorothy sang. "I don't hear unpleasant things. I've trained myself to be deaf when I have to be, so you might as well stop talking about it. Let's talk about you again. Tell me about this place . . . this coal mining town and how you came to live in Provincetown," she said. "I'm actually fond of the Cape, but we only stay in Hyannis. That's where the Kennedy's live, you know. Spike, please take the fastest route to The Vine," she told him when he got behind the wheel. "I'm absolutely starving to death back here."

"Yes, ma'am," he said and winked at me as he pulled out of the parking lot and onto the road.

With all that had happened, I hadn't even looked up at the magnificent blue sky. We shot into traffic and we were soon on one of California's famous freeways. I was really here, and somewhere, not far away, my mother might be, too. If I ever needed her, I thought, I need her now.

# 3

## ❦

# *Hopes Dashed*

Traveling through Los Angeles was very different from traveling through New York City. Everything seemed so much farther apart and there weren't nearly as many tall buildings, even though there seemed to be many more streets. However, Spike obviously knew his way around because as soon as we ran into a line of heavy traffic on the freeway, he took an exit and began to wind the limousine through the city streets. Dorothy said it wasn't the nicest area of Los Angeles, but even the poorer areas looked bright and dazzling to me. Sidewalks glittered and giant billboards advertised new movies. However, I did notice there weren't as many people walking the sidewalks as there were in New York. Here, everyone seemed to be in cars. Minutes later, Dorothy eagerly pointed out the sign that read CITY OF BEVERLY HILLS.

"Home," she declared with a deep, grateful sigh. The way she spoke about it made it seem as if Beverly Hills were an island on which she felt safe and secure from the rest of the world.

Spike drove up to the front of The Vine, a restaurant

with a hunter green railing smothered in vines and bright pink and red bougainvillea. There was an outdoor patio that looked nearly filled with patrons. Waiters and busboys in starched white shirts and black pants with black suspenders scurried about gracefully, moving like invisible people past the obviously well-to-do clientele, all of whom were thick in conversation.

The restaurant's valet hurried to help us out once Spike came around to open the door.

*"Merci,"* Dorothy said with a wave of her glove.

When Spike got back into the car, I wondered where he would go to eat, but I didn't have time to ask. Dorothy swept us down the cobblestone path to the gate of the patio, where a very attractive young woman waited at the hostess station.

"Mrs. Livingston," she said, flashing a smile made for toothpaste commercials, "how are you?"

"Starving, Lana. Meet my sister's young friend, Melody. She's just flown in from New York. This is her first time in Los Angeles and I thought I would introduce her first to The Vine. So get us a good table," Dorothy insisted.

Lana turned and studied the patio.

"I have number twelve open," she declared as if it were an amazing accomplishment.

Why was it so important where we sat? I wondered. All of the chairs looked the same and the patio with its fountain and bright flowers looked beautiful no matter where you were sitting.

*"Bellissimo,"* Dorothy approved. Lana started down the cobblestone patio and we followed until she stopped at a table nearly perfectly centered. Dorothy beamed with satisfaction and after we sat Lana handed us the menus encased in leather folders the same hunter green shade as the railings.

"We have an angel hair pasta special with red peppers and portobello mushrooms today, Mrs. Livingston."

"Oh, that's good. *Merci.*"

As soon as Lana left us, Dorothy leaned toward me.

41

"This is usually a table reserved for movie stars," she said. "It's where everyone can see you."

"Oh." Why did she want everyone to see us? I wondered. It made me feel more self-conscious about my hair, my clothes, everything I did.

I looked at the menu. The prices were shocking. Everything was à la carte and the salads were almost as expensive as the entrées. Simple things were described so elaborately, I wasn't sure I recognized them. What was a heart of celery?

"Don't you think a second about the prices," Dorothy said, anticipating my reaction. "My husband Philip writes off everything I spend one way or another." She laughed. "He says since I do so much to help the American economy, the least the government can do is subsidize me."

"What does your husband do?" I asked. "I don't remember Holly telling me."

"He's an accountant and a financial manager with some very impressive clients," she replied, lifting her eyebrows. Then her face filled with the excitement of a starstruck little girl. "Oh, I think that's somebody sitting in the corner over there," she said, nodding right. I turned.

"Somebody?"

"A television star, right?"

"I don't know," I said.

"I'm sure it is. Well, let's see," she said, turning back to the menu. "Why don't we have the angel hair special after the goat cheese salad, okay? Do you like iced tea? They make it with a touch of mint."

"Yes, ma'am."

"Please don't call me ma'am, Melody." She gazed around nervously to see if anyone nearby had heard. "That makes me sound so old. Call me Dorothy."

"Yes, ma' . . . Dorothy," I said and she smiled and nodded with approval, holding the brim of her hat as she did so. The waiter came. He spoke with a thick Spanish accent. I had trouble understanding what he said, but

42

Dorothy had no problem. She gave him our order and added, *"Por favor,"* the Spanish for "please." I already had noticed how she liked to throw French, Italian and Spanish expressions into her conversation, flicking her wrist as she did so.

"I don't imagine you ate very well on the plane, did you, you poor thing?"

"I was too nervous," I admitted.

"That's okay. I'm always too nervous to eat when I travel. Philip's never too nervous to lose his appetite over anything. Now, let's get right down to your problem," she said, pausing only when the busboy brought us our iced tea. "As I understand it, you want to find out if this woman is your mother, a woman who came out here to be a movie star. You were told she was killed in a car fire and they even shipped her body back to Provincetown?"

"Yes."

"It sounds very, very complicated. I discussed it with Philip and he agrees we should simply hire a private detective. After all, why should a young girl go investigating such a thing?"

"Oh no," I moaned. "This is something I have to do myself. Thank you, but I do," I insisted.

"Really?" She stared at me a moment and then rolled her eyes. "Well, I suppose you can start yourself. I'll have Spike take you around. He's very good when it comes to weird things, as you saw, but you must listen to him," she admonished. "I wouldn't want anything to happen to you while you're my guest," she said. Then she thought about what she had said and added, "I wouldn't want anything to happen to you under any circumstances."

"Thank you, Dorothy. I do appreciate your concern for me and what you're doing," I said.

"Now, now, let's not think about it. I'll become deaf," she threatened again. I started to laugh. "So," she continued without catching her breath, "tell me more about my dear little sister. Does that crippled man still live with her in the rear of that hole-in-the-wall shop?"

43

"I don't think of Billy as being crippled," I began and described my trip to New York and what Billy and I had done together in so short a time. She listened, a small smile on her face. I had the feeling she was studying me rather than paying attention to the things I said.

"It's so wonderful to be young and impressionable," she declared with a sigh. "It's almost a shame to introduce you to the hard realities of the real world. Holly always refused to face them. But you saw how my sister lives, like some hippie, some gypsy. And she's so pretty and bright when she wants to be. I could find her an adequate husband in a heartbeat, if she would let me, but *que sera, sera.*"

I was about to protest and explain that I thought Holly was happy as she was and lived a good life, but our salads arrived. They looked delicious. However, the portions made me smile and shake my head. A half dozen forkfuls would clean the plate. I felt guilty having her pay for it.

"It seems like a lot of money for this small amount of food, Dorothy."

"Nonsense. It's more than enough. You've got to watch your diet, especially here, my dear. Just look around at these women. Look," she ordered and I realized she really wanted me to do it now.

I looked around the restaurant as subtly as I could. There were many attractive women, all with beautiful hairdos and expensive-looking clothes. It was obviously a place for the rich and beautiful.

"Everyone watches her figure. Competition, competition, competition, my dear. Every woman is competing with every other woman here."

"For what?" I asked.

She laughed.

"For what? For the eyes of a man, what else? Many of these women want to be in pictures or with powerful men. But don't worry, I'll explain it all to you later. Just from the little you have told me about your background, I know you have so much to learn, and I do enjoy helping a young woman become . . . sophisticated," she declared. "Now don't eat too quickly. You don't want to seem like some naive young girl from the Midwest. Besides, this is the best table. We should enjoy our moment in the spotlight. See, people are wondering who we are already," she said, nodding at people at other tables. She was right—they were looking our way. Dorothy adjusted her hat and smiled at someone.

"You can be friendly," she said, still nodding and smiling at people, "but don't speak to anyone first. Let them come to you. Always wait for them, and never tell anyone too much," she warned. "The more mysterious you are, the more your stock goes up. That's the way Philip would put it." She nodded at someone to our right. "Don't worry, you'll learn. After a while," she assured me.

"I'm really not here for any of that, Dorothy," I said softly. "I'm just here to see about my mother."

"Of course, but like everyone else who comes here, you'll soon fall in love."

"Fall in love? With what, with whom?" I asked.

"Why, with yourself, dear. Who else?" she said and laughed. "I'm sure," she added when I just stared at her, "that that is exactly what happened to your mother."

After what proved to be one of the longest lunches of my life, our meal followed by cups of cappuccino and fruit tarts that cost as much as the meal itself, we finally left. Spike was right there with the limousine, waiting. He held open the doors and I did feel like someone very special because of the way pedestrians paused to look at us and the way the hostess and other staff members fawned over Dorothy. She was like a sponge, soaking up their artificial smiles and growing fatter on that than the miserly portions we had been served. I did get a glimpse of the bill and Holly wasn't far off when she had told me what it would cost. Dorothy had paid over seventy-five dollars for lunch!

We rode past other expensive-looking restaurants, up

Santa Monica Boulevard to what Dorothy announced was the world famous Rodeo Drive.

"I'll take you there tomorrow, my dear, to find you something adequate to wear."

Spike made a right turn and drove us past beautiful large homes, one more elaborate than the other with their Grecian columns and tall hedges. As we drove, Dorothy rattled off the names of movie stars, singers and dancers I had seen in films. She also knew the names of film directors and producers who lived in various houses because her husband Philip had some of them for clients.

Finally, we slowed before a two-story English Tudor bigger than any house I had ever seen. It had a steeply pitched roof, side-gabled, with tall, narrow windows with multi-pane glazing. There was a massive chimney on the left crowned by three decorative chimney pots. The walls were brick contrasted with wooden claddings. It was the sort of house I had seen only on the covers of romance novels.

"Home sweet home," Dorothy declared as Spike turned into the pink tile driveway lined with Tiffany glass lamps. The lawn looked like an emerald carpet, with every blade cut perfectly. There was an enormous weeping willow on the left, its tearful branches nearly reaching the ground, and on the right was a thick oak that looked proud and majestic as it towered over the flowers, rock garden and yellow, white and pink bougainvillea that clung to the tall wooden boarder fence beneath it.

"Your house is so big!" I exclaimed. "I didn't think houses could be so big in a city. It's a mansion!"

"I suppose it is a mansion. We do have twenty rooms," she said, "if you count the help's quarters, Philip's office, Philip's gymnasium . . ."

"Gymnasium. Twenty rooms!"

Dorothy laughed.

"Philip complains that it's never big enough, especially when I host my women's club meetings."

Alongside the house was a three-car garage, but because the entrance was on the side, it made the house appear even longer. I saw windows above the garage, too.

Spike parked in front of the arched doorway and quickly came around and opened Dorothy's door. As soon as she stepped out, he rushed around the limousine to open mine and reached in to take my elbow and help me out. I felt silly having someone do the simplest things for me, but I was afraid to make a social error.

"Take her bags to the pink room, please Spike," Dorothy commanded. "We have many guest rooms, but I think you'll enjoy this one the most. It suits young people," she said. Spike glanced at me with a small smile on his lips and then opened the trunk.

"Let me acquaint you with our house before you settle in for what I'm sure is a much needed rest," Dorothy told me. I followed her to the front door, which seemed to open magically as we approached.

A short, stout, bald-headed man with bushy gray eyebrows and a pug nose greeted us. He wore a dark blue suit and tie and had a light complexion with rust-tinted spots along the crests of his cheeks and the base of his forehead. His skull was peppered with what looked like freckles dropped randomly along the middle and down his temples. His thick lips were almost the same shade of orange.

"Hello, Alec. This is Melody. She will be staying with us for a while."

He nodded.

"Very good, madam," he said in sharp, clipped tones with just the slightest nod. His light gray eyes swept over me, making me feel as if I had to pass inspection before entering the house. After a moment, he stepped aside and we entered.

The entryway had dark, rich-looking brown tile that complemented the walls paneled with dark cypress. Above us a teardrop glass chandelier glowed. The stairway, winding up with a mahogany balustrade and detailed spindle work, was polished to a pristine glow.

Spike started up with my bags, Alec right behind him, but I followed Dorothy deeper into the house.

On the right was a very large living room with a dark pine grandfather's clock that bonged the hour of three. All of the pieces of furniture were oversized to fill the great space. Light blue satin curtains draped the windows and the marble floor was covered here and there with large Persian oval area rugs in a matching blue. There was so much to visually gobble, I could only shake my head: great oil paintings depicting scenes in cities like Paris and London, as well as grand gardens, all in elaborate gilt frames, glass sculptures that looked like they cost hundreds of dollars, porcelain figurines so dainty and perfect they were surely hand-painted, silver and gold candelabra, antique swords . . . how could anyone be so rich?

"Cozy, isn't it?" Dorothy asked proudly.

Cozy? It was a room in which one could run tours, not relax, I mused, but only nodded.

She showed me the den, with its rich, plush leather sofas and chairs, Philip's office, the dining room with a table that could seat twenty at a time and the kitchen that looked more like a kitchen for a restaurant. She was especially proud of her ovens, although she was quick to say she never even boiled water for tea.

"That's Selena's job," she declared and introduced me to her cook, a very short and very plump Peruvian woman with eyes as dark as peat moss. "Selena lives in the rear of the house," Dorothy explained. "Spike has an apartment over the garage, but my maid, Christina, lives in West L.A. She arrives here at seven in the morning and leaves after dinner, usually about eight. Philip pays them all off the books," she added in a whisper.

"Off the books?"

"Things accountants do to stave off the greedy government. Let's go settle you in. I'm sure you want to shower and freshen up after your trip."

"Yes, I do. Then I'd like to visit the address."

"The address?"

"Where my mother might be," I said.

"Right away?" She grimaced. "Surely, you want to wait until tomorrow."

"I'd rather do it as soon as possible. It's why I'm here," I emphasized. She raised her eyebrows.

"I keep forgetting how much energy young people have," she said. "Very well, if you insist. We'll have Spike ready for you in an hour."

"Thank you, Dorothy, and thanks for showing me your house. It's wonderful."

She beamed.

"I've done most of the decorating myself. With the help of professionals, of course. Holly's been here only once. Can you believe that? I think she's afraid to return, afraid to face the fact that she might like it here," she added with a wink.

I doubt that, I thought. Holly was impressed with spiritual, not material things, I wanted to tell her, but I kept my lips sealed tight.

We climbed the stairs. Alec had already unpacked my things, hanging up what had to be hung and putting my other things in the dresser drawers. It embarrassed me to realize he had done all this and especially handled my underthings.

I was so shocked by the bedroom though, that I didn't even have time to feel embarrassed. This wasn't a room, but a chamber fit for a princess. I couldn't believe the posh splendor, the opulence! The walls were covered in silk damask, colored a delicious strawberry pink, richer than the pale mauve of what I thought had to be at least a two-inch-thick carpet. There was a king-size white pine bed, the wood somehow treated so it had strands of blush pink through it. There was a canopy and over the bed itself was a soft, furry coverlet. Even the walk-in closet was bigger than any room I had slept in. It had shelves for shoes and a mirror and a small dressing table at the rear. But there was also a vanity table and matching dressers in the room itself.

All of the fixtures in the bathroom were brass. The

floor was a whitewashed tile. There was a whirlpool tub, a glass stall shower that looked like it would fit a whole family and double sinks. Mirrors everywhere caught my look of amazement. This was the guest room! What could Dorothy and Philip's master bedroom be like?

"I can't believe how wonderful your house is, Dorothy," I said again.

"I'm glad you'll be comfortable," she replied.

"Comfortable! This is a palace. How could anyone not be comfortable?"

She laughed.

"Are you sure you want to go dragging yourself into West Hollywood so quickly? Why not pamper yourself a bit, dear? Take a whirlpool bath, rest, watch some television on your own set. We'll have some hors d'oeuvres before Philip gets home and then we'll have a nice dinner—"

"It sounds wonderful, Dorothy, but I'd feel guilty. I'm not here to enjoy myself. I'm here to find my mother," I reminded her.

She sighed and shrugged.

"Everyone is in such a rush these days. Well, I'll tell Spike to be ready."

"Thank you. For everything," I said.

She flashed a smile and left me to take a shower and change my clothes. I was tired, nearly exhausted, but my excitement over being here and being so close to finding Mommy was stronger. I got into the shower and let the warm water wash over me until I tingled and then I got out, put on a pair of jeans and my best blouse, brushed out my hair, took a few deep breaths, closed my eyes and thought about Billy Maxwell and Holly sitting beside me, advising me on how to calm my nerves and gather my energy, energy I needed now more than ever.

Then I rose and set out to find my mother.

Thinking about the time that had passed since Mommy had left me with my stepfather's relatives in

Provincetown, I was suddenly plagued by a new, albeit foolish fear. Had time and events changed me so that she might not recognize me, especially if she was suffering from some form of amnesia? It hadn't been all that long, but I felt so different. When I confronted her, how would I begin? It seemed ridiculous to walk up to someone and say, "Hello, remember me? I'm your daughter. You're my mother." If there were other people standing around, they would surely think I was mad.

As I stepped down the carpeted winding stairway and through the entryway to the front door, I felt myself shrink. It was an illusion, of course, stimulated by the size of everything around me, but more important, by the size of the task I was about to begin. I took a deep breath and stepped outside.

Spike was leaning against the limousine reading a copy of *Variety*. He looked up at me and smiled. Then he folded his paper and opened the rear door, stepping back in one graceful motion with a very affected and deliberate theatrical bow.

"Madam," he said.

"Thank you," I said in a voice barely above a whisper. I started to get in and paused. "Oh, here's the address," I said, handing him the slip of paper that might have held the key to my future. "Is it far away?"

"Nothing's far away in this town except a good part," he commented.

I got in and he closed the door and went around quickly to the driver's seat.

"Would you like to look at this?" he said, offering me the copy of *Variety*.

"No thank you," I replied.

He shrugged.

"I just thought you'd like to see what a Hollywood paper looked like. It's filled with all sorts of news about actors and actresses. You've never read one before, I bet," he muttered.

"No. I haven't had a reason to," I explained.

He laughed as he started the engine.

"I'm not trying to be an actress or anything," I added when the smirk remained on his lips.

"Every woman is an actress and therefore would love to be in movies," he quipped.

"Not me. And every woman is not an actress," I snapped back at him.

He laughed again. The patronizing smile that remained on his face was infuriating.

"I want to go to college and do other things," I continued, wondering why it was so important to me to explain myself.

"Your mother came out here to be an actress, didn't she?" he asked as we proceeded down the long driveway. My shoulders stiffened.

"If you're trying to be an actor, why are you a chauffeur?" I asked in reply.

He turned and looked at me to see if I were being serious.

"It takes a lot of time, intense studying, knocking on doors, hundreds of auditions until you get that one big break," he whined. "In the meantime, unless you were born with a silver spoon in your mouth or unless you have some rich friends who are willing to stake you, you take any job you can that pays for groceries and rent. This isn't a bad job for me. Mrs. Livingston gives me a lot of leeway. Whenever I have an important audition, she gives me the time off, even if it means she has to use a taxi service."

"How long have you been here trying to be a successful actor?" I asked him.

"Three years, seriously at it," he replied.

"Have you been in any movies?"

"I had a few bit parts. I have my Screen Actors Guild card. That's more than a lot can say. I was in a play six months ago. It ran nearly a month, too."

"Then you must be good," I said. He turned to flash me one of his handsome smiles.

"I am. I just have to get everyone else, the important

people, to see it," he said. "After a while it's all just your lucky stars anyway," he added. "Being in the right place at the right time."

"Do you believe in astrology?" I asked.

"Hey, I'll believe in anything they want me to believe in as long as it means I get the part," he said.

"It's that important to you?"

"Are you kidding?" He turned back and gazed at me as if I had just arrived from another planet. Then he smiled. "After you're here for a while, you'll understand," he said. "It's in the air."

"I hope I'm not here that long," I muttered and gazed out the window. Spike continued to watch me in the rearview mirror. I allowed my eyes to meet his briefly before I turned to stare almost blindly at the passing scenery. I couldn't help but be nervous about what was only minutes away. My stomach was doing somersaults. Spike finally noticed my anxiety and took some pity on me.

"It's been some time since you've seen your mother, huh?" he asked softly.

"Yes."

"And you're not even sure it is your mother?"

"No," I said, "although everything points to her being my mother."

He shook his head.

"What a gig. This address, it's an inexpensive condo development. Most of the owners sublet to people tying to break into the business."

"The business?"

"That's what we call Hollywood, the biz," he said. "We have our own lingo." He laughed.

"It's like another country," I muttered, but loud enough for him to hear, which made him laugh even harder.

"You really wouldn't want to be famous, in show business? I bet you have some sort of talent."

I continued to stare out the window.

"I play the fiddle and some people say I'm very good."

"There, you see. A number of country music stars have become famous actors," he said.

"I'm far from a country music star," I said, shaking my head. How easy it was for someone to fall into the trap and start believing in his or her own fantasies, I thought. Was that what had happened to Mommy?

"You gotta think positive about yourself. Look at me. I must go to ten, twenty auditions a week and most of the time, I don't even get a call back, but do I let that discourage me? No. I just keep coming back at them. Sooner or later . . . sooner or later," he chanted.

I gazed at him, wondering if he, not me, was the one who should be pitied.

"It's just down this street," he finally said, after making a right turn. My heart seemed to stop and then pound, pound, pound like someone beating on a locked door. I held my breath as he slowed the limousine.

"That's it," he said, "The Egyptian Gardens. I just love the names they give these places."

I peered out the window. Tall hedges walled in the pink stucco complex that wound around the pool in an ell shape. The buildings were only five stories high, each unit with its own small balcony. Some had flower boxes with plants overflowing the sides. All had a small table and chairs. Although the pink shade was bright, the buildings looked worn, tired, chipped and battered in places. The lawn was spotty, some of the bushes looking sickly with many branches without blossoms.

There was a directory of the residents just to the right of the main gate above which was the name of the complex scrolled in dark pewter. Spike was right. I saw nothing Egyptian or even vaguely Arabic about the place and like him, wondered why it was called The Egyptian Gardens. The main gate opened and two young men in shorts and polo shirts, wearing sneakers without socks, walked out laughing. They were both slim and good looking, both with wavy dark hair. They were so identical, in fact, they looked like they could be twins.

"Pretty boys," Spike mumbled. He got out and opened

54

my door. For a moment I thought my legs wouldn't work, but I pushed myself up and stepped out. "I'll wait right here for you," Spike said.

"Thank you," I said, or at least I thought I had. I wasn't sure I actually made the sounds. He tilted his head.

"You okay?"

I nodded and crossed to the main gate. I looked up at the directory and read the names until I found Gina Simon. My fingers trembled as I reached up to press the button next to the name.

"No point in doing that," I heard a female voice say and turned as a young woman with bleached blond hair came up beside me. She was in a pink tank top and white spandex shorts and had her hair tied in a ponytail. She jogged in place as she spoke, her pretty face flushed, small beads of sweat across her brow. "It doesn't work. They were supposed to fix it last week and the week before and the week before, but nothing gets done fast around here." She took deep breaths and continued to lift her feet in rhythm. "Who you looking for?"

"Gina Simon?"

"Oh, Gina. Sure. She's right across from me. Four-C. Come on," she said and jogged through the main gate. She paused, holding the gate open, and continued to lift and drop her feet as she did so. "It's not locked. So much for security here."

I followed her in and she continued to jog down the walkway. I walked quickly, just about jogging myself to keep up. She paused when we reached the pool. Three young women in bikini bathing suits were sunning themselves on lounges. I gazed about quickly to see if Mommy was at the pool as well. I was relieved she wasn't. I didn't want to meet her in front of all these people.

A tall, very thin young man with short light brown hair sat dangling his legs over the diving board.

"Hey Sandy, how was your workout?" he asked the young woman who had let me into the complex.

"I nearly got hit by an idiot on a motor bike near Melrose," she said.

One of the women on the lounges sat up and braced herself on her elbow. She had long, reddish brown hair. Except for her nose, which was very pointed, she had nice features, too.

"Did you lose the five pounds?" she asked, rolling her eyes and smiling like a cat.

"I'm getting there," Sandy said. She spun on her heels and looked at me. "C'mon, before they eat you alive," she said and the three young women laughed. I hurried after her. She took me around the pool, down a walkway to the steps of the second building. Once inside, she stopped jogging.

"I'm trying to lose weight for an audition. It's a photo shoot and you know how the camera puts the pounds on you. The elevator's right down here," she said, indicating the corridor on her left. "I'm Sandra Glucker, but my show business name is Sandy Glee."

"My name's Melody," I said.

"Perfect," she said, shaking her head. "I love it. Actress, dancer, singer?"

"No," I said.

"No?" She stopped walking and turned back to me. "Are you a writer?"

"No," I said, smiling. "I'm not in the business."

"Oh. Oh," she repeated as if just realizing there were other kinds of people in California. She looked at me again. "You're pretty enough to be."

"Thank you."

"Gina Simon. How do you know, Gina? Oh, don't mind me. You don't have to tell me. I'm just someone addicted to gossip, but it's not as bad as some of the other addictions around here."

We stepped into the elevator and she pushed the button for the fourth floor.

"We know each other from someplace else," I said and hoped that would be enough for her.

"Someplace else? Is there someplace else?" She

laughed at her own remark. I smiled and the elevator door opened. "You're from Ohio?"

"Ohio?"

"That's where Gina's from, some small town near Columbus, I think. So, what, did you meet in school or something?"

"School? No." How old did she think I was? Even more important, how old did she think Gina Simon was?

"What, is it top secret? There's Four-C," she pointed to the door down the hallway. Instead of going into her own apartment she watched curiously as I walked toward apartment 4C.

I gazed back at her and flashed a nervous smile. Then I took a deep breath and knocked on the door.

"The door buzzer works," she said. "At least, it should."

"Oh. Thanks." I pushed it and waited. So did she. No one came to the door. I pushed the buzzer again. The seconds seemed more like minutes.

"She's probably not there. Maybe she went to an audition. Didn't you call first?"

"No," I said sadly.

"Too bad. In L.A., you should always call first. I'll probably see her later. You want me to tell her you were here?"

"No," I said and realized I said it too quickly. I smiled. "I was hoping to surprise her."

"Oh. Oh! I love surprises. So does Gina, I'm sure." She snapped her fingers. "You're not her sister, are you? She told me she has a younger sister. You are, aren't you?" she followed before I could speak. "That's terrific. She'll be so happy. She misses her family so much."

"She does?"

"Of course. Deep down inside, no matter how beautiful she looks and sophisticated she seems, Gina is a simple girl. That's why everyone loves her. You want to wait in my place?"

"Er, no. I'll just come back later. Thanks," I said.

"You sure. Because—"

"No, thanks," I said, my heart thumping fast. I hurried into the elevator and hit the button for the first floor. As the doors closed, Sandy Glee stepped out to look at me one more time, her face full of confusion.

The minute the doors opened, I rushed out. Then I did jog down the walkway, past the pool, where everyone looked at me, and to the gate. I hurried out and to the car.

"What happened?" Spike asked, stepping out to open my door.

I shook my head.

"She wasn't there, and . . ."

"And what?"

"I don't think it's my mother!" I cried.

# 4
## ❧

# A Different World

"Do you want to go right back to the house?" Spike asked me.

"I don't care," I wailed and curled up in the corner of the seat. I've come all this way for nothing, I thought, for a dream, a child's dream. I should have done what Dorothy suggested: had a private detective do the footwork first. But even that idea was silly. Where would I get the money to pay him? Grandma Olivia wouldn't have given it to me for that. She couldn't care less whether or not my mother was really alive unless it meant I was out of her hair, out of Provincetown and away from her precious family.

"I'm sorry you were disappointed," Spike continued, "but in L.A. you've got to learn how to live with disappointment."

"I don't want to be in L.A.!" I cried.

"Sure you do. You haven't seen the best of it yet," he replied. "Look at those houses up there. They call that the Hollywood Hills. The views are terrific. See how some of them are built on the edge of the hill? I bet they get a thrill when the earth shakes, huh?"

Despite myself, I peeked through my hands to look at the houses.

"And you're so close to the ocean here. If you want to go and relax or get some sun, hey, all you do is drive a few miles. I'll show you," he said and made another turn, sped up and headed west. "Say you're at work, see, and you've had a bad day, so before you go home to the old lady, you take a little detour," he rambled. "Back in the boondocks, you'd stop in some grungy tavern and moan over your suds. But here . . . hey, look over there. See that building. That was used as the front shot in *Gone with the Wind*. That's Tara!"

I glanced out the window.

"This is a movie studio," he continued. I sat up and gazed at the long white buildings and the trucks. Minutes later, Spike told me to look straight ahead, and there it was . . . the Pacific Ocean. Just the sight of the waves and the vast silvery blue water pulled at my heart. I thought about Cary and May and walking on the beach with Kenneth's dog Ulysses at my heels. I remembered the wind in my hair, the smell of the salt air, the sound of the terns above me, the wonderful feeling of being alive and part of nature.

Spike was right. We started out in a city and moments later, here we were, parking on a bluff overlooking a long stretch of beach.

"Let's walk over to the fence and look down over the Pacific Coast Highway." He got out and opened my door. I took a deep breath, felt myself relax, and then stepped out. "C'mon, follow me," he urged.

We walked over the grassy area where there were benches and where some older people were sitting around their portable folding tables and playing cards.

"This is Santa Monica," Spike explained. "It's a great little beach community, full of European tourists as well as locals. There's the Santa Monica Pier," he said pointing down the beach. "See the Ferris wheel. There's a merry-go-round there, too. It's fun! People are just coming off the beach," he added, nodding toward the shoreline below us. Cars rushed by on the Pacific Coast Highway and in the distance, the sun hovered between two clouds and just over the horizon. "That's Malibu," Spike said, continuing his explanation. "Pretty, isn't it? Sometimes, when I don't get anywhere in an audition, I stop by and just gaze out at the sea. It gives me a fresh outlook, boosts my morale, know what I mean?"

"Yes," I said. "I've been living in Cape Cod. I know the power of the sea."

"Oh yeah, right. I forgot. For some reason, I keep thinking of you as small town, West Virginia. You can't get away from that accent," he kidded. "Actually, it's cute and I bet some casting directors would love it."

I nodded and bit down on my lower lip, trying hard not to show my emotions.

"My parents were a lot older than most when they had me," Spike volunteered. "My mother was nearly forty and my father was in his fifties."

"When you were born?" I asked, thankful for the change of subject.

"Yeah. I guess they woke up one morning and looked at each other and said, 'You know what? We forgot to have children.'" He laughed. "Dad passed away last year. He made it to seventy-nine."

"Where are you from?"

"Phoenix. My mother still lives there with her sister in one of those golden age communities. She's a golfer, addicted. Whenever I do call her, all she talks about is her handicap and the great putt she made. I told her when she dies, I'll have people ride in golf carts behind the hearse." He laughed again and then shook his head. "She didn't think it was funny."

We both stood there, staring out at the sea. There were sailboats that looked like they were pasted against the darkening blue horizon, and farther out was what looked like a cruise ship heading southwest.

61

"If you want to go to the beach one day, I'd be glad to take you," Spike offered.

"Thank you, but I don't know if I'll be here all that much longer."

"I bet the Livingstons wouldn't mind how long you stayed. You should take advantage."

"I don't want to take advantage of their hospitality," I said, "and besides, I have people waiting for me back in Provincetown."

"People? You mean, a boyfriend?" he asked with an impish glint in his eyes.

"Yes," I admitted.

"What's he do?"

"He takes care of his father's lobster fishing boat right now and in the fall, he'll be harvesting cranberries."

"Sounds . . . nice," Spike offered, but his head was turned in a way that kept me from reading his eyes. Did he mean it? Did he really have a longing for something more substantial than acting or trying to be an actor, or was he just humoring me?

"It *is* nice," I said defensively. He glanced at me with a small smile on his lips.

"You're too young to cash in your chips and settle down, Melody. Look out there. It's a big, wide world to explore. There's so much to do and see."

Our eyes met. If he wasn't being sincere, he was a good actor after all, I thought.

"So what convinced you the woman wasn't your mother?" he asked finally.

"She comes from the Midwest, Ohio, and she's apparently a lot younger than my mother," I said.

"But she looks like your mother in that catalogue?"

"A lot like her. Different hair color, but that's nothing," I said.

"Well, people lie about their age here. It comes with the territory. Hollywood is a young person's world, especially for women, and triple especially for a woman who wants to be a model or in films."

"Really?"

62

"Absolutely," he said.

"This woman claimed to have a younger sister though, and my mother has no brothers or sisters," I said.

"So? People manufacture their pasts here. It's as if they stepped out of a movie of their own making," he continued. "Before you give up, I'd try again. Why don't you try calling her later?"

"I didn't get a phone number," I said.

"She'll be listed, especially if she wants to be an actress or model. She wants to be easily contacted."

I nodded.

"I guess we should get back," I said. "Dorothy wasn't too happy about my shooting off right away as it was."

"Sure," he said. He flashed me one of his warm smiles, took my hand and led me back to the limousine. When he opened the door for me, the people who were playing cards looked up to see who I was and drivers slowed their cars to glance our way. Everyone here was so eager to spot a celebrity, I thought. For the first time since we had arrived, I actually wished I was one. Was I starting to catch the disease?

When I returned to the Livingston's mansion, Dorothy came rushing down the hallway to greet me.

"What happened? I've been sitting on pins and needles waiting. I should have had Spike call me from the limousine. Well?" she asked.

"I still don't know anything for sure," I said and explained what had happened and why I was filled with new doubts.

"You poor thing. To come all this way and be so disappointed. Why couldn't that dreadful woman have been there?" she said, bunching her lips together.

"Spike says I should try to call her now."

"He does? Well, I suppose you can do that, too. But we're going to have dinner in about a half hour. Philip's already home and getting dressed."

"Dressed?"

"We always dress for dinner. Don't worry. Just put on the nicest thing you have to wear," she said. "Tomorrow,

I'm taking you to Adroni's on Rodeo to get you something fashionable."

"Oh, I really don't think—"

"Remember," she sang, "I get deaf."

I smiled.

"Thank you, Dorothy."

"My sister, the psychic, you should excuse the expression, called before to see if you arrived all right. I asked her if she was such a psychic, how come she doesn't know the answers to her questions before she asks them." Dorothy laughed at her own joke. I smiled, imagining Holly's reaction. "I forgot all about the little gift you handed me at the airport, so I had to pretend I had looked at it. I did a few minutes ago. Where does she expect me to wear these things?" she added shaking her head. "Anyway, I told her you would call her tomorrow. She was off to do some sort of hoodoo, voodoo thing."

"Thank you," I said, heading for the stairway. "I'll be right down."

"Don't worry yourself about the woman, dear. If she's not your mother, you're still welcome to stay here and enjoy Los Angeles for as long as you like."

"Thank you," I called back and hurried up the stairs to my plush room.

It wasn't until I plopped myself down on the bed that I realized just how tired I was. Young or not, I finally realized the time difference. After all, for me it was three hours later than it was for everyone here. I'll just rest for a few minutes, I thought and lay back, closing my eyes. A sharp rap on my door woke me immediately. I sprang into a sitting position.

"What? Yes?"

The door opened and Alec gazed in at me.

"Mr. and Mrs. Livingston are waiting for you in the dining room," he announced.

"Oh. Oh, I fell asleep! I'll be right there," I cried and hopped off the bed. He grimaced and closed the door.

I splashed cold water on my face, practically tore off my blouse and jeans, and pulled on my dress. I ran my brush through my hair once and then hurried out of the room and down the stairs.

The Livingstons were at the far end of the long table. Mr. Livingston sat at the end. He was dressed in a dark sport coat and navy blue tie. His thinning dark brown hair was parted on the right side and cut neatly around his ears. He glanced up at me, his hazel eyes sweeping over me quickly before turning downward again to look over the bridge of his narrow, bony nose, under which he wore a well-trimmed mustache. He had thin lips and a soft, almost round chin.

"Hello dear. I'd like you to meet Philip. Philip, this is Holly's little friend, Melody."

"Hello," he said quickly and flashed a smile that swept across his lips so fast, it was as if someone had turned a light on and off.

"Just sit right there, dear," Dorothy said, nodding at the seat across from her. She wore a black evening dress with puffy sleeves and a frilly, square collar, a pair of teardrop diamond earrings with a matching necklace and bracelet, and at least two more rings than she had on when I had first met her.

I took my seat and Philip looked up instantly at Alec. He moved quickly to begin serving us.

"I told Philip all about your little episode today," Dorothy continued, "and he made a wonderful suggestion. Tell her, Philip," she said.

"You're doing fine," he replied, glancing at me and then at his plate as he drummed his fingers on the table. Alec began serving us bowls of what looked like clear chicken broth with some rice and carrots.

"Philip says this woman has to have a social security number. Everyone has a social security number. He will call the business manager at the catalogue company and check the number to see if it's under her name or your mother's name. Isn't that a wonderful suggestion?"

I nodded and looked at Philip. He began eating his soup.

"Just common sense," he muttered between slurps.

Then he paused, his spoon perfectly still before him, not a tremble in his hand. "Of course, people have been known to produce phoney identification and get a new social security number. We'll see," he added.

"So you see, dear, you don't have to spend any more time chasing down this woman. Just relax and enjoy your visit," Dorothy said.

Philip twisted the right corner of his mouth so deeply it looked like his lips were made of pale pink clay.

"It won't be something I can do overnight," he muttered.

"That's all right. I'll still want to meet this woman," I said.

"Philip thinks that might be dangerous."

"I didn't say dangerous. I said unpleasant."

"Well, that's practically the same thing," Dorothy insisted.

He put his spoon down and sat back. Alec moved instantly to remove his soup bowl. I had barely eaten half of my small portion and took two quick spoonfuls when I felt Alec hovering over my shoulder. Dorothy didn't dip her spoon into the cup more than twice, but that seemed to be enough.

A small dinner salad followed, accompanied by the thinnest slices of bread, paper-thin slices that crumbled in your fingers.

Our main course was veal medallions in a lemon sauce, accompanied by string beans and mashed potatoes with a flavor I couldn't recognize. Everything was delicious, but as I ate, I noticed Dorothy watching me and recalled her warning about eating too much. I could have eaten more, but I stopped.

Philip made little conversation but he was interested in my description of the lobster fishing business and the Cape Cod tourist business. He said he had some clients interested in investing in a hotel chain that serviced the Cape and he was not keen about it.

Dinner was followed by coffee in a silver service and a

custard dessert. It had been a wonderful meal and I said so as I thanked them.

"Maybe we should ask Selena to prepare lobster for us tomorrow night, Philip, in Melody's honor," Dorothy said as the meal came to an end.

"Lobster's overpriced these days," he grumbled.

How could anyone with this much money worry about the price of lobster? I wondered.

"Oh nonsense," Dorothy said.

"I don't enjoy eating things that I know are overpriced," he insisted.

"I really don't need to have lobster, Dorothy."

"Of course she doesn't," Philip said, nodding. "She gets it dirt cheap back on the Cape and it won't be as good here. Think of something else," he said. "I've got some work to finish in my office," he explained as he rose. I realized he was not quite as tall as Dorothy. "It was nice meeting you," he added, nodding as he walked away.

"Philip's the most efficient man I've ever known," Dorothy said shaking her head. "He reviews the household accounts once a month and makes brilliant suggestions to save money. He says he does it for his clients, why can't he do it for himself? I suppose that's true. Well, do you want to find something to read? You can look in our library. I try to keep up with everything. I belong to three book clubs."

"First, I'd like to try to call Gina Simon," I explained.

"Oh. Well then, why don't you use the phone in the parlor. You'll have some privacy there," she suggested.

"Thank you," I said, trying to remember where the parlor was in this big house. She must have read that in my face.

"Just go down the corridor to the third doorway on the left, dear. There's a phone book on the shelf of the small table."

"Thank you."

"You're welcome. I'll be in after a while and then we

can go to the den and watch some television if you like. *Desperate Lives* is on tonight. Do you watch it? Philip calls it nothing more than a soap opera, but it's so much more than that, it's . . . just more," she said.

"No, I haven't heard of it," I said.

"Haven't heard of it? Oh dear. Well, maybe you'll like it," she said and I went to the parlor. I found the phone book and discovered three Gina Simons, but the address pointed out the right one. With my fingers trembling again, I lifted the receiver. It was an antique brass and ivory dial phone and I misdialed the first time and got a phone number that was disconnected.

I dialed correctly the next time, but after only three rings, an answering machine came on.

"This is Gina Simon. I'm sorry I'm not able to take this call. Please leave your name, the time of your call and a brief message at the sound of the beep," the voice directed. I listened closely. It did sound like Mommy, but there was an affectation, an attention to diction I didn't recognize. I waited and called again just to hear the voice. It sounds like her, I told myself. It must be Mommy.

Dorothy entered the parlor, a small white angora cat in her arms.

"This is Fluffy," she said. "Isn't she beautiful?"

"Yes, she is."

"Philip won't let me keep her in the house proper. She stays with Selena. He says whenever she's permitted to run through the house, she leaves hairs everywhere. He's so finicky about the house. If a piece of dust is out of place, Philip knows it."

She sighed and sat in the soft cushioned chair across from me, the cat purring in her lap.

"So, did you try calling that woman?"

"I got an answering machine," I said. "It sounds like my mother."

"Did you leave a message?"

"No. I wasn't sure what to say."

"She might have been there, listening," Dorothy said,

nodding. "People often do that here. They wait to see if it's someone important and then they answer. If it's not someone important enough, they let the machine take the call. It's a power thing, Philip says."

"Power thing?"

"Yes, you just don't speak to anyone. It diminishes your importance."

"I can't imagine my mother thinking that way."

"Well, if this woman wants to be someone in the industry, she behaves that way, believe me. I've met enough of them."

I thought about it. What was it Billy Maxwell had told me just before I had left New York . . . be prepared to find a very different woman, even if she was my mother. Perhaps that was very true.

"I wish the world we lived in wasn't so conscious of every little thing," Dorothy said, dreamy-eyed as she petted the purring cat in her lap. "Philip wants me to be perfect, to remain perfect. If I have a hair out of place, he asks why I didn't go to the beauty salon this week," she said a bit more mournfully than I would have expected.

"He doesn't seem like that," I told her. She snapped out of her reverie and raised her eyebrows.

"He's a man, isn't he? They're all the same, waving a magnifying glass over you, checking for wrinkles, for age spots, measuring your bosom, your waist, your hips, looking for an ounce of ugly fat.

"I have a personal trainer," she continued, "who comes to the house three times a week. It's such a bore, but I bear it for Philip's sake. And my own, I suppose," she said with a sigh. "Well, a woman has to do all she can, doesn't she?" she added.

"I'm not sure. I've never really thought about it I guess," I said.

"Of course you haven't. You're still young and beautiful. You have a way to go, but believe me, one day you'll wake up and look in the mirror and notice a little wrinkle here, a little more puffiness there and you'll realize it's going to take some work to look beautiful.

"Of course," she continued, "if you're bright enough, you won't settle for just anyone and you'll marry someone substantial as I did, so he can provide you with the best there is when it comes to cosmetic surgery."

"Surgery?"

"Now don't sit there and flatter me and tell me you didn't notice how firm my buttocks are for a woman of my age without thinking I had something done," she said smiling.

"I didn't really notice, but . . ." An operation on her rear end?

"It's nothing more involved than a tummy tuck. I can't tell you how many times I've had that done. Oh, and my eyes of course. Some people are so lucky. They're born with genes that help them to remain young-looking longer. Philip's mother, for example, hardly had a wrinkle in her late seventies and look at Philip. Well, it's always different for men anyway. They can have wrinkles. It makes them distinguished-looking, but we girls . . .

"Well," she said with a little more animation in her face, "do you think our sexual relationship would be as strong as it is if I didn't keep myself attractive? There's an article about it in my latest issue of *Venus*. According to scientific studies, a successful relationship means a husband and wife make love on the average of five times a month, even at our ages. I told Philip about it and he said his own research indicated between four and six times. We mark the calendar. You probably noticed it on the wall by our bed. Philip appreciates order in his life.

"Oh, I know what men do when they have ugly wives," she continued, ignoring my gaping mouth, "especially in this town," she said, nodding. "A woman has to work on her relationship. That's her job. And I don't mind telling you I'm very successful at it.

"You saw how the young male waiters were gazing at me at The Vine," she said, batting her eyelashes and smiling. "They have no idea how old I am, and they'll never know," she said firmly. "You guard your age like

70

you guard your life. Never tell a man your true age. Always subtract five to seven years at the least," she advised.

"Oh no," she said suddenly, rising to her feet. *"Desperate Lives* has started. Quickly," she ordered and marched out of the parlor.

I sat there for a moment, trying to digest the things she had told me the way you would try to digest food that was far too spicy. The words kept repeating themselves.

"Come along, dear!" she shouted.

I rose and joined her in the hallway. She turned in to the den and flipped on the television set. Then she plopped herself into her overstuffed chair, curling her legs under her lap, and gazed at the television screen like a teenager about to see her teen idol. I sat on the sofa beside her and listened to her little moans and sighs as one handsome young man after another paraded before us on the large television screen.

But fatigue began to rise in my body like mercury in a thermometer. I felt my eyelids getting heavier and heavier and drifted off a few times, only to be wakened by her shouts at the television set, complaining about something a character said or did, as if she thought they could actually hear her.

"Doesn't that just get you infuriated," she railed, turning my way. I nodded, even though I had no idea why she was so upset. "And I hate it when they leave you hanging like that. But," she said, smiling suddenly, her mood swinging radically in the opposite direction, "as Philip says, that's how they get you to tune in night after night and how they get to sell all those products. You look tired, dear. Perhaps you should go to bed. I know it's late for you."

"Yes, I guess it's all finally caught up with me," I said, rising. "Thank you so much for everything."

"Nonsense. Tomorrow, right after breakfast, we'll go to Rodeo Drive and get you something proper to wear. Don't," she said, raising her hand to stop any protest, "say anything that will make me deaf. Philip and I have

71

no children. I was never fond of the idea of being pregnant and Philip really can't tolerate little people very well anyway. But we both enjoy doing things for young people now and then. When they're deserving, as you are, of course." She smiled. "Have a good night's rest."

"Thank you," I said again, too tired to argue anyway, and went upstairs, taking the steps as if I were already walking in my sleep.

Despite my exhaustion, before I turned out the lights and crawled under the cover, I lifted the phone receiver and dialed Gina Simon's number. It rang and rang until the answering machine came on again, and again, I listened closely to her voice, feeling more and more confident that it sounded like Mommy's voice. Or was I just wishing it did?

And why wasn't she picking up? Had she gone away? Maybe it would be days, weeks, before I stood face to face with her.

I lay my head back on the pillow and closed my eyes, grateful I was too tired to continue thinking, but still apprehensive as to what tomorrow would bring.

# 5

### &

# *A Bitter Pill*

Once again it was a gentle knock on my door that woke me, but this time a pleasant-looking woman with strands of gray running through her dark brown hair entered. The breakfast tray she carried was laden with a silver coffee pot, cup and saucer, a plate, silverware, eggs in a dish, a croissant, jelly and butter and a tall glass of freshly squeezed orange juice. Alongside everything was a small vase with a single fresh red rose.

"Good morning," the woman said. She had a pretty smile brightened with the warmest blue eyes I had ever seen. She was about five feet two with a small bosom and hips definitely too wide for Dorothy's taste. Her forearms were strong, but she had small hands. "I'm Christina, Mrs. Livingston's maid. She asked me to bring up your breakfast this morning."

"Oh, you didn't have to do that," I said, sitting up and struggling to get my eyelids to stay open. "What time is it?" I gazed at the clock in the belly of a light blue ceramic seagull. "I've never slept this late."

"It's all right, dear. Mrs. Livingston insisted," Christi-

73

na said, placing the tray on a bed table she'd retrieved from the closet.

"You have two, two-minute soft-boiled eggs," she said, lifting the cover to show me. "Did you want anything else? Hot cereal, different juice? I have freshly squeezed grapefruit or prune."

"No, this is fine, but I could have come downstairs," I said, uncomfortable with all her fussing.

"Only Mr. Livingston comes down for breakfast as a rule," Christina replied with a smile. "He reads the morning papers and doesn't mind eating alone. Mrs. Livingston always takes her breakfast in bed. Do you have everything you need?" she asked, walking into the bathroom. "More towels, anything?"

"I'm fine at the moment," I said, drinking my juice. "Thank you."

She nodded at me and watched me take a few bites of the croissant.

"I hear you're from the East and this is your first trip to California," she said.

"Yes."

"I've never been to New York, but I hope to go one of these days. I have a daughter who can't be much younger than you," she added. "Her name's Stacy. She's starting community college this year, working at a department store and taking some courses. She wants to be a grade school teacher."

"That's great," I said. "I guess she likes working with children."

"Yes, she's a great help with my others. I wish we could afford to send her full-time, but . . . we just can't at the moment."

"How many children do you have?"

"I'm raising four," she added.

"Four?"

How did she manage raising four children while working as someone's maid, and have such a pleasant personality? I wondered.

"The youngest is six, a boy." She paused at the

doorway. "Just leave everything beside the bed. I'll be up later," she told me. "Let me know if you need anything," she added as she left.

I couldn't help feeling quilty about being pampered so much while I had yet to make contact with Mommy, so I ate the delicious breakfast quickly, then showered and dressed, taking more time than usual with my hair. Dorothy had made me so self-conscious about my looks I was afraid she would rush me off to the beauty parlor if I didn't look pretty enough to greet the California morning.

Mr. Livingston was just leaving the house when I came down the stairs. He wore a pin-striped suit and maroon and white tie. He stopped at the front door to look up at me as I descended.

"Good morning," he said.

"Good morning."

"I hope you had a good night's rest," he said without a smile.

"Yes, thank you."

"Well, enjoy your day," he added. He looked uncomfortable speaking to me alone. He fumbled with his briefcase and then hurried out the door.

I thought about dialing Gina Simon's number again, but imagined I would only get the answering machine. It was better to go over there in person. I had to wonder if Sandy Glee had told her she had a visitor and then described me to her.

"Excuse me, miss," Alec said, seemingly appearing out of nowhere. "You have a phone call."

"A phone call? I do?"

"Your name is Melody, is it not?" he asked sharply, as if he thought I was being critical.

"Yes."

"Then, you have a phone call. You can take it in the parlor," he said nodding in that direction.

"Thank you."

I hurried in and lifted the receiver.

"Hello."

"Hi," Holly said. "Sorry I missed you yesterday, but I had a reading to do and by the time it was over, I thought it might be too late."

"That's all right."

"How are you doing? Did you meet the woman in the catalogue yet? Kenneth called me early this morning to see if I had heard from you."

I told her about my visit to the apartment complex and the things Sandy Glee had told me about Gina Simon.

"I'm not getting good vibes, Melody. Remember what I told you. Pack up and come back if things aren't what you hoped they would be," she said.

"I will," I promised.

"Good. How's my sister treating you?"

"Like royalty," I said. I told her about my room and my breakfast in bed.

Holly laughed.

"I hear you. She's a character, huh? And Philip, did he say more than two words?"

"About seven or eight," I said, laughing. It was so good hearing Holly's voice, hearing the sincerity and the warmth. "It's nice of you to call, Holly. It's nice of you to care."

"Would you be any different if roles were reversed?" she asked. "Billy sends his regards, too."

"Tell him hi and I'll call you guys as soon as I know . . . anything," I said.

"Okay. Take care and don't let Dorothy talk you into a face lift while you're there," she warned before hanging up.

Before I had even set the phone down, Dorothy appeared.

"Good, you're up," she said as she entered the room. "The stores are just opening."

"I'm sorry I overslept. I'm usually up a lot earlier than this."

"Overslept? Nonsense. A woman needs her sleep.

76

That old fashioned idea about beauty rest happens to be true. If you don't rest your skin, it gets old faster. I never get up much earlier than this unless I have a very important reason. Anyway, I've called for the car. I just have to tell Selena what Philip wants her to make for dinner tonight and then we'll be off to the shops."

"Dorothy, really, I just want to go back to the apartment complex, see Gina Simon and—"

"You need something decent to wear first. Then you'll go," she insisted.

"Really, I—"

"Deaf," she said, shaking her head with her hands over her ears. "Meet me outside. Spike's bringing the car around."

She left for the kitchen. There was nothing to do but let her be generous, I thought, and then pay another visit to The Egyptian Gardens.

Anyway, I couldn't help but be impressed with the stores on Rodeo Drive. Papa George and Mama Arlene, who had lived next to to us in Sewell, West Virginia, used to say their grandparents came to America thinking the streets were paved with gold. This was the closest anything came to that, I thought. The designer clothing stores with their richly draped mannequins in the windows, the grand art and antique galleries, the beautiful restaurants and expensive jewelry stores all made it look like shopping for the rich and privileged. Everywhere I looked, I saw Rolls Royces, Mercedes, and other expensive automobiles, as well as limousines like ours with chauffeurs in uniforms opening doors for people who looked like they were all in a contest to outdress each other.

"Right here, Spike," Dorothy ordered and turned to me to say, "I know this boutique well. They have the sort of clothing young girls like these days. You'll see," she promised.

When we entered the store, I thought it was going out of business. There were so few things on display, each item was treated like a special work of art. Toward the rear of the store was a bar where a bartender prepared cappuccinos, lattes and espresso for the customers. The saleslady recognized Dorothy immediately and hurried over, her high heels clicking on the Spanish tile.

"Enchanted, Mrs. Livingston. How have you been?" she asked, her hand out limply. A gold bracelet filled with diamonds dangled from her small wrist. She looked like she had spent a half a day preparing her makeup and hair. Not a hair was out of place and she had the most even pancake complexion I had ever seen, which made her look tan down to the base of her neck, after which there was a milk-white line. Dorothy just squeezed her fingers quickly.

"Very well, thank you, Farma. This is my sister's friend from the East Coast. She had to rush here and wasn't able to pack her better things. So I thought we would just pick up something nice for her to wear during the day and something for the evening."

"Oh, how nice," Farma replied and gleamed at me with dollar signs in her eyes. "We just received this Italian pants suit in a perfect color for . . ."

"Melody," Dorothy said. "I knew you would have something appropriate."

"Come dear," she said, drinking me in to measure my size. "What a delicious little figure you have."

"Doesn't she?" Dorothy said.

I never felt anything as soft as the material out of which the pants suit had been made. It was a creamy white color with swirls of pink through it and it did fit perfectly. When I gazed at myself in the mirror, I felt my ego swell. Then I glanced at the tag dangling from the left sleeve and I almost fainted. It was fourteen hundred dollars!

"She looks fantastic," Dorothy said. "What a wonderful choice for day wear," she said, without even checking the price. "Now, let's think about something for the evening. I plan to take her to Chasens tomorrow night, and you never know who might walk in."

"Oh, I have a darling black dress, just in from Paris." Farma hurried off to get it and I spun on Dorothy.

"Dorothy, look at the price of this!" I exclaimed. She gazed indifferently at the tag.

"What of it, dear? Decent things are going to be expensive these days."

"But this—"

"Please," she said widening her eyes, "don't embarrass me. I know all the salespeople in these stores and they know me. Oh, that does look sweet," she said when Farma brought out the thin-strapped evening dress. Reluctantly, I tried it on and it also fit perfectly, flattering my figure, but it was eighteen hundred dollars! I couldn't swallow after Dorothy told her to wrap up the evening dress.

"She'll wear the pants outfit now," she declared.

"Very good," Farma said.

"Dorothy . . ." I stood, astounded.

She stepped up to me so she could lower her voice.

"If I don't spend my money, Philip will only invest it in one of those dreary annuity funds and tie up the money for years. As it is, I never get to spend all of my monthly allowance."

"You have an allowance?" I asked, amazed at the idea of a grown woman being given an allowance.

"Of course I do. And if I don't use it, I can't get him to raise it, can I? He's too smart. He'll simply say I don't spend what I get now, so why raise it? All of my friends get allowances and I happen to be at the top. I don't intend to lose that position," she added.

"Besides," she continued, "I don't enjoy giving my money to charity as much as I do buying something for a pretty young girl. It makes me feel . . ." She smiled. ". . . feel younger myself. I used to have a figure like yours . . . naturally. Now go put on that suit. We're going to go someplace special for lunch and many of my friends will be there."

She smiled triumphantly.

"When Spike takes you back to the apartment complex, people will pay more attention to you and be more impressed with you. They'll take you more seriously. You'll see. Here everyone's impressed by clothes and cars first, and then they consider the person wearing the clothes and driving the car. You'll learn."

"I feel like they should have given me a passport when I left the East Coast," I remarked and she laughed so hard she had to tell Farmà what I had said. Then they both laughed again.

While I changed into the Italian pants suit, Dorothy bought herself three blouses and two skirts. The bill at the end of our visit was enough to keep a family of four in food and shelter for months back in Sewell, I thought, but I dared not utter another complaint.

Before Dorothy had Spike take us to lunch, she insisted on buying me a pair of shoes to match the pants suit and a pair for the evening dress. Then we had lunch at a little café off Rodeo Drive where a sandwich cost as much as an entire meal anywhere else in America. Dorothy seemed to know everyone there, introducing me as her sister's close friend. I listened to them chatter about clothes and jewelry, and all the things they had bought that morning. Everyone managed to get in how much they had paid, as if the higher the cost, the more justified they were in buying it.

My head was spinning from this spending whirlwind by the time Dorothy had Spike drive her home. Alec was brought out to carry my packages up to my room, and then I was finally excused to pay another visit to the apartment complex.

"You look great," Spike said. "You belong in expensive clothes."

"Nobody belongs in things that cost this much. It's outrageous," I said. He laughed.

"It's supposed to be. This is Hollywood. Later, I'll take you up to Grauman's Chinese Theater and you can look at the footprints and handprints of the stars."

"I'd rather find the footprints of my mother," I

mumbled and sat back, hoping this time I would have more success.

Now that I knew the buzzer on the directory at the front of the complex didn't work, I simply entered through the main gate and followed the path past the pool. There were a half dozen young men and women sunning themselves on the lounges, some holding reflectors under their chins. Unlike the first time, no one paid any notice to me. I didn't see Sandy Glee anywhere. As I approached the building in which I knew Gina Simon's apartment was located, I heard a loud, familiar laugh. A woman I was sure was Mommy came out of the entrance accompanied by a short, stout man with thinning gray hair and a bulbous nose. He had thick lips and was wearing a pair of thick-lensed eyeglasses that made his eyes look like the eyes of a dead fish.

I knew it was Mommy because when she saw me, she gasped, brought her hand to the base of her throat, and paused. Her escort looked at her curiously and then at me. Mommy regained her composure with a deep breath and smiled at the man.

"Anything wrong?" he asked. I stood waiting, my heart thumping like a parade drum. "You forget something?" he followed when she didn't reply.

"No," she said quickly. "It's all right."

"Well, we had better move along. Gerry Spindler is the sort of producer who likes to be the one who's late for a meeting, not the person he's interviewing. Not that I think there's a doubt about you, sweetheart. He'd have to be made of stone to pass on you," the stout man said and laughed grotesquely, his jowls shaking and his lips curling. Mommy fixed her eyes on me as they continued toward me.

"Mommy!" I exclaimed when she was only a few feet away.

"Pardon me?" she said.

The stout man brought his head back.

"Mommy, what's going on? Alice found your picture in a catalogue and sent it to me in Provincetown and Kenneth found out who you were and where you were," I said quickly. "Grandma Olivia gave me the money to come out here. Mommy, don't you recognize me?"

"What?" she said laughing.

"Who is this?" the stout man asked.

"I have no idea," Mommy said. Her eyes turned as cold as two small stones in a West Virginia mountain brook.

"It's me, Mommy. Melody. Don't you recognize me? Really?"

"First, honey," she said in a sharp, hard voice I didn't recall, "I could never be your Mommy. I'd have to have been six when I had you."

The stout man roared with laughter.

"And second, I never saw you before in my life. I wish they would fix that damn security system here," she told the stout man. "Any riffraff can walk in off the street and you know what we have walking the streets around here these days."

"Yeah," he said nodding and gazing at me.

"Mommy . . ." Tears burned under my eyelids. I tried to swallow so I could continue, but the lump in my throat felt like a chunk of coal.

"Maybe it's someone's idea of a joke," the stout man offered. "Anyway, don't worry about the security system. You get this job and you'll be able to move into a classy place, honey. And so will Mr. Marlin."

"Please, listen," I finally uttered. Mommy glanced at me and then quickly threw her head back to brush the hair from her eyes. I was shocked by how empty she could make her eyes, as if she knew how to turn all her emotions off. She tightened her hand around the arm of her fat escort and continued down the walkway as if I didn't exist.

I stood there, gaping after them, watching her disappear around a turn. She laughed at something the man said and then threw me one final disdainful look before she disappeared. I sank to the stone bench at the side of the walkway, stunned, feeling cold, actually shivering in the hot California sun. Despite her coldness, there was something in Mommy's eyes that told me she had recognized me, that she wasn't suffering from amnesia, but at the same time, there was something that said, "Be gone, don't you dare come back into my life, especially now."

How could she pretend to be a woman in her twenties? She looked it, but she knew she wasn't, and how could she leave me standing here, amazed and in shock after I had come so far? I buried my face in my hands and started to sob. I had come all this way to be ignored and rejected by my own mother, who I had hoped would be so happy to see me it would even cure amnesia. I took a deep breath and sat back. I remained there, staring, shaking my head, feeling nauseated and sick. Tears streamed down my cheeks, dripping off my chin, but I made no attempt to wipe them away.

A handsome dark-haired, young man and a very pretty blond-haired woman came hurrying down the walkway. They both glanced at me and smiled as if seeing someone bawling on a bench was just part of the scenery around here. They hurried into the building, their laughter tinkling behind them. Above me, a window was open and Latin rhythms came pouring out. This was not a place to be mournful, I thought and rose to my feet. I actually wobbled for a moment, the world around me taking a spin. I held on to the back of the bench and waited for the vertigo to pass, but it lingered like cramps that wouldn't dissolve.

"Hey, what are you doing?" I heard and turned to see Spike standing there. "You all right?"

"No," I wailed.

"What happened? I've been waiting and waiting. I thought I had better come in and see if I could find you. Hey," he said and lunged at me to prevent me from crumpling to the cement walkway.

Only minutes later I woke in his arms. He was sitting

on the bench with me in his lap, gently slapping my cheek.

"Melody . . . Melody . . ."

"What happened?"

My eyes fluttered open again and the world came back into focus.

"You fainted," he explained.

"Oh. I'm sorry," I said, feeling horribly embarrassed. Fortunately, no one else had come by to gawk. We were still alone. Spike helped me sit up.

"You all right? Take a deep breath. Go on. That's it. What happened?" he asked when the color returned to my face.

"I met her," I said. "Right here. She came out of the building with some man and I was no more than a foot away from her."

"So?"

"It was my mother, but she pretended she didn't know me. She said she couldn't be old enough to have had a daughter my age and she laughed at me." I started to sob again. "She told the man I was some sort of riffraff coming off the street. She wished they had fixed the security system so I would be kept out."

"Take it easy," Spike said and put his arm around my shoulders. "She was probably putting on an act for that guy."

"But why? Why was that more important than me? I came across the whole country to find her and she hasn't seen me for so long. Why?"

He shrugged.

"She probably had an audition or something and maybe the guy was a producer she was stringing along. I don't know. This is Hollywood."

"You keep saying that as if it justifies everything that goes on around here," I snapped back at him. "I don't care if it's Hollywood. People should still be decent to each other, especially mothers to their daughters."

He smiled at me as if I had said the silliest thing.

"You know something," he remarked, nodding as he

gazed at my disdain, "you could be quite an actress. You've got integrity. You can reach down into the emotion well and draw up the right responses."

"I don't want to be an actress! I don't want to be in Hollywood! I'm not pretending to feel bad. I *do* feel bad! I want my mother to acknowledge me and explain why she has done these terrible things," I cried.

"Maybe she will, one of these days," he said calmly. "But now's obviously not the right time. Come on. Let's get out of here. I hate complexes like this, filled with people trying to make it in the business. You can cut the desperation in the air. It's depressing," he said as he stood. "Come on." He held out his hand for me. I took it and stood up. "You okay? You think you can walk?"

"Yes," I said.

"Great." He kept his arm around me and we started down the walkway. The sight of a chauffeur walking with his arm around a young woman in an expensive Italian pants suit drew some eyes as we passed the pool again. It almost made me laugh, but my heart was too heavy for any sort of joviality. All I could think of was Mommy's cold, indifferent eyes and her voice cutting through me like a band saw.

I got into the limousine and Spike drove us away. He continued to make excuses for Mommy as we went along.

"If she is your mother, when you confront her alone, she'll be different," he assured me. "You caught her by surprise, that's all."

"She's definitely my mother," I said. "The instant I set eyes on her in person, I knew and she knew me. She just . . . made herself so different."

"That's—"

"Don't say it," I warned. He laughed.

"Hey, you've got to step back, catch your breath and try again. You'll get to the bottom of it all, I'm sure."

I didn't reply. I gazed with empty eyes at the scenery that flew by, no longer seeing the beautiful flowers and plush lawns, the glitzy stores and exciting billboards.

This was a place I'd rather not be in, I thought. I closed my eyes and wished I was walking on the beach. I concentrated as hard as I could until I could hear the waves lapping at the shore and could see the whitecaps sparkling in the New England sunshine. It put a smile on my face.

"You okay?" Spike asked, watching me in the rearview mirror.

"Yes."

"Good. Hey, did I tell you I have a chance for a really great part tomorrow?"

"No."

"It's a recurring role. Know what that means?"

"No."

"Well, if I get the part, I'll be in this episode and then the writers will write me into others, so I'll work on a regular basis and really get some exposure. From there, the sky's the limit," he said. "It's not a very big role to start, about thirty lines, but it's the impact on the show that counts. You want to see the script, maybe help me rehearse?"

"Help you rehearse? How can I do that?"

"I'll do my lines and you'll read the others. I'd like to have you hear me recite. You've got a fresh ear and would probably hear my mistakes."

"I don't know anything about acting, Spike."

"That makes you an expert around here," he said and laughed. "Come on. You don't want to just hang out with Dorothy, do you?"

"Not really," I said. It was probably unkind to say that about someone who had been so generous and hospitable to me, but I really wasn't in the mood to hear about expensive clothing or beauty tips. How I wished I could drop in on Holly and Billy. If only they weren't so far away. I longed to run up the stairway to Cary's private workroom and throw myself into his arms, too.

But I was here, among strangers, with my own mother being the biggest stranger of all.

"Will you? Please," he said.

"Okay," I replied.

"Great," Spike said. "I appreciate it."

When we arrived at the Livingston residence, Spike pulled the limousine around to the garage instead of to the front of the house. He opened my door and directed me to a side door that took us upstairs to his apartment.

"Don't mind any of the mess in here," he said, throwing some clothing into a pile behind the sofa. "Between driving for Mrs. Livingston and preparing for auditions, I don't get much time to be a housekeeper. Is it stuffy in here?" he asked, throwing open a window.

"It's all right," I said. There was a pile of scripts on the sofa. He hurriedly cleared them away to make a space for me. "How about something to drink? Beer, juice, water?"

"I'll just have some water, thank you," I said.

"Sure." He rushed into the kitchen. I gazed around the bland apartment. There was nothing on the walls and except for the scripts piled here and there and the clothing and dishes scattered about, there was no personality to the place. It reminded me of the thrifty motels Mommy, Archie Marlin and I stayed at during our trip up to Provincetown. Now that seemed ages and ages ago. It was hard to believe the woman I had just confronted was the same woman, but she was. I was positive about that and right now, it started to make me angry.

"Wow, what a look on your face!" Spike said returning with a glass of ice water. He handed it to me and I drank.

"She had no right to treat me like that. I don't care who was with her," I said.

He nodded.

"You'll tell her, I'm sure," he said. "I'll tell you something," he said, stepping back and scrutinizing me from head to toe as he nodded, "when you get angry and your face gets all flushed and your eyes look like they have candles burning behind them, it's rather exciting."

He put his hands together, thumb to thumb like a film director and gazed at me through the opening, moving about as would a camera director searching for the best perspective. I shook my head and laughed.

"You're always in a movie," I said.

"That's life, a movie. I'm trying to get good reviews, that's all," he said, laughing at his own joke. He poured himself a glass of beer and then handed me a script with the pages marked.

*"Desperate Lives?"* I said, looking at the title page. "This is Dorothy's favorite show."

"I know. I haven't told her I'm going for a part in it yet. She would make me too nervous. Okay, here's the setup. I'm Trent Windfield, who has discovered he's more in love with his girlfriend's sister than with his girlfriend. Her name's Arizona."

"Arizona? That's a state," I said, finding the name on the page.

"That's what her parents named her because they have this multimillion-dollar ranch there. In this scene, Trent decides to tell Arizona how he really feels about her. The problem is he's a graduate student and she's only a high school junior. Her father, a man with a fiery temper, would have him shot."

"How does Arizona feel about Trent?" I asked, gazing at the lines.

"She's always had a crush on Trent, but she never dreamed it would turn into anything. She's over-whelmed, but excited, titillated. It's a dream come true. Ready?" he asked, standing before me.

"Okay, I guess."

"Top of the page," he said. I watched him lower his head and then raise it slowly, his face changing, his eyes filling with emotion.

"No one knows I'm home," he said. "I drove right to your house." He fell to his knees at my feet. It took me by surprise and I gaped at him. "Read your lines," he coached out of the side of his mouth.

"Oh." I looked at the pages. "Why? Why did you come here first, Trent?"

88

He took my hand.

"Because the things I said to you just before I left . . . the things I told you I was feeling haunted me. I couldn't study. I couldn't talk to anyone. All I've been doing is thinking about you. Every time I look at another girl, she has your face, Arizona." He leaned on my knees and drew closer.

I gazed at the pages again.

"If you're teasing me, this is cruel," I said.

"It would be like teasing myself, like being cruel to myself," he said. "I know this is biting into forbidden fruit, but I would chance being thrown out of Paradise just for one of your kisses," he said.

I started to look at the pages again when his fingers slipped under my chin and gently lifted my face so he could lean over and kiss me softly on the lips. My eyes went wide.

"Arizona," he said. "Your name is branded on the front of my brain."

He kissed me again, this time putting his hands on my shoulders to hold me and draw me closer, making his kiss harder, his tongue moving through his lips and slipping in between mine. Surprised, I sat back.

"I knew you loved me just as much. I knew it," he said and flooded my face with kisses, running his lips down to my neck. His hands went to my waist.

"Spike," I said.

"Trent," he replied, and covered my mouth with his again, his kiss forcing me back on the sofa. His right hand moved off my waist and up over my ribs until he reached my breast.

"Wait," I cried.

"There is no time to wait," he said, still acting as if we were in his scene. But my words were my own. I wasn't reading off a page. In fact, the script had fallen from my hands. Spike pushed me down on the sofa, his lips moving to my chin, my neck and then his fingers separating the jacket of the pants suit so he could lift it and slide his hands under my silk blouse. When his fingers reached my bra, I twisted and turned to break free.

"Don't be afraid," he whispered in my ear. "This is the way grown-ups make love."

"Spike, stop!" I cried. His lifted my bra and soon the tips of his fingers were sliding over the top of my breast, strumming my nipple as his lips continued searching my neck, my face, his left hand against my head, trying to get me to return his kisses.

I brought my knees up higher and then, with all my strength, pushed into his stomach. He lost his balance and fell off the sofa. I didn't wait to give him a chance to recuperate. I shot up and turned away from the sofa, straightening my clothing quickly.

"Are you crazy?" I demanded.

He sat back, a wide, silly grin on his face.

"I'm just getting into my scene. What are you getting so excited about?"

"That's not in your scene," I accused.

"It's what we call improvisation. It helps you to build your part. You get into the character. That's all. Come on," he said, patting the sofa again. "Let's try again and when you get into it—"

"I'm not getting into anything," I said, backing away. "If this is acting, I'd rather do someone's laundry," I added.

He laughed.

"Melody, really—"

"Thanks for the introduction to dramatics," I said, heading for the door. "You should do real well. Good luck," I said and charged out of his apartment, down the stairs, bursting into the sunshine.

Maybe everyone was crazy here. Maybe like Spike said, everyone was moving in his or her own movie. Mommy certainly seemed to be.

Instead of heading back into the house, I walked down the tiled driveway and out to the street. The sky was hazy now and there was a nice cool breeze even though the sun was still strong. Traffic went by at a leisurely pace, people glancing at me curiously. Gardeners trimmed hedges and swept leaves and debris from the fronts of beautiful homes. I walked with my arms folded under my breasts, my heart still pounding from my episode with Spike.

And then I paused to watch a little girl with long golden pigtails being lifted out of a car by a woman who had to be her mother. She clung to her with loving desperation and gazed over her mother's shoulders at me. Happy, secure, she flashed me a sweet smile and then waved as if we knew each other. I waved back and for a moment I felt as if I were waving at myself, years and years ago, when I was about her age and my stepdaddy was alive. Of course, I didn't know then he was my stepdaddy. I thought he was my real daddy. He loved me just as much as any real daddy could.

The woman carried her little girl into the big, beautiful house where she would be secure and safe and where even the thought of something unpleasant was left at the doorstep. I stood there, smiling and thinking about her. I don't know how long I was standing there, but suddenly I realized there was an automobile stopped nearby and someone looking at me.

It was Mr. Livingston.

He waved.

"You all right?" he asked.

"Yes," I said. "Thank you. I was just taking a little walk."

"In Beverly Hills, that's considered strange," he remarked. "Don't go too far," he said, raised his window and drove on. I watched him turn into the driveway and then I headed back myself. Maybe it was strange to be alone here and think.

I would do what Spike had suggested. I would confront Mommy again, hopefully when she was alone, and if I had the same result, I would get myself back on the plane as quickly as I could and I would fly away, leaving Mommy and my past behind me.

# 6

## Devil's Bargain

Alec greeted me at the door when I returned from my short walk and in a very stiff and formal voice informed me that Mr. and Mrs. Livingston wanted to see me immediately in the parlor.

"Melody, dear, where have you been?" Dorothy asked the moment I appeared. She was seated on the settee and Philip was sitting across from her in the thick cushioned arm chair, his posture regal. They looked like they had been having a very serious conversation. "Philip just told me he saw you wandering aimlessly about Beverly Hills. Why didn't you come right in and report to me about your second visit to that Egyptian whatever?"

"I just wanted to be alone for a while," I said. I certainly wasn't going to say anything about Spike and the little drama in his apartment. "I wasn't wandering about aimlessly. I knew where I was going. Doesn't anyone just take a walk here? Why did they build sidewalks?"

"You poor dear. Come in here this instant and give us the details about your visit," she insisted and patted the seat beside her.

Philip sat staring at me, his fingers pressed together in cathedral fashion, his beady dark eyes looking quite disapproving. I walked in slowly and sat. Then I took a deep breath and began.

"I met her," I said in a voice that even sounded like the voice of doom to me, "and she pretended not to know me."

Philip nodded and glanced sternly at Dorothy.

"It was what I anticipated," he said, "even from the little I knew about this bizarre situation. Dorothy—"

"Now hush, Philip. We will solve the matter ourselves," she said, but he didn't look relieved.

"This is not one of your social games, Dorothy. I told you what I thought when I first heard about this. We sympathize with your situation, Melody," he said, directing himself to me, "but we're certainly not equipped to solve the problem as Dorothy implies. This sounds to me more like a police matter. Someone is surely defrauding someone here," he continued. "Perhaps an insurance company. I simply can't have myself attached to the issue in any way. I have a major responsibility to my clients, who are all high-profile, and I can't afford to have any negative publicity. You seem like an intelligent enough young woman to appreciate that."

"Yes sir. I'm sorry. I'll leave tomorrow."

"You don't have to leave so quickly," Dorothy said, but not with the same firmness she said most everything else to me.

"I don't want you to feel we're throwing you out. You're a friend of my sister-in-law and Dorothy made her sister some promises," he added, eyeing her disapprovingly. "You can stay for a while as long as you don't bring any of this mess to our doorstep, but from what it sounds like to me, my best advice to you is to return to where you call home and the people who care for you," Philip said.

"Yes sir," I replied in a small voice that started to crack.

"You can report what you know to the proper authorities and let them take the necessary action," he continued. "I'll assist you in doing that, if you wish."

"That's not why I came here. I don't care about any of that. I wanted to find out what really had happened to my mother. I wanted to see if she needed me."

There were tears in my eyes as I spoke, but they defied gravity and remained firmly under my lids.

"I see. Well, Dorothy knows that if you require some money for your return trip . . ."

"I have everything I need. Thank you," I said.

"Okay. I'm sorry for your trouble. You're a very nice young lady and I'm sure you'll regain your composure and go on to do something worthwhile with your life."

"Oh, she's going to do a lot more than that," Dorothy said. "She's an exceptional young lady."

"Yes, well, I'll just go up and get ready for dinner." He shot another, even sterner look at Dorothy. "Don't put yourself in a position where you're giving advice you shouldn't be giving, Dorothy."

"I think I know what I can and can't tell someone, Philip."

"I certainly hope so," he said with his eyes full of warning. He glanced at me and then rose and left the room.

"I'm sorry," I said. "I don't want to make any trouble for you. Maybe I should leave right away. I can stay in a motel until I make travel arrangements."

"Of course you won't do something like that. Don't you listen to him. He's just being . . . just being Philip Livingston," she said, as if that explained or justified it. "Now I want to hear all the details. Go on. Tell me everything from start to finish," she begged, leaning toward me, her eyes wide. For a moment I had the feeling she was treating me and my problem as if it were all another episode of her favorite soap opera. Nevertheless, I related the events as they occurred, leaving out my scene with Spike. When I was finished, she sighed deeply.

"Maybe Philip is right, dear. Maybe you should get on with your own life. Not that I want to chase you away, but . . ."

94

"My mother is part of my life," I said.

Dorothy smiled and shook her head at me as if I had said something ridiculous.

"Family can be such a burden. Look at what I have with Holly."

"Holly is a very happy person and she has a lot of friends and knows a lot of wonderful people," I shot back. "I can't think of anyone who's been nicer to me."

"Oh she has a heart of gold, especially when it comes to helping other people, but will she ever help herself? Not Holly. She was always like that, always off on a cloud. I tried to get her to be more substantial and do more with her life, but there's just so much you can do and then, then you've got to do what Philip said, go on with your own life. Philip does give the best advice. He always has. Sometimes, I feel he's more like a father to me than a husband." She smiled. "Are you all right, dear? Is there anything else you want to tell me?"

"I'm tired," I said. Dorothy was so wrapped up in herself, she would never hear anything she didn't want to hear anyway, I thought. "I'll just go up and rest for a while."

"Of course. Take a whirlpool bubble bath and suddenly the world will look much better to you. Believe me, it will. If I'm depressed, I just go to the spa and get a facial and take a mud bath and a massage. What good is money if you don't use it to make yourself happy and drive away the gloomies?" she added with a thin little laugh. What she said reminded me of our shopping spree and all she had spent on me. I was sure now that Philip would be very upset once he found out, despite what she had told me.

"I'd like you to bring that evening dress back to the store, Dorothy. I won't be needing it now and—"

"You certainly will. Won't you go to some nice affair back East? And just think how envious all the other young women will be when they see you in a designer dress."

I stared at her, too tired to argue.

She rang a bell and a few seconds later, Christina appeared in the doorway.

"Christina, will you please draw a bubble bath for Melody?"

"I can do that myself," I said.

"Please, just do it, Christina," Dorothy emphasized firmly.

"Yes, Mrs. Livingston," Christina said and left to do it immediately.

"Really, dear. You have to let the servants do their work otherwise . . ." She laughed. "Otherwise we won't need servants and they would be without jobs, and Christina is someone who can't afford to be without a job. She has a flock of children to feed. Enjoy your bath. Alec will call you to dinner."

She rose and stood there for a moment gazing at me.

"I wish you were able to stay for a while longer. I have so much to teach you," she said and then shook her head with a twist of pity on her lips and left.

You have so much to teach me? I thought and gazed around at this palace in which two people shared wealth beyond my imagination, but seemed to be like strangers to each other. I don't want to learn about getting the best table in a restaurant or how to keep a wrinkle off my face. No, I wanted to learn something much deeper. I wanted to learn where I truly belonged. If I stayed here ten years more, I didn't think I could get Dorothy Livingston to understand that.

My legs felt like they had turned to stone beneath me when I rose and started for the stairs. It was another bright day outside, but inside my heart the sky was overcast with long, thick clouds of despair. As I approached my room, I heard Christina singing by the whirlpool tub.

"I've put in some scented bubble bath for you," she said when she heard me enter.

"Thank you."

She looked at me closely.

"Did you have a bad day?" she asked.

I started to shake my head, but my lips trembled and my chin quivered. I had to bite down to keep from releasing a sob.

"You poor girl," she said, coming to me. I couldn't help myself. I started to cry. She wrapped her arms around me quickly and held me to her, stroking my hair. "There, there, now, nothing is as bad as all that."

"Yes it is," I wailed. "My own mother refused to recognize me today. She ran off and left me with relatives back East and then I think she pretended to die so she would be rid of me forever," I blurted.

Christina looked shocked for a moment and then she nodded slowly, her lips firm.

"Any woman who denies her own child must be in trouble," she declared. "It's not natural and it has to be painful for her."

"Do you think so?" I asked, wiping my eyes.

"Oh yes. When you become a mother, you'll understand," she said with a smile. "Your child is part of you, always your baby. It hurts to see them grow up because you know they're growing away from you, but that's a different and healthy kind of letting go.

"I'm sure your mother will contact you," she said and squeezed my hand softly.

"She doesn't know where I'm staying."

"Then she expects you'll be back," Christina assured me.

"I don't know," I said, thinking about it. I wanted to share her optimism, to make everything terrible look small and insignificant, to believe that after a storm there was always a rainbow, but I had been disappointed so many times already.

"Have more faith, dear," she said. "Relax, eat a good dinner, get a good night's rest and tomorrow, tomorrow will look a lot more promising."

Her smile was like the sunshine after the rain. I couldn't help but smile back.

"Thank you," I said. "Your children are lucky to have such a good mother."

"Oh, I tell them that all the time," she joked. She had me laughing again and for an instant I felt like my old self, full of sunshine and laughter.

I enjoyed my whirlpool bath, soaked and relaxed and practiced meditating. I thought about Billy Maxwell overcoming his personal disaster and I grew stronger. I was even hungry and looking forward to dinner.

Right after I got dressed, there was a knock on my door and Christina poked her head in.

"Everything all right?"

"Yes, thank you, Christina."

"You have a call," she said. "Just leave the bathroom as it is. I'll come back before I leave and take care of it all," she added, closing the door so I would have privacy. I imagined it was Holly calling again. Maybe Dorothy had called her and told her what Philip had said. Holly would want me to fly back to New York and stay with her for a while. I had to admit it looked like the best idea.

"Hello."

"Melody," Cary said. What a surprise it was to hear from him.

"Cary!"

"I called Holly and got her sister's number. Are you all right? How was the trip?"

I spoke quickly, in minutes summarizing everything that had happened, beginning with the near disaster at the airport. He listened silently until I was finished. I realized it was already late in the evening back East.

"Sounds like you've had a terrible time from the day you left New York," he said.

"But how are you?" I asked.

"Things are not too good here, Melody. I'm actually calling you from the hospital."

"The hospital! What happened to you?"

"It's not me. Dad's back in the cardiac care unit. He had another heart attack. I think he brought it on himself

98

this time, complaining about being restricted, insisting on doing more than he should."

"Oh Cary, I'm so sorry. How's Aunt Sara?"

"You know Ma. She just keeps herself working so she won't think about it."

"And May?"

"Not so good. She misses you a lot," he said. "Which is about half as much as I do. But I understand why you have to be away," he added quickly.

"I do miss you very much, too, Cary."

"What are you going to do now?"

"I'm not sure yet. I'll call you as soon as I know," I promised. "If you can, tell Uncle Jacob I hope he feels better."

"I will."

"And take care of yourself, Cary. You can't do everything for everyone," I said, knowing him.

He laughed.

"Look who's talking. Guess who I saw this morning at the hospital?" he said. "Grandma Olivia. She couldn't help herself. She had to ask me if I had heard from you. I told her I was calling you tonight and she made me promise to give her the latest news."

"She's just hoping her investment pays off and I stay away forever," I said dryly.

"But you're going to fool her," he said and then laughed nervously.

"Right now I think the only person I've been fooling is myself," I moaned.

"I saw Kenneth in town this afternoon. I didn't speak to him. I saw him just as he was driving away. He looked . . . more straggly, if that's possible. I guess he's not taking very good care of himself."

"That's too bad. I was afraid something like that might happen."

"We're all just falling apart without you around here," Cary said.

"Oh, Cary."

99

"I don't know if I said it enough to be sure you believed me, Melody, but I love you. I really do."

"I believe you, Cary, and I do miss you."

"Take care of yourself and don't fall in love with any movie stars," he kidded.

"You don't have to worry about that," I said, laughing.

His good-bye was like a ribbon in the wind, lingering for a moment and then drifting away with the end of the phone call. I held the receiver for a few minutes after the line had gone dead, as if by doing so I could hold on to Cary's voice and my warm memories of him longer.

When I went downstairs for dinner, I found the air even thicker than usual, if that was possible. Philip uttered barely a word, eating and staring ahead as if he were alone in the room. Dorothy tried to make small talk, telling me about a new makeup she had discovered and a skin cream that made her feel as soft as a baby.

The food was a treat, a Mexican dish called a fajita. Dorothy told me Mexican food was very popular in Los Angeles.

"Because there are so many of them here and most of them are good cooks," she explained.

After dinner she wanted me to watch television with her; it seemed Philip rarely did anything with her at night. He usually had work to do in his office, or if he wasn't working, he was reading. Dorothy had said he hated television unless he was watching the financial reports, which she thought were abominably boring. I wondered what had brought these two people together at an altar to pledge undying love and devotion until death did them part. It seemed the only romance in Dorothy's life was the romance she watched with religious devotion on her soap operas.

I thought about the things Christina had said and I thought about Cary and May and Kenneth, and all the people who needed me back in Provincetown. Wasting any more time seemed sinful. I would do no more of it, I pledged.

"I'm going back to The Egyptian Gardens one more time," I declared after dinner. That brought animation into Philip's face. "And I'm not going to leave until I get some truthful answers."

"Tonight?" Dorothy asked.

"Yes, right away," I said.

"Really, Melody, do you think that's wise, especially at this time of night?" Dorothy asked. She looked to Philip for support.

"I wouldn't suggest you do that," he said. "It's not very intelligent in light of what you have already experienced."

"Sometimes, we have to do what our hearts command more than what our minds demand," I replied.

"Inevitably that leads to disaster," he retorted.

I said nothing more, but they both understood I was going.

"I'd rather not have our limousine involved," Philip said as he rose from the table.

"I'll just call a cab."

"Philip," Dorothy said.

"I'm afraid I have to be firm on this," he told me.

"I understand. You've both been very kind and I'm grateful for your hospitality."

"It's not the first time my sister-in-law has put me into a difficult situation," Philip remarked.

"Why don't you wait until morning, Melody? Maybe then things—"

"Regardless of whether it's day or night, I don't want our car involved," Philip repeated, raising his voice. Dorothy sat back as if she had been slapped.

"I'll just go catch a cab," I said rising.

"You don't catch a cab in Los Angeles. You call for one to pick you up," Philip said. "I'll see that Alec does that for you."

He marched out of the dining room.

"Please be careful, dear," Dorothy said.

"I will." My heart racing ahead of me, I hurried upstairs to get my purse. Actually, I was happy Spike wasn't going to be driving me anyway. I wasn't sure I could look him in the face after what had happened in his apartment.

The cab was just pulling in when I stepped out of the house. I hurried to it and gave the driver the address. I was off for what I had decided would be my final attempt to approach Mommy. If I failed, in the morning I would go back East.

The Egyptian Gardens looked different in the evening, even seedier, if that was possible. Some of the lights in the lanterns along the walkway didn't work and some of the lights on the buildings were dead as well. The shadows draped longer, deeper, darker. The gate squeaked when I opened it and entered. Ahead of me at the pool, two young men were talking and drinking something from tall glasses. They turned my way as I continued past them. Just as I reached the far corner and started toward Mommy's building, I saw a man step out of the doorway and pause to light a cigarette. The flame of his match danced on his face and hair for a moment and I gasped and retreated into the shadows. It was Archie Marlin. I'd recognize him anywhere.

He still had short orange-red hair and skin the shade of milkweed, with freckles on his chin and forehead. Everyone back in Sewell always said he looked ten years younger than he really was, although no one knew his exact age. No one knew very much about Archie Marlin. He never gave anyone a straight answer to questions about himself. He always joked or shrugged and said something silly. But he had filled Mommy with enough promises to sweep her off her feet and have her go off with him.

I held my breath as he walked past me, a slick, small smile on his orange lips. He strolled down the walkway and went around the corner. I let out my breath, my heart pounding. I didn't want to face him just yet, if ever; but seeing him was the last and final assurance that the woman upstairs in that building was beyond a doubt my mother.

My legs felt as thin and weak as a scarecrow's legs of straw as I entered the building and went to the elevator. When the doors opened, I stepped in quickly and pressed Mommy's floor. My heart seemed to have risen into the base of my throat. How horrible, I thought, how horrible that I should have all this trepidation about seeing my own mother. In moments I was standing in front of her doorway, hesitating, my fingers lingering over the buzzer. Finally, I stabbed at it and waited.

The door was thrust open and Mommy was standing there in a bathrobe, her hair unbrushed, no makeup on, her eyes glassy. She wobbled and spoke before she saw who it was.

"What did you forget now, Richard?" she asked and then focused on me. Her expression froze, first with a glimmer of delight and then quickly with a look of annoyance. "You again?" she said.

"Mommy . . ."

She stared, then she leaned out farther to look up and down the hallway.

"I see I won't get rid of you so easily. Get in here," she ordered as she dragged me into the apartment.

Mommy closed the door quickly behind me, gazed at me sourly and then walked into the living room. She kept her back to me.

"Why are you pretending not to know me, Mommy?" I asked and wiped one of my tears away quickly.

"Because I don't know you," she said. "I don't know anyone from that life. I can't, I just can't," she said, slamming her fists against her thighs and spinning on me. "Why did you come here? How did you find me?"

"Alice saw your picture in a catalogue and sent it to me. I brought it to Kenneth and he studied it and said he felt sure it was you. Then he called a friend in Boston who helped track you down for me."

"Kenneth?" She relaxed her lips into a tiny smile, and

then realizing what she had done, drove the angry, hard look back into her eyes. "I don't know anyone named Kenneth, except Ken Peters at ICM. You've got to go back," she said. "Tell them . . . tell them I'm not who you thought I was and—"

"But why, Mommy?"

"It's better for everyone all around," she said. She folded her arms under her breasts and stiffened her shoulders like one of Kenneth's statues, firming up her resolve, strengthening her resistance. I just started to cry more openly. "Stop it," she said. "Don't you see? You'll mess everything up, ruin my chances just when I was starting to get someplace. I might have a good part in a movie and another, better modeling job. I'm meeting important people. Just when it's finally happening, you pop out of nowhere and nearly sink my boat."

"I don't understand, Mommy." I took a deep breath. "How did you do this? You had everyone back home believing you died. There was a body. You're buried in the family plot back in Provincetown."

She laughed, went to an imitation ivory cigarette box on the yellowish brown coffee table and took out a cigarette.

"You mean Olivia Logan permitted the poor corpse to be deposited in her precious family ground even though she believed it was me?" She laughed again, found a match and lit her cigarette. Then she fell back into the worn, cotton print easy chair and stared at me as she puffed away. "You look good," she said. "You filled out nicely. Jacob didn't throw you out on the street, I guess."

"He's very sick, Mommy. He had a heart attack and nearly died. Now he's back in the hospital."

"Doesn't surprise me. He's too much like his mother to enjoy life or let anyone else enjoy it. Probably finally soured his own heart." She took a deep breath, shook her head and gazed through the sliding glass doors of the balcony. "I can't have a daughter your age," she said. "I wouldn't get a decent job in this town."

"Why not?"

"It's just the way it is. Young people get everything here, especially women. Look, you don't belong with me, honey. I'm not a good mother. I never was and I never will be. It's just not in my nature."

"Why not?" I asked.

"Because . . . because I'm too self-centered. Chester was right about that. Don't you remember? It was always Chester who did the important things for you, not me. And you spent most of your childhood next door with Arlene and George."

"Papa George died, Mommy," I said sadly.

"Did he?" She nodded. "He was pretty sick when I left. I didn't think it would be too much longer. You see," she said, snapping her head up and firing a look of fear my way, "you see how short life is, how quickly your chance to do something fades? I won't get a second chance out here, Melody. This is it for me. That's why I did what Archie suggested when the accident happened."

"I don't understand, Mommy. What happened?"

"Archie was really in an accident," she said, waving her cigarette. "He was returning from a party at a bar where there was supposed to be a gathering of producers and agents. He had one of his younger clients with him. The girl was really very young, but had everyone fooled, except Archie of course. Anyway, he had me lend her my identification for the night. On the way back, Richard, as you know he's called now, lost control of the car and as soon as it crashed, it caught fire. He was thrown, but the girl was trapped and killed.

"When the police found the body and my identification, Archie and I discussed it and decided it would be better if I took advantage of it to cut myself off from family. So I took on a new identity. I'm Gina Simon, Gina Simon, do you hear? Everyone here thinks I'm years younger than I am!" she added in defense. "I can't get anywhere unless I'm this young, so I did it. Don't look at me like that," she fired. "I knew you were doing well and you were with family. It wasn't as if I left you stranded somewhere."

"Family," I said, my face twisting with rage. "You left me with a family that you knew disliked you."

"Yes, but you're not me," Mommy said. "I figured that in time they would see that and not punish you for being my daughter. And they're all well off, even Jacob."

"Not anymore. His business is struggling and it's hard work and now that he's very sick—"

"You can't live with me. Why did you come here? How can I take you in? Go back and wait until I get established and make a lot of money and then I'll send for you," she promised. "You've got to go before anyone realizes who you are. Where are you staying?" she asked quickly, realizing there might be people who already knew.

"I'm staying with Holly Brooks's sister, Dorothy Livingston, but not after tonight," I said.

"Holly Brooks? I know that name."

"She's a friend of Kenneth's."

"Oh. Oh yeah. Is she living with him?"

"No, she lives in New York City. She's been very nice. She helped me get here."

"And this Dorothy . . . what does she know about us?"

"Just what I've told her . . . how you pretended I was someone you didn't know."

"Good. Go back and tell her you came here again and you had made a mistake. Then go back to Jacob and Sara."

"I can't go back to Jacob and Sara," I said. "If I go back, I have to live with Grandma Olivia."

"Olivia? Why?" she asked. I sat on the sofa and began to tell her the story of my discoveries, how I had visited with her mother, my grandmother Belinda, and how I had learned that my mother's father was really Judge Childs.

"I finally understood why Kenneth and his father don't get along. He blames his father for his losing you," I said.

Mommy smiled.

"Kenneth," she said softly, reminiscing. "I suppose if things had been different, he and I would have married.

You don't know how handsome he was and bright. All my girlfriends were crazy about him. He was always different, always exciting to be with." Her smile faded. "But when I learned the truth and brought it to him, it was as if I had hit him with a sledgehammer.

"They're all so prim and proper on the outside, the blue bloods who made me feel inferior. I was the poor, discarded little girl, the waif living off of Olivia's kindness and generosity. How she continually reminded me of it. She took me in just to reduce the embarrassment, but she hated every moment I was there and she brought her boys up to think of me as contaminated. Only I fooled her, didn't I? I won Chester away from her and for that, she hated me forever.

"Was she smiling at my funeral? I wish I had been there just to watch the hypocrites," Mommy said and puffed her cigarette violently.

"No, she wasn't smiling. She was dignified. It was a very nice funeral. Kenneth was there, too."

"Poor Kenneth. Was he very upset?"

"Yes."

She sat back, pleased.

"It's not so bad to bury yourself once, especially when you're burying the ugly past too." She stared blankly at me. "But that's all gone, six feet under, Melody. You can't dig me up. It's not fair. I've finally thrown off the chains, the weight of my past, and I have opportunities now, new friends . . ." She gazed around. "This is just temporary. After my next few jobs, I'll be living in a plush condo, maybe in Brentwood. Archie assures me," she said.

I looked down, my heart so heavy I thought it might fall out of my chest.

"Why does Olivia want you to move in with her now?"

"Because Uncle Jacob's so sick and because she wants to keep the lid on any scandal. I told her I wanted to live with Kenneth since he's really my uncle, but she says that will only stir gossip."

"Oh, she's right about that. Olivia knows her territory.

Maybe it's not a bad idea anyway. It's a beautiful house. I did enjoy living there when she wasn't breathing down my neck or screaming at me for one thing or another."

"She wants to find a proper school for me and she said I have an inheritance from Grandma Belinda's half of the Gordon fortune."

"That's great. So you see, you should go back and quickly."

"But . . . it's not money I want or a snobby girl's school, Mommy. Olivia isn't my mother. She's not even my real grandmother. I'm afraid to live with her, afraid she'll make my life as miserable as she made yours."

"She wasn't completely at fault. I brought a lot of it on myself," Mommy confessed. "I was angry at them, all of them, and I wanted them to pay for my unhappiness."

"They'll always see you when they look at me," I said. "Olivia does, no matter what she tells me, and Uncle Jacob certainly does. Even Kenneth," I added and she perked up.

"Oh?"

"He had me model for him just the way he had you model," I said.

She widened her eyes.

"Really? And you did it?"

"Yes. He's created a wonderful new piece of sculpture. He says it's his greatest work, *Neptune's Daughter*. But the face on the sculpture is more your face than it is mine," I told her. I saw she liked that.

"Stand up," she asked suddenly. I did so. "You really did fill out. You're a very attractive young girl. Kenneth doesn't miss much." She thought again for a moment. "Didn't you like it at all back there, meet anyone nice?"

"Cary's nice, very nice. I miss him and I love May, but I've missed you, Mommy. I really have. I don't like being . . . alone. It's not fair."

She nodded and crushed her cigarette.

"It did bother me to leave you, to lie to you," she said. "Maybe not as much as you would have liked it to have bothered me, but it did. I didn't like leaving you behind, but there was just no other way to do all this. You understand?"

I nodded, even thought I really didn't.

"I had to listen to Archie. He's had much more experience with all this," she said in defense. "What are we going to do?" she asked herself.

"Please, let me stay with you, Mommy."

She gazed at me and smiled.

"You were always a sobering influence on me, weren't you, Melody? When I stayed at Frankie's bar and grill too long in Sewell and came home, I would take one look at your face and feel so damn guilty I lost my buzz in an instant. I hated you for that, too," she admitted, "but later, I would love you for it, as much as I could love any child, I suppose."

She straightened up.

"I don't have very much here, yet," she said. "It's not even a drop in the bucket compared to what Olivia has and what she can offer you."

"I don't care about that, Mommy. I should be with you."

"You can't be with me," she whined. "I just can't have a daughter your age."

I thought quickly, remembering what her friend Sandy had thought.

"I could be your younger sister. You told people you had one," I suggested quickly.

"How do you know that?"

"I met some woman here the first time I came. Her name was Sandy and she thought I was your younger sister surprising you," I said.

"She would." She smiled and looked at me. "We do look like sisters. I mean, I look young enough to be your sister, don't' I?"

"Yes, Mommy, you do."

"See," she pounced jabbing her forefinger at me. "That's just the problem. You can't call me Mommy. A younger sister doesn't call her older sister Mommy, does she?"

"I won't."

"You'll forget."

"I won't," I insisted.

She relaxed as she thought about my suggestion.

"If I had a younger sister here, it would certainly make everyone believe me even more," she thought aloud.

"That's right, it would," I said nodding.

"You can only call me Sis or Gina. You can't even forget and call me Haille."

"I never did, Mommy."

*"Mommy!"*

"Well, there's no one here right now," I said quickly.

"Archie's not going to like this. He'll be furious with me," she said with a shake of her head.

"He has no right to be furious with you. You've done everything he wanted, haven't you?"

"Yes, yes I have," she said. She stared at me and then she smiled. "He won't be unhappy when I tell him he has another prime client anyway," she said.

"Another prime client?"

"You, silly. You're beautiful. You can become a model and an actress, too. We'll tell everyone I called you out here to develop your career. Just like me. Then we really will be sisters!" she exclaimed. "Maybe we'll even get to do something together."

I shook my head.

"I could never—"

"Sure you could. It's so easy. You smile when they want you to smile and you bat your eyelashes when you have to and before you know it, you have an assignment and they're paying you hundreds of dollars an hour just to pose."

"I don't know if I can do that," I said, recalling what I had learned from Spike already about the business.

"Believe me, you can do it," she said. "Okay, you can have the second bedroom and we'll try it. If it doesn't work out, you have to promise you'll return to the Cape and go back to school. Well? You wanted to be with me, this is how you can be with me. Make up your mind."

I stood there, speechless for a moment. Could I really turn down a chance to be with Mommy again? To wait for the perfect opportunity to find out who my father was? Before I had a chance to really think about her suggestion, we heard the doorbell.

"Who the hell is that so early?" she muttered and rose to go to the door. It was Sandy Glee.

"I saw you," she sang looking past Mommy at me. "I saw you from my patio coming up the walkway. So, Gina. Aren't you going to introduce me to your surprise?"

"Melody," Mommy said turning to me, "you see why you can't keep any secrets here. Everyone's a snoop. This is my kid sister," she said, eyeing me warily.

"I knew it," Sandy remarked with a clap of her slender hands.

"She's coming to stay with me for a while and try her luck in Hollywood like the rest of us nitwits."

"Richard's going to represent her, too?"

"Yep."

"Good. Welcome to the fight," Sandy said. "I'm having a few people over tomorrow night for a pot luck dinner if you want to introduce her around," Sandy said. "About seven."

"We'll be there," Mommy promised.

"See you later, Sis," Sandy said waving. She left the apartment and Mommy spun around to me with a wide smile on her face.

"It worked. I knew it. I do look young enough to be your sister. In this town everyone believes everyone else's lies. It's a perfect place for people who hate the truth.

"Welcome home, Melody," she said sincerely. "I can finally throw my arms around you."

Even as she hugged me, giving me the affection I so desperately needed, I had to wonder: What had I gotten myself into?

# 7
## &

# New Beginnings

Mommy made us some coffee and we sat and talked in her small kitchen, catching up on what had happened to both of us since the day she had left me in Provincetown.

"I really did hate leaving you behind," she said. "You remember how hard it was for me to do that, don't you? I think I cried all the way from Provincetown to New York City, but Archie, I mean Richard, was right in advising me not to take you along. It was a hard trip, struggling for work along the way, trying to get meetings with important people in the big cities, going from one cheap motel to the other, sometimes barely having enough money to feed ourselves. You would have hated every minute. Many nights you would have been left alone in some crummy motel room. Some of them didn't even have television sets in the rooms.

"How could that life compare to being in the fresh ocean air, going to a good school, eating well . . . You understand why I did it, don't you, honey? You don't blame me anymore?" she asked, her voice shaking.

I took a deep breath and shifted my eyes away so she

couldn't see how deeply I had been hurt. Kenneth had once told me I might as well have had translucent skin. It was that easy to see my thoughts and feelings. However, there was no sense being dishonest and lying to my mother now that I had found her, I thought.

"I used to hate you for it, Mommy," I admitted. "I used to sit there in Laura's room and listen hard through the walls for the phone to ring and hate you for not calling, hate you for making promises you wouldn't keep."

"I know. And that bothered me, too, but Richard kept saying, 'If you call her and can't send for her, it will be even more cruel, won't it?' He was right."

"He wasn't right. I needed to hear your voice, Mommy," I insisted.

She slammed down her coffee cup so hard it nearly shattered on the table.

"You've got to stop blaming me for things. I can't have any stress," she whined. "Stress brings on age and wrinkles and makes you look terrible and then you can't get jobs. The camera picks up every little detail, you know. They don't want you if they can't use you for close-ups. I won't get any work. Is that what you want to happen? Richard won't stand for it anyway. He won't let you stay here," she warned.

I gazed around the apartment, just realizing what she was saying.

"Does he live here, too?"

"Well what do you think? You have no idea how expensive it is to live and work in Los Angeles. Apartments like this are hard to come by. What would be the point of both of us having our own apartment and paying two rents?"

"Are you married?" I asked, holding my breath.

"No, we never got married. I don't want to get remarried for a long, long time; but Richard is . . . well, he's more than my agent; he's my financial manager. He takes care of all our money needs. He does that for all his clients."

"How many clients does he have?" I asked.

"A half dozen, but none earn as much as I do right now, so you see why it's so important everything remains smooth for us," she repeated. "No more talk about the terrible past," she said, waving her hands over the table. "I don't want to hear about how you suffered and I don't want to be reminded about what I did when I lived there. Don't ask me any questions about any of them, and don't even bring their names up in front of me," she ordered. "That's the rule if you want to live here, understand? I mean it, Melody." She glared at me, her eyes colder than I ever recalled them.

"Even Kenneth?" I asked.

"Yes, yes, yes, even Kenneth. Nobody. I forbid it. I didn't have a life before this. That's the way I want to think now. It's what Richard says I should do. These are changes we had to make for our own well-being. I hate being selfish, but it's a good selfishness because it helps us find success."

"Why did he have to change his name, Mommy? I never believed that story about Archie being his nickname."

"You're right. Archie was never his name. It was his older brother's name and he took it so he could be thought of as older when he first left home. That's a big difference between men and women. Men like to be thought of as older. They don't get punished for being older and turning gray with wrinkles, but we do.

"Anyway," she continued, "his brother got himself into big trouble with loan sharks and the like and as soon as Richard found out, he dropped that name like a hot coal so they wouldn't mistakenly come after him. That's why he never liked to talk about his family. He was ashamed of them. His father wasn't any better. Now, don't mention any of this in front of him. Understand? He would be furious with me. He's very sensitive about it."

"I won't say a thing," I said, not really believing the story anyway.

"Good. As long as you do what you're told, we'll be fine. I think," she said, still not sure.

She looked at me hard again and then tilted her head, smiling.

"I like that outfit you're wearing."

"Dorothy Livingston bought it for me."

"Did she? You and I are almost the same size. We can share things, but you've got to take good care of whatever I give you to wear, okay? Some of my things are very special and designed for auditions. Did you bring a lot of your own stuff to California?"

"Not a lot, no."

"Where are your things?"

"At the Livingstons'."

"Well, I guess you'll have to go get your stuff. Don't tell her too much when you go back." She thought a moment. "I know what you should say," she added with excitement. "Tell her you're going back to Provincetown. You probably won't see her again anyway, and that way, she'll tell everyone else who asks about you that you left."

"Why don't I just tell her the truth?" I asked. She laughed.

"You never tell anyone the truth if you don't have to, honey. That's something you keep in your back pocket as a last resort. Take it from someone who's had to make her way on the road of life the hard way. I know from where I speak. The less you tell people about yourself, the better off you'll be later. There's always a jam to get out of and the truth can reduce your options. Richard taught me that lesson real well," she said, nodding.

"Okay," she continued, "let's look at where you'll sleep." She rose to go to the doorway of the second bedroom.

I followed her and she snapped on the light. A dull glow fell from the ceiling because the fixture was full of dust.

"This is going to be your room. We have only one bathroom, as you see, so don't hog it. You can help me keep the whole place clean. It's too much for a working girl to do that and stay pretty enough for an audition at a moment's notice anyway. That's why it looks a little disorganized right now," she said, but I remembered that Mommy was never a very good housekeeper. My stepfather Chester and I did most of the heavy cleaning in our trailer back in Sewell.

I studied the small bedroom. The walls were a faded pink, scratched, scuffed and chipped. Even the guest room at Holly's in New York with its one window was more comfortable and cozier-looking than this bare-walled, dusty room with a bed now covered with clothing, cartons of files, old issues of movie magazines and trade papers. The thin rug was badly worn in places, its thin threads frayed and unraveling. The curtains on the two windows were limp from dust and bleached from the sunlight. Large cobwebs dangled in the corners of the ceiling. I noticed a pile of what looked like thin briefcases in the right corner.

"You'll have to clean up a bit in here, but don't lose anything."

"What's that in the corner?" I asked.

"Oh, that you can't touch. Those are Richard's watches, antique watches. He sells them on the side. A friend of his got him into it here and he's made a nice bundle of pocket money doing it."

"He sells antique watches? I thought he was an agent with a half dozen clients."

"Everyone trying to break into the business does something else in the meanwhile, Melody. Most of the people living here work as waiters or waitresses in restaurants, some valet park cars, some even pack groceries. Anything to keep food on the table and pay the rent until you hit it big."

"I know. Dorothy's chauffeur is an actor. He told me he was in a few movies."

"What's his name?" she asked quickly.

"Spike. I don't remember his last name."

"Spike. I know ten Spikes if I know one," Mommy said with a laugh.

We both turned as the door opened and Archie Marlin entered. The moment he set eyes on me, his face became flushed with surprise and then anger.

"What the hell? How did she get here?" he demanded. He closed the door sharply and stood facing us with his hands on his hips, a cigarette dangling from the corner of his mouth. He pulled it out. "Huh?" he said pointing the cigarette at me. "Did you send for her behind my back?"

"No, Richard. A friend of hers from Sewell saw my picture in the *En Vogue* catalogue. She sent her the catalogue and Melody brought it to someone who knew advertising. He tracked me down for her and she came out to L.A. to find me."

"That's just great," he said throwing up his arms. "That's just what we need right now. Your daughter," he said with disgust.

"But no one knows she actually found me, do they, honey?" she asked me.

I shook my head.

"Big deal. What are we going to do with her now?" he asked, as if I were some puppy left on their doorstep. "And just when I had everyone believing you were young enough to play their parts."

"That's not going to be a problem. We worked it out," Mommy told him.

"Yeah? How?" he said. He dropped himself into the worn easy chair, ashes from his cigarette raining down on his pants and the chair. He didn't seem to notice or care.

"Sandy thought she was my younger sister. Remember the story you told me to tell? That I have a younger sister back home in the Midwest?" she said, nodding to get him to remember. I imagined he had trouble keeping track of all the lies they had spread from West Virginia to California.

"Yeah, I remember. So?"

"So don't you see?" She turned to me. "Melody came after me, following me, looking for a career herself," Mommy said. He turned from her and gazed at me with sudden interest.

"Younger sister? Looking for a career herself, huh?" He sat forward. "Come a little closer," he ordered.

"Go on, honey. Richard doesn't bite," Mommy said with a smile.

I took a few steps toward him and he raised his lusty green eyes to look at me, lingering over my body in a way that made me feel naked beneath his gaze. His lips curled.

"Yeah, she's a looker now, ain't she? How old are you again? Never mind. From now on, you're twenty-one, see?"

"Twenty-one?" I looked at Mommy, but she just smiled and nodded. I turned back to Richard. "No one will believe that," I told him.

"Of course they will. They won't care if you're lying or not anyway, which is more important. Yeah," he said nodding and smiling as his eyes burned through my clothes, "I can find her some work."

"I'd rather find my own," I said and he stiffened.

"You got any money?"

"Yes. Grandma Olivia gave me traveling money."

"Well, that's not much. The rent here's high and groceries and everything else costs a lot. If you're going to stay with us, you're going to have to pull your fair share, right Gina?" he said.

For a moment I had forgotten that was the phony name Mommy had taken for herself. I squinted with confusion and then remembered and looked at her.

"He's right, Melody. You're big enough and old enough to make your own way now. And besides, Richard might just make you a star too."

"I might," he said nodding. "I always thought she was a pretty girl, being she's your daughter," he said, smiling at Mommy. She beamed. "So," he said sitting back, "you saw your mother in the *En Vogue* catalogue. I got her that job," he bragged, "and we made some money on it, didn't we, Gina?"

"Yes, we did, Richard."

"Course, we spent it all, but I got her another job yesterday too. I just wrapped up the deal, honey," he said.

Mommy squealed.

"Oh, that's wonderful. See, honey? I am making it here. What's the job?"

"You're going to demonstrate some new perfume over at the Beverly Center and then be a model for makeup demonstrations," he declared.

Mommy held her smile, but it lost most of its bright light.

"Well, what about that role in the movie, Richard?" she asked softly.

"We'll see. They're still thinking about you," he said. "You might get a call back tomorrow in fact."

Her smile warmed again.

"Good. Well, Melody has to return to where she was staying and get her clothes and things, Richard."

"Oh yeah? Where were you staying?" he asked me.

"With the sister of a friend in Beverly Hills," I replied.

"Beverly Hills? Well, well, well, ain't we coming up in the world?" He laughed. "You sure you want to lower yourself and come live here with us common folk?"

"I was leaving their house tomorrow morning anyway," I said. "Mrs. Livingston was just doing her sister a favor by helping me."

"All right. I'll take her to go fetch her things. I like driving around Beverly Hills, gives me a chance to pick out the house I'm going to buy real soon," he said with a faraway look in his eyes.

"Oh, that's so nice of you, Richard. You see, honey? We'll work it all out as long as you listen. Isn't that right, Richard?"

"That's right," he said sternly gazing at me. "As long as you know who's running things around here and do exactly what I tell you to do."

"He knows what's best for us, honey," Mommy said. I looked from her to him, his glaring eyes full of self-satisfaction and I nodded to myself, recalling Christina's words and thoughts. Mommy did need me now more than ever. Somehow, someway, I would free her of the hold this slimy man had over her, I pledged.

He seemed to sense the challenge I threw back at him. He pulled his shoulders up, curled his lips and nodded at the door.

"Let's go. I have important things to do."

"Thank you, Richard," Mommy told him. "It's very nice of you." He shrugged.

"As long as she does her fair share, it's no skin off my teeth," he said. "And," he added firmly, threateningly, "as long as she remembers she's your sister and not your daughter."

"She won't forget. See you soon, Sis," Mommy said with a laugh. Richard gazed at me, his head tilted, a wry smile on his lips now.

"Well, what do you say?"

I looked back at Mommy, whose face coaxed me to do what was expected.

"See you soon . . . Gina," I managed, even though the word wanted to choke my throat.

Richard Marlin roared with satisfaction and opened the door.

"Miss Simon," he said stepping back with an exaggerated bow, "shall we fetch your things at the Livingstons'?"

I walked out, my heart pounding, but my spine as straight as Grandma Olivia's could be when she was faced with a challenge. Maybe she was right, I thought. Maybe I was more like her than I wanted to admit.

"So, tell me how you've been since we left you back at the Cape," Richard said as we drove out of the parking lot. He had a different car, an older car with dozens of dents and scratches and a crack in one of the rear windows. The passenger seat in front had a deep tear in it, too. He glanced at me. "You don't look the worse for it. I'd say they fed you well, didn't work you too hard."

"I managed to get along," I said and he laughed.

"I bet you did fine living with those clam diggers."

"They're not clam diggers. They're lobster fishermen and they harvest cranberries. It's hard work and you've got to know the sea and—"

"Right, right. It's great if you want to get up with the worms and break your back every day. That's not for me, not for Richard Marlin," he boasted. "I'm going to have the easy life and soon, too. I've already started doing better than most out here."

From what I saw, I thought he had been living better when he was a bartender back in Sewell.

"What happened to your other car?" I asked. "It was much nicer."

"What? Oh. It don't pay to have a nice car in the city. People are always knocking into it, and if you have a nice car, someone's bound to steal it for parts anyway. Lots of big actors and producers have old, beat-up-looking cars like this one," he assured me. "So they won't be noticed so easily, see? Once people find out you're an agent and a manager, they hound you to death hoping you'll take them on as clients."

"So you're afraid of having too many clients?" I asked, incredulous.

"I've got more than I can handle now. We're going to make it big, your mother and me. You'll see." He looked at me closely and then turned back to the road. "You sure you want to stay with us?" he asked. "We won't have time to do any baby-sitting."

"I don't need baby-sitting."

"This is a place for grown-ups, people who can deal with hard realities," he bragged.

"Really? From what I've seen, it looks like a land of make believe, a big sandbox," I replied. He turned to me, his eyebrows raised and then he laughed.

"Maybe you will get along here after all."

When he saw the Livingstons' home, he whistled through his teeth.

"Why the hell do you want to leave this?" he asked. "Why don't you just stay on until they throw you out?"

"That's about what Mr. Livingston's doing," I remarked as we pulled into the driveway.

"You better wait in the car," I suggested when he went to get out.

"What's that supposed to mean? You too haughty now? Think I'm an embarrassment? Think these people are better than me?" he asked angrily.

"No, but if Dorothy Livingston sees you, she might describe you to her sister, who will tell people back in Provincetown, who might be angry enough to tell the police about what you and Mommy have done. There's a stranger buried in the Logan family plot and Olivia Logan is not the sort of woman who would look fondly on that," I said. "She's a powerful woman, too, with friends in high places. She might even get the FBI after you," I added.

He thought a moment, looked at the house, and then nodded as he sat back.

"Yeah, right. Good thinking. You do have a head on your shoulders. That's good. I'm tired of doing all the thinking for everyone," he said. "Go on. Make it fast. I got things to do," he ordered and I got out of the car quickly and went to the front door.

Alec came to the door almost immediately after I had pressed the buzzer. He looked out at the car in the driveway and then stepped back with that habitually disapproving grimace on his face. Dorothy and Philip appeared in the hallway, both coming from the den. Alec closed the door and walked away without a word as they approached me.

"What happened?" Dorothy asked. "I've been very worried since you left and so has Philip," she said. I glanced at him, but he still looked more concerned about his own reputation than anything else.

I thought about Mommy's advice concerning the truth and decided she wasn't right. I wasn't going to get caught up in her and Richard's web of lies.

"We met and I'm going to stay with her," I said quickly. "She needs me."

"You mean she owned up to who she was?" Philip asked.

"Yes."

"Well, why did she do such a terrible thing before? Why did she deny knowing her own daughter?" Dorothy demanded.

"She had her reasons," I said, "but it's all cleared up now. I'll just go get my things."

I started for the stairs.

"But . . . will you really be all right?" Dorothy asked.

"I think she knows if she'll be all right, Dorothy," Philip said, obviously happy to be rid of me. "She's old enough."

"No she's not. She's—"

"Dorothy," he snapped.

She bit down on her lower lip and watched me climb the stairs. I hurried into the room and threw my things together quickly. I gazed at the black evening dress in its box, thinking that if I just left it there, Dorothy would have to take it back.

"I won't take it back," I heard Dorothy say as if she had been reading my mind. I turned to see her standing in the doorway. "You might as well take it with you, Melody. Otherwise, it will just collect dust."

"I don't mean to be ungrateful, Dorothy. You've been wonderful and kind and generous, but—"

"No buts, ifs, or maybes. I just want you to know I hope the best for you, Melody. You're a sweet young lady," she said, coming into the room and sitting on the bed. "Actually," she said, looking down at her hands, "I wish I could do something as significant for my own sister, but she and I . . . we never saw the world the same way. Oh, we love each other, I suppose, as much as two sisters can, but I know Holly thinks I have no purpose to

123

my life other than satisfying myself. She doesn't know who I am," she said with tears in her eyes. "I have my mountains to climb, too."

I smiled at her.

"I'm sure she knows that, Dorothy. She cares a lot about you and she thinks a lot of you. She told me you would be wonderful to me and she was right. Thank you very much." I took the box with the dress in it and she smiled.

"Good luck to you and please, please don't hesitate to call me if you need someone. Don't worry about Philip. He'll growl, but he'll do the right thing in the end."

I nodded and she hugged me.

"I do wish I had had a daughter like you," she said. "I wish I had someone else, someone who needed me. Philip's about as self-sufficient as anyone can be. It's good to be needed and wonderful to be able to help someone in need."

"I know. That's why I want to be with my mother," I said.

She nodded.

"She's very lucky. I'm sure she doesn't deserve you."

Dorothy followed me out and down the stairs. At the doorway we hugged again. Philip was nowhere in sight. He wasn't the sort who cared to say good-bye anyway, I thought. Tomorrow, he would forget my face.

I hurried out and to the car, turning once to wave. Dorothy lifted her hand and held it for a moment before she closed the door softly. Loneliness, I thought, had nothing to do with money or wealth; loneliness had to do with the heart. If it beat only for one, it was only half used.

"What did you get, a good-bye present?" Richard asked, eyeing the box when I got into the car.

"Mrs. Livingston was very generous. She bought me some clothes."

He glanced at the box and saw the name inscribed on the cover.

"That's a pretty expensive boutique in Beverly Hills," he said as he started the engine. "What is it?"

"A black evening dress."

"Oh yeah? Well, what do you need with something that expensive now?"

"She wanted me to have it," I said dryly.

He backed out of the driveway and looked at me. "I got an acquaintance who can turn a new dress like that into hard cash, which we could use. Especially since you ain't worn it yet and I bet it still has the tags on it, right?"

"Yes."

"Good."

"I don't want to sell this," I said. "It was a present. It meant a lot to her to give it to me."

"Is that so? What are you, a millionaire? You going to pay the first six months rent for us? You going to buy tomorrow's groceries, pay the electric and gas bills? Pay for my car insurance? I gotta cart you girls around town to the auditions, to the jobs. That takes gas money, upkeep. There's expenses here," he whined. "If you want to be part of this, you gotta put in your share. How much money did the old lady back in Provincetown give you for traveling?" he demanded. "Huh?"

"She bought my tickets and gave me . . . five hundred dollars," I said. She had given me two thousand, but I knew where Richard's questions were heading.

"Well, where's the money?"

"I spent nearly all of it coming out here," I said.

"What's left?"

"A hundred dollars."

"That's all? All right. Give me seventy-five and keep twenty-five for pocket money so I don't have to give you any for a while. Go on, give it to me," he said. "I'll need to have some seed money to find you a job now, too."

I opened my purse and counted out the seventy-five without his seeing how much was really there. When I handed it to him he shoved it into his pocket without another word.

"Good. That makes sense. I'll find you work," he promised.

I curled up in the corner of the seat and gazed out the window as Beverly Hills fell behind us.

"There's my house," Richard claimed, nodding at a large home with Grecian columns in the front. "It's only a matter of time," he said with a confident laugh.

Matter of time? Matter of centuries, I thought, but kept it to myself. My eyes filled with tears of determination. Somehow, somehow soon, I had to get Mommy away from him and away from all this.

As soon as we returned to the apartment, Richard told Mommy about my evening dress, but when Mommy saw it and then tried it on, she moaned and pleaded for him to let us keep it. She did look absolutely beautiful in it.

"I'll get a job where I'll need to wear something nice like this, Richard. Won't I?" she asked, spinning in front of the mirror. "And then, instead of having to rent something, I'll have it. And how about the wonderful, important parties you told me we would be attending soon? I'll need to look good for you, won't I? Oh please, let us keep it."

"People will be impressed Mommy has something so expensive," I added, "and clothing is important to people in the business, isn't it?" I offered to support her.

Richard glared at me.

"How do you know what's important to people in the business?"

"I met an actor who told me all about it," I said.

"Oh, you met an actor. Big deal."

"She's right though, isn't she, Richard? You've told me that. That's why you needed the money for your nice jackets and suits," Mommy added.

He squirmed in his seat.

"We could get a nice piece of change for that."

"Mommy's got work and you said you were sure you could get me work soon anyway," I chimed.

He reddened with fury.

"That's right, Richard," Mommy said, checking her reflection in the mirror.

"You're going to keep calling her Mommy," he snapped at me. "You're bound to make a mistake in front of strangers."

"I won't," I insisted.

"You better call me Sis or Gina even when we're alone, Melody," Mommy advised. "Get into the habit."

"All right. I will. You look beautiful in that dress, Gina," I added, enjoying the way Richard twisted in his seat as the prospect of losing the money for the dress sunk in deeper.

"Richard," she whined. "I've waited so long for something nice."

"All right, all right. Just this once, I'll change my mind, but next time when I decide something—"

"We'll listen. We promise," Mommy said.

He smirked, turned a suspicious eye at me and then went to watch television while Mommy and I got my room organized.

"The Livingstons must be so rich, Melody," Mommy said. "Such expensive gifts. But soon, I'll be able to buy myself things like this. I'll be driven in my Rolls to Beverly Hills and stroll into the most expensive stores, too," she said and pretended that my dingy room was a designer's boutique. "The salespeople will come rushing over, each eager to help me, to show me the latest fashion," Mommy continued. I sat on the bed and watched her pose as if she were gazing at a dress. "Yes, that might work. What's that? Only five thousand dollars? What, is it on sale?"

She laughed and then spun around to look at herself in my evening dress once more. I laughed, too.

"It's beautiful," she said and sighed. Then she looked at me. "But it's really yours."

"No, it isn't Mommy, it's yours. I want you to have it, keep it in your closet."

"Really? Thank you, dear. But please," she said,

whispering, "try, try to call me Sis or Gina." She gazed at the doorway. "Especially when he's here."

I nodded. She gave me a quick hug and then left to be with Richard.

It felt strange going to sleep in their apartment that first night because it reminded me of the trip from Sewell up to the Cape. I recalled the nights on the road, sleeping in motel rooms with them sleeping together nearby, just as they were tonight.

Back then I could only think of my stepdaddy and wonder how Mommy could hold and kiss someone else so quickly after my stepdaddy's death. Maybe she was afraid of being alone, so afraid she would even cling to someone like Archie Marlin. He took advantage of her vulnerability and replaced her fears with pipe dreams. Was Mommy just too grief-stricken to notice? But what about now? What was her excuse for letting him rule her life now?

I felt so small and alone myself, sleeping in this dismal little room. If Mommy hadn't realized what sort of a man Archie Richard Marlin was by now, how could I hope to open her eyes? He held up the promise of glamour and fame, riches and respect. What could I offer in its place except the truth? And for Mommy, the truth might be too painful a pill to swallow.

Like so many other people in Los Angeles, dreams, no matter how false or impossible, were something she would much rather have. At least, I thought, I had found her, and at least now, there was a chance.

I was up before either of them the next morning. I made coffee and toasted some nearly stale bread. They didn't have much more to eat for breakfast, no cereals or eggs and very little jam or butter. Nevertheless, the aroma of freshly brewed coffee brought them out of the bedroom.

"Now this is more like it," Richard said. "I usually have to go out for some coffee. Your sister can't get her eyes open fast or wide enough to boil water first thing in the morning."

"Oh, Richard."

"What, am I telling her something she didn't know about you?" he said and laughed.

"We need some groceries," I said.

He raised his eyebrows.

"So, you still got a few bucks. While we're off to the mall for your sister's job, you go buy what you want," he said.

I made up my mind that was just what I would do.

"Clean up our room, too, while we're gone," he ordered. "I'm tired of living in a pigsty and until you start working and bringing in money, you'll earn your keep that way."

"I gave you money," I reminded him. He reddened.

"What money?" Mommy asked.

"Just some of her pocket money, hardly anything, but I need it to go riding up and down the valley seeing people and trying to get her a job, don't I? Well, don't I?" he pursued.

"Yes, I suppose so," Mommy agreed. It seemed there wasn't anything he couldn't make her think or say.

They drank their coffee, nibbled on some of the toast and then went to get dressed. I waited until they left and then I called Holly and told her where I was and what had finally happened.

"So you've decided to stay?"

"Yes," I said. Although I didn't tell her how Philip wanted me to leave, I did tell her how sad I thought Dorothy really was.

"She can't buy enough things to keep the darkness from her door," I told Holly.

"I know. It's a conversation she and I have had before. Maybe I should make another trip out there soon."

"I wish you would. She does miss you," I said.

"Listen to you, giving other people advice and trying to help them while your future is still uncertain. Don't take on more than you can handle, sweetheart, and call me if you need me."

"I will. Thank you, Holly."

As soon as I hung up, I called Cary, hoping he might just be home. He wasn't, but Aunt Sara was eager to talk.

"Jacob's very sick," she told me. "It was worse this time. And now Cary's got me worried, too. He barely gets any rest between going on the boat, looking after our business and running up to the hospital. I'm on my way up there now."

"I'm sorry, Aunt Sara. I wish I were there to help you."

"Are you all right, dear? I haven't even asked you how your search is going. I'm sorry."

"That's all right. You have enough on your mind. Just give Cary my phone number, please, but tell him not to call until he really has a free moment. It's not any sort of emergency."

"I'm afraid it is here," she said in a tiny voice. "We all try to be strong for Jacob, but it gets so hard to keep our spirits up."

I heard her start to sob and then she quickly excused herself and hung up. I felt awful about being away from Aunt Sara and the family when things were going so poorly. I felt myself pulled in every direction. Mommy also needed me, but she seemed to have chosen her predicament. Cary and Aunt Sara and May had no choice.

Where did I really belong?

It seemed like I had been searching for home forever. Just when I thought I'd found it. . . .

# 8

*A Star Shines*

After I got dressed, I went downstairs and asked a man working on the grounds where the closest grocery store was. He spoke broken English mixed with Spanish words, but I remembered enough from my high school Spanish class to communicate with him. The supermarket was a little more than three long blocks away. When I got there and saw all the delicious produce, I wanted to fill my cart, but thinking about the long walk home kept me from going wild. It was already hot and sticky, with only little puffs of clouds lazily sliding toward the horizon. A nice day for a stroll but not for lugging groceries around.

A handsome young man with dark brown hair was just turning in his apron at the next counter when I checked out, and I caught him looking my way as I was paying the cashier. As I walked from the store, struggling not to spill anything out of my two bags and hoping the bottoms wouldn't burst, I heard someone behind me say, "You look like you could use a third arm."

I turned to see the handsome young man from the

store. In the sunlight, his hair held hints of copper. His laughing eyes were hazel with long eyelashes. Although he wasn't what I would call muscular, he was well proportioned, sinewy, sleek, his face very masculine, especially around his mouth.

"I could carry one of those for you," he offered. "I won't steal your food," he added with a soft smile when I hesitated.

"How do you know where I'm going?" I asked.

"The Egyptian Gardens, right? I saw you there yesterday. I was at the pool when you went by. I live there, too," he said. "I'm walking that way anyway," he added, "going home." He shrugged when I didn't reply. "Light's changing."

"What?"

"We can cross now," he said, indicating the traffic had stopped.

"Oh."

He reached out and took one of my bags.

"Better hurry up," he said. "This is one of the shortest lights in L.A."

He grabbed my elbow and gently directed me across the street. We walked quickly and didn't speak again until we were on the sidewalk.

"I don't blame your hesitating to accept my offer. I don't trust my groceries with strangers either," he said with that silly, impish grin again. "Strange women are always approaching me and offering to carry one of my bags."

"Very funny."

"My name's Mel Jensen."

"Melody . . . Simon," I said.

"There. Now we're no longer strangers," he quipped. "I can carry your groceries all the time."

"Just because we exchanged names doesn't mean we're not still strangers," I replied and he turned very serious.

"You're right. Besides, around here, you're never sure the person is giving you his or her real name anyway," he said with a tiny turn in the corner of his mouth, and I felt myself turn a bright crimson. He was looking straight ahead, so he didn't notice. "But that's my real name and I intend to make it a household word," he bragged, now turning to see my reaction.

"What are you selling?" I asked and he laughed, the light in his eyes getting even brighter. He paused when he saw I wasn't kidding. "You're serious? You think I'm a salesman?"

"Well, you said household, so I thought . . ."

"What are you doing in L.A.?" he asked, suddenly very curious and suspicious. I looked away before replying.

"I'm visiting my sister," I said.

"Sister? Simon," he thought aloud. "Oh, you're Gina Simon's sister?"

"Yes," I said. I never thought of myself as a good liar and I had doubts that I would be able to fool people the way Mommy and Richard Marlin wanted. I was positive people would see through me or hear the hesitation in my voice and know immediately I wasn't telling the truth, but if Mel Jensen saw my deceit, he ignored it.

"Of course," he said nodding, "you two do look a lot alike. I suppose you want to be an actress and a model, too?"

"Not really, but my sister's agent thinks I can be. He says he's going to try to get me a job while I'm here," I replied.

"Stranger things have happened. The doorman at the Four Seasons got offered a small part in a television pilot. The pilot was picked up and he got a recurring role in it. Now he's an actor who drives up to the Four Seasons in his own Mercedes and has doors opened for him."

"Are you an actor, too?"

"No, I'm a dancer, jazz, interpretive, that sort of thing. However, if they made musicals the way they did when Gene Kelly and Fred Astaire were alive, I'd be in the movies," he claimed. "Anyway, this job packing groceries and stocking shelves is just something to keep a roof over my head while I fight the good fight. I share an apartment with two other guys, who both happen to be actors. Aren't you and your sister from the Midwest someplace?"

"Yes," I said quickly, hoping he wouldn't press me for details. I didn't know all the lies Mommy and Richard had spread about themselves.

"I'm from Portland."

We turned into The Egyptian Gardens and I stopped to take back my second bag of groceries.

"That's all right," he said. "I'll go up to your sister's place with you. I'm not in any rush. I'm not waiting for anything. I have an audition tomorrow morning and then I'll be hovering around the phone." He laughed and we walked down the pathway to Mommy's building. "You should see the three of us when we've all gone for something and the phone rings. It's a mad dash. Lately, all three of us have been disappointed, but my luck's changing. I can feel it."

"I hope so," I said.

"Thanks. See, we can't be strangers any longer. You're already wishing me luck."

He stepped into the elevator with me and carried my bag of groceries to the door of Mommy's apartment.

"Thank you," I said as he put the bag into my arms.

"Just an added service we provide at the Bay Market," he replied with a soft, beguiling smile on his lips. "What are you doing with the rest of your day?"

"I'm . . . cleaning," I said.

"It's so hot today."

"I have to do it," I said.

"When you take a break, come on down to the pool and I'll introduce you to some of the other tenants."

"I'd like that," I said hesitantly.

"See you later then," he replied and started for the elevator.

I don't know why I said I might go to the pool, I thought. I don't even have a bathing suit. I put away the groceries and began to clean the apartment. From the gobs of dust and the cobwebs I found, I realized neither Mommy nor Richard had ever done much cleaning since they had moved into this place. The pail of water turned black from my dipping the mop in it after two or three swipes of the kitchen floor. The windows were so crusted with grime, they made the outside world look gray even on a beautiful day.

The bathroom was even dirtier. Stubborn mildew had formed in every crack and space, and when I moved a small rug near the tub, I jumped back a foot because of the size of the bugs that came crawling out.

Finally, I turned my attention to the bedrooms. The little balls of dust under the beds were like tumbleweeds. There wasn't any vacuum cleaner either, so I had to sweep under the beds and wash by hand the places the mop wouldn't reach. I didn't know whether Mommy would want me to go into her and Richard's dresser drawers, but I saw she wasn't folding her clothes any better than she used to fold them back in Sewell. I did most of our washing and ironing back then, too.

Clothes were draped over chairs and there was a pair of jeans and a blouse crumpled on the floor. While organizing one of her dresser drawers, I found a light pink two-piece bathing suit and I thought about Mel Jensen's invitation. It was still very sunny and warm outside and I was about due for a break.

When I tried on the bathing suit however, I realized it was very revealing. I was going to take it off and look for another, more modest suit, but all I found was another bikini, this one even skimpier.

I stood up and gazed at myself in the mirror again. The suit fit well. I was a little bigger in the bosom than Mommy so the top was snug. My hips were more narrow, but the suit was like new and not stretched. I turned around, gazing at myself from different angles, not unhappy with what I saw. I didn't approve of girls who flaunted themselves, but I didn't see why I should be ashamed of having a nice figure. I could use a little tan, I thought, and conjured up Mel Jensen's soft, handsome, inviting smile. Did I have the nerve to go down to the pool in this suit? Just the thought of it was titillating.

While I was considering it, the phone rang. It was Cary.

"I tried calling earlier," he said, "but when the answering machine came on, I decided not to leave a message. You wouldn't know when to call me anyway. I'm in and out so much."

"I went shopping for groceries."

"Shopping for groceries? Where are you? What did you tell Ma? She can't remember anything these days. What's happening?" He fired questions at me without taking a breath.

I told him about my confrontation with Mommy and summarized her story quickly.

"So they sent a strange woman's body to Provincetown? I can't believe it. That's against the law, isn't it?" he asked.

"I suppose so," I said.

"What about the woman who's in the grave? Isn't anyone looking for her?"

"I don't know all the details, but there are a lot of people here who have left their families behind forever. Besides, I think it was mostly Richard Marlin's doing," I added. "Mommy seems . . . under his control, but I'm going to get her out of here," I said and explained why I wanted to stay in Los Angeles and try to save her from Richard's evil grip.

"Maybe she doesn't want to be saved, Melody," Cary said.

"I've got to try."

"Why? She didn't care about you. Look at what she did. If your friend back in West Virginia hadn't found that picture in the catalogue, do you think your mother would have ever called again?" he argued. "She was just like those other people you mentioned, people who forgot their families."

I knew he just wanted me to go home to him, although what he was saying was not untrue.

"That's just it, Cary. I did see the picture and I did find her and I know she needs me. One day she's going to find herself all alone here. Once Richard decides he can't get anything more out of her, he'll leave her stranded."

"She should have thought of that herself. You don't belong there," he insisted. "They're criminals, sending a stranger's body to be buried as if it were your mother's. Grandma Olivia's going to be furious."

"Maybe you shouldn't tell her anything just yet."

"What do I do when she asks, lie? Is that what you're learning how to do out in L.A.?"

"No."

"Your mother's a good teacher," he muttered. "We both know that."

"Look Cary, no matter what she's done, she's still my mother. You'd feel the same way."

"No, I wouldn't," he said quietly and I could hear the sadness in his voice.

"How's your father doing?" I asked.

"There's been no change. He's still in the cardiac care unit in the hospital. It was raining here this morning, a small storm, so we didn't go out in the boat. I'm depending on the cranberry crop to get us through the year anyway," he added. "There's going to be a lot of work to do soon."

"Maybe I can come back to help," I suggested.

"And then what, return to L.A.?"

"I just don't know, Cary."

"You probably like it out there. Hollywood," he spat. "It's a lot more glamorous than living in an old house and harvesting cranberries. I don't blame you," he said in a tired voice. "I wish I could run away from my responsibilities, too."

"I'm not running away from my responsibilities, Cary Logan. I'm running toward them. I'm trying to help my mother," I said firmly, determined to make him understand.

"Right. Well, you know where I'll be. Give me a call sometime, if you *have* time," he said, not disguising his frustration and anger.

"Oh, Cary, you know I'll call."

"I gotta get back to the hospital," he said. "I left Ma up there with May. Bye."

"Cary."

The phone went dead. I held the receiver in my hand a moment and then put it back on the cradle, my heart feeling like cold stone. Cary didn't do well with sadness and hardship. He turned inside himself and bitterly closed up like a clam. It was the way I had found him when I had been left there to live with Uncle Jacob and Aunt Sara, and it had taken a while to get him to say two friendly words to me. I felt just horrible not being there at his side when he needed me so much.

But when I gazed around this small apartment and thought about Mommy completely under Richard's control, I knew I had to stay. I had to try. It was times like this I wished there were two of me. I would send my other self back to Provincetown. I should have been the one to have a twin, not Cary, I thought.

A rich peal of laughter came flowing up from under the patio. I went out and listened. Two young women were walking down the path toward the pool. They were both in bikinis, even skimpier than the one I was wearing.

I do need a break, I thought, just a small intermission from all these troublesome thoughts. Just for a little while, I'll pretend to be one of them. My only fear was that whatever madness drove them would be contagious and what Cary suggested would come true. I'd find it was easier to just run away into my dreams and fantasies, and like everyone else here, not worry if they had any reasonable relationship to the truth.

Despite that fear, I searched for and found a beach towel at the bottom of the closet and a pair of sandals. I scooped up Mommy's coffee-stained and cigarette-burned terry cloth robe and slipped it over myself. Then I headed down to the pool, telling myself it was just for a little while. No harm done. Right?

"This is Melody Simon," Mel Jensen told the stout, light-brown-haired man on the lounge beside him. "Melody, meet Bobby Dee," Mel said.

"Greetings," Bobby Dee muttered. He held the sun reflector under his chin and glanced at me quickly.

"Bobby's the drummer for the Gross Me Outs, a rock band who cut their first single last week."

"Oh. Congratulations," I said. Bobby Dee grunted. Mel pulled up a lounge chair so I could be beside him. Across the pool Sandy and two of her friends were sunning themselves, surrounded by two other young men. Everyone looked at me when I took off Mommy's robe and laid it neatly on the lounge. Mel's smile widened.

"You better put on some suntan lotion," he suggested. "You're a bit pale in places that have obviously not seen the sun in a while." He handed me his bottle of lotion.

"Thank you," I said and rubbed some lotion over my legs and arms.

"I can get your back for you," he volunteered.

"Watch out. That's how he starts," Bobby Dee mumbled. "First it's the back and then it's the arms and then—"

"Never mind, big mouth," Mel said. He took the lotion and stood behind me. His hands felt warm on my skin, but the lotion was cold and I jumped.

"He's the guy with the magic touch." Bobby lowered his reflector and really looked at me. "You don't sing, do you? We're looking for a new lead singer."

"I sing when I play the fiddle," I said. "But I'm not good enough to be in anyone's band."

"Fiddle. You mean as in hoedown music?"

"I guess so," I said. Mel rubbed the lotion into my

arms and then spent some time on my shoulders and neck. "Thank you," I told him. I had the feeling if I didn't speak up, he'd keep at it all afternoon.

"No problem."

"Hell's a Poppin' has a fiddle player in their band," Bobby said. "They got a gig in the valley, at Market Square off of Ventura. Ever hear of them?"

"She just got here, Bobby. She doesn't even know what you mean by the valley," Mel said.

"Oh yeah?" He studied me a moment and then went back to his sun reflector.

Sandy and one of her girlfriends dove into the pool and swam over to us. The young men jumped in after them.

"Hi again," Sandy called and raised herself up to look at me.

"Hi."

"You've met Mel, I see," she said.

"At my office," he told her.

"Watch out, he bites," she warned, laughing as she pushed herself away.

"Why is everyone warning me about you?" I asked him.

"Jealousy," he said. "Beware of the green-eyed monster. It possesses everyone around here eventually."

Bobby grunted.

"Look who's talking," he said. Mel spun on him.

"What, you're not jealous of Tommy and the Loafers?" Mel asked him.

"It was just luck that they got that contract instead of us," Bobby replied.

"You're still jealous," Mel said. "See?" he told me. I smiled, lay back and closed my eyes. Someone turned on a radio and the music drifted our way. The sunlight was warm. There was laughter around me. It was easy to forget problems. I could get used to this, I thought shamefully.

"Are you going to Sandy's party tonight?" Mel asked.

"I think so," I said.

"Good."

I opened one eye and glanced at him. He was on his side, turned toward me.

"Why don't you bring your fiddle to Sandy's tonight," he suggested.

"I didn't bring it to California," I said.

"You didn't? Why not?"

"I . . . didn't think anyone would want to hear a fiddle player," I said.

"Doesn't Jerry have a fiddle?" Mel asked Bobby.

"Yeah. We'll dig it out for you. I'll bring it tonight."

"No, I'd rather not. I'm really not that good," I said.

"If there is one place in the world modesty doesn't work, it's L.A.," Mel said. "Here, you're considered weird if you don't blow your own horn."

"Then I'll be considered weird," I said firmly, "because I don't."

Bobby laughed.

"She plays the fiddle, stupid," he said, "not the horn."

"I bet you're good," Mel insisted. I didn't reply. "Come on," he said poking me, "let's get wet."

He got up and dove into the water, a smooth, graceful dive that barely made a splash.

"Come on in," he said when he surfaced. "It's great."

I looked at Bobby, who shrugged and said, "I took one bath already this week."

Mel treaded water and Sandy and the other girls began to splash him. He splashed back. It looked like they were having fun so I got up and sat at the edge of the pool. Mel swam over and seized my ankles.

"Come on. You won't drown. It's only five feet deep." He tugged and I went forward, falling into his arms and into the pool. The girls came to my rescue, splashing him so much he had to dive under. I joined in, but when they turned to me, their eyes widened with shock. I paused, curious.

"What's wrong?" I asked.

Sandy swam forward.

"Your suit," she said and I looked down at the top of

my mother's bikini. In water the suit became transparent. I was as good as naked.

"Oh no," I wailed, wrapping my arms around my breasts.

"Just wait a minute," Sandy said and climbed out of the pool. She got my towel off the lounge and returned. I got out and she wrapped the towel around me. Everyone was looking at us, and some of the men who had arrived were shaking their heads gleefully. Even Bobby Dee was laughing at me.

Embarrassed to the bone, my face and even my body turned so red I looked like I had gotten a bad sunburn.

"Thanks," I told Sandy. "It's one of my . . . moth— my sister's suits. I didn't know it would do this," I explained. I looked at the others and then grabbed the apartment keys off the table by the lounge and fled.

When I got up to the apartment, I looked at myself in the mirror. This suit was obviously not meant for bathing, I thought. I got out of it quickly, dried off and put on my clothes. As I was drying my hair, I heard the buzzer. It was Mel, bringing the rest of my things.

"Now that was a dramatic exit," he said when I opened the door. "You're definitely an actress. You made a big first impression."

"Thanks a lot. I'd rather not have been noticed. I didn't realize that suit wasn't meant for swimming. I borrowed it from my sister's dresser drawer."

"No explanations necessary. I kind of liked it," he said, leaning in close to me.

"I wonder why," I said sarcastically, and then reached for my robe and sandals. "Thanks for bringing these."

"No problem. I'll see you at Sandy's," he said. "Dressed?"

"I'm not showing my face," I wailed.

"That's silly. Everyone understands. Something like that happens around here regularly."

"Not to me," I cried. He laughed as I closed the door.

When Mommy and Richard Marlin came home, I took Mommy aside and told her what had happened.

"Oh, I haven't been down at that pool ever," she said. "Those suits are for modeling jobs. You don't want to get too much sun when you're my age. It brings out wrinkles," she explained.

"It was very embarrassing," I said and she just laughed.

"I bet it made you instantly popular with the young men around here," she said, with a tinge of jealousy in her voice.

"I'd rather not be that popular."

"Of course you would. The more men looking at you, the more important you are," she told me. "Take your time giving any one of them your individual attention. You've got years and years to go before you do what I did, chain yourself to one man."

"Is that what it was like for you, Mommy? You felt trapped all the time?"

"Yes," she confessed easily. "And please, remember, don't call me Mommy," she whispered.

Richard came out of the kitchen.

"You bought quite a bit," he said. "There's actually some real food in this house for once."

"Well, we don't have to worry about it tonight. We're going to Sandy's party," Mommy reminded him.

"I can't go, Sis. Not after what happened this afternoon."

"Nonsense, Melody."

"What happened this afternoon?" Richard asked. Mommy told him and he laughed. Then he looked at me seriously.

"I think I got you a job. I described you to this producer and he wants to see you tomorrow. After I drop Gina off at the mall, I'll take you to the studio."

"Oh Melody, that's terrific, and so fast, too. Now the girls around here will really be dying with jealousy."

"The green-eyed monster," I said nodding, recalling Mel's words.

"What?"

143

"Nothing. What kind of a job is it?" I asked Richard. "What do I demonstrate?"

"Don't be so smart. It happens to be an acting job," he said, "in an independent movie."

I looked at Mommy, who beamed.

"But I've never acted," I said.

"So you'll learn," Richard said. He looked around and nodded. "She did a good job with the place, didn't she, Gina?"

"Yes. Thank you, honey."

"Maybe, maybe this will work out after all," Richard said, smiling like a Cheshire cat. It was a smile that sent chills down my spine. Suddenly, I was feeling like a cornered mouse.

My little incident at the pool made me the star at Sandy's party. The moment the three of us came through the door, there was a cheer. I was embarrassed by the attention, but thought everyone was very friendly. The party was already in full swing by the time we arrived since Mommy had taken forever to put on her makeup and decide on how she wanted to wear her hair.

"Besides," she'd told me, "in Hollywood, being on time is a sign of weakness. Always be fashionably late."

Mel had helped Sandy with the food, bringing her things that were ready-made at the supermarket. They started with recorded music, but Bobby Dee and his band began to play as more guests arrived. The apartment wasn't much bigger than ours and it seemed to me everyone who lived in the complex was there, and it wasn't long before everyone was dancing. Even people standing and talking were moving to the rhythm of the music as they spoke. If ever fun was infectious, it was infectious here, I thought, unable to keep myself from swinging and moving to the music and laughter around me.

Almost all the conversations I heard were about auditions, parts, agents and producers. What amazed me the most was how easily everyone accepted Mommy as

144

about their age. In her micro mini and her black tank top with her hair pulled back into a ponytail, she did look more like my sister than my mother. I understood why the lie was so easily accepted.

My thoughts were interrupted when Mel asked me to dance with him. As we spun around the room I noticed Richard had moved off to talk to two pretty women while Mommy danced with someone who called himself Stingo. He had hair as long as mine and wore two silver earrings. Mommy's laughter was soon heard over the music. Every once in a while, she glanced my way and beamed a smile. She looked happy, like someone who had been rejuvenated. Was it possible to really turn back time, to be young again?

Suddenly, Bobby's band stopped playing and he announced to the crowd that there was a new talent in their midst, a fresh, innocent voice. I had no idea who he was talking about until he produced the fiddle and called out my name. Mommy looked as surprised as I was.

"No," I said shaking. "I told you I wasn't that good."

"We'll be the judge of that," Bobby declared. "Come on, we're all bitter friends here," he added with a smile.

"Go ahead," Mel urged.

"I can't. I—"

"Just do it or he'll keep bugging you. That's Bobby."

Reluctantly, I stepped forward and everyone cheered. Mommy and Richard stood beside each other watching with interest and surprise. Although Richard looked pleased, a strange look came over Mommy's face. If I didn't know better I'd have thought she was jealous.

"This is a song an old friend taught me," I began as I took the fiddle. The crowd grew still, but I tried not to think of them and instead thought of Papa George and his pleasure whenever I played for him. "It's an old mountain folks song about a woman whose lover dies in a feud. She mourns him so much that her heart turns into a bird and flies away, up to join his soul."

Someone laughed and someone else said, "Shut up, you idiot."

145

I lifted the bow and began, singing softly at first and then lifting my voice and closing my eyes. When I ended, there was dead silence.

"That was great," Mel said just loud enough for everyone to hear. There were murmurs of agreement and then there was loud applause and cheers.

"Looks like you got a real good new client, Richard," Bobby shouted across the room. Richard smiled and nodded.

"Do I know talent when I see it or don't I?"

"Is that a question?" Someone shouted and there was more laughter. Bobby and his band started again and the wild, happy mood returned.

"That was very sweet," Mommy said coming up to me. "You didn't waste much time getting to know everyone and letting them know you played the fiddle."

"I didn't. It just—"

"But I really don't think that kind of music is successful in Hollywood these days, Melody, so don't get your hopes up."

"Oh, I don't expect the fiddle to make me famous. I didn't even want to play it now. I didn't come here for that."

She laughed.

"Oh, maybe you did," she said with a wink. Without another word, she grabbed the arm of a tall, dark young man and went off to dance again.

As I walked through the room everyone congratulated me on my performance and Sandy gave me a big hug.

"You're great," she declared. "You're going to make it."

"Make it? Make what?"

"Success, silly," she said before rushing off to dance. Mel stepped up beside me.

"You're a hit. No one has moved into this complex and won everyone's attention so quickly," he declared.

"I'm not looking to do that."

"What are you looking for then? A job in the supermarket? I can help you get that," he teased. "Somehow, I think you want more, just like the rest of us."

"No," I insisted.

I looked around at the gathering of young hopefuls, everyone believing something wonderful would happen if only they tried hard enough. They came from all over, the East, the Midwest, northern California, each of them waiting to get their big break. It wasn't wrong to have ambition, but there was a line, a difference between ambition and false dreams, dreams that would only bring pain and disappointment. I had no idea where the line was or who was crossing it, but I wasn't going to be one to do so, I vowed. Yet I could see how easily someone could be tempted to believe in fairy tales. I couldn't deny the compliments and encouragement had me daydreaming about being a famous musician.

Cary's words came thundering through my memory. *It's more glamorous than living in an old house and harvesting cranberries. I don't blame you.*

"I'm tired," I told Mel as my thoughts came back down to earth. "I've had a big day." I flashed a smile at him and grabbed Mommy's arm as soon as she danced near me. "I'm going back to our place. I'm tired, Sis."

"Whatever," she said, barely hearing me. She was too involved in her dancing.

"Hey, it's so early," Mel said as I headed for the door.

"Jet lag, I guess," I replied shortly.

"You're going to miss a good time. Things haven't even begun yet," he coaxed, still holding onto my hand.

I pulled it away gently.

"There'll be other good times," I said. "Thanks."

His disappointment was written across his face.

"Yeah, you're welcome. Anytime," he said turning away.

I slipped out of the party quickly and went across the hall to our apartment. Once I closed the door behind me, I let out my long-held breath. My face was flushed. The breeze coming through the window was too warm to bring any relief so I went out onto the patio and sat there, looking over the tops of the buildings at the brilliantly shining constellations.

I wondered if Cary thousands of miles away was looking at the same stars. I missed seeing the way they sparkled over the ocean, making wishes on shooting stars as I walked along the beach. Was the ocean calm tonight? Were the waves gently lapping at the shore? As much as I wanted to hear Cary's voice, I knew it was too late to call him. Everyone was probably asleep anyway, I thought.

I heard a car alarm go off on the street in front of the complex. It sounded like a wounded animal, an injured stray dog, its high-pitched scream lasting a good two minutes before it stopped. Then, it was relatively quiet again. My eyelids drooped. I got up and got ready for bed. The moment my head hit the pillow, I was asleep.

But a few hours later, I was woken by the sound of Mommy and Richard's laughter. They came bursting into the apartment, both sounding drunk and not caring how much noise they made. Mommy shouted.

"Where's my talented little sister?" She laughed and came to my doorway. "The hit of the party. How'dya like that, Richard?"

"I love it," he called to her and she laughed again. I pretended to be dead asleep, but I opened my eyes and saw her wavering in the doorway. "Everyone thinks that was very cool, Melody . . . being a hit and then walking out of the party. Very cool. Looks like I taught you more than I thought," she said, "but just don't forget who's the teacher."

"Come on to bed, Gina."

"I'm coming."

She stood in the doorway glaring in at me. I didn't move.

"Sleep tight, Sis," she said. Then she laughed, wiped her forehead and stumbled away. I heard something fall on the floor with a crash and I heard her curse.

"Get to bed before you destroy the place and ruin all the good work your sister done," Richard teased.

Mommy cursed again and then she went into their bedroom and slammed the door. The whole apartment shook.

I heard their muffled voices through the walls, Mommy raising hers and then Richard yelling something. After that, I heard Mommy's sobs and wails. Finally, it grew quiet.

She can't be happy here, I thought. She just can't. Tomorrow, tomorrow I'll start talking to her about going back. I'll remind her about my inheritance and how we'll have money and how she could do whatever she wants if she would only stop trying to be someone she isn't.

It was like I was in the land of ghosts, everyone trying to be another person and their true selves floating around them, waiting to return to their lost bodies. Ironically, that's what Mommy had to do . . . return to her body, to her name, to the identity she had buried in a grave back in Provincetown.

Would she ever want to be Haille Logan again?

I hoped so, because Haille Logan was my mother.

# 9
&

# *Take One*

*I* woke to the same sound of shouting and muffled cries I had heard before falling asleep. By the time I rose, got dressed and went out to put on a pot of coffee, however, it was quiet again. Richard emerged first, looking furious. He poured himself some coffee and began mumbling aloud.

"It's like pulling teeth sometimes. Why do I have to put up with this?" he muttered. "She acts like she's doing me a favor. LET'S GET IT STRAIGHT WHO'S DOING WHO A FAVOR HERE," he shouted toward the bedroom.

"What's wrong?" I asked and he spun on me.

"What's wrong? Everything's wrong. She drank too much, as usual, thanks to you, and then she went into one of her crying jags and kept me up all night. Finally she passed out and now she's miserable and hung over."

"Because of me?" I asked, confused, but he ignored my question.

"She moans and fights me. She knows she has to get up and look good. MY REPUTATION IS AT STAKE

150

HERE!" he added, again shouting in Mommy's direction. She finally emerged wearing sunglasses and walking with small, careful steps like someone who was walking on eggshells. She went directly to the coffee pot.

"You can't wear those sunglasses all day, Gina. I told you to stop drinking ten times last night if I told you once, didn't I? Didn't I?" he asked furiously.

"I'll be fine," she said.

"Sure. You'll be fine. You'll look and act half dead and they'll fire you and once again, they'll blame me. Another market will be lost to me and my other clients!" Richard exclaimed.

"Your other clients?" She tried to smile, but that seemed to make her head ache, because she immediately grabbed her forehead.

"Does anyone want anything to eat?" I asked. Mommy didn't reply, but Richard turned away from Mommy and looked at me.

"No. And get dressed," he snapped. "You have to go with us. I'm not coming all the way back here to pick you up. Your appointment is in West L.A."

"Dressed? I am dressed."

"Put on something . . . sexier. Don't you have a mini-skirt or something?"

"No, I—"

"Go look in Gina's closet," he ordered. Mommy smiled.

"Yes, go do that, Melody. Only, don't wear my other bathing suit."

She laughed.

"Oh, you're so funny," Richard said. "I have all the responsibility here. I'm the one putting his neck out. It's about time I was appreciated. I mean it," he said sternly.

She raised her sunglasses off her nose. Her eyes were bloodshot and very tired looking.

"I appreciate you, Richard. You have no right to say I don't."

"Well, if you're not in tiptop shape when I deliver you, you put me in a bad light," he said. He turned to me.

"Didn't I tell you to pick something out? We're behind schedule because it took so long for me to get her out of bed."

I gazed at Mommy. She lowered her glasses again and sipped her coffee. She hadn't even said good morning to me. I went into their bedroom. It looked like war had been fought in their bed: the blanket twisted, the sheet pulled up, one of the pillows on the floor. Mommy's clothes from last night were piled over her shoes beside the bed. I found a miniskirt and matching blouse in her closet and put them on.

"That's more like it," Richard said. "You women have got to understand how to put your best foot forward when I bring you someplace," he lectured.

"It's not our feet they're interested in," Mommy quipped and then laughed.

"Very funny. Let's get moving," he ordered.

He didn't give me time to clean anything up. I barely had time to turn off the coffee pot before he marched us out of the apartment, mumbling angrily behind us that we put pressure on him by taking so long to get ready.

"He's a slave driver," Mommy said loud enough for him to hear. "But he's right. I'm lucky I have him looking after me."

"If he was looking after you, why did he let you drink so much?" I asked her.

She glanced at me and then stiffened.

"He didn't let me. You heard what he said in the kitchen. He tried to get me to stop."

"Why did you do it?" I pursued.

"Because I'm not the hit of the party like you, Melody. I'm not perfect, but there's a lot worse than me around here," she added in a louder voice, mostly for Richard's benefit.

"I'm not perfect, Mom . . . Sis, and I didn't go there to be the hit of the party. Honest."

"It doesn't matter. Who cares what these losers think around here anyway? Most of them will be gone in six months. You'll see," she said.

I got into the rear of the car and Mommy got into the front. None of us spoke as Richard made his way through the city streets, cursing at drivers, mumbling about why he should be living in a nicer neighborhood by now.

"And I would be, too, if I'd only got the sort of cooperation I need."

"I'm sorry, Richard," Mommy said when we pulled into the mall parking lot. "I know I was a bad girl."

"Just try to do a good job in there. Important people come to this plaza and someone could easily spot you. Remember what I told you . . . exposure, exposure, exposure . . . that's the name of the game."

"Right. I'm sorry," she said and leaned over to kiss him. He didn't soften much, keeping his back straight, his eyes forward.

"I'll be back to check on you later," he said. It came out as a threat. Mommy turned to me before getting out.

"Good luck, honey," she said, "and listen to whatever Richard tells you."

"I don't know what I'm doing or—"

"Will you get going, Gina," Richard ordered. "You're already a few minutes late."

"Yes. Right away," she said and left the car. Before I could get into the front seat, Richard started away.

"Where exactly are we going?" I asked.

"Live Wire Studios," he said. "A friend of mine is doing us a favor, giving you a chance."

"But I don't understand. How do I start acting without a single lesson?"

"The director teaches you everything you have to know right on the spot. It pays real well. We could make a half a year's rent on this one assignment if you do it right," he said.

"A half a year's rent?" So much money, I thought, and dependent on me.

"That's right and that's only the beginning. I've been telling your mother how good it could get, but she goes off on a bender like this and nearly ruins things from time to time," he said. "It hasn't been easy for me, no matter what you think."

"Maybe she's not really happy here then," I offered. He was silent. "Why did you say it was my fault, what happened last night?"

"You upstaged her," he said, "and Gina hates being upstaged, especially by someone who's supposed to be her younger sister."

"Upstaged? But . . . I didn't mean to do anything like that."

"Sure," he said with a smile. "None of you women mean anything."

"It happens to be the truth," I snapped.

I glared at the scenery. The buildings and the neighborhood began to look more seedy and run-down. Where were we going?

Finally, he made a turn into a driveway. I saw a building with something called an Adult Reading Store in front of it. The driveway wrapped around behind it to another building that looked like an attached garage, but above the doorway was a sign that read LIVE WIRE STUDIOS.

"Here we are," Richard said.

"This is a studio?"

"Most of the studios look like this," he explained. "People who don't know Hollywood have this fantasy, this glamorous view of it. It's just another warehouse, just another factory churning out fantasy instead of shoes or chairs. That's all. Now remember," he warned, "you're twenty-one years old. Oh, I told them you were in a small film back in West Virginia."

"What?"

"It's nothing. Everyone makes up his or her resumé here. The film was called *Cherry Blossom*. You played Cherry."

"What?"

"Stop saying 'what,'" he ordered, turning around. "Now don't tell them any more than they need to know about you. And do what the director wants quickly, without questions, understand? You'll be here most of the day. I'll pick you up at five."

"You're not coming in with me?"

"I have other clients, other meetings," he said testily. "I can't be baby-sitting you. You want to be a movie star, this is how you start."

"I don't want to be a movie star," I said gazing at the worn-looking doorway to the dull brown stucco building. I noticed there were no windows.

"So? You'll grin and bear it, fame and fortune. I should be so unlucky." He opened my door. "Come on, get going. I'll be right here at five," he said and stepped back.

I got out slowly, too slowly for him. He reached in and pulled me by the arm.

"Will you get going," he said. "Everyone has to do his part to keep this operation going. You want to be with us, earn your keep or go home?" he threatened. "Now what's it going to be?"

"I'm just going to make a fool of myself," I said.

"So what? Besides," he said with a sly smile on his lips, "something tells me you won't make a fool of yourself. In fact, you might just be a bigger star than your mother will ever be. And then you'll only have me to thank."

He got into the car again and nodded at the studio door.

"The director's name is Parker, Lewis Parker."

He turned the car around and drove out of the yard, leaving me standing in front of the studio. I took a deep breath, swallowed back my confusion and fear, and went to the door. It opened to a dim, shallow hallway. There was a very tiny office on the right with paper piled on the small desk and stacks of what looked like scripts scattered on the floor. A poster of a woman clad in a see-through nightgown, hovering over a man wearing handcuffs was on the wall above the desk. The poster read SLEEP WALKER. SHE WAS HIS BEST NIGHTMARE.

I continued down the hallway to another door above

which was an unlit red light bulb with the words DO NOT ENTER WHEN LIT beneath it. I knocked on the door and waited and then knocked again. Maybe there was no one here, I thought. It looked deserted.

Suddenly, the door was opened and a curly-haired, young black man in dungarees and a loose fitting T-shirt greeted me.

"Can I help you?" he asked.

"I'm Melody Simon," I said, my voice cracking.

"Oh, yeah. Good. Parker, the other girl is here," he called over his shoulder. "I'm Harris. Follow me," he said, turning back to me.

"Get her in here," someone shouted from behind him and Harris stepped back, smiling.

"Come on," he said.

I entered slowly. There were wires everywhere and lights on poles. I saw the cameras, three of them all pointing toward what looked like a bedroom, where a cameraman was adjusting some lights. A very buxom platinum blond–haired girl who didn't look much older than I was sat on the edge of the bed, her arms behind her as she leaned back, her breasts bare. She had a tattoo of what looked like a snake coming up and out of her cleavage. She wore nothing but a pair of flimsy panties, and she chewed bubble gum, blowing a bubble and snapping it before wiping it back in with her tongue. I must have gasped aloud.

A plump bald-headed man spun around in a chair.

"Over here," he called. "I'm Lewis Parker. You the girl Marlin sent? What's your name again?" he asked.

I was still too stunned to speak. I shook my head instead.

"Hey," he said. "We haven't got time to waste. I have to do four scenes and two setups today."

When he rose from his chair, I could see he was very fat and I wondered how he'd fit in the chair. He waddled rather than walked toward me and stopped, drinking me in from head to foot, a pleased smile spreading like melted butter over his jowls and thick, fleshy lips.

Because he was so heavy, his eyes looked small, sunken in his large head.

"Marlin was right," he said. "A looker. Great. Delores," he cried and a woman who looked like she was in her fifties, but who also had bleached blond hair and wore lots of makeup, came out from behind a rack of costumes. "Get her dressed and on the set, will ya? Make sure she looks . . . innocent. I like that. Good."

"Yes, Lewis."

She marched toward me.

"Hello," she said. "Step over there. We don't have a dressing room."

"Dressing room? Why would we need a dressing room?" Lewis Parker said and Harris and the cameraman laughed. "We're all friends here."

"I don't understand," I said, shaking my head and stepping back. The half-naked young woman sat up and suddenly took interest in me. "What is this? What kind of a movie are you making?" I asked.

"What's she talking about?" the woman asked, looking at Lewis Parker.

"What is this? What kind of a movie are we making? This is Live Wire Studios," Lewis Parker said. "You're Melody . . . somebody, right? You were in a blue film before, something called . . . what's it called, Harris?"

*"Cherry Blossom.* She was the lead," Harris said.

"Right. So. You know what to do. We're on a tight schedule."

Lewis Parker started back toward his chair. The cameraman looked my way and stopped fiddling with the equipment. I shook my head again and took another step back.

"No, I don't do things like this," I said. "I never did."

"What?" Mr. Parker spun around as quickly as his heavy legs allowed. "What do you mean, you don't do things like this?"

"I don't know what Richard told you but . . . but I can't do this," I cried.

"Hey!"

157

I turned and ran out the door, down the short corridor and burst out to the parking lot. For a moment I stood there, confused, undecided as to which direction to take. Then I hurried down the driveway to the busy city street, my heart thumping. When I reached the sidewalk, I started in one direction and then another, unsure of my surroundings. I took a step off the sidewalk as cars whizzed by, and one driver blared his horn, sending me flying back, my stomach almost in my throat. Tears streaked down my cheeks. I took a deep breath and closed my eyes. Richard must not have known what kind of assignment he'd gotten me. He just couldn't have expected me to actually take the job. . . .

"Get hold of yourself," I ordered my frantic body. When I opened my eyes again, I saw a phone booth by the gas station across the street. I thought I might call Dorothy and ask her to have Spike pick me up. This time I waited until the light changed and then I hurried across to the booth and dug into my purse to find some change. It wasn't until I took off the receiver and started to put in the coins that I realized I couldn't call Holly's sister. Her husband would be furious with her, especially if she got involved in something like this. It wasn't fair for me to do this to her after all she had done for me, I thought.

But I didn't know where I was and I had no way to get back to the apartment. I thought a moment and then dialed information and asked for Mel Jensen's phone number. There were three Mel Jensens, but I knew I had the right one when I mentioned The Egyptian Gardens. I got the number and dialed. Someone picked up after only one ring.

"Hello."

"I'm looking for Mel Jensen," I said.

"Oh," the voice said, dripping with disappointment. "Just a minute. Someone for you," I heard him say and Mel got on.

"Hello."

"I'm sorry to call you, but I didn't know who else to call. My sister is working at a mall and—"

"Melody?"

"Yes," I said.

"Where are you? I hear a lot of traffic."

"I'm on a street corner. I'm lost and . . . I don't know how to get back and I thought—"

"What's the address? Where are you?"

"The address?" I looked at the street sign and then read it to him.

"Okay. I know where that is. Wait right there," he said. "It'll be a good twenty minutes."

"Thank you."

After I hung up, I looked for a place to sit and wait, but there weren't any benches around so I went into the coffee shop on the opposite corner and sat at the counter. I ordered a cup of coffee, but barely sipped it, watching the clock. When fifteen minutes had passed, I went out again and stood on the corner. While I was waiting I saw a man I thought might have been Harris come out of the studio and disappear into an alley. Almost ten minutes later, just when I was starting to get nervous, I heard a car horn and saw Mel. I was never so happy to see anyone. He pulled over and I got in quickly.

"What the hell are you doing down here?" he asked.

I started to cry, sucked in my breath, and told him.

"Marlin wanted you to be in an X-rated film? Some break," he said. "They can make good money. I'm not saying he lied about that. Does your sister know?"

"No. So you think Richard knew it was that kind of job?" I asked.

"Are you kidding? Those jobs are right up Marlin's alley. Well you did the right thing walking out like that. These things can come back to haunt you when you do get decent work and become a star."

"I'm not going to become a star, any kind of star. That's not why I came here," I protested. Wouldn't anyone believe me?

"Why did you come here?"

"Just to visit," I said. After a moment I added, "But

159

now that I'm here, I hope I can talk my sister into going back home with me."

Mel laughed.

"I don't know your sister that well, but she looks like she's been bitten, just like the rest of us. Don't get your hopes up."

Now that I was in his car and we were driving away from Live Wire Studios, I swallowed back my panic and felt my heart stop pounding.

"Thank you so much for coming to get me," I said.

"You sounded terrified. I borrowed my roommate's car. I don't have a car myself."

"Oh. It was nice of him to lend it to you."

"Yeah. So why did you leave the party so quickly last night?"

"I was feeling exhausted. You didn't see how dirty my sister's apartment was and how much work I did."

He laughed.

"I bet. She's no Suzy Homemaker, huh?"

"No. She never was."

"What, did your parents spoiled her?"

"My father did," I said. It wasn't such a lie, I thought. "He and I ended up doing most of the work, even the cooking."

"What about your mother?"

"She died when we were very young," I said.

"Oh, sorry."

"I can't believe what Richard wanted me to do," I muttered, still half in shock.

"It doesn't surprise me. To a manager or an agent, it's easy money."

"I have to find some other way to earn money while I'm here," I moaned.

"I can always get you a job at the supermarket," he said, half kidding.

"Could you?"

"You'd like that?"

"I'd do anything, anything but what Richard was trying to get me to do," I replied.

160

"Okay, I'll see about it. I'd take you somewhere for something to eat, but I have to get to work. I have the afternoon shift today."

"That's all right. You've done a lot for me already."

"How about paying me back by going to dinner with me later?"

"How's that paying you back?" I asked, laughing.

"I like your company," he said and smiled. "Well? I'll be out at six-thirty. We can go around seven. You like Italian? I know a great little place only two blocks south of us."

"Okay," I said. "But I should be taking you out. I wish I could afford to."

"Don't worry about. It's my treat."

I thanked him again when we arrived at The Egyptian Gardens. After he dropped me off I hurried up to the apartment and quickly changed out of Mommy's mini-skirt and blouse, putting my own clothes back on. I was calm enough to make myself some lunch and settle down. I did some more cleaning to keep my mind off what had happened and spent the remainder of the afternoon reading Mommy's movie magazines on the patio. A little after five I heard her and Richard come in. I got off the lounge and entered the apartment to meet them in the living room.

Richard stood there with his hands on his hips, glaring at me furiously. Mommy looked almost as angry, her hands clenched in fists at her side.

"What did you do, Melody?" Mommy asked softly. "What did you do to Richard?"

"What did she do to me? I'll tell you what she did," Richard said, stepping toward me before I could offer any response. "She put a nail in my coffin here. She hurt my reputation and completely destroyed a lucrative market for me. I had three other girls set to get jobs with Live Wire Studios and they canceled all of them. You lost those girls a lot of money and they needed it badly," he said. "I'm not even counting my lost commissions."

"Melody, how could you do this?"

"Mommy, you don't understand," I cried.

"There," he screamed, his forefinger jabbed at me. "She keeps forgetting. She'll call you Mommy in front of these people here and you might as well kiss your career good-bye."

"Melody, I've pleaded with you not to call me Mommy."

"I know. I'm sorry," I said. "I'm just upset. I won't forget anymore." I took a deep breath. "I did what he told me to do. I went into the studio and there was a half-naked woman sitting on a bed and they wanted me to . . . to be in this movie."

"So?" Mommy said. "Richard told you how much money you were going to make. I bet it was twice if not three times what Kenneth paid you to model naked for him," she added.

I felt my heart stop and then start racing. The blood seemed to drain from my face. I tried, but I couldn't speak for a moment. The lump in my throat was as hard as a rock, unmovable.

"What? You get undressed only for certain men when you feel like it?" Richard quipped. "When I get you a job where you can help us, you decide to be Miss Prim and Proper? You run out of the studio, make me look like the fool of the year?"

"Sis, that was different. What Kenneth was doing was art. You know that," I finally said, unable to believe she didn't see the difference.

"A lot of people think of this as art too, Melody. You have to be understanding and you can't be a snob," she said.

"A snob? But Sis, they wanted me to get undressed and be in bed with this other woman and—"

"What of it? I've done it," she said.

"You have?" I asked, not wanting to believe her.

"Of course. How do you think we got the security and first and last month's rent for this place? You know how much money that is? And I got it with just two days' work," she said proudly.

I just shook my head in disbelief.

"You can't stay here without earning your keep," Richard insisted. "We're not running a shelter for the homeless."

"I'll earn something. Mel Jensen thinks I can get a job at the supermarket," I spat back at him.

"The supermarket? That's what you want to do?"

"Yes. I'd rather sweep floors and stack groceries forever than do what that fat man wanted me to do back in that so-called movie studio."

"Well, you raised a pretty smart girl," Richard said to Mommy. "Supermarket Wonder. Great. In the meantime you can keep this apartment spotless and see to our laundry. If you won't be a movie star, then be a servant. Maybe that's all you're capable of being."

I looked at Mommy for support, but she just nodded.

"Richard's right, honey. With the three of us now, we won't be able to afford a housekeeper or dry cleaners if you don't work where Richard wants you to work."

"I don't mind doing the cleaning and looking after the laundry," I said. Surely Mommy didn't fully understand what Richard was doing to her and what he would have done to me if I had let him. We're the ones exposing ourselves, embarrassing ourselves, lowering our self-respect and he was the one collecting the money for it. I had to make her understand and if it took my having to be someone's little slave for a while in order to do so, I thought, so be it.

"Good," Richard said, marching out of the living room to the bedroom.

"Sis, you don't know how terrible this place was. You couldn't have done something like that."

"Don't be stupid, Melody. You can't be a child anymore. You're here, make the most of it, take advantage. You have a built-in manager and agent. Do you know how hard it is for new talent to get representation?"

"Talent? What kind of talent does it take to strip off your clothes and do X-rated things in front of a leering cameraman?"

"You'd be surprised," Mommy said. "The camera doesn't lie. If you're not sincere when you perform, the camera will expose you."

"Oh, you're exposed all right, and then some. Sis, listen," I said, but Richard came marching back into the living room. His arms full of shirts and pants and a few pairs of shoes on top.

"See that these things are washed and ironed. We can't afford the laundry. And I want these shoes polished so I can see my face in them. I've got to look twice as good now that you have screwed things up," he claimed as he dumped everything at my feet.

I looked from the pile to Mommy, but she just turned and walked into the bedroom.

"Of course," Richard said softly after she was gone, "if you want to turn around and go back to Cape Cod . . ."

I glared at him with hot tears in my eyes and then I started to scoop up his clothes.

"Not yet," I said. "I haven't finished what I came to do."

He saw the firmness in my face and his smile evaporated.

"Just watch yourself," he said. "You're playing out of your league and you're playing on my turf."

"I'm not playing," I replied and began to take everything into my room.

An hour later while I was ironing Richard's shirts, Mommy poked her head into my room to tell me they were going out to dinner.

"We can't afford to take you, honey," she said. "I'm sure you'll find something for yourself here."

"Someone's taking me to dinner," I said softly, not looking up at her.

"Oh? Who?"

"Mel Jensen," I said. When I looked up at her I saw a look of surprise on her face.

"Really? Well, you be careful," she said. "Watch what

you say, what you tell him. Men can get you to trust them too much too fast," she warned.

"I suppose you'd know," I said. Her back straightened and a sharp look came into her eyes.

"Don't be disrespectful, Melody."

"I'm not. I'm just . . . Sis, when can you and I sit down and have a real conversation? When can we be like we used to be, just for a little while?"

"I don't know," she said, a little sadly. "I don't know if we ever can. That's why . . . that's why it might have been better if you never came looking for me, Melody. I'm sorry," she said. "I just don't know."

We stared at each other a moment and then she returned to the living room and left with Richard. My heart felt as if it had sunk like a chunk of coal into my stomach. I sat on the bed and buried my face in my hands, choking on dry sobs. Billy Maxwell was so right when he said people changed because of where they were and what they were doing. He warned me to expect Mommy might be a very different person. But was she different? Perhaps she was the same woman she had always been, but the woman I had refused to permit myself to see. I took a deep breath and sat straight, wondering what I should do. Should I just leave her, try to forget I had a mother, or should I remain and do battle with her fantasies and her phony knight in shining armor? How would I ever get her to listen to anything I had to say?

I was in such a confused and troubled state of mind I forgot all about Mel until he came knocking on the apartment door.

"Ready?" he asked when I opened the door.

"Oh Mel. I forgot. I'm sorry." I looked down at myself wearing an apron over dungarees. "I'll just be a minute," I said. "Come on in."

I rushed into the bedroom to pick out something to wear and then I hurried into the bathroom to brush my hair and put on some lipstick. Mel sat on the sofa laughing as I paraded back and forth.

"It's all right. Take your time," he called.

I took a deep breath, closed my eyes and tried to calm my nerves before appearing before him again.

*"Voilà,"* he said, standing. "Remarkable metamorphosis. You look great."

"I don't feel great," I moaned. He opened the door and stepped back so I could pass.

"So, tell me, how did Marlin take your not going through with the assignment?" he asked as we descended in the elevator.

"He was furious. He said I hurt his reputation."

"I bet. Not to mention his pocketbook. I was offered those kinds of films, too."

"You were?"

"Sure. A lot of would be's think that's the way to get into the business, and unfortunately they get taken advantage of. This is a tough place, a city with sharp teeth that devours the pure of heart," he remarked.

"Then why do you stay?" I asked.

"It's where it's at," he replied with a shrug. "And, I'm not so pure at heart." He put his arm though mine and led me out of the complex.

The restaurant was small and cozy, just as he had described and the food was delicious. Mel talked about himself, telling me all about his home and his family. Every time he asked me questions, I had to check myself to be sure I wasn't saying anything that would give away all of Mommy and Richard's lies. I tried to say as little as I could. Finally, he sat back and narrowed his eyes.

"Getting you to talk about yourself is like pulling teeth. Why is that?"

"I don't know," I said shifting my eyes down quickly. He continued to stare.

"Are you really just visiting or did you run away from home?" he pursued. I raised my eyes and smiled.

"Run away from home? What makes you think that?"

"I've met a number of runaways and they act a lot like you, evading, giving only the bare minimum when asked a question."

166

"Well, I'm sorry to disappoint you. I'm just visiting," I said and he laughed.

"Fine."

"I am!"

Why was it every man I met could be so infuriating, thinking they knew me better than I knew myself?

"They've got great spumoni," he said and ordered some for us.

"I hate to see you spend your money on me," I told him, calming down slowly. "I know how hard it is for you."

"That's okay. Actually, I asked you out both to be with you and to have you celebrate with me. I got a part in a theatrical production that will open in two months. I had auditioned for them so long ago, I forgot all about it and wrote it off, but out of the blue, my agent received a call and called me just before I left to pick you up tonight."

"Congratulations. That's wonderful, Mel."

"I expect you to be in the front row opening night," he said. "Now," he continued, turning more serious, "what this means, I realized, was I have to give up my job at the supermarket. I spoke to the manager this afternoon and told him I had someone responsible to take my place. He thought it was fine. So, congratulations to you. You'll get your job in about three more days, if you really want it."

"Good," I said. "Now Richard won't be able to complain about me. Thank you."

"Of course, I think you should aim higher. You have talent and you look great," he said. "But you've got to want it, be hungry for it."

"But I *don't* want it," I said and he stared at me with that curious smile on his face.

"Maybe that's what intrigues me the most about you," he said.

"What?"

"Your ability to resist the temptation, your lack of ego. You're just the type who succeeds," he added.

I looked at him, at that impish grin on his face. It

amazed me how other people saw things in me I never saw in myself.

After we walked home, Mel asked me if I wanted to come up to his apartment.

"We could listen to some music. My roommates are out for the night."

"I don't know," I said. "I promised my sister I wouldn't stay out late."

"It's not late," he insisted. "I'd like to dance for you, too."

"Dance?"

"Sure. I'll show you what I did at the audition for this show. Okay?"

It sounded interesting so I agreed and we went up to his apartment.

"You'll have to excuse the mess," he warned me at the door. "Remember, three guys live here."

It didn't look anywhere near as cluttered and dusty as Mommy's apartment had been before I had started to clean it. I told Mel and he laughed.

"Want something to drink? More wine, perhaps?"

"I suppose wine's all right," I said and he poured me a glass. After he did, he went in to his bedroom to put on his dancing clothes. I heard the music first and then suddenly, he leaped into the room, wearing the tightest top and pants I had ever seen, so tight they left nothing about him to the imagination. He spun on his toes and lifted his legs so high, I lost my breath, especially when he did it right in front of me.

The music became faster, the beat harder. He mixed ballet steps with slides and turns that were dazzling. Finally, he stopped and stood before me, breathing hard, his face flushed with excitement. I felt flushed myself from the wine and his performance.

"Well?"

"You're wonderful," I said. "I can't imagine you not succeeding."

He laughed and stepped closer. The music continued, softer, slower. He reached out to take my hand.

I started to shake my head, but he pulled harder until I stood and we were dancing cheek to cheek, his hard, fast breathing on my neck. When I caught sight of us reflected in the window, it looked like I was dancing with a naked man. My own breathing quickened as his slowed and then he smiled at me and kissed me softly. I felt him push against my thighs.

"You're so sweet," he said. "I really like you." He kissed me again, but I didn't let his lips linger on mine. I stepped back, bowing my head and, when I looked down at him and saw how excited he was, I felt my heart flutter and my breath grow short.

"I've got to get home," I said.

"Melody . . ."

He stepped toward me.

"I really do, Mel. Please."

"Okay," he said. "I don't force myself on anyone, but I hope you like me."

"I do, but not that way. I'm sorry," I said. "I'm sure there are a lot of girls who would love to be up here with you," I added.

He smirked.

"Very few like you. Okay, I'll give it time," he said. "Consider this my first audition. Maybe, you'll give me a call back, okay?"

I laughed and tried to shift my eyes from his very revealed body. I found my purse and headed toward the door.

"If you wait for me to change again, I'll walk you home."

"No, that's all right. Thanks for dinner."

"I'll call you about the supermarket job," he said.

"Thanks."

I hurried out the door and when I looked back, I saw him standing there, smiling after me. I waved and descended the stairs, feeling as if I were fleeing.

But was I fleeing from him or from myself? For the first time, I thought I was really more afraid of my own weakness and desire. This was a place filled with many

169

different kinds of temptations. The Egyptian Gardens might as well be the Garden of Eden, I concluded and half expected a snake to come up and whisper in my ear as I crossed the courtyard to our building and made my way up to our apartment.

The phone was ringing as I entered. I hurried to it and after my first hello, I heard nothing.

"Hello?" I said again. I heard a deep breath and then . . .

"Where were you?" Cary asked.

"I was out to dinner, Cary. What's wrong?"

"Dad's dead," he said. "He had another heart attack in the CCU and he died." He laughed strangely. "I couldn't think of anyone else to call but you and you were out to dinner."

"Cary, I'm so sorry."

"Yeah, well, it won't be the wrong person in his grave, will it?"

"Cary—"

"I'm tired. It's very late here. I ran down to the docks when I came home and I just stood there looking out at the ocean and thinking about all the trips he and I made together. Funny," he said huskily, "now you and I are both without fathers."

"I'll be back as soon as I can, Cary. I promise."

"Okay," he said in a small voice.

And then he hung up and left me crying for both of us.

# *10*

## ❧

# *Revelations*

After I hung up the phone, I sat on the sofa in the dark living room and cried softly, thinking about Cary, little May and Aunt Sara and what they all must be going through. I wondered how Grandma Olivia and Grandpa Samuel were taking the news of their son's death. Nothing could be worse than losing a child, I thought, no matter how old the child was at the time, or how aloof and cold at heart you were.

Uncle Jacob had resented my coming and living with him and his family, but most of the time I thought that was because my presence made the loss of his Laura that much harder to bear. Right from the beginning, Aunt Sara treated me as if I had been sent to replace Laura, but I knew as far as Uncle Jacob was concerned, no one could ever replace his daughter. He had been hard, sometimes downright cruel to me, but I also recalled moments when he gazed at me with softer, kinder eyes, especially after he had heard me sing and play the fiddle, and often, when he didn't think I was aware of his gaze.

He was a hardworking man who wanted to provide for

his family as best he could. His religious zeal often made him cold and unpleasant to me, but on more than one occasion, Cary hinted that his father had become more devout and sterner after Laura died, somehow blaming himself for her death. When he was in the hospital the first time, he had asked to see me at his bedside, and because he thought he was dying, he confessed to me that he and my mother had done something sinful together when they were young. At the time he made it seem that he blamed himself for my mother's wild ways later on when she was older. Afterward, he denied saying these things. Ashamed of what he had told me, he found my presence even harder to bear. I'm sure he was happy when I decided to leave to find my mother, as happy as Grandma Olivia was to see me go.

I closed my eyes and took a deep breath. Minutes later, I fell asleep and didn't waken until I heard the door open, followed by loud laughter.

"Why is it so dark in here?" I heard Richard say before snapping on a lamp. The shock of light made me blink and rub my eyes as I sat up quickly.

"Well, well, look who's waiting up for us," he said.

"Why are you still up and dressed? How was your dinner, Melody?" Mommy asked. "You didn't drink too much wine or anything, did you? Did you bring Mel up here?" she scanned the room as if to look for evidence of his having been in the apartment. She wobbled a bit but took a step closer and focused on me with some effort, finally noticing how red my eyes were and the streaks tears had made down my cheeks. "What's going on now?" she demanded.

"Uncle Jacob," I said and swallowed, taking too long for her.

"What about him? I can't imagine anything about him that would interest me," she told Richard, who laughed. "Well, what did he do?"

"He died," I said. "His heart gave out at the hospital." She stared, the news having a sobering effect on her. I saw her face move through a myriad of emotions, from shock to sadness, to anger and then indifference. She smirked first at Richard before turning back to me.

"His heart, as you call it, gave out a long time ago. I don't wish anything bad on anyone, but I can't pretend to be terribly upset about it," she said, the mirth all gone from her eyes and lips.

"But you grew up with him and Daddy. You can't be so uncaring," I replied.

"You don't know anything about what my life was like growing up with Jacob as a so-called brother, Melody," Mommy flared back at me, "and I can't forget how he treated me afterward when all the trouble began for me and Chester."

The anger in her eyes stunned me so much I was speechless.

"I don't like anyone bringing bad news to Gina," Richard said, suddenly pretending to be very protective. "Especially news about her past, and especially the night before she has an audition."

"Yes," Mommy said, smiling with a proud gleam in her eyes. "I have something exciting to try out for tomorrow, a part in a television sitcom. I've got to get right to bed. That's why we came home so early," she added.

I looked at the clock. Early? It was a little past one o'clock. What was late supposed to mean?

"You should go to sleep yourself," Richard said. "You have a lot of work ahead of you, too." He laughed and headed for the bedroom.

"I do feel sorry for Sara and the children," Mommy said, her voice somewhat softer. "Sara was always nice to me." She sighed and pulled her head back a little as if to swallow back some errant tears. Then she looked at me with a small smile on her lips. "If you think you should go back for the funeral, it's all right. I . . . can't have anything more to do with them. Whatever tears I would spill would be one more tear than his mother will anyway. Believe me," she said.

"You hate her very much, don't you?" I asked.

The corners of her mouth whitened with her rage.

"Yes. I won't deny it. I do, and she has no love for me either, Melody." Her eyes glared hotly and then her expression returned to one of self-pity. She groaned. "I hate going to sleep feeling upset," she said as she turned toward the bedroom. "I wish you hadn't told me about it."

I watched her go in and close the door and then I rose and went to bed myself. Maybe I should return to the Cape, I thought. Maybe the mother I had hoped to find did die and was buried back in Provincetown. What had happened to Mommy to make her so selfish? Or had I been too blind to realize that that was her true self?

Mommy was right about going to sleep with sadness like a rock on your chest, however. I tossed and turned, sobbed and sighed through most of the night, unable to get Cary's sad eyes out of my mind.

I finally fell asleep just before morning and slept so soundly, I didn't hear Richard and Mommy get up. I did wake when I heard him shout my way.

"Well, this is a fine thing. We don't have coffee made. What sort of a maid did you hire, Gina? Turns out she's lazier than you."

I got up quickly, throwing on one of Mommy's light cotton robes, and stepped out into the living room. Richard was already dressed and Mommy, dressed rather nicely, I thought, came out of her bedroom, too.

"I'll make some coffee," I said. "It won't take long." I started toward the kitchen.

"We can't wait," Richard said, his eyes fixed hard on me. I realized I wasn't wearing much and he seemed to be able to look right through my flimsy night clothes. "We'll get something at the studio. Clean up our bedroom while we're gone. I left some more of my things for you to iron," he added and started toward the front door.

Mommy looked at me, her face somber.

"Wish me luck," she finally said.

"Good luck."

"Thank you," she said, flashing a smile. Then she followed Richard out of the apartment. I listened to their footsteps disappearing down the hallway toward the elevator and then I went into the kitchen and put on some coffee for myself. I sat there, more or less in a daze, sipping coffee and nibbling on some toast and jam. Before long, my mind wandered back to memories of myself and Cary on the beach. I thought about Kenneth and his dog, Ulysses, and remembered first meeting Holly and the fun we had talking like sisters.

How could Mommy want this kind of a life? I thought. Despite herself and the mean things she had said to me last night after I had told her about Uncle Jacob, her eyes did soften occasionally. Deep in her heart, I told myself, she wants to go home. I've just got to get her to realize it.

Still wearing my nighty and Mommy's robe, I cleaned up their bedroom and began ironing Richard's pants and shirts. I worked without thought, moving like some kind of a robot, dazed by the tragic events. A little after noon, I finally put the work aside and went into the bathroom to take a shower. I stood there letting the warm water beat on the top of my head, my eyes closed, the stream flowing over my face. Finally, I shut off the shower and stepped out from behind the curtain.

For a moment, I was confused. I knew I had brought in a towel and my clothes, but there was just a hand towel on the rack and none of my clothes were in sight. Not trusting my own memory, I figured I had intended to do these things, but because of being in such deep thought, hadn't. Dripping wet, I ran out of the bathroom to my bedroom. As soon as I entered, the door closed behind me, only I hadn't been the one to close it.

Richard stood there, leering at me, and he was stark naked himself!

Silent screams stuck in my throat.

"What are you doing? Where's Mommy?" I finally shouted and rushed to the bed to pull the top sheet off and throw it around me. Brittle as thin glass, his laughter

175

crackled across the room. He stepped forward, not making any attempt to hide his manliness from my sight.

"I told you to stop calling her Mommy," he said, still smiling.

"Where is she? What are you doing?"

"She's at her audition. She'll be there most of the day. There are a lot of actresses trying out for the part, so I thought, why hang around? I decided, while waiting, I might as well make myself useful. I've been wondering why you would run out on such an easy job for a lot of money yesterday, and I figured out it's simply because you're too innocent. You need to grow up, and fast, or you'll never amount to anything. Consider this an extra service. Call it my generosity," he continued, moving closer and closer until he was only inches away.

I turned and looked down rather than into his face. His breath stank from alcohol and began to upset my stomach. I felt it do flip-flops.

"Come on," he said, "I know you're looking forward to this."

"Get away from me!" I cried.

He put his right hand on my shoulder and his left on my waist, forcing me to turn to him.

"Relax and enjoy," he said bringing his lips close to mine. I swung my head and tried to pivot out of his grasp, but he tightened his hold and pressed his lips against my mouth. I gagged and kicked out, catching him between his legs with my knee. His face exploded like a balloon bursting and he crumbled, clutching his lower stomach.

I didn't wait. I pushed past him and started to run from the room, holding onto the sheet. Somehow, he managed to reach out, clutching the end of the sheet and holding on. It tugged me back until I let go and fled the room, totally naked. I returned to the bathroom and slammed the door shut, locking it after me. Then I stood there for a moment gasping, sobbing, listening. My heart was pounding so, I had to lean against the door to brace myself. The memory of the stench coming from his mouth made me dry-heave.

"You little bitch," I heard him shout. He came up to the door and tried the handle. "Open up. How dare you knee me like that? I'm letting you stay here, aren't I?"

He pounded the door with his fist and I screamed. Then he stopped and all was quiet for a long moment. I tried to hold my breath so I could listen, but my lungs were stretched to bursting and the thump, thump, thump of my heart was echoing in my eardrums.

"You'll be sorry," he finally said in a loud whisper between the door and the doorjamb. "I could have taught you something, made you grow up overnight. You would have been sophisticated enough for anything, but Richard Marlin doesn't allow himself to get turned down more than once. It's your loss," he added. "You hear?"

He punched the door again. I cried out and backed away, afraid he would break the door down. After a while I heard only silence and then, when I drew closer to the door and put my ear against it, I heard him walk away. I didn't come out. I sat on the tub and waited, my arms folded tightly under my breasts, my sobbing slowing and my breathing returning to normal. I heard the front door open and close. All was quiet. Was it a trick to get me to open the bathroom door?

I waited and waited, listening, hoping he would grow impatient if he were still out there, but I heard nothing. Suddenly the phone rang. It rang and rang and I imagined that if he were still there, he would be too concerned the call was for him and he would have answered it. More confident that he was gone, I unlocked the door as carefully and as quietly as I could. I hesitated and then in fractions of an inch at a time, opened it until I could peer out.

I didn't see him anywhere. I looked across the dining area to my bedroom. The door was wide open. Was he waiting inside the room again? I tried to swallow, to stop my heart from its racing again, but I couldn't. His attack had made my legs weak and my whole body trembled as I opened the bathroom door wider and wider until I stepped out, and then waited, terrified he would suddenly appear and lunge at me. He didn't.

My courage growing, I practically tiptoed across the floor to the doorway of my bedroom. There I paused to listen. I heard nothing. I took a deep breath and walked into my bedroom, gazing around quickly, clenching my hands into little fists with which to pummel him should he pop out at me. He wasn't anywhere in sight. I closed the door quickly and then, my heart fell. What if he were hiding in my closet?

I waited, listening again for a moment. Hearing nothing, I went to the closet door and pulled it open. The wind from my jerking open the door shook the clothes on the hangers, but thankfully, there was no Richard Marlin hiding and waiting to pounce out at me.

I got dressed as quickly as I could and then I fled the apartment, feeling trapped and in danger of a horrible repeat performance if I remained there. I didn't look at anyone when I hurried down the walkway. Like someone in a race, I shot through the main gate and charged down the sidewalk. I walked as quickly as I could, not looking back, crossing streets, fighting traffic, hurrying along as if I knew where I wanted to go. It felt good to move quickly. It stopped my body from trembling and the farther away from The Egyptian Gardens I walked, the safer I felt. Finally, tired, my body in a heavy sweat, I paused at a corner, undecided in which direction I should continue. I gazed at the street sign that read Melrose Avenue, and then I looked around at other people.

Up until this moment, I hadn't noticed anyone or anything. I had walked with blind eyes, focused only on fleeing Richard's awful grasp. Now I found myself in a very curious area of the city. Young people with blue, green and pink hair, dressed in leather jackets and jeans walked past and in front of me. Many had tattoos covering their arms and chests. Two girls even had rings in their noses! I felt like I had stepped onto another planet.

I backed up, turned and started walking in the opposite direction. Everyone in this city really did seem to be in his or her own movie, I thought, feeling as if I had wandered onto a movie set. I didn't know whether I should laugh or cry. After I walked a few minutes, the neighborhood changed again and I slowed my pace, quickly realizing that I was lost. I stopped again and gazed around, this time seeing a small store window on my left that read MADAM MARLENE, READINGS. I saw the crystals and the tarot cards and thought about Holly and Billy. It brought a smile back to my lips. Impulsively, perhaps searching for good memories at a very troubled time, I stepped into the small shop.

There was a dark cherry wood table and two chairs at the center of the little room. The crystals were in a small glass case on the right and at the rear of the shop the was a doorway like the one at Holly's shop, curtained with strings of beads. When I entered, a small buzzer had gone off. A short, dark-haired elderly lady came through the doorway of beads. She wore a shimmery white shawl over a dark blue dress and had silver earrings with crystals that glittered like diamonds in between the long strands of hair falling over her shoulders. Her dark eyes were large but she made them appear even larger with smudgy kohl eyeliner.

"Hello," she said. "I'm Madam Marlene. Would you like a reading?"

I shook my head.

"Um . . . I . . . I just . . ."

"You look upset," she said. "Please," she added pointing to the seat by the table. "Rest a moment and tell me what troubles you."

"I'm lost," I said. "I'm new here and I don't remember how to get back to my apartment complex."

"Which complex, my dear?" she asked, her smile soft and friendly. She looked to be about fifty and not much more than five feet tall.

"The Egyptian Gardens," I said.

"You're not very lost. Just go down two streets, make a left and you'll run into it after about ten minutes. I think there's more troubling you though, isn't there?"

I nodded and gazed around her shop.

"I have a friend in New York City who has a crystal shop and who does astrological readings for people. Her name's Holly."

"That's interesting," Madam Marlene said, and a knowing twinkle came into her eyes. "You really came in here because you wanted to know something, yes?" she pursued, her head tilted slightly and her eyes even more luminous as the dim overhead light caught them in its warm glow.

I thought a moment and then nodded.

"I wanted to know if someone I loved would ever return to me," I said.

She nodded as if she had always known I would show up on her doorstep.

"Sit down. Please," she said.

"I just left my apartment quickly," I said. "I don't have any money on me."

"Oh, that's all right," she said. "You can send me something later." She sat at her table, motioning for me to sit down across from her. She reached out immediately and took my right hand into her hands and held it, closing her eyes. Then she nodded to herself and looked down at my open palm.

"You have already been on quite a rugged road," she said, "with many twists and turns. Your life has more valleys than most, but I see some very high places too. I see you have lost loved ones, yes?"

"Yes."

"Yet you have strong energy. What is your name?"

"Melody."

"I see music in you, yes. This person, this loved one who is lost has been lost for a while."

"Yes," I said.

She looked at my hand again and then she reached out

180

to touch the locket Billy Maxwell had given me. She turned it in her fingers a moment.

"Lapis lazuli. Someone you like very much and someone who likes you very much gave it to you."

"That's right," I said.

"You are like a comet, something beautiful and full of energy floating through space, searching . . . searching for a home, your real home."

"I am," I said, excited that she seemed to know so much about me.

"Someone you're searching for is coming," she said, closing her eyes again. Seconds later she opened them, and this time there was no smile on her lips. "Where you are looking for love, there is no love. You will have to change direction. But don't worry. Your energy is too strong to be defeated. Do not be afraid to turn toward the darkness, for often what we think is sunlight is merely the reflection coming from our own glow. Do not look for love in the usual places," she concluded and sat back as if reading my palm, feeling my energy and predicting my life had exhausted her.

"Thank you," I said standing, uncertain if I'd be able to follow her advice.

"Oh, it's my pleasure. It's always a pleasure to read a heart as big as yours. Here," she said opening a drawer in the desk to pluck out a business card. "This has my address. I usually get twenty dollars, but you can send me fifteen."

"Thank you," I said, taking the card from her wrinkled hand.

"Your locket will bring you much luck on your journey. Keep it with you always," she called as I went to the door.

"I will. Bye."

I stepped out, feeling revived, calmer. It would take time to understand all she had said, but I would think about it. Since I had been with Holly and Billy I paid more attention to these things and I wasn't so quick to laugh at anyone or anything that seemed new and different to me. I was leaving myself open to new ideas and experiences. But there were still some things I could definitely do without.

Dreading facing Richard again, I headed back to the apartment, following the directions Madam Marlene had given me. A little over half an hour later, I turned into the main gate and with great trepidation, made my way to our building and then to the elevator. When I stepped out and walked to the apartment door, I paused. I had to tell Mommy what he had tried to do, I decided. Maybe now, maybe finally, she would see him for what he truly was.

I opened the door and entered, surprised to find them both sitting in the living room. Mommy looked like she had been crying all afternoon. Her eyes were bloodshot; her face streaked with makeup that had run. Richard sat there looking calm, his legs crossed, a drink in one hand and a cigarette in the other. He gazed up at me with a confident smirk that put a chill in my heart.

"So you decided to come back," Richard said.

"What did you do, Melody? Run away afterward?"

"Yes," I said defiantly gazing back at Richard as I spoke. "I did. I was too scared to stay here. I was afraid he would come back and try again."

"Ha!" Richard said and crushed his cigarette in the ashtray. "Listen to that."

"Melody, how could you?" Mommy asked.

"How could I what?" I looked from her to him and then back to her, realizing he had told her some lie. "It was him, Mommy. And I don't care if I called you Mommy," I added quickly for his benefit. "He attacked me in the bedroom. He came into the bathroom while I was taking a shower and he—"

"Liar. She's just like I said," Richard interrupted. "Conniving, sly. Tell the truth for once, will you."

"The truth?"

"I was sitting here, right where I am now, relaxing, planning on making some important calls, when all of a sudden, she comes out of the bathroom after taking a shower and parades naked right in front of me," he told Mommy. "She walked right up to me as if she were fully dressed and smiled. Go on, tell her," he challenged me.

"No," I said, shaking my head. "That's not what happened, Mommy. He took all my clothes out of the bathroom and when I came out and went to the bedroom, he was waiting for me and he was naked!"

"Did you ever hear such a story, Gina? Look, Melody, you've been trying to compete with Gina ever since you arrived. You made a spectacle of yourself down at the pool and then you tried to steal the limelight at the party. I get you a job, but it's not good enough for you. Oh no. You'd rather we support you, too."

"Mommy, listen . . . he was there, in the bedroom, waiting for me. He told me he was going to educate me. He—"

"Educate you? This story gets more and more stupid every time she opens her mouth. Listen, sweetheart, you're going to have to do better than that if you want to make it in Hollywood."

"I don't want to make it in Hollywood! And neither do you, Mommy. You have to come home. You have to leave this place," I cried.

"See?" Richard Marlin said jabbing his finger at me. "That's been her plan all along . . . to mess things up for you so you would leave. She's jealous of her own mother. I've seen it a hundred times, and especially out here. Now she says she doesn't care if she calls you Mommy. She'll do it deliberately in front of people and make you the laughingstock of the whole industry. She's already made us a mountain of trouble because of what she did at Live Wire."

"Mommy . . ." I said, turning to her. She shook her head at me.

"I'm very disappointed in you, Melody. I really don't know what to say."

"Say you believe me. Say you know he's lying and that he's a phony who can't do anything for you out here, that

183

all he's doing is getting you silly little jobs or selling you to sex merchants," I begged.

Richard sat back looking very satisfied. Mommy bit down on her lower lip and looked away.

"Mommy—"

"Keep it up; keep it up. Keep calling her Mommy," Richard chanted like a cheerleader at a football game.

"Maybe Richard's right, Melody. Maybe it's better for all of us if you go back. This isn't working out."

"You believe him, Mommy?" I choked, barely able to whisper the words.

She didn't reply. I saw the grin on Richard's face and I glared back at him hatefully. He looked so confident and Mommy looked so weak and under his control. My frustration and pride overflowed.

"Maybe you deserve him then," I said and fled to my bedroom to pack my bags.

Twenty minutes later, after the phone had rung, I heard Richard yelling, blaming Mommy for not getting yet another part. Then I heard him leave the apartment. Minutes later, Mommy came to my bedroom. She wore her sunglasses again and she looked very pale and unhappy.

"I guess you heard," she said. "I didn't get a call back from today's audition. Richard says it's because I'm too distracted these days."

"Maybe it's because you're not meant to be an actress, Mommy," I said and closed my bag.

"No, I can do it. I know I can. It's just taking a little longer than we expected, that's all."

"I didn't do what he said I did, Mommy. It was the other way around. I swear it."

"It doesn't matter, Melody. Richard's right. You don't belong here. I don't know what I was thinking when I agreed to let you stay."

"You were thinking like my mother," I told her. "You were thinking about doing the right thing."

She smiled.

"You were always the dreamer."

"Me?" I started to laugh. "Look around you, Mommy. Look where you are. This place grows dreams like . . . like we grew weeds back in Sewell."

"I meant you were a dreamer because you saw more in me than there is. I'm sorry, honey. I'm not the mother you want me to be."

I nodded. Maybe, finally, she was speaking the truth. I sat on the bed and stared into my lap.

"What are you going to do? Do you have any money?" Mommy asked.

"Yes, I have most of my money. I didn't tell Richard the truth. He would have taken it all. I have my return ticket, too. I'll go to the airport and get myself on the first flight I can," I added.

"And go back to Provincetown?"

"Yes."

"Good. I'll be happier knowing you're safe, and you'll be safe there," she said.

"You mean then your conscience won't bother you, don't you, Mommy?" I shot back at her.

She started to get angry and then her shoulders sank and she nodded.

"Yes," she admitted. "I guess it's time for the lies between us to stop."

I stared at her, trying to blink away my disbelief.

"Chester was always a better father to you than I was a mother," she said and then she laughed. "And the funny thing was he wasn't your real father. Though that didn't bother him at all."

"Mommy," I said sucking in my breath, "when you left me in Provincetown and I discovered the truth about you and my stepdaddy, I started to think that Kenneth was my real father. I just knew you had to be lying about Grandpa Samuel. Please, please, tell me the truth."

She looked at me for a long moment and I thought she was just going to shake her head and walk away, but she came farther into the room instead.

"I hated them," she said, "as you know. When Judge Childs told me he was my real father and therefore

185

Kenneth and I were half-brother and half-sister, I felt as if he had reached his hand into my chest and ripped out my heart. I felt so betrayed, Melody. You can't imagine. Here were all these high and mighty people always making me feel like someone inferior because my mother had me out of wedlock and Olivia had to take me in like some wayward orphan. They never stopped reminding me how grateful I should be, how lucky I was.

"And all the while . . . the lot of them were no better, and in fact, much worse. They were deceitful, greedy people, liars and charlatans, so I decided I would get back at them. When they realized I was pregnant, Olivia was ready to pounce, to point her finger at me and shout, 'See, see, this proves how low-down and no good she is, how she's nothing more than a tramp.'

"But I fooled her, I fooled the whole lot of them when I turned the tide and accused Samuel of being the father of my unborn baby. Olivia," Mommy smiled at the memory, "almost died of embarrassment. She was sick and in her room for days. I told her I would expose the whole sinful lot of them. I would shout it in the streets.

"Chester . . . Chester always loved me. He was quick to take my side, especially when I went to him and cried on his shoulder. He promised to look after me, no matter what. I played them all against each other. Chester and Jacob fought. Olivia pulled her tail between her legs and crawled into a hole. I felt sorry for Samuel, but he was someone to pity anyway, letting her bulldoze him all the time, pretending he didn't know she was really in love with Nelson Childs, who had an affair with her sister, my mother. They were hideously cruel to her. They put her away in that institution and made me ashamed of my own mother.

"Nothing I did to them equaled what they had done to me, Melody. I regret nothing except . . . except what I had to do to you. I'm sorry, but I know you're going to be all right."

"Not until I know the whole truth, Mommy. I want to know who my real father is. You've got to tell me."

She nodded and turned her back to me as she turned her gaze to the window.

"I was wild. I wanted so much to hurt them all, to keep hurting them, embarrassing them. I drank, hung out with older friends, flirted with everyone. And then one night, after I had been out drinking, I decided to walk home. It was a warm night, full of stars. I remember getting dizzy every time I looked up at the sky.

"Suddenly, he was there in his car beside me. I turned and he rolled down his window and asked me why I was walking alone so late at night. He sounded so protective, so concerned. He said he would drive me home so I got into his car, only he didn't drive me home. He drove me to a beach road and he talked about his unhappy life, how he was married to a beautiful woman and making a lot of money, but how he was still dissatisfied. His life was missing something, some excitement, and he said whenever he saw me, no matter where I was or what I was doing, he was filled with that once-in-a-lifetime excitement."

Mommy turned to me.

"You have to understand how it was for me, Melody. No man had ever spoken to me like that. I was swept off my feet and this man . . . he was successful and well-to-do and he was telling me I was more important to him. How could I resist?

"I made love with him and it was special. We met often, secretly and then I became pregnant with you and it all went out of control. It wouldn't have done me any good to reveal his identity. He wouldn't leave his family for me, and when Olivia attacked me, I made my decision to get my revenge. I never told anyone the truth, not Chester, not Kenneth, no one."

I held my breath until I could hold it no more.

"Who was he, Mommy? Is he still in Provincetown?"

"Yes, honey, he is," she said. "His name is Teddy Jackson. They call him T.J.," she said.

I know my heart stopped beating for a moment. I know my blood drained from my face. I felt the room spin. Mommy grasped my hand. I closed my eyes and battled for a breath.

"Are you all right?"

I didn't reply. I waited until my heart started beating again, swallowed and nodded.

"His son," I said, "Adam Jackson, tried to be my boyfriend when I first arrived."

"Oh no. Did you want to be his girlfriend?"

"No, I hated him. He's arrogant."

"Good," she said. "For a moment I thought I did to you what Judge Childs had done to Kenneth and me."

"I think I had a feeling about Mr. Jackson, Mommy."

"He's spoken to you?"

"From time to time, and whenever he has, he's been very nice."

"He'll never come forward and admit it, honey. He has a family, a position in the community—"

"I don't care. I just wanted to know who he was," I said. "Thank you for that, Mommy."

I stood up. Madam Marlene had been right when she read my palm. I was looking for love in the wrong place.

"Maybe you shouldn't go yet, Melody. Maybe you should stay another day."

"No. I don't belong here, Mommy, and Cary needs me. He needs me far more than you do," I said.

My mother stared at me as if I was a stranger and then she nodded.

The lies would end between us and like two people who had finally lifted the masks from their faces, we finally saw each other for who we truly were.

And we both knew we would have to live with that forever. For better or worse.

# 11

## Home Again, Home Again

*I* decided to leave without any other good-byes. I felt confident that Mommy would make up a story to tell to Mel Jensen and the others. Lying came as naturally as breathing to her now. Maybe it always had. I took a cab to the airport and arranged to fly what they called the red-eye from Los Angeles to Boston. For a while I flirted with the idea of returning to New York to visit with Holly and Billy, but the summer was drawing to a rapid end. I still had my last year of high school to complete, and I was tired of throwing myself into other people's lives.

It was time to grow up anyway I told myself, to put my childhood beliefs back into my box of fantasies and close the lid forever on my past, on my hope of having a real mother and a real father. I was truly an orphan. The only man who had wanted to be my father was dead, and the man who really was my father had kept it a secret and was happy that he had escaped responsibility.

In a real sense, my mother had died twice: first, when she and Richard Marlin had invented their deception and sent a dead stranger back in my mother's coffin; and now, when I had found her and had failed to revive any real mother–daughter feelings in her. She was truly a stranger to me. I shed no tears walking away from her and I could hear her sigh of relief as she closed the door behind me. Her ordeal was over. She could go back to living the life, and the lie, she always wanted.

On the flight back to Boston, there wasn't anyone in the seat beside me on the plane, and for that I was grateful. I was in no mood to make conversation, and after my near tragic experience with that man in New York who had tricked me into taking his drug-laden briefcase, I was wary of strangers anyway. I simply closed my eyes and welcomed the drowsiness. I slept for most of the trip.

When I arrived in Boston, I made my way to the bus stop and bought a ticket to Provincetown. It was late morning by the time the bus headed out on the highway. I didn't leave enough time to get breakfast, but I had little appetite anyway. I felt numb, beaten, drained of any resistance and energy. The monsters in the shadows were too big and too powerful and there were far too many. It was better to retreat and to accept and be what fate seemed determined to have me be.

With that darkness well entrenched in my heart, I thought it was best to take a taxi to Grandma Olivia's and Grandpa Samuel's as soon as I arrived in Provincetown. Grandma Olivia was the true monarch of this family. She seemed to be the only one capable of determining destiny. She was the one who had decided how my grandmother Belinda would live and where she would live. She was the one who ruled Uncle Jacob and Aunt Sara's family. She even dominated Judge Childs. Certainly, she was the one who ruled her own house, and despite what my mother believed, Grandma Olivia was the one who had banished Mommy to a poorer, harder life in the coal mining town of West Virginia.

It was time to recognize that power and bend to it. I had no more defiance in me. I felt like a flag at half mast.

When the taxi pulled up the driveway of Grandma Olivia's house, my sense of defeat thickened. I moved lethargically, exhausted, my head down, up the walkway to the front of the house and pressed the buzzer, resembling someone who had come to offer her surrender.

Above me, the late afternoon sky had turned a deep, dark blue. The air smelled fresh, crisp, but I was much too nervous to enjoy the beautiful day. Grandma Olivia's maid, Loretta, opened the door and stood looking at me, her face wearing a mask of indifference. I imagined working for Grandma Olivia had toughened her. She moved through her day like some cog in a machine, reliable, consistent, but uncaring. She revealed no reaction to my appearance. I could have been a traveling salesman, for all she cared.

"Will you please tell my grandmother that I am here, Loretta," I said in a tired voice and stepped into the house. She lifted her eyebrows and gazed at my suitcases.

"She doesn't have to tell me," I heard and turned to see Grandma Olivia at the top of the stairway, gazing down at us with her regal posture. She wore clothes of mourning, a black blouse and a black ankle-length skirt, which somehow made her look taller than she was. Her white hair was brushed and pinned back as usual, and there wasn't the trace of any makeup on her pallid face.

"That will be all, Loretta," she continued as she took a step down. "You can return to your dinner preparations."

"Yes, ma'am," Loretta said with a slight curtsey. She hurried away.

"So you've returned, as I knew you would. Giving you that traveling money was a waste, but it's your waste, not mine," she added. "I will keep the document you signed and deduct it from your trust fund."

She continued her descent, sliding her hand along the mahogany balustrade as she walked, her head high, her shoulders and back perfectly straight.

"I don't have to ask you what happened. I can see it on your face: disappointment, disillusionment. Or should I say a final awakening? At last you see her for what she is?" she asked, not hiding her pleasure.

"It's because of the man she's with—" I began.

"Oh, don't blame it on someone else," she interrupted with a wave of her hand. "It was always that way with Haille. Someone was eternally making excuses for her, finding someone or somewhere else to place the blame and the responsibility for her selfish, cruel acts." She paused and smirked. "I assume she faked her death in order to end even a semblance of responsibility for you," she said smugly. Her eyes were unflinching. She had the confidence of a predator who knew she had her prey trapped.

"Yes," I murmured, my own eyes down. Even now, even after all I had been through, I still couldn't help being ashamed of Mommy.

"Humph," Grandma Olivia said. I looked up at her, tears burning under my eyelids, but kept trapped there, the last vestige of my pride. She shifted her eyes away from me, but when her gaze returned to my face, I thought I detected a hint of sympathy. "Well," she continued, "I suppose it was something you had to do, something you had to see for yourself. You can provide the details at some later time, if you like. I certainly have no burning desire to hear them.

"But," she continued with that characteristic strength I hated, respected, and envied all at the same time, "that part of your life is over and we must go on. This family must continue to strive to maintain its position of respect in the community. It would be best, obviously, if no one hears of this scandal. As far as I'm concerned, we buried your mother. I'm not going to go and dig up some unfortunate soul. Haille's as much dead to me anyhow, and from the looks of you, you feel the same. Who have you told about all this?"

"Just Cary," I said. "Kenneth Childs will know, too."

She thought a moment.

"Kenneth will keep it to himself. I'll have a word with

Cary to ensure he does the same," she said with a curt little nod of her head.

"You don't have to worry. Cary doesn't gossip, especially about our family," I said and she smiled, but a cold, hard smile that turned her stone eyes into glittering glass.

"Our family, is it? That's good. That's what I want to hear." She nodded, her smile softening just a bit. "You did right coming here," she said. "You have good sense. As we discussed before you went on this futile journey, you will live here from now on." She paused, her face hardening again. "You know, I am sure, about my son's passing while you were away?"

"Yes," I said. "I'm sorry."

"So am I, but we bury the dead so the living can continue to strive. Jacob was a good man, but he was a sufferer. He took things too much to heart and his heart was so weighed down, it collapsed. There's a lesson to learn," she said widening her eyes at me. "You have to build a casing around your heart to protect it. You don't give away your affections, your sympathies, your feelings cheaply, because every time you do, it costs you.

"There are many lessons you will learn here," she said, continuing to fix her gaze on me so intently, I dared not look away.

"As I told you before you left, you have, I have noted, demonstrated some qualities of character that, although in the rawest form now, can be cultivated so that you will grow into a stronger person, a capable person. But this will happen only if you listen and obey. I don't intend to relive the painful past I endured with your mother," she warned. "You will behave while you are under this roof and you will do nothing that will bring discredit to this family."

"Maybe this isn't such a good idea," I suggested. "Maybe I should go back to live with Aunt Sara."

"And learn what? Self-pity? Ha. Besides, she has enough to do caring for her handicapped child."

"I can help her. I can—"

"Waste your life," she concluded. Her cold eyes softened a bit. "Everyone expects I will look after you, now that your mother is supposedly dead anyway. How do you think it will look if I permit Sara to endure another burden immediately after losing Jacob?"

"So you're worried about your own reputation," I said and she stiffened so quickly it was as if an electric shock had passed through her.

"I was hoping you would see that what I am offering you is an opportunity other girls your age would die to have. Yes, I have selfish motives, but they're not motives for myself. They're for this family. Family name, honor, reputation, these are the really important things, Melody. You will learn that and understand it after a while.

"People without family pride are weak, and their weakness and lack of control affects their entire family. Look at that woman you insist on calling Mother. Does she have any pride in herself? Well, does she?" she demanded.

"No," I admitted hesitantly.

"Do you want to be like her?" she pursued. I raised my eyes and she smiled after one glance at the fire in them. Then she nodded. "There's more of my family blood in you than you care to recognize," she said. "Very well. You'll take the room that once belonged to Haille. I've had it prepared for you, anticipating this day. Even though you have come to live here, you are to look after yourself and your own things. Loretta is my maid and will not have time to wait on you hand and foot. Besides, that's how we went wrong with Haille: we gave her too much, spoiled her. Actually, Samuel was the one who indulged her, and you know the thanks he got for that.

"I expect you to continue to do well in school. I also expect, no *demand,* that you conduct your social and personal affairs only on the highest levels. Never do I want to hear even a hint that you've been doing some of the terrible things young people your age do these days. No drinking, no drugs, no promiscuity and you are not to parade around in any of those silly, risqué clothes young people today think are fashionable.

"I will arrange for your preparatory schooling after high school graduation so that there will be a smooth transition after you complete this last year," she said in a calmer tone. "However, as I said, there are things you will learn from me just by living here and observing, things you can't learn in any school. You can go up and rest now. You look tired. If you want some supper, come down in two hours."

"Where's Grandpa Samuel?" I asked.

"He's asleep on a lounge in the back. That's how he spends most of his time these days . . ." Her voice was so low it was as if she forgot I was in the room. Then suddenly she noticed me staring at her. "Well? Is something wrong?"

"I'm not sure which room was my mother's," I said quickly, gazing up the stairway.

"First door on the left," she said. "It's been cleaned and so has the bathroom. Make sure it all remains that way. You'll find some clothes in the closet and the dresser drawers to wear. I had them bought for you the day after you left, anticipating this day," she added triumphantly.

"I wish I had the same crystal ball," I replied dryly.

"You will," she said with confidence. Then she looked at me as if she was deciding whether or not to say, "Welcome home." She remained silent, nodded, and then turned to go down the hallway to her parlor.

Feeling like someone who had been given the key to a motel room and told to find her way herself, I started up the stairs. When I reached the first door on the left I paused, took a deep breath, and opened it. My new home, I thought as I gazed inside the room.

If there had been any trace of femininity in this room before, Grandma Olivia had erased it. It looked almost as Spartan as a room in a nunnery. The walls were papered dark brown with no pattern and there were plain white curtains on the windows. The bed was a simple one without a headboard and was covered with a beige blanket and pillow case. There was a small desk in the corner, and it was equipped with a few pads, pens, pencils and a sharpener. The only other furniture was a plain dark pine wood dresser with six drawers and a nightstand of matching dark pine next to the bed.

There was no vanity table and no mirror other than the mirror above the sink in the bathroom. Of course, there was no phone in the room and no television set or radio. When I opened the closet, I found a half dozen simple dresses, two ankle-length skirts and some color-coordinated blouses. In the dresser drawers I discovered underthings, socks, and a few wool sweaters, for which I would be grateful when the weather turned colder.

I opened my suitcase and took out the two expensive outfits Holly's sister had bought me and I hung them in the closet. They almost looked comical next to such simple, inexpensive and practical clothing. I put the matching shoes on the closet floor and completed my unpacking, finding a place on the nightstand for the Chinese fan Billy Maxwell had bought me. I promised myself I wouldn't let too much time go by before calling him and Holly and thanking them both again for all they had done.

My unpacking completed, I sat on the bed for a moment and stared through the opening in the curtains at the ocean in the distance. The blue sea looked inviting, peaceful, soothing. At least I had that view whenever I felt trouble, which I imagined would be often in this house.

Gazing around, I wondered what this room had been like when my mother lived here. Grandma Olivia must have gone through it with the fury of a hurricane and torn away anything that suggested my mother had lived here. It was a good-size room. I could make out where some shelves had once been hung on the far wall. On them my mother probably had her dolls and stuffed animals. From the little Cary had told me, I understood that Grandpa Samuel had spoiled her and bought her whatever her little heart desired. I wondered if it had all been consigned to the basement along with those pictures Cary had once showed me, or if it all had been given away, even burned. Grandma Olivia was not incapable of doing something like that.

I lay back on the bed. The trip had been exhausting even though I slept on the plane and on the bus. I realized what I was feeling was a deep emotional fatigue. The kind of weariness that gripped my very bones. Just dozing on a plane or bus wasn't enough to quench it. I was hungry, though. I thought I would just close my eyes and take a short rest, and then, as Grandma Olivia said, go down to dinner.

But when I opened my eyes again, it was so dark I couldn't see the door. The sky had become overcast, shutting out the stars. I blinked, sat up, and listened. The house was quiet, barely creaking. I fumbled for the light switch on the small lamp by the bed and squinted when it came on. Then I looked at the clock. It read two A.M. I had not only slept through dinner; I had slept right into the night!

A feeling of panic like a little trickle of ice water ran down my spine. I had intended to phone Cary right before or after dinner and let him know I was back. He would be upset that he wasn't the first one I had called or seen. Now it would be hours before I would be able to tell him I was back. And I wanted to get over to see Kenneth as soon as possible, too. There was so much to do and here I was sleeping the valuable time away.

After waking to such alarm, of course I couldn't fall back to sleep. That famous jet lag everyone warned me about was taking its toll. My body didn't know what time it was and my stomach, angry at being forgotten, growled and churned. I rose, went to the door and peered out. I could see a faint light in the hallway and over the stairway. The door creaked as I opened it farther. Then I practically tiptoed out and down the stairs, each step on the staircase betraying me with a groan as I descended. I didn't want to disturb anyone, but I needed to eat something, some milk, a piece of bread, anything.

On my way down the hallway toward the kitchen, I saw there was light coming from the parlor. When I reached the doorway, I paused and gazed in to see Grandpa Samuel slouched in an easy chair, his hands on his stomach, his mouth open as he slept. On the table beside him was a decanter of brandy and a partly filled goblet. I continued on to the kitchen where I made myself a turkey sandwich, which I ate quickly, feeling like a thief.

Suddenly, I heard a gasp and looked to the kitchen doorway to see Grandpa Samuel standing there looking as if all the blood had drained from his face.

"My God," he said, stumbling forward and stopping, his eyes wide. "Haille?"

"No, Grandpa. It's Melody," I said. "I'm sorry I woke you but—"

"Melody?" He scrubbed his face hard with his palms and then looked at me again, a dazed look in his eyes. "Melody?"

"Yes, Grandpa. I was hungry. I fell asleep and missed dinner and—"

"Oh. Oh, yes, Olivia told me. She had Loretta look in on you." He shook his head. "For a moment there . . . your mother used to come home late like this and go to the kitchen to gobble something. Lots of times she'd had too much to drink," he added in a whisper, "but I wouldn't tell Olivia. I'd make sure she got some food in her and then I'd send her up to bed.

"Well now," he continued, still sounding a bit confused, "well, I guess it's late. I should go up. Olivia's probably given up on me again." He looked at me askance. It was as if he still didn't trust me, trust reality. "I didn't hear you come in, Haille," he said after a long moment. He shook his head. "I'd better go to sleep. I'll lock the front door again. Olivia locked it when you didn't come home on time and said to let you sleep in

198

the streets, but as usual, I unlocked it when she went upstairs."

"What? Grandpa . . . it's me, Melody," I said softly, puzzled by his behavior. Maybe he was sleepwalking. And talking.

He smiled.

"Let it be another one of our little secrets, okay? Now don't you oversleep tomorrow morning," he warned, waving his right forefinger at me. Then he smiled. "Good night."

He turned, and slowly made his way toward the stairs, looking more like an old man than ever, as he shuffled away. I cleaned my dishes and wiped up the table, careful to erase all traces of my midnight snack. When I got to the stairway, however, Grandpa Samuel was just pulling himself up the final steps and groaning as he made his way to his and Grandma Olivia's bedroom.

I went up to my room quickly and closed the door. Then I got undressed, put on one of the new nightgowns that were in the dresser drawer and crawled into bed. Finally my stomach was settled, but now my mind raced as I tried to figure out Grandpa Samuel's strange behavior. I didn't look that much like my mother, did I? I wondered. And after I had told him who I was and he seemed to remember, why did he forget again and talk to me as if I were Haille, as if he was living twenty years in the past?

"There, you see. It's Melody, our grandaughter. Melody, not Haille," Grandma Olivia insisted when I entered the dinning room to have breakfast the next morning. I was still lounging in bed when I heard the two of them walk by my room earlier that morning, and I scrambled to shower and dress as quickly as I could. Grandpa Samuel gazed up from his bowl of oatmeal and nodded, smiling at me as I took my seat at the table.

He was dressed in a sports jacket and wore a tie, but he had done a poor job shaving his face. There were patches of gray stubble on his chin and along his jaw.

"He was raving last night," Grandma Olivia continued, "talking stupidity again, telling me Haille was back."

"Good morning, Grandpa Samuel," I said, concerned that he'd give away my early morning wandering. His eyes looked glassy, distant, however. I gazed questioningly at Grandma Olivia.

"He's slipping away," she muttered, "into his dotage."

"What's that, Olivia?" he asked. "What about the cottage?"

"I didn't say anything about any cottage, you fool," she snapped. "I want you to see the doctor about that hearing aid today. I told Raymond to take you over there."

"Oh. Fine, fine. I've got time today," he said and she laughed.

"You hear that? He can find the time in his busy schedule today."

I gazed at him. He was so different and it had happened so quickly, I thought. I turned again to Grandma Olivia, who saw the confusion in my face.

"He's been like this ever since Jacob's death," she explained. "It hit him like a sledgehammer and aged him years in minutes."

Grandpa Samuel blew on his spoonful of oatmeal and gazed absently ahead, looking through me.

"Oh, how sad," I said.

"As is much of life," Grandma Olivia instructed. "That's why it's important to learn how to deal with unpleasantness, how to accept what you can't change and move on to what you can. Don't ever waste your time again on lost causes. Time is too precious. You're young now, so you think you'll be young forever, but one day you'll wake up and find yourself unable to count the wrinkles and the gray hairs and you'll have aches and pains where you never had them before."

She turned back to Grandpa Samuel.

"If you keep blowing on that same spoonful, Samuel, it will turn to ice. Eat it already."

"What's that? Oh, yes. I have time today. I have time," he muttered.

"I don't know why I bother," Grandma Olivia said. "He'll soon be in the room next to my sister. You'll see."

"Maybe with time—" I said.

"With time he'll grow worse. There's no sense wasting tears over it. What are your plans for today? Do you have everything you need for the start of school? I believe that's next week if I'm not mistaken."

"Yes, it is. I've got everything I need. I was hoping to go visit Cary and Aunt Sara and May," I said.

"That pathetic woman. All she does, day and night, is cry. Her eyes are so bloodshot, it's a wonder she can still see out of them."

"I'm sure it's been very hard for all of them," I said, remembering how awful I felt after my stepdaddy Chester died.

"Jacob had a good insurance policy. There's adequate money for the way they live, and I made sure they had a little more. They won't starve or go without necessities," she said tersely.

"I'm talking about more than money," I said, amazed that she showed no emotion when she talked about the death of her son.

She laughed as if I had said something hilarious.

"Yes, when you find out what that is, let me know."

"I already know. It's love, concern, friendship . . ."

"No one loves anyone more than he or she loves him or herself. You'll discover that."

"I hope not," I said.

"You already have," she replied. "What could be more intense than a mother's love for her own child? And yet, your mother loves herself more. Don't think romantic love is any different. Men and women crave each other, pledge all sorts of things to each other when they're young and in love, and then, time goes by and they begin to grow apart. Their own interests become most important again. Before you know it," she said gazing at Grandpa Samuel, who was blowing on another spoonful

201

of oatmeal, "thirty-five years have gone by and you hardly know the man who shares your bed. And if he doesn't end up calling you by some other name, you're fortunate.

"Don't place too much faith in romantic love, Melody."

"What *do* you believe in, Grandma Olivia?"

"I told you, family, name, reputation, self-respect." She dabbed her lips with her napkin and rose. "For today and only today, I'll permit Raymond to cart you over to Sara's before he takes Samuel to the ear doctor, but I don't intend to have him do that every time you get it into your head to go there.

"Samuel," she snapped. "Do you intend to play with your food all morning?"

"What? Oh? Is it time to go?"

"It was time to go a long time ago," she said wistfully. The sadness in her voice caught my ear and I stared at her for a moment. She quickly realized I was looking at her and rose from the table. "Finish your breakfast, Melody. I'll have Raymond wait for you in the drive."

As soon as I had finished breakfast, I joined Grandpa Samuel in the car. When Raymond brought me to Aunt Sara's, I expected Cary would have already left to go on the lobster boat, but when I got out of the car and knocked on the door, it was he who opened it and gazed out at me, his eyes first full of surprise and then, full of joy.

"Melody! You're back!"

"Hello, Cary," I said smiling.

He started toward me to embrace me and then saw Grandma Olivia's car pulling away.

"What was Raymond doing here? Where are you suitcases? How long have you been back in Provincetown?" he asked, rapidly firing his questions at me.

"I got in yesterday, but I was so tired from the trip that I fell asleep as soon as I put my head on the pillow and slept into the night," I said.

"Slept? Slept where? You went to Grandma Olivia's house first? Why?"

"Where are Aunt Sara and May?" I asked instead of replying.

"Inside. What's going on? Why did you go to Grandma Olivia's first? You're going to stay with her after all, aren't you?" he demanded.

"Yes, Cary. I am."

"Why?"

"You remember we had this discussion before I left, when I had learned Judge Childs was my real grandfather and Kenneth was my uncle."

"Yes, but—"

"None of that's changed, Cary, and with my mother really not dead and buried—"

"But no one knows it and with Dad gone—"

"That's just it. I . . . just think it's best for now. Your mother has enough to do and, well, now, especially with everyone believing my mother's dead and buried, Grandma Olivia thinks this is better for all concerned. But just as I promised before I left, I'll see you every day," I added quickly.

His green eyes seemed to pierce right through me as his lips curved up in a disdainful smile.

"I didn't think you'd go through with it after your trip to California, but I guess now that you've tasted wealth and glamour, you'd rather live in the mansion, right?"

"No, that's not it," I protested, shaking my head.

"There's no question she can do far more for you than we can," he continued, folding his arms across his chest and pulling his shoulders back. "I don't blame you."

"Stop talking to me like that, Cary. You don't understand."

"Oh, I understand. That's my trouble. I understand too much," he said.

This time I permitted the burning tears to course down my face.

"Visiting my mother was a disaster. First, her boyfriend Archie, or Richard Marlin, or whoever he really is, tried to get me into a pornographic movie and Mommy approved," I said. Cary's cold smirk evaporated a bit. "Then he tried to . . . tried to rape me and she believed him when he said it was my fault. She was happy to see me go. She has everyone believing she's not much older than I am. She told them I was her sister and I had to pretend to be her sister.

"I have no parents anymore. No one who truly cares about me!" I cried.

"You have me, Melody, and May and my mother. . . . You know she needs someone to fill Laura's place in her heart."

"That's just it . . . Laura's place. I appreciate that, but I've got to become myself and I'm afraid, Cary. I'm afraid that now, more than ever," I confessed, hiding my eyes as I did so, "your mother will want me to be Laura. I'm sorry," I said. I wiped away more tears. He was silent.

"I know what you mean but . . . . I just . . ."

"You think I want to live with Grandma Olivia? She's cruel in ways I don't even understand, but she's strong, Cary, and if ever there was a time I needed someone strong, it's now."

"I'm strong," he proclaimed.

"You are, but you have to be strong for your mother and your sister first, especially right now," I said. "Later, when the time is right, I want you to be strong for me, too."

That brought a warm smile to his face. He thought a moment and then he nodded and stepped closer to embrace me. I loved the feel of his strong arms around my body. I wished I could sink into him and be safe and secure behind the walls of his love forever and ever.

He kissed away a lingering tear and brushed back my hair.

"I thought I had lost you forever," he said. "I thought you would fall in love with Hollywood."

"I hated it, Cary, at least the part I saw. It's not the

place for me or for my mother, but she just hasn't realized it yet. I'm afraid that when she finally understands, it will destroy her."

"Grandma Olivia is right, Melody. You need to forget about Haille. You've come home to us. You need to start thinking about the future." He looked up at me sheepishly. "I never thought I'd ever agree with her about anything."

"I know. I hate to say this, but I think we both have a lot to learn from her."

He laughed and then grew serious.

"You saw how bad Grandpa Samuel is, I suppose."

"Yes. It's as if something snapped in his head when your father died."

Cary nodded and tears glistened in his eyes, too. He swallowed quickly and then smiled again.

"Well, May will be very happy to see you, and so will Ma. Come on in," he added, stepping aside. He kissed my cheek again and we entered the house.

May was at Aunt Sara's feet reading and Aunt Sara was doing some needlework, her hands working mechanically, her mind obviously elsewhere. Aunt Sara lifted her eyes slowly and when she saw me, her face softened into the most loving and wonderful smile, the smile I had wished to find on my own mother's face but didn't.

"Melody!" She put her needlework down and the action caught May's attention. The moment May saw me, her face exploded with happiness and she jumped up to run into my arms. I held her tightly and then she pulled back and began signing with such speed, I couldn't keep up.

"Slow down," Cary signed. "She's so full of questions she will exhaust you much quicker than any cross-country trip."

I laughed and stepped forward to embrace Aunt Sara.

"I'm so sorry, Aunt Sara."

"I know, dear. He fought hard. The doctors said he fought until the end. He did not go 'gentle into that good night.'"

"Not Dad," Cary said proudly. "He was a real Logan."

For a moment I thought about Grandma Olivia's words concerning family dignity and I smiled at Cary's pride.

"Come, sit with me and tell us all about your journey. Where are you suitcases? Has Cary brought them upstairs already?" she asked looking from me to him. Cary didn't say anything.

"I'm going to stay with Grandma Olivia for now, Aunt Sara. With Grandpa Samuel the way he is and all, I think she wants my company," I explained. It wasn't such a terrible white lie, I thought. Actually, I hoped it was true.

"Oh. I see," she said fighting hard to hide her disappointment. She forced a smile. "Well, she can do so much for you. Of course you should stay with her. That's very good. So then, that woman wasn't Haille after all?"

I looked at Cary, whose eyes told me he hadn't said a word to her.

"No, Aunt Sara, the woman I found was not the mother I was hoping to find."

"Oh, how sad." She nodded with a small smile. "But at least you're back here, home with us, with your family again. You must tell us all about California. I've never been there."

I sat beside her on the sofa and told them about my trip. May sat at my feet, watching my hands, and Cary sat in what had always been his father's chair, listening, his eyes fixed on me.

We had lunch and then Cary and I took May for a walk along the beach, just as we used to do.

"While you were away, May and I came out here often. I'd pretend you were with us. It was easy because she can't hear, so I could talk aloud to you. I don't know how many times I told you I loved you."

"I heard you each time," I said. He tightened his hold on my hand.

"Can you stay for dinner?"

"I think I'd better go back for dinner, but I want to see

206

Kenneth this afternoon and I was hoping you'd drive me out there," I said.

He turned away quickly.

"What's wrong?"

"I was out there yesterday," he said. "Kenneth's . . . different. I think all of it, finishing his big work, your friend's discovery of Haille, your leaving . . . all brought back painful memories, memories he was able to bury in his work."

"What's wrong with him?"

"He was drinking a lot. Actually, I found him sleeping on the beach, Ulysses whining beside him. I helped him into the house. He had obviously been out there all night."

"Oh no, Cary."

"I don't know if you should go there."

"More than ever, Cary. I should go there more than ever," I said.

I said it with such determination and strength, I even surprised myself.

"With all your unhappiness and all your own problems, you think you can go and help someone else?" he challenged.

"Because of all that," I replied, thinking about some of the things Grandma Olivia had said. "It's important to learn how to deal with unpleasantness, how to accept what you can't change and move on to what you can."

"And you think you can change Kenneth's unhappiness?" he asked with skepticism and amazement.

"Yes," I said gazing out over the blue waves that rolled toward us. "Yes, I do."

# 12

&

# *The Downward Spiral*

*T*he wind picked up considerably as we drove down the bumpy beach road to Kenneth's house. I could see the ocean spray bouncing off the rocks, and the seagulls looked like they were struggling to stay on course. The sky was still quite blue, but over the horizon long somber clouds with ominously gray faces were snaking toward us.

"Bit of a nor'easter coming," Cary said. "We'll get some heavy rain tonight."

We stopped beside Kenneth's jeep, and noticed that he had left the driver's side door wide open. Getting out of the truck slowly, I stepped up to the jeep and peered in at the empty beer bottles and the empty fast food bags on the floor, some old french fries and packets of ketchup beside them.

"I think he burned out his battery," Cary said, gazing over my shoulder. He nodded at the dashboard. "Looks like he left the headlights on all night after he returned from whatever bar he was at."

I shook my head, my heart thumping in anticipation as we turned toward the house. The door was unlocked as usual, but it, too, was partially open. The house was even a worse mess than it had been before I had begun working for Kenneth. It looked like he hadn't washed a dish in the kitchen since I had left. Food was caked on plates. Glasses, some still with wine, whiskey, beer and flat Coke in them, were scattered everywhere, even on the windowsills.

I knocked on the bedroom doorjamb before gazing in, but Kenneth wasn't there. I didn't know how he could sleep in the bedroom anyway. The blankets were half off the bed, as were the sheets. There was a pillow on the floor, along with clothing and shoes he had discarded. I waded through the mess and then stopped and stooped down to pick up the picture of Mommy and me I had once found under the bed.

"Boy, it smells in here, doesn't it?" Cary said. I saw some rotted food and what looked like a pile of vomit in the corner. "Disgusting. What's that?"

"A picture of myself and Mommy. Did you check the bathroom?"

"Yes. He's probably in the studio," Cary said. He shook his head as he gazed around the room. "I told you things were bad, but I didn't know how bad they were."

"Okay. Let's go find him," I said and we walked through the house, both grateful for the fresh air. I gazed down at the small pool where Kenneth kept Shell the turtle and some fish. Two dead fish floated on top of the water and Shell was nowhere in sight.

The door to the studio was wide open. I stood in the doorway, sweeping my eyes over the bottles, the plates, the paper and cans. A chair was overturned and the small sofa looked as if it were missing some of its stuffing.

Kenneth was sprawled at the foot of *Neptune's Daughter*. He was folded in the fetal position, one hand holding a nearly empty bottle of whiskey. His cheeks were unshaven, his beard very straggly, his hair long and untrimmed. He wore a stained pair of dungarees, no shoes and a faded brown T-shirt ripped down the right side. His eyes were shut tight and his mouth was twisted in a grimace. It looked like he was having a terrible nightmare.

Ulysses, sleeping at his side, rose with great effort, and came to greet us, his tail wagging emphatically.

"Oh, Ulysses, you poor baby," I said as he licked my hands and my face. "When was the last time you were fed?"

"He's probably been eating off plates, leftovers," Cary remarked.

We both looked at Kenneth again. He hadn't stirred.

"Maybe we shouldn't wake him," Cary said. "I told you I did that before, but I didn't tell you he wasn't so nice about it."

"We can't leave him here like this," I declared, took a deep breath and went to him. He smelled awful but I knelt down and carefully pried the bottle of whiskey out of his fingers. Cary rushed over to take it and put it on the table. Then I shook Kenneth's shoulder gently. His mouth closed and opened, but his eyes remained shut. I shook him again, harder.

"Kenneth. Kenneth, wake up. It's Melody. I'm back. Kenneth. Kenneth!" I jerked his arm and his eyes snapped opened with a start as he groaned. He shot up so quickly, I nearly fell backward to avoid being struck by his swinging left arm. Then he fixed his eyes on me and rubbed them into focus.

"What?"

"I'm back, Kenneth. It's Melody."

"You're back?" He scrubbed his face with his palms, dropped his head as if he were going to fall asleep again, and then lifted it slowly, gazing at me harder. "You're not a vision, a dream? You're really here," he said smiling.

"Yes, Kenneth. I'm really here. What's going on? What have you done to yourself?"

He smiled.

"Done to myself? Nothing. What you see here has been done to me, not by me," he replied. "So . . ." He finally noticed Cary standing to the side. "Oh, the beach rescue service has arrived, huh?"

"Hi, Kenneth. I think you drained your battery in the jeep. You must have left the lights on last night."

"Most likely," he said nodding.

"I have some jumper cables in the truck. I'll give it a boost and get it running for you."

Kenneth brought his hand to his temple, to his mouth and then bowed.

"My family thanks you."

Cary laughed and then looked at me and saw I didn't think any of this was funny.

"I'll just go charge the jeep while you two talk," he said and hurried away, Ulysses at his heels.

"Talk? We're going to talk?"

"What's happened to you, Kenneth? You weren't like this when I left."

"I don't know," he said quickly and struggled to get to his feet. I moved to help him, but he pushed me away. "I can do it myself," he said, but he wobbled when he stood and had to put his left hand against the statue. He opened his eyes and smiled. "I knew I created this for a reason."

"It has a lot more reason to be than that, Kenneth. It's spectacular," I said, glancing at *Neptune's Daughter* again. There was no question the face was my mother's face.

"Right. Art for art's sake, to bring out the beauty that is otherwise unseen, unheard, untouched around us. I am a prophet, a singer of songs, a . . ." He groaned. ". . . a man with a terrific hangover."

He staggered over to the sofa, grabbed a pillow and flopped down, nearly turning the sofa over at the same time.

"Why are you drinking like this? You're killing yourself," I said.

"No, it just looks that way. I can go on like this indefinitely. So," he said coming more to his senses, "I did hear from Holly a few times. Apparently, our Miss Cape Cod did pull a fast one, huh? She performed a death and resurrection, just as we all suspected?"

"Yes, she and her so-called agent took advantage of a situation to fake her death. The woman in the car with

211

Richard Marlin was borrowing my mother's identification and was first mistaken for Mommy and then deliberately made out to be her."

"Olivia's not going to appreciate less than blue blood bones in her sanctified ground."

"Why is everyone so worried about what Grandma Olivia thinks?" I moaned.

"I don't really worry about it. I'm amused by it, actually." He thought a moment. "I shouldn't be at all surprised. Haille liked to pretend she was someone else all the time, especially movie actresses. When she met strangers, she would give them a fictitious name, make up a whole history for herself and do it rather convincingly."

"Then she's in the right place," I said and began cleaning up the studio.

"Don't do that. I don't care about it being clean and organized anymore. You are looking at my last work," he said staring at *Neptune's Daughter*.

"Stop it, Kenneth. You're not going to let this be your last work. You're too young to retire."

"Retire?" He laughed. "Yes, retire is a good word for it. Kenneth Childs, renowned New England sculptor, has declared his retirement. I like the sound of that."

"I hate it because it's full of self-pity," I said. His eyes widened.

"Whoa. Et tu, Melody? Then fall Kenneth Childs."

"I understand, Kenneth, because I've been wallowing in it as well." I put another pillow back on the sofa and sat beside him. Then I told him what had happened in California and why I had left. He listened, his eyes regaining some of their spirit and light as I spoke, especially when I described my mother and how young she looked.

"Then she's still very beautiful?"

"Yes, but there are many beautiful women in Hollywood, most with more talent, and all probably with more reputable and reliable agents. Richard Marlin is just some lowlife that has her beguiled," I said.

He nodded.

"I feel sorry for her. She was just as much a victim as I was. I feel sorry for you, too," he added quickly.

"I don't want you to. I'm not going to think about it anymore and I'm not going to try to make something happen that can never happen."

He looked at me with new interest.

"I see. You're learning to grin and bear it, huh?"

"Yes, and I want you to learn as well." I paused and then added, "You were actually lucky you didn't end up with my mother. Grandma Olivia is right about people making excuses for her. She is what she is not because of what happened between you two, not because she discovered your father is her father, but because it's in her to be who she is. She was always selfish, Kenneth. You know that's true."

He laughed.

"Where did you find all this wisdom and knowledge?"

"It was a long journey," I said dryly, "through a rain forest of tears. Just because she lost you as a lover doesn't mean she had to turn me away, to deny me as her daughter, does it? When do you stop blaming your father for every mistake you make and start blaming yourself?"

His eyes widened.

"You don't understand," he said in a hoarse whisper, his head shaking.

"I understand. Don't you think I wanted to love her, too? Don't you think I wanted to have a mother? When I was growing up and I had so many questions, girl-talk questions, don't you think I longed to have her spend hours and hours with me and not talk about herself and her pimples or her new ounce of fat? Do you think if you had been able to marry her, you would have changed her?"

"I don't know," he admitted. "All I do know is I would have liked the opportunity." He sighed deeply. "Okay, Melody, okay," he said. "I'll stop wallowing in self-pity, but I don't know about my work." He looked at

*Neptune's Daughter.* "This project just seemed to drain me. Maybe I gave it everything I had."

"I doubt it," I said. We heard the jeep's horn and looked toward the doorway. Cary gave us the thumbs-up sign.

"He's a good kid. Hard news about his father. There's a lot falling on his shoulders now. Did you come back to live with them?"

"No, I'm going to be living with Grandma Olivia. Remember how the arrangements were already made just before I left for California?"

"Yes, I remember, and I remember thinking it was a good idea. You'll learn a lot from her."

"That's what she keeps telling me," I said dryly. He laughed and then he reached out to stroke my hair.

"It's nice to have you back, even though for your sake I was hoping it would have worked out otherwise."

"Thank you, Kenneth. Um, can I make a small suggestion at this time?"

"Why not?"

"Could you take a shower or a bath soon?"

He roared with laughter and pulled his hand away from my hair.

"Okay, I deserve that."

"In the meantime, I'll clean up some of this mess."

He shook his head and sighed.

"You're a bad influence on someone who wants to wallow in self-pity, Melody."

"Good," I said, which brought another smile to his face. I had the feeling there hadn't been too many since I had left.

"You did wonders with him," Cary said as we drove away some two and a half hours later. We left Kenneth eating some warm food and promising to rest and stay off the whiskey for a while.

"I don't know how long it will last though," I said sadly. "He's come to the point where his art isn't enough. He needs someone real to love and to love him."

"I can understand that," Cary said, reaching to squeeze my hand softly.

"Yes, me too."

As we bounced over the beach road, I gazed back at Kenneth's house. Ulysses had come to the gate, but he didn't, as usual, follow the truck most of the way down the beach road barking after us. Cary gazed in his side mirror.

"Ulysses is showing his age, huh?"

"Yes," I said sadly. "And he's the only companion Kenneth has."

During the drive back to Grandma Olivia's we watched the clouds blow in from the north, creeping over most of the sky. By the time we turned into the driveway, it had begun to rain.

"What are you doing about the lobster business?" I asked Cary as we came to a stop in front of the house.

"Roy's been running it. Theresa's been helping him, too. She asks about you often."

"She turned out to be the nicest girl at school, as far as I was concerned. I don't care what the snobs think of the Bravas."

Cary laughed. The Bravas, as the half black and half Portuguese residents of Provincetown were called, weren't easily accepted by the girls Grandma Olivia considered of respectable lineage.

"I've got the cranberry crop to worry about now anyway. Because of the warmer weather this year, they're a little ahead of schedule," Cary said. "Most of the berries are already a bright red. Usually, we don't begin harvesting until October, but I think we'll be at it by the third week in September this year."

"This will be my first cranberry harvest. What do I need to know so that I can help you?"

"Well, these cranberries will all be for juices and sauces so we do what's called a 'wet harvesting.' First, we flood the bog until the cranberries are completely covered with water. Then we bring in fat-tired trucks called 'water reels' or 'eggbeaters.' They're driven through the bog and the spinning reels on the machines loosen the berries from the plants and they float to the surface. That's when the hard work begins."

"What do you mean?"

"We assemble a corral using boards and canvas hinges, and encircle the cranberries, drawing them to one end of the bog. A pipe is placed just beneath the surface of the water, and this pipe leads to a pump on shore which sucks the berries into a metal box called a hopper. The hopper separates everything and then the berries are loaded into trucks."

"You sound like you know exactly what to do," I said.

"Maybe, but I've never done this without Dad."

"You'll do fine, Cary, and I'll be there beside you."

He laughed.

"You'll be in school," he said.

"I'll take some days off," I promised.

"Play hooky? You have a chance to be class valedictorian, don't you?"

"It's not as important to me," I said, "as helping you."

He smiled and leaned over to kiss me. It was a short, sweet kiss, and when he pulled back, I looked so deeply into his green eyes that I felt I was really connecting with him, with his soul, with who he was. His eyes were like magnets. I moved my lips toward his again and we kissed, only this time longer, harder, embracing each other tightly.

"I'm glad you're back," he whispered. "I had nightmares that I would never see you again."

"Fill your head with only good dreams, Cary. I'm back and I won't ever leave you again," I promised.

He was so happy it brought tears to his eyes. We started to kiss again, when I looked out over his shoulder at the house and saw a window curtain move on the second floor. I was sure it was Grandma Olivia gazing down at us.

"I better go in, Cary, before it really starts pouring."

"Right. When should I come by tomorrow?"

"Wait for me to call you. I'd like to visit Grandma Belinda, if I could."

"Sure, I'll take you," he said.

"You should be spending all your time with your mother, Cary. She must be so sad. And lonely."

"I can't sit there all day and watch her cry, Melody. It makes me crazy to see how sad she is. The best I can do is work hard and show her that everything will be all right. I'll take care of things."

"I know you will," I said, nodding. "I'll call you tomorrow."

I gave him a quick kiss and hopped out of the truck. He watched me cross in front of it and smiled at me as I walked to the front door. He didn't start the engine until I opened the door to go in. I waved and he started away.

With the sky so overcast and the lights either off or turned low, it was dismal and dark in the house. I felt a chill run through my body and folded my arms across my chest as I hurried up the stairs. When I reached the second floor and turned toward my room, I found Grandma Olivia waiting at my door. Without a greeting, she opened the door for me and stood back.

"Let's talk," she said, grimly.

Keeping my head down and my arms still folded, I walked by her and into the room. She closed the door softly behind her.

"Where were you all day?"

"I went to Aunt Sara's and spent time with her and May, and then Cary took me to see Kenneth," I replied.

"It would probably be better if you stopped going out to that beach house so much now," she declared.

"Why?"

"There's enough suspicious gossip going on. It will only add to it."

"I can't hide from every whisper in Provincetown," I said.

She stiffened.

"You will lead an exemplary life here. No one will have any reason to utter the smallest suspicion or tale of indiscretion," she demanded as if she could order the future at will.

"I'm not going to stop seeing Kenneth. He's my uncle, my real uncle."

"Don't ever say that to anyone, do you understand?" she snapped, moving to stand over me. Her eyes looked more haunted by her own fears than rage at me. Nothing appeared to terrify her more than the community learning Judge Childs was my grandfather and had been her sister's lover.

"I have no intention of rattling any of the skeletons in our family closet, Grandma Olivia. It wouldn't serve any purpose except to hurt people who have already suffered too much because of them."

She smiled, relieved, and nodded.

"That's right. That's good thinking."

"How is my grandmother?" I asked firmly.

"Belinda is . . . Belinda. She was taken off the medication that turned her into a vegetable, if that's what you mean."

"Good. I'm going to see her tomorrow. Don't worry, you won't have to waste any gas. Cary's taking me," I said quickly.

"That's the main reason I wanted to talk to you," she said. "You've grown too close to Cary. I understand why," she continued, crossing to the window. The rain had become harder and the wind was flinging the heavy drops at the house, drumming a wild beat upon the roof. "You were alone; you were in strange surroundings but you had a contemporary to talk to and befriend you. However, now that you are here, you've got to create some distance between the two of you."

"Whatever for?" I asked and she pivoted quickly.

"Cary is a good, responsible young man, but too limited for you now. You can't make the mistakes I made," she warned. "There would be no purpose for taking you in if I didn't teach you that," she added.

"Being with someone you love can never be a mistake," I replied.

She shook her head.

"When you've grown out of these foolish romantic notions, you will be strong enough to take on the responsibilities I have in mind for you. Besides, you're not thinking of your immediate future. You will finish this school year, go to a prestigious prep school which will prepare you for the best colleges, where I am sure you will meet someone from a distinguished family and form a meaningful relationship."

"You talk like you have my whole life planned out for me."

"I will do the best I can, but you must be cooperative and obedient," she continued, obviously not at all concerned with my feelings. "I've been thinking about you all day and I've concluded that you can begin your training immediately. For that purpose, I have contracted with an excellent tutor, a Miss Louise May Burton, who happens to be a retired charm school teacher. You will begin your lessons the day after tomorrow, so don't make any silly plans to wander the beaches, or go sailing or visit anyone."

"Lessons? In what?"

"Etiquette, manners, behavior. You are going to attend schools populated by the daughters of only the best families, people of stature, good breeding, pure blood."

"There's nothing wrong with my manners," I complained.

She laughed.

"How would you know, my dear? Have you ever been with people who recognized the difference?"

I stared at her a moment, my anger simmering my blood into a rolling boil. Yes, my mother was a great disappointment, but there were many people in my life who were warm and decent. Why, Papa George and Mama Arlene would make any of Grandma Olivia's blue bloods look like savages when it came to true and good feelings and decency, I thought.

But Papa George was dead and Mama Arlene had moved away, a small voice reminded me.

"That's settled then," Grandma Olivia continued. "You will limit your contact with Kenneth Childs and with Cary and you will be a good student of manners."

"I won't limit my contact with Cary," I challenged.

"If you won't on your own accord, I'll have to speak with Sara. And," she said smiling, "you know what sort of influence I have with Sara. They are, despite what dribbles in from that dying lobster boat business and their silly cranberries, dependent upon my charity to an extent you don't fathom. Why even that pathetic house really belongs to me," she revealed. "My son needed to borrow the money for the mortgage."

"You wouldn't dare do anything to hurt them," I countered.

She fixed her eyes on me with a firmness that put ice into my veins.

"Not unless you force me too," she said. Then she smiled. "I suppose you could always run away and live like your dead mother. Think it all over and I'm sure you'll conclude that your best chances for a decent life are here with me and with what I will do for you."

"Why are you really doing all this for me?" I asked her, suddenly more curious than angry.

"I told you, for the family's sake," she said.

I shook my head.

"There's another reason."

"There is no other reason . . . for anything," she declared and then turned to leave my room.

The rain grew heavier, its drum beat pounding on my heart as well as on the house. I saw Cary's loving smile, his deep green eyes revealing his great need for me and great trust. How could I disappoint him? Grandma Olivia's threats scared me. I thought about the fury in her face.

Some time ago, she had trusted her heart to someone who had betrayed her and from that betrayal my mother was born, a woman she couldn't control or mold. I was her last chance for revenge.

But revenge against whom? Against what?

Was it someone or was it merely a world she had come to despise? Maybe it was both, I thought.

I was sure that in the days to follow I would find all the answers, only I was just as terrified of making the discoveries as I was of not.

I was floundering in a world of adult quicksand. Who would throw me a line to pull me out? Kenneth? Judge Childs? My Grandmother Belinda? Cary? Everyone seemed to be floundering just as much.

Only Grandma Olivia, only she seemed to walk on firm ground. I had to admire her for that, and suddenly, I was filled with a new fear.

What if she got her way and I became the woman she wanted me to become?

Would I become her?

Then surely, she would have her revenge.

Grandpa Samuel did not join us for dinner. When Loretta began serving, I inquired after him.

"Samuel's not up to coming down to dinner tonight," Grandma Olivia said and began to eat her soup.

"Isn't he hungry?"

"He doesn't remember when he ate and when he didn't," she remarked acidly.

"Well, that's terrible, isn't it?" I pursued.

"Yes," she said and paused. "I'm debating whether to have a nurse move in to help take care of him or—"

"Or what?"

"Have him placed in the home Belinda is in. The doctor will be examining him again in a few days and we'll know what he thinks we should do."

"Surely, he'll get better. He's just overcome with grief," I said.

She dabbed her mouth daintily and signaled for Loretta to remove her bowl.

"Really Melody, I don't know if we have room on our door to hang it," she said.

"Hang it? Hang what?"

"Your medical degree. I didn't know you had one," she said humorlessly.

"I'm just saying that it's possible, isn't it? He just needs some tender love and care. It's very painful to lose someone you love," I shot back. Sarcasm dripped from those thin, smug lips of hers.

"Of course it's painful, but tragedy and sadness must be subdued if you are to be of any value to anyone, including yourself. If all you are going to do is wallow in tears, you might as well throw yourself into the grave with your loved one. I may sound insensitive to you, Melody, but I am a realist, pragmatic. All the success, all that we have, is a result of that strength.

"And the irony is," she continued, "the weaker, more sensitive members of my immediate family are totally dependent upon my strength. Where would they be without me? Where do you think Samuel would eventually end up, and Belinda and Sara? All of them. Even you," she added.

She nodded at Loretta, who began serving the entrée, but who looked terrified of doing anything that would interrupt. Grandma Olivia continued.

"I don't expect gratitude. I don't need to be continually stroked with thank-yous, but I won't be despised for my actions either. Is that clear?" she demanded.

I glanced at Loretta, who looked like she was waiting for my reply before she would serve me, too.

"Yes, ma'am," I said.

"Good." She began to eat while I poked at my food. "You may go visit Belinda tomorrow. You should, now that I think about it. Tell her about Haille. Give her all the details about her daughter. A good dose of reality might be beneficial," she said, nodding and smiling.

We stared at each other a moment and then we ate quietly, neither of us saying another word until we were finished. Loretta was there to remove the dishes in an instant and quietly announced that she'd be bringing out dessert momentarily.

"I'm tired and I've had enough to eat. You should take your time. Try the crème brûlée. It's very good," Grandma Olivia said and retreated to the parlor.

I had no more appetite and left the dining room soon after her. When I passed the parlor, I saw her sitting in her grand cushioned chair, suddenly looking very small, exhausted and alone. She had a book in her lap, but she wasn't reading anymore. She was staring out the window at the slow downpour, watching as the sky poured out the tears she'd never allow herself to shed.

I went upstairs to my room, but when I reached the second floor, I heard a door open and close and saw Grandpa Samuel coming down the hallway. He spotted me and hurried toward me. He wore a pair of pajamas and a dark blue velvet robe, but he was barefoot. His hair was disheveled. It looked like he had been running his fingers through it for hours.

"Haille," he whispered. "I'm glad you're back."

"No, Grandpa. I'm Melody," I said softly with a smile. "Melody."

He shook his head and looked back as if he was afraid of being overheard.

"She's gone and done it. I told her it wasn't right, but she forbade me to utter a word. She said it was a family disgrace and if I should so much as drop a hint in public or to Jacob and Sara, she would have me thrown out. She would tell everyone I was responsible for your pregnancy after all. Can you imagine? I think she meant it."

"Grandpa."

"I'm not saying she's not right. Maybe she is better off where she is, but Haille, you—"

"Grandpa, it's me, Melody," I said. I reached out and took his hand. He turned and looked into my face.

"What?"

"Look at me closely. I'm not my mother."

"You mustn't tell her I told you," he said. He looked very frightened.

"Tell her what? Who are you talking about? Belinda?"

He shook his head.

"I'm not responsible," he said, pulling his hand from mine and backing away. "You can't blame me."

"Grandpa."

"I'm going to bed. Things will look different in the morning. They always look different in the morning. But if you don't believe me, you go into the basement and you look. You'll find the papers. Shh," he said bringing his finger to his lips. "Don't say a word. Don't let her know I told you," he warned me. "Just pretend you found the papers yourself," he added and hurried away, looking back only once before going into his bedroom and closing the door.

What papers?

Was it all part of his madness? Like Ophelia in *Hamlet*, had he been driven insane by the death of someone he loved? If he didn't come out of his constant state of confusion he would end up in a rest home, I sadly thought.

Or were there more skeletons dangling in a closet I had yet to discover? Was it not just madness but painful memories that did this to him?

I heard footsteps below. Grandma Olivia was coming up the stairs, and for now, I thought, I would keep Grandpa Samuel's words to myself.

In my room I lay on the bed, my thoughts tumbling through my mind, making it impossible to sleep. Grandpa Samuel's words echoed in my ears and when I did finally drift off to sleep, it was of secrets and lies and whispers from beyond the grave that I dreamt. I tossed and turned for most of the night before I finally gave up on sleep.

I lay there with my eyes wide open for the longest time. The rain had stopped but the wind continued to whistle and blow over the big house, scratching at the window and whispering a name. My nightmares had stirred a voice. I could not make it out, but I knew it was a secret deeper than I had ever fathomed.

# 13

## *How Sweet It Is*

After breakfast the next day, Cary came by to take me to see Grandma Belinda. I waited at the parlor window so I could rush out to meet him as soon as he pulled into the driveway. I didn't want him to have to see the look of disapproval on Grandma Olivia's face. He would surely ask me about it and I would have to tell him her feelings concerning us. If there was anything I wanted to avoid at the moment, it was family turmoil, especially when it could be traced back to me.

Yesterday's storm had passed and the small vanilla scoops of clouds looked like they were melting over the powder blue sky. The instant I saw Cary's truck, I ran out to greet him. As we drove away from Grandma Olivia's dreary home, Cary and I remarked on how bright the sun seemed, how clean and clear the air, how beautiful the grass and flowers. It filled me with a renewed sense of hope and reminded me of when I was younger and I believed life would be like one long and perfect summer day, a day just like this one.

I was about to see my closest relative again. I hoped

that taking her off her medication had cleared her head. I couldn't wait to hug her and talk to her about everything, especially all my dreams and plans for the future. At least Belinda had time to listen, I thought. At least I had someone neither Mommy nor Grandma Olivia could take from me.

As we drove up to the rest home, Cary talked about the times his twin sister Laura had gone to see my grandmother before Uncle Jacob had forbidden any further visits. Cary hadn't talked about Laura for quite a while. When I had first come to Provincetown, just pronouncing her name seemed to bring pain to his lips.

"Why did Laura visit her so often, Cary?" I asked. He thought for a moment, his memories brightening his sea-green eyes.

"Belinda took to Laura the first time she met her. It was as if they recognized something soft and loving in each other, some secret the two of them shared. No matter who else was present, Belinda directed herself only to Laura. No one knew about the first time Laura visited her up here. In fact, if I recall, my father didn't discover it was going on until the third or fourth time, and only then because some spy of Grandma Olivia's told her about the visits. She called Dad and he chastised Laura for going; after all, Belinda was the black sheep of the family. We weren't supposed to mention her name, much less visit her.

"But Dad always had trouble forbidding Laura to do things," Cary continued. "Whenever Laura and I did something he didn't approve of, Dad would direct himself mainly to me, barely looking at Laura, as if she hadn't been involved at all. He never thought he let his soft spot show, but it was obvious he always thought things were my fault anyway, as if I was the one who should have known better or should have been more responsible. Laura would fly to my defense, of course, taking as much blame as she could, but Dad wouldn't hear of it. He would accuse her of trying to protect me."

Cary laughed, as he continued remembering.

"'But Dad,' she would exclaim, 'Cary wasn't even there!'

"'No matter,' Dad would growl back. 'He should have been there to stop you or warn you.'"

"Once," he said turning to me as we drove up the side road toward the rest home, "I took quite a beating for the both of us. He whipped me with a thick leather strap and I had so many welts on my rear end I couldn't sit for days. I had to lie on my stomach. Laura came into my room and sat beside the bed, crying as if she felt the pain as much as I did. I tell you, I stopped feeling sorry for myself and didn't feel as much pain. One of my tears would draw ten of hers, so I had to stop crying or she would drown the two of us," he explained with a laugh.

"Anyway, she would bike all the way up here to visit Belinda, and Belinda really looked forward to her visits, from what I heard. I think Grandma Olivia was jealous. Laura never biked over to visit her." He smiled, turning to me. "Like you, Laura cared more about other people than she cared about herself, especially those who were less fortunate, whether it was because of lack of money or lack of love."

We pulled into a parking space and got out of the truck and made our way to the entrance of the home. A pretty nurse greeted us just inside the lobby. Her name tag read MRS. WILLIAMS. I hadn't seen her before. She didn't look much older than her late twenties.

There weren't as many residents sitting there as the last time I had visited, but once again, my appearance, and especially Cary's, too, drew all their attention, quieted their conversations, interrupted their checkers and card games.

I explained who we were and whom we had come to visit, but before Mrs. Williams could respond, Mrs. Greene stepped out of her office and drew our attention as she came toward us, her high heels clicking over the tile floor.

"Well, it's been some time since your last visit," she

said. "You led me to believe you would be here frequently," she added as if she had caught me in a lie.

"I've been away," I explained. She smirked and turned to the nurse. "I'll see to them, Mrs. Williams."

"Yes, ma'am," the nurse said and returned to the other residents.

"Your grandmother is in the garden," she said, glancing quickly at Cary. "This is a family member, I assume?"

"Yes, he is. How is she doing?"

"Quite well, actually. I should warn you that since you've been here, Miss Gordon's formed a friendship with one of our other residents, Mr. Mandel, and the two of them spend most of their time together."

Cary smiled but Mrs. Greene didn't even acknowledge him.

"It's just a companionship, of course," she continued, speaking through her tight jaw as she led us through the lobby and down a corridor to a side door that opened on the gardens and walkways, "but we encourage such things. We find it's good for their mental health to develop relationships with other residents."

"You talk about them as if they're some other species," I remarked. Cary's eyes widened, surprised at my tone of voice and confrontational demeanor, but I recalled this woman's attitude about me the other times we had met, and I was sure she was somehow on Grandma Olivia's payroll.

"The elderly practically are some other species," she replied, not skipping a beat. "However, only someone who has to work with them day in and day out would understand, I'm afraid."

She flashed as artificial a smile at us as I had ever seen and then nodded toward Grandma Belinda and a short, bald man sitting on a bench. He had a dark wood cane and leaned on it as he sat. His glasses had slipped down the bridge of his nose until they tottered at the very crest of his narrow nostrils. He wore a blue suit jacket, but pants of a lighter shade, almost gray actually. His tie was awkwardly knotted with one half far longer than the other and his socks sagged around his ankles.

As we approached I was hoping Grandma Belinda would remember me. When her face brightened, I thought she had.

"Well, look who's here, Thomas, my grandnephew and grandniece," she said and I realized that because I had come with Cary, she assumed I was Laura.

"No, Grandma," I said. "It's Melody, not Laura."

"Melody?" She looked at Cary.

"That's right, Aunt Belinda. It's your granddaughter, Melody. How are you?"

She looked from him to me and blinked rapidly. Even though she appeared to be struggling with her memory, she was far from as pale and drained as she had been the last time I had visited. She looked bright, her cheeks a little rosy. She had taken care to brush her hair neatly, and she even wore a little lipstick. I saw she was holding on to Mr. Mandel's left hand. He smiled up at us, nodding.

"Oh," Grandma Belinda said. "I want you two to meet Mr. Mandel. He used to be an accountant and can still add lots of numbers in his head, big numbers!"

"Don't exaggerate, Belinda. I'm not anything like I was," he said jovially. "Pleased to meet you. I guess I'll let you visit with your family, Belinda," he said, rising and patting her softly on the back of her hand.

"You don't have to leave, Mr. Mandel," I said, seeing the disappointment on Grandma Belinda's face.

"No, no, I have to talk to Mrs. Landeau about her tax shelter investments. I promised her. You go on. Here, take my seat," he said to me.

Grandma Belinda looked sadly after him as he wobbled away on his cane. Then her eyes shadowed, growing deep, dark, her face turning angry and resembling Grandma Olivia's face.

"I know what she's up to, asking him for advice," she muttered. "She had her eyes on him the moment he came over to sit with me in the dining room. Green with envy, that one. I bet she hasn't a cent invested in anything anymore. She's just lying to get him to pay attention to her. I know that type. They can't stand to see someone else happy."

Cary laughed. I shook my head at him so he would stop; I didn't want Grandma Belinda to think he was laughing at her. Then I sat beside her, taking her hand into mine.

"Grandma, don't you remember my coming to see you before?" I asked. "Don't you remember our talks?"

She glanced up at Cary and then smiled at me.

"Of course, I remember. How are your parents?"

Cary and I exchanged looks of disappointment. Should we confront Grandma Belinda with doses of reality or was it better to assume the roles her confused mind assigned us?

"Look at me, Grandma Belinda. I'm Melody, Haille's daughter, your granddaughter. I'm not Laura. I've come to tell you about Haille. I went to see her in California."

She stared at me, pressing her lips together. Then her face turned harder, her eyes colder.

"I don't have a daughter," she said. "Everyone has to stop saying that." She turned to look after Mr. Mandel, her voice full of rage. "Now you've gone and chased Mr. Mandel away and that Corina Landeau is going to get her claws into him. Every time I find someone, someone tries to steal him away. My sister's no exception either." She turned back to us and her face suddenly softened again with a sweet smile. "How's your mother? You tell her I enjoyed the cookies and if she wants to make me some more, I won't object."

"Grandma," I said with more desperation, "please, try to remember my other visits. I'm Melody, Melody, Haille's daughter."

She continued to look after Mr. Mandel and from the faraway look on her face, I could tell she wasn't listening to me. I sighed deeply and Cary put his hand on my shoulder.

"Grandma Olivia wanted me to come up here and give

her a dose of reality. I think she knew what I would find," I said bitterly.

"She was here," Grandma Belinda said, her gaze still fixed away from us. "She paid me a visit. I suppose I'm to be honored."

"Who was here, Grandma?" I asked.

"Her majesty, who else?" she said, turning back to us. "She told me Haille was dead, killed in a car accident long ago. So you see, I can't have a granddaughter. I don't have anyone. I had Mr. Mandel, but now—"

"That's not true, Grandma. She lied. You have me, Grandma," I said. "Please, look at me, remember me. I visited you before. Don't you remember?" I cried, practically pleading with her. She stared at me, her eyes empty.

I turned to Cary and so did Grandma Belinda.

"How's your mother, Cary?" she asked. "Does she still do that beautiful needlework?"

"Yes, she does, Aunt Belinda." He smiled and she nodded.

"I used to do needlework, but my fingers are too clumsy now. That's what happens. You get older and your fingers get clumsy." She shook her head sadly and then turned back toward Mr. Mandel and pressed her lips together so hard little white lines of rage formed.

"Just look at her beaming over there," she muttered under her breath. "He's talking and she's beaming. She doesn't have a penny invested. I told him, but men don't listen. Some other woman bats her eyelashes at them and they go chasing after them. You understand, don't you?" she asked turning back to me as if she just realized I was sitting beside her. She smiled. "Just look at you. Look at you. You look so grown up, Laura. So grown up. Don't fall in love too fast," she warned as she turned back to look at Mr. Mandel. "Why don't we just walk over there and I'll pretend to need him to help me with my money, too. Yes," she said, pleased that she'd come up with a solution to the problem.

"Grandma . . ."

She continued to stare after Mr. Mandel.

"It's no use, Melody," Cary said. "She's not going to remember. You're just wasting time and facing more disappointment."

"But she is all I have left, Cary. I have no other family," I moaned.

"You've got me," he said emphatically.

"I thought she'd remember," I said, gazing at her wistfully. "I thought we'd have some time together, but obviously Grandma Olivia made sure we wouldn't," I added. "She came up here and confused her. She did it deliberately."

"Let's go, Melody."

"She's jealous of everything, even the fragile relationship I was building with my grandmother. She just came bursting in here and swept it all away."

"Melody, you're getting yourself all worked up. Come on," he urged.

"Do me a favor," Grandma Belinda said when I stood up. "Just go over there and ask Mr. Mandel to come back. Tell him I need him right away."

"He'll come back to you, Grandma," I said. "You're much prettier than she is."

"I am?" She brightened again and nodded. "Yes, I am much prettier, aren't I?" she agreed, brushing the sides of her hair with her palms. "He'll see that. She's got that mole on her chin with tiny hairs. I don't even have many wrinkles, do I?" She turned to us, raising her face to the sunlight, her eyes closed, her lips pursed like a young flirt.

"No, Grandma, you don't," I said and touched her cheek. She opened her eyes and gazed up at me.

"You look like an angel now," she said. "Your mother must be very proud of you."

"She is," Cary said quickly. "Very proud."

"That's nice. That's the way it should be."

She turned back to glare in Mr. Mandel's direction. Cary tugged my hand and I stood up beside him.

"She'll be all right," he said.

"You're right," I said. I leaned over and gave her a kiss on her cheek, but she didn't notice. Her gaze was locked on Mr. Mandel. "Bye Grandma. I'll come back. I promise."

"Don't forget the cookies," she called as we started away. I looked back at her once before we left the garden. Mr. Mandel had left the other woman and was hobbling down the path toward her and she looked very contented, very happy.

"Maybe it's time you started thinking more about yourself, about us," Cary said as we left the rest home. "Maybe it's time we both looked to the future and not to the past, huh?"

"Maybe," I agreed, but I wasn't as confident as he was that the past would let us do that.

I said nothing to Grandma Olivia about her visit to the rest home. I wasn't going to give her the satisfaction of knowing that she had once again gotten her way. When she asked about my visit, I said it was fine and left it at that. If I was to survive in her world, I had to learn to play the game her way. For the time being, I would pretend to be the young woman she wanted me to be.

The next day, as Grandma Olivia had promised, Miss Burton arrived at the house to begin my education in etiquette, making me feel from the start that I wasn't much better than some hick who had just arrived on these precious Cape Cod shores. I was sure it was how Grandma Olivia had described me to her.

She called me down to the parlor and introduced me.

"Miss Burton, I'd like you to meet my granddaughter, Melody," Grandma Olivia said, and I looked at the tall, thin woman who stood so straight, I thought she had a steel rod for a spine. She had very small shoulders, the bones of which pressed up sharply against the dark blue cotton dress that hung over her body in a straight line. Its hem reached her ankles and it was buttoned at the collar.

Miss Burton said nothing but held out her hand.

"Hi," I offered, shook her hand quickly, backed away

and looked at Grandma Olivia, whose head bobbed slightly in approval.

"Until school begins, Miss Burton will meet with you promptly at nine A.M. each weekday morning. After school begins, you will arrange your schedules accordingly."

"For how long?" I asked.

"For as long as it takes to turn you into a lady," Grandma Olivia replied curtly.

"I think I am a lady," I returned. Grandma Olivia grinned coldly and looked at Miss Burton.

"As you see, you have a real challenge here, Louise."

"I'm sure we'll do what we can," Miss Burton said, still scrutinizing me intently.

"Then I'll leave you to begin. I know you need all the time allotted for your lesson. And then some," Grandma added and walked out of the parlor. For a moment Miss Burton and I just looked at each other, sizing each other up like two combatants. Then she cleared her throat and took a step toward me as if someone had given her a shove from behind.

"I can help you only if you want to be helped," she said grimly.

"I don't think I need to be helped," I replied honestly, since she wanted to be frank.

"Oh, my dear," she said smiling and shaking her head, "you most definitely need to be helped."

"Really?" I said dryly. "And how can you tell so quickly, or are you basing everything on what my grandmother has told you about me?"

"I make my own evaluations of people. Let's simply begin with your entrance this morning. Mrs. Logan introduced you properly to me. A young person is always introduced *to* an older person, but you don't say 'Hi.' The very least you say, is simply 'Hello.' This is acceptable in any situation except, of course, after a very formal introduction. We had a somewhat formal introduction. You should have said, 'Hello, Miss Burton, I'm glad to meet you,' or 'How do you do, Miss Burton.' Furthermore, a formal verbal greeting should be accompanied by direct eye contact, which indicates that you are actually paying attention to the person you are acknowledging. You let your eyes wander to Mrs. Logan, the room, me, Mrs. Logan, back to me again," she lectured. "Should I continue?" she asked.

"I guess," I said, feeling a tight knot form in my stomach.

"An older person extends his or her hand first to a younger one, as I just did, but you don't take someone's hand limply as if yours is boneless or as if you're grasping an empty glove. Of course, you don't squeeze too hard, but you should be firm and you should look the person directly in the eyes when you shake.

"Next," she continued without skipping a beat, "is your dreadful posture. A person who stands erect and sits erect looks best, looks confident, looks like someone of worth. Rounded shoulders, slouching, folding your arms across your body as you are now doing . . . all this shows your sloppiness and lack of refinement immediately. Your shoulders should be back, chin in and slightly up, abdomen and stomach in, back straight and knees relaxed. You may keep your arms at your sides, relaxed, as well. Now, let me see you take that seat," she said nodding toward the overstuffed chair to my left.

I eyed it like a challenge of great proportions, positive that whatever I did would be wrong. Nevertheless, I stepped up to the chair, turned, looked directly at her and sat. She laughed.

"What's so funny?"

"You don't really sit like that. You would never be so stiff, nor do you flop into a chair. Sit softly and keep your knees together," she added, nodding at my legs. "The only people who want a view of your undergarments are degenerates. You should sit a bit sideways to keep from sprawling into the chair."

"These pillows are so soft that I—"

"More reason to be aware of your posture and how you appear to others in the room."

"I don't think I look especially sloppy," I protested.

"You don't look sloppy, but you don't look like a young woman of refinement, a woman of quality, stature, a woman who would attract someone of like ilk," she insisted. "You are part of a very distinguished family now. You have a responsibility to be distinguished yourself, and sitting in a chair with your knees wide enough apart to drive a truck between them, slouching when you stand, moving in jerky motions, gawking, all of that makes you look more like someone brought up by uneducated, unsophisticated people of low quality."

"That's not true. I was brought up by good people, decent people who cared about other people and—"

"Then why don't you try to make them proud of you, proud of what you can become and proud of who you now are?" she retorted before I could continue my protest.

I swallowed back my pride and indignation.

"I will be only as good a teacher as you permit me to be and you will be only as good a student as you allow yourself to be. Shall we begin or for the next hour would you rather we debate whether you need my help or not?" she asked firmly, never relaxing her proper posture or letting any warmth into her cold brown eyes.

"I'll try," I finally said, breathing deeply, determined not to cry.

"Good. Then let's begin. Walk out and walk in again, pretending we are meeting for the first time. Keep thinking about your posture as you enter the room."

I rose and left the parlor. For a moment I was tempted to rush out the front door. Then I gazed down the corridor and saw Grandma Olivia watching me. I knew the satisfaction she would get from seeing me flee. She would just nod and say she knew I didn't have it in me to rise to her level. Furious at the thought of her ridicule, I pulled back my shoulders, held my head high, and returned to the parlor.

Miss Burton offered her hand and I shook it firmly and said, "Hello, Miss Burton. I'm pleased to meet you."

She smiled and nodded toward the chair. I sat as she had instructed and placed my hands in my lap.

"Very good," she said. "We'll make a lady of you yet."

"I think being a lady comes from more than knowing how to say hello," I told her.

"Of course it does my dear. The guiding principle of etiquette is thoughtfulness. There are ten commandments of everyday behavior. Never," she began, wagging her long, thin and bony forefinger at me, "talk only about yourself, never gossip, never ask personal questions or pry, never intentionally embarrass anyone, never stare or point at someone, never chew gum with an open mouth or snap it, or make bubbles, never display affection in public," she said, pausing for breath. "From what I understand, that's a commandment you young people today violate often."

"I don't," I protested.

She shook her head.

"You must become your own best critic and to do that, you must not lie, especially to yourself. That's what happens when you lie to others; you end up lying to yourself."

"But —"

"Didn't you kiss someone right out here in this driveway recently?" she asked.

I sat, my mouth agape. Grandma Olivia told her about my kissing Cary?

"Don't keep your mouth open like that. It's not only impolite, it's unbecoming."

"I—"

"Kissing in public is showing affection, wouldn't you agree? Let's move on," she said standing. "Today we want to concentrate on eating."

"Eating?"

"Mealtime manners, my dear. Please, follow me to the dining room."

I rose and started toward the door.

"Always permit the older person to leave first," she instructed. Embarassed, I stopped and allowed her to walk out first. "Please, come along," she said. "There is no need to wait that long behind me."

I shook my head and followed her to the dining room, feeling like a puppy being housebroken. As we passed the stairway, I noticed Loretta standing in the shadows, gazing down at me. Her face was shrouded in the gloom, and I could only wonder whether Loretta would turn out to be my only friend in this cold and heartless home. Or would she, too, prove to be another of Grandma Olivia's minions, too frightened to do anything but her bidding?

If only I knew I could trust Loretta, I would reach out to her and tell her to watch closely, I was about to beat Grandma Olivia at her own game.

My first opportunity came at dinner that night. As I headed toward the dining room, I heard voices in the parlor and paused by the doorway in time to hear Grandma Olivia say, "He's become impossible, a blithering idiot. I can't permit him to be seen in public anymore. I want you to call in some favors and put him at the head of the list, Nelson."

"But I thought the doctor said that might only exacerbate his condition," Judge Childs replied.

"What about my condition? Don't you think it's been more than exacerbating for me?"

I stepped forward and the Judge saw me.

"Oh, Melody!" he exclaimed getting up to greet me.

I held out my hand the way Miss Burton had instructed, standing erect and holding out my arm fairly stiffly to prevent him from embracing me. I was uncomfortable with him showing me any affection in front of Grandma Olivia. I knew that if she suspected the relationship I was developing with my grandfather she would destroy it as quickly as she had my fragile bond with Grandma Belinda.

"Good evening, Judge Childs," I said. "It's nice to see you again."

He paused as if struck dumb for a moment and then smiled and took my hand for a very quick greeting, glancing at Grandma Olivia as he did so. She nodded approvingly.

"I'm happy to see you've come back."

"Thank you," I said with a tight smile, hoping he would go along with my ploy.

"Er . . . we were just . . . relaxing before dinner," he explained with some awkwardness.

He looked as dapper as ever, albeit a little older, grayer, his face a bit thinner. He wore a navy sports jacket and khaki pants, a striped cravat tied loosely around his neck.

"Isn't Grandpa Samuel coming to dinner?" I asked. "I haven't seen him all day."

"No," Grandma Olivia said sharply. "His condition is worse. The doctor will be seeing him in the morning."

"Is there anything I can do to help?" I asked, wishing I could will Grandpa Samuel well again.

"There is nothing any of us can do," she replied dryly. Just then, Loretta came to the doorway, and with a small curtsey announced dinner was ready.

"Finally," Grandma said, rising. Judge Childs held out his arm to her and she took it quickly, the both of them heading for the doorway. I stepped aside to let them leave first and then quickly followed them down the corridor.

"You must tell me about your trip West," the Judge said when we were all sitting at the table. "Perhaps you can come by one day to visit," he added, after throwing a nervous glance at Grandma Olivia.

"I'd like that, Judge Childs," I said, unfolding my napkin and placing it in my lap. Grandma Olivia studied my posture as I sat straight, my spine pressed firmly against the back of my chair.

As soon as the soup was served and Grandma Olivia picked up her spoon, the Judge and I began to eat. Except for Grandma Olivia's house, I had never eaten anywhere where there were so many pieces of silverware next to the plate. Miss Burton had explained that we always start with the implement of each type that is farthest from the plate. We ate quietly for a moment, Grandma Olivia and I eyeing each other. When the level of our soup became too low for the spoon, Grandma Olivia scraped the bottom of her soup dish, loud enough to be heard.

I tipped mine, lifting the near edge and pointing the bowl away from myself.

"I believe this is the proper way to do it, Grandma," I said, delighted to see her face redden. The Judge started to laugh, but stopped the moment he saw the rage in Grandma Olivia's eyes.

"I know the way to do it. I wasn't ready yet," she replied.

"Your spoon sounded as if you were," I said. Although I was determined to see my plan through, I was beginning to think I might have to take things a bit slower.

She pressed her lips together and tilted her bowl properly, but she only took one more spoonful. When we had both finished, we left our spoons in the soup dish, moving almost simultaneously and looking like two competitors vying for a prize in mealtime etiquette. I saw the question marks in the Judge's eyes.

Trying not to grin, Loretta removed the dishes and returned with our appetizers, clams on the half shell.

"I assume you've visited with Sara and the children since your return," the Judge said. "How are they doing?"

"As best as can be expected. Cary and May really miss their Dad. And, of course, Aunt Sara is just so sad," I replied.

"Please give Sara my best when you see her again," he said. "I will have to do something to help that poor family," he added, shaking his head sadly.

When Grandma Olivia began to eat her clams, the Judge and I dug into ours. The clams were served on cracked ice arranged around containers of cocktail sauce. We speared the clams with our shellfish forks and dipped them into the sauce and ate them in one bite.

"Sweet," the Judge said, patting his belly contentedly.

Our salads followed and then our entrée, which tonight was lambchops. I almost choked on my meal when the Judge took one by the bone and gnawed at the meat. I could only imagine what Miss Burton would say to that! Grandma and I cut ours daintily and ate in small bites. When I was finished, I put my knife and fork on the plate and sat back. Loretta took my dishes and silverware, and then collected Grandma Olivia's. The Judge didn't relinquish his until every morsel was gone. Then he smacked his lips and remarked about the flavor of the meat.

"This is one of the best restaurants in Provincetown," he quipped.

"And the price is right," Grandma Olivia muttered. The Judge roared with laughter and then sat forward, his elbows on the table as he clasped his hands.

"So, Melody, you're about to start your senior year, then," he said. "I bet you're excited about that."

"Yes, I am," I replied honestly.

"I'm thinking of Rosewood for her as a prep school," Grandma Olivia said, always anxious to put in her two cents' worth.

"Oh yes, a fine place. I think Congressman Dunlap's daughter is there this year, if I'm not mistaken."

"You're not," Grandma Olivia said.

Loretta brought in our coffee and a lemon cake, which the Judge eyed covetously. When Grandma Olivia lifted her cup, she spilled some of her coffee into the saucer. It was as if a solo performer at a concert had hit a sour note. She froze for a moment and then continued, sipping her coffee and then putting the cup back, her attention shifting to the lemon cake.

"Shouldn't you replace that saucer, Grandma?" I asked her. She fired a look at me and sat back.

"Loretta," she called. Loretta appeared. "I'd like a new saucer, please."

"Right away, Mrs. Logan," Loretta said and hurried back to the kitchen. The Judge's smile widened. Grand-

241

ma reached forward again for the lemon cake. She cut herself a piece and passed the cake plate to the Judge.

"I was told that the plate is to be passed counterclockwise, Grandma. Wasn't that correct?" I asked, trying to sound as innocent as I could manage, considering my knees were knocking. Her face turned so purple, so fast, that I was worried she might do some actual harm to herself. She took the cake plate back so quickly, her hand trembling so much the cake slipped to the edge. In an effort to balance it again, she overcompensated and the cake fell, splattering in front of the Judge, who pulled back to avoid being hit by the icing.

"Whoops," he said with a laugh. Loretta came charging toward the table.

Grandma Olivia, as red as a sunburnt tourist, jerked her chair away from the table to permit Loretta full access to the mess.

"No harm done," the Judge said. "I'll eat that anyway it looks, Loretta."

She smiled at him but shifted her eyes toward Grandma Olivia as if she felt she would somehow be held responsible.

"Nonsense," Grandma Olivia said. "Loretta, take that back into the kitchen and make it look presentable again."

"Yes, ma'am," she said, hurrying away with the smashed cake.

"I would have eaten it off the table," the Judge said to lighten the moment, but Grandma Olivia glared daggers at him until he sat back like an obedient little boy. Then she turned slowly to me.

"If you hadn't interrupted like that—"

"I was trying to practice what I've been taught, Grandma. I'm sorry, but Miss Burton says we shouldn't save our best manners for the outside world. She says the people with whom we live deserve our best manners even more."

"Miss Burton?" the Judge asked.

"Someone I hired to teach her the finer ways," Grandma replied quickly.

Loretta returned with the cake somewhat repaired, only this time she went around the table and served us each our piece.

"Looks scrumptious, doesn't it?" the Judge said.

"Yes, it does," I said and cut my piece with my fork. Grandma Olivia only nibbled at hers and left more than half on the plate.

Just as Loretta returned to take away the dishes, we heard the doorbell. She paused for orders.

"See to that first, Loretta," Grandma said.

"Expecting someone?" the Judge asked.

"Not at all," she said, obviously annoyed to be disturbed. A moment later, Loretta returned with Cary behind her. He was carrying a covered pie dish.

"Oh, sorry I got here too late, Grandma," he said, "but Ma sent over a homemade cranberry pie. I picked some early berries and she made it just this afternoon."

"Hmm . . . I've never cared much for cranberry pie," Grandma Olivia said, sniffing haughtily.

"I love it," the Judge said, winking at me.

"Then you take it," she said with a wave of her hand.

"Thank you. And Cary, you thank your mother for me," he said as Cary stepped forward with the pie.

"Put that in a box for Judge Childs, Loretta," Grandma Olivia commanded. "You should have brought it earlier if you expected us to eat it tonight," she told Cary.

"I had some things to do at the dock and . . ."

"Oh, don't worry about it," the Judge said. "It won't go to waste, that's for sure."

Cary stood there awkwardly, waiting for an invitation to sit at the table, but Grandma Olivia wasn't offering any. He glanced at me and then smiled at the Judge.

"May I be excused?" I asked. "I'd like to go for a walk on the beach."

She glared icily at me.

243

"It's getting late," she said sternly.

"Late?" the Judge asked and looked at his watch as if he were the one who somehow mistook the time.

"For walks on the beach," she explained. "I thought you had problems at the dock, Cary."

"It's all been fixed, Grandma. I can stay for a short visit," he said, practically pleading. Reluctantly, she nodded.

I rose.

"Thank you, Grandma. Judge Childs, I enjoyed dining with you tonight. I hope I'll see you soon."

"Anytime you want, my dear. Just come right over," he said, smiling happily. Thankfully Grandma Olivia was too wrapped up in her own steam to think the Judge's invitation odd.

I left the table and accompanied Cary to the back door. When we stepped outside, I felt as if I had thrown off shackles. The night air never felt so refreshing.

"What's going on in there?" Cary asked. "You could cut the tension with a knife."

"Grandma and I are practicing good table manners," I said and laughed. "It appears she is not as perfect as she thinks she is. I think I'm going to have some fun with all this proper this and proper that."

Cary took my hand and we walked down to the beach. The ocean was calm, the tide lapping softly at the shore. In the distance I saw the tiny lights of a tanker. Stars glittered just above the water, some looking like strings of sparkling diamonds. There was no moonlight, but the evening was clear enough so that the heavens glowed down over us.

"You sure you want to live with her?" Cary asked. "She looked meaner than ever tonight. Where was my Grandpa? After the whole pie thing, I was afraid to ask," he explained.

"She has him shut up in his room. I overheard her talking to the Judge. I think she's getting Grandpa Samuel placed in the same home my grandmother is now in," I said.

"Is he that bad?" Cary asked, unable to keep the tremor from his voice.

"He's babbling, confusing things I don't understand and he's not looking after himself, Cary. Unfortunately, I think she might be right. He needs help."

"It's like everything's falling apart around us," Cary said sadly. "Ma won't break out of her depression. And May is so unhappy."

"I'll come by tomorrow," I promised, "and spend time with them."

"Thanks. I know they both miss you terribly."

We paused, both gazing out at the water. He slipped his arm around my waist and I leaned my head on his shoulder. I felt his lips on my hair, my forehead and then on my temples. I lifted my head toward him and we kissed, a long, soft kiss. Then he embraced me and turned me around toward him so he could kiss me again. I heard his breathing quicken.

"I love you, Melody. I don't think an hour goes by that I don't think of you, even when I'm asleep," he said.

"Cary, We have a problem," I said pulling away and taking a few steps down the beach.

"What?" he asked, following me slowly.

"Grandma Olivia doesn't want us to spend so much time together. She's practically forbidden it."

"What? Why?"

"She's planning out my life, designing it, and in her design, there is no place set aside for you," I told him, uncertain how to soften the blow.

"What? But—"

"So, I think it would be best if we don't let her know how much time we spend together. The less she knows about it, the better. She'll only make trouble for us, for you," I said.

"How can she do that?" he asked worriedly.

"Any way she wants. And every way you *don't* want." I said. "Why cause problems anyway, if we don't have to? The more I see of the adult world, the more I realize it's built around millions of white lies that get strung into chains of illusion and deception anyway. I'm tired of fighting it, Cary. If we have to steal our happiness, we'll steal it," I said firmly.

He smiled.

"As long as I'm with you, I don't care how we do it," he said.

"For the time being, I'm going to let her believe I'm doing everything she wants. It will make things easier for all of us. Your mother doesn't need any more turmoil in her life at the moment. None of us do," I said. He nodded.

"You're getting to be a pretty strong person, Melody."

"Whether I want to or not," I replied. He laughed and then embraced me again for another long kiss. This time his hands moved over my arms and my waist, climbing to my breasts. I moaned and sank against him, my legs weakening.

"Cary."

"I missed you so much," he said. "When can we be together like we were?"

"Soon," I promised. "Soon. We better get back now though."

He nodded reluctantly. As we approached the rear of the house, I gazed toward the basement stairs, recalling when Cary had first shown me pictures of my mother and revealed she had been living with Grandpa Samuel and Grandma Olivia, growing up with my stepfather and Uncle Jacob as if she were their sister.

"Grandpa Samuel mumbled about some other secrets hidden in the basement, Cary. Do you think it's true? Or just his delusions talking?"

"I'm sure that's all it was," Cary said, but as we passed the stairway, I felt the shadows drawing me, beckoning, promising revelations that would chill me to the bones.

Someday I would have the courage to see.

But for now, I needed my courage just to make it through the day.

# 14

## ❧

# *Sacred Moments*

*E*xcept for Theresa Patterson, whose father had worked for Cary's father and now Cary, I had made few friends at the high school. After I had played my fiddle and sang in the variety show at the end of the school year, people took more notice of me, but since I was in California I hadn't spent time with any of the other girls during the summer. A few were curious about where I had been, and when I told them I had been to Hollywood visiting friends, they were more than interested. Since I couldn't really reveal the details of my trip they soon grew bored and stopped finding excuses to drop by my locker and chat.

On Tuesdays every week after school, I spent an hour or so with Miss Burton. Since our initial first meeting, I felt less defensive and even began to like her. Her husband had died five years ago, and both her children lived in Florida. In many ways she was just as lonely as I was.

"Etiquette," she explained during our second session, "is really nothing more than the Golden Rule put to

247

work. You are simply developing ways, manners, behavior to treat people as considerately as you would like them to treat you. You show them respect and expect them to show you respect. You treat older people with veneration and hope that when you are older, that's how you will be treated. You practice etiquette at meals so you don't do anything unappetizing. You wouldn't want it done to you. And there are always the problems that come from wondering how to behave at special occasions, how to behave with royalty, with high government officials, et cetera. Etiquette gives us the guidelines that make us comfortable in these settings.

"Isn't it nice to know how to introduce someone to somebody whose name you've forgotten? Why embarrass that person or make him or her feel bad? Isn't it comforting to know how to properly thank people, invite people, console people, what to do at weddings, funerals and birthdays? All of this will certainly come in handy when you're in the business world or looking for a career," she explained.

I stopped resisting, and listened and learned. Whenever I could, I pointed out Grandma Olivia's failures and mistakes, although now I usually chose them one at a time. I especially liked to do it in front of one of her distinguished guests.

Finally, one day she paused at the dining room table when we were eating alone and said, "I know why you're criticizing my table manners or my dinner invitations, but I want you to know it no longer bothers me as much as you hope it will. Furthermore, I am happy you are learning these things and despite yourself, are becoming refined. In the end when you are finished being a brat, you will come to me and thank me," she predicted. Deep down I couldn't help but wonder if she was right and from that day forward I stopped correcting her.

I really did have to try and keep some peace since it was just the two of us in the house now. At the end of the first week of school, I had returned home to learn that

Grandpa Samuel had been taken to the rest home. I didn't realize it until Grandma Olivia and I sat at the dining room table that night. After Loretta served us our appetizer, Grandma Olivia announced Grandpa Samuel's fate without a crack in her voice or a tear in her eye.

"I had to have Samuel taken to the home," she said. "He's become impossible."

"He'll be there forever then?" I asked.

"As long as forever is, yes," she replied.

I nodded.

"I'll visit him whenever I visit Grandma Belinda," I declared.

"Don't be surprised if he forgets who you are entirely. According to the doctor, he's only going to get worse," she said.

"I'm so sorry. I wish there was something we could do to help him."

"That's old age. The weight of grief, disappointment, a lifetime of struggling take their toll sooner on some than it does on others. It will be your fate as well as mine. It's best to prepare for it rather than try to deny it. Only the weak live in illusion. I don't expect you to like me, but I'm hoping you will come to respect what I'm trying to do with and for you," she continued.

"Both my sons are gone. My daughter-in-law remains a frail, pitiful creature. I have a deaf mute for a granddaughter and a grandson who keeps hoping his pipe dreams will come true. Yes," she said with a smile, "I do know about Cary's foolish dreams of building boats."

"They're not foolish."

"It's foolish from a business standpoint. He'll always be a plodder, not much of a student, not much of a businessman and certainly not capable of supervising the family fortune. You, on the other hand, will be. It's a great responsibility . . . family. Each great family is like a kingdom unto itself. Whether this one survives or not will rest solely on your shoulders some day. That means you, too, will have to make decisions that won't be popular, but will be best for everyone. Either you will have the strength and will to do it or you won't.

"Every decision you make now, every choice has an impact on the fate of this family. Remember that and you will do well," she advised. "It wasn't easy putting my husband into a home, but it had to be done and it was. Moaning about it won't help him or me," she said, sounding like she needed to convince herself more than me.

"I'll stop in to see him," I repeated.

"Do that, but don't come begging me to bring him home if that's what he asks you," she warned. "I will not allow it."

She looked like an alabaster statue set in the dining room chair. Her decision was unquestionable. I nodded, ate my supper in silence and eagerly retreated to my room to do my homework and leave the long, lonesome shadows she cast through the house.

The days and weeks went by. I devoted most of my time to my schoolwork, not only because that was what Grandma Olivia wanted, but because I truly enjoyed it. The dramatics teacher tried to talk me into trying out for the fall production, but I resisted. I wanted to give Cary and May all my free time. I was there when Cary began the cranberry harvest, and although I didn't play hooky, I was beside him right after school, sometimes bringing May home so he could be free to supervise the work.

Aunt Sara snapped out of her sorrow as best she could. She had spent so much of her adult life caring for Uncle Jacob, anticipating his needs and wants, it was hard for her to stop the routine, stop wondering what favorite food of his she would prepare each night. For a while she continued to wash and iron his clothes, under the guise that Cary might use them. Cary did try to wear some of his father's things, but he had trouble doing it. To take for himself Jacob's possessions, however few, was to admit, each time, that his father was truly, finally, gone.

When I came home from Aunt Sara's I occupied my time by writing letters to Alice Morgan in Sewell, telling her all about my mother. I thought Alice deserved to know since she was the one who had discovered Mommy's picture. Alice called after she had read my first letter. She consoled me and promised to come to Provincetown the first opportunity she had. I never heard from Mommy, of course, but I did call and speak to Holly and Billy a few times. Holly was very concerned about Kenneth and I promised to visit him as often as I could and give her a report.

Kenneth was much better than he had been when I had first returned from California, but he still hadn't started working on anything new. He spent more time than usual at his favorite local pub, and some days he fished or visited a friend in Boston. I felt like a spy, but a good spy since I was making my reports to Holly.

Another sore point around my new home was that Grandma Olivia refused to permit me to get my driver's license or take driver's education. She said the car was the downfall of young people today, and I, a budding debutante, should have men driving me around or use our chauffeur. She did allow me to have a bicycle and I was soon a regular sight along the sides of the Provincetown streets. Although it was quite a ride, I peddled my way out to Kenneth's occasionally on weekends.

One Saturday, I found him walking alone on the beach. He was dressed in his ragged jeans and a T-shirt and was barefoot. I caught up with him, but he didn't acknowledge my presence for quite a while. Instead, he just stared at the water, and when he finally did turn, I saw his eyes were bloodshot, as if had been crying. Or on another drinking binge.

"What's wrong, Kenneth?" I asked, holding my breath.

"Haven't you noticed anything different?" he asked, spreading his arms wide and gesturing across the beach, back toward his house.

"Different?" I gazed around and then it hit me. "Ulysses," I said.

"I buried him this morning."

"Oh Kenneth, no,"

"I woke up this morning, but he didn't. It was like him to die quietly. That dog was never a problem, even as a puppy. He was patient, undemanding, sensitive to my moods." He smiled. "Better than any woman I've known. No wonder they call them man's best friend. We were a team," he said, his voice catching. "I'll miss him."

"I'm sorry, Kenneth. I'll miss him, too."

"I know you will. He took right to you, as I recall," he said trying valiantly to smile. He took a deep breath and we walked along the beach together, the deep silence of sadness linking us during our somber thoughts. Finally, he paused and turned to me with a genuine smile.

"So, you're burning up the academic playing fields, I hear, and look like a shoe-in for class valedictorian."

"Who told you that?"

"Cary," he replied slyly.

"He's been here?"

"Often, lately. I've decided to hire him to build me that sailboat," he said.

"Really, Kenneth?"

"Really."

"That's wonderful. He must be so excited!"

"He's got some good ideas. In his own way, he's a very creative young man, and, he's crazy about you."

"I know," I said blushing.

"What's Her Highness think of it?"

"Forbids the thought," I said.

"Hmm. What are you going to do? She rules with an iron hand," he warned. "And when she brings it down, she usually smothers the victim like an ant."

"She's hard, but we've come to a bit of a truce these days. She hasn't had much to complain about. I'm doing well in school. I'm Miss Burton's favorite pupil, and I listen attentively to Grandma Olivia's nightly lectures about people, responsibility, the importance of family, family, family," I added in a pretend deep voice. Kenneth laughed.

"You little devil. You're humoring her to death, aren't you?" he asked.

"I'm being . . . diplomatic," I said and he laughed harder. We heard a horn and turned to see Cary bouncing down the beach road in his truck.

"Here comes my sailboat engineer," Kenneth said. "I wonder if he's come to see me about it or if there's been some diplomatic maneuvering here for a rendezvous," he teased. My cheeks turned crimson. He laughed and we started toward the house.

"Cary Logan," I cried as we approached him, "why didn't you tell me about the sailboat you're building for Kenneth?" I stood with my hands on my hips. Cary looked at Kenneth, who wore a wide grin.

"I wanted it to be a surprise," he said, shifting the rolled up papers he carried under his arm. "I've got the plans completed, Kenneth," he said.

"All right. Let's spread them out on the table in the studio and study them. I bought some Portuguese bread this morning and your favorite cheese, Melody," he told me.

"Is that a hint to make everyone a sandwich?" I asked suspiciously.

"Now I see," Kenneth said to Cary, "that she is just as quick as you said she was."

Cary roared as the two of them went in to the studio. I joined them fifteen minutes later with our sandwiches and some lemonade. Cary's sailboat plans were on the table and I thought they looked very impressive and professional.

"It looks huge," I remarked.

"Six thousand eight hundred thirty-four pounds with a twenty-nine-and-a-half-foot deck. The cabin will hold up to six people comfortably," Cary said. "You see it has a relatively long waterline, which gives us optimal volume and at the same time favors speed. This double-chine hull with a flat-bottom plate gets us quick immersion of the upper—"

"Cary, you're losing her," Kenneth gently pointed out.

"What? Oh. Sorry," he said.

"I think you might safely say he's got a passion for this," Kenneth remarked.

"It looks . . . beautiful," I said lamely.

"Well I'm sure you can understand this," Cary said, refusing to give up on me. "It's very roomy and has a lot of storage space. Starting at the bow here, there is a chain locker followed by a double berth. There's a twenty-five gallon fresh water tank, storage under the seats, and behind the seats there are lockers and a bookcase. Here's the folding table hinged on the center board case. The hull is built upside down on a framework made from the bulkheads. No temporary molds means no waste."

"Sold," Kenneth said. "Now, can we please eat?"

Cary looked up from the plans, first at Kenneth and then at me and then he smiled.

"Sure," he said. "I'm starving."

Later, when we were alone on the beach, I pretended to be still upset that he had kept all this a secret.

"I just wanted to surprise you," he protested. "Besides," he added sotto voce, "I couldn't be sure Kenneth was serious. You know how erratic he's been these days. I know he's serious now though. He's put the money up for the plans and given me the green light to start. I'll be building the boat here," he said.

"What about the lobster business?"

"I'm making a deal with Roy Patterson, giving him more responsibility and more of the income. I talked it over with Ma, but she doesn't really understand what I'm trying to do and naturally she's afraid for us. I hope I'm doing the right thing," he added. "I just feel like this is my chance. Once I build one boat and others see it . . ."

"You'll do well, Cary. I'm sure you will."

He nodded with a weak smile.

"I hope so. I know if Dad were alive, he'd be furious about it."

"He never wanted to do anything differently, Cary. It wasn't in him to change, but you're creative and you

254

heard Kenneth say you have a passion for it. If anyone knows about being passionate over something creative, it's Kenneth. In the end you'll make us all proud of you."

"I hope, but for the time being, maybe it would be better if you didn't mention anything about it to Grandma Olivia," he said.

"I don't mention anything about you in front of her and she never asks me anything. It's part of the truce that's fallen between us these days," I said.

He smiled, grateful for that.

"Well, since I'll be here most of the time now, maybe you and I can see more of each other and—"

"I'll stop by as often as I can and bring May, too."

"Kenneth's going to Boston this weekend," Cary said quickly. "He told me it would be all right for me to use his place, if I want."

We stared at each other a moment.

"I can't get away overnight, Cary. She would have the dogs at my heels," I said.

"It doesn't have to be overnight, but we could have dinner here and just for one day maybe, feel like we were . . . you know . . . together."

I thought about it. Somehow, lying to Grandma Olivia didn't seem to be such a bad thing.

"I have an idea. I'll talk to Theresa tomorrow. She'll cover for me," I promised. Cary brightened with hope and we kissed. The wind swept through our hair and the ocean spray sprinkled our faces. It made me feel fresh and alive.

Cary insisted I put my bike in the back of his truck so he could drive me most of the way home. I rode the last mile and a half on my bike. When I arrived, I saw that Judge Childs was visiting with Grandma Olivia. He had been coming over more oft n since Grandpa Samuel had been taken to the home. The two of them usually spent their time sipping sherry in the gazebo. Often, the Judge stayed for dinner.

I hadn't yet paid him the visit he expected. I didn't want to talk about Mommy. It was too painful to think about her. Since I had returned from California, she hadn't phoned or written. It was still difficult to accept the fact that she wanted to be out of my life forever. Sometimes I would walk past the cemetery and see the stone with her name on it. Once, I even stopped to pay my respects to the poor anonymous soul who had been made to take Mommy's coffin and grave. In my secret-put-away heart, I mourned for her the way I mourned for myself, imagining her wishing to be with her own people, whoever and wherever they might be.

Maybe she was, I thought. Maybe being next to the bones of your loved ones wasn't what mattered. Perhaps there was something stronger that bound us after death, some linking of the soul that would someday find me greeting Papa George, my stepdaddy and whoever else I loved and who loved me.

The week after I met Cary at Kenneth's I talked to Theresa in the cafeteria during lunch, planning a way for me to spend most of the following Saturday and Saturday night with Cary at Kenneth's house. With midterms coming up, it was easy to claim we would be studying together. What I wasn't prepared for was Grandma Olivia's reaction to my choice of friends. The way she glared at me when I told my story made me feel she had seen right through the subterfuge, but her irritation was drawn from a more polluted well.

"Patterson? Is that the same Patterson who works for Cary? The Brava?"

"Yes, her father is Roy Patterson."

"That's the best you can do? The best friendship you can form at school? What about the Rudolph's daughter or Mark and Carol Parker's daughter? Isn't Betty Hargate, the accountant's daughter, in your class also?"

"I don't get along as well with those girls and they are nowhere near the student Theresa is, despite her being what you call a Brava. I not ashamed of my friendship with her; I'm proud of it."

"I see I'm not getting you out of this town fast enough," she replied.

256

"I'm not moving in with the Pattersons, Grandma Olivia. I'm merely preparing study sheets. You want me to be the valedictorian, don't you?"

She raised her eyebrows, considering.

"There's no mother in that house."

"Her father will be home and you know he's a nice man, a hardworking man."

"You intend to eat dinner with them?" she asked, as if I were going to eat with Aborigines.

"I ate there often last year," I said, "before I realized I was so important."

"Don't be impudent. Very well," she said after another thoughtful pause, "Raymond will take you and pick you up promptly at nine P.M."

"It's Saturday night!" I protested.

"Ten then," she said relenting a bit.

"No one else in my class lives under such strict rules," I complained.

"No one else has your destiny and responsibility," she replied dryly. "Let's not have these silly discussions."

I retreated, feeling I had won as much as I could from her at the moment. When I told Cary, he was ecstatic.

"I'll bring some lobsters and clams for dinner," he said. "We'll have May with us for a while, but I'll take her home in the afternoon."

"That's fine, Cary."

"She wants to know if she can bike out to Kenneth's with you one day. I explained how dangerous it is for her to go on the road by herself. She can't hear cars and trucks."

"I'll come by and get her one day. We'll be all right."

"It'll be a real treat for her," he said. "I haven't been able to do much for her these days and with Ma the way she is . . ."

"It's no problem, Cary. I want to do it," I assured him.

The next day Theresa and I made our final plans at school. The first time I met Theresa I thought she was a very serious girl, pretty but dour to the point of being angry. Since I was new in school, the principal asked her to show me around. We got off to a bad start because she assumed I would look down on her the way other so-called blue bloods did.

I thought she was one of the prettiest girls in the school, with her caramel complexion, black pearl eyes and ebony hair. After she realized I wasn't like the others, she permitted me to get closer to her and we quickly became good friends.

Theresa enjoyed the idea that we were conspiring against my grandmother. She thought of her just as most others did, The Iron Lady, Queen of Snob Hill.

"If she calls for you on the phone, I'll have my brother say we went to the library. Don't worry about my father. He won't ask questions. Since my mother died, he treats me like an adult. Are you going to spend the whole night with Cary?" she asked, her eyes bright with interest.

"No, I have to be back at your house before ten. That's when Grandma Olivia is sending Raymond to pick me up."

"Bummer," she moaned for me. "But, at least you'll have some time alone."

"Theresa Patterson, just hear you," I teased and we laughed. Everyone in the cafeteria gazed at us with jealousy, wondering what delicious secret we shared. Our sealed lips only stirred their curiosity more.

When Saturday came, I was so nervous I was positive Grandma Olivia would become suspicious, but she was preoccupied with a dinner party she was having for Congressman Dunlap and two of his legal aides. The only thing she said that put butterflies in my stomach was that she was sorry I wasn't going to be at the dinner.

"It's important for you to meet important people now," she declared. I thought she would insist I attend the dinner, but she hesitated and added, "but being named class valedictorian is important too. You'll be the first Logan to do so."

The tone of her voice was explicit: Don't fail to do it.

Shaking when I got into the limousine, I took deep breaths and tried to calm down all the way to Theresa's.

As soon as Raymond dropped me off and left, Theresa gave me her bike and I started for the beach. Cary and May were already there, Cary working on the boat. He looked like Adonis, shirtless, his muscles glimmering in the sunlight.

"I was afraid you weren't coming," he said as I walked Theresa's bike over the sandy part of the road. May came running to me. We hugged and I looked at Cary. Neither of us had to say much to each other; it was all in our eyes.

I spent most of the afternoon with May, walking along the beach, searching for shells, telling her about school. She wanted to know more about boys. If any girl needed a big sister, it was May. Aunt Sara wasn't very comfortable explaining things to her. Sex, love and romance embarrassed her. I was the one who had explained what a menstrual cycle was, what changes would happen to her body, what her feelings would be like. Once, we had a long talk about what it meant to fall in love and she told me about a classmate she liked, a boy who had kissed her. Apparently, since I had been away, she had learned much more from her girlfriends at school, for when she looked at Cary and me and the way we spoke, touched and looked at each other, she smiled at us knowingly.

While Cary was bringing May home, I prepared our dinner and set the table. Constantly aware of my curfew, we savored the hours and minutes we had. I waited in front of the beach house, watching the twilight flood the sky with its rosy farewell to the day, flaming the clouds crimson, streaking violet shot through with saffron. Cary returned in the quickest time ever, his truck bouncing hard over the beach ruts.

"Everything's almost ready," I said when he hopped out of his truck and followed me into the house.

"Looks great," he said, but his eyes never left my face. Every time I turned, every time I lifted my gaze from the pots and dishes, I found him staring at me hungrily. My body filled with an ache, a hunger for his lips and his touch. Perhaps it was because we were so far from anyone, alone, in a domestic setting, behaving like married people, whatever the reason, I never felt more desire and passion for him than I did that night. We could barely eat, neither of us saying very much.

Cary leaped out of his seat at the end of the meal to help me clean up. Everything we did seemed designed to keep us under control. It was as if we both understood that the minute we were free of any other distraction, the moment we turned to each other, we would be in danger of consuming each other. Finally, I dried the last dish.

He stood back, gazing at me.

"Melody," he said softly and held out his hand. I took it and he led me out to the guest bedroom. Next to the bed, we kissed and held each other tightly. "I love you," he said.

I took a deep breath, closed my eyes and nodded.

"I love you, too, Cary. Very much."

I kept my eyes closed as his fingers undid the buttons of my blouse. In fact, I stood there, unmoving, waiting as he peeled my blouse down my arms, undid my skirt and drew it below my knees, lifting my leg gently for me to step out of it. Then he kissed my shoulders, my neck and undid my bra, drawing it from me while at the same time, he brought his lips to my nipples and nudged my breasts with his cheeks. My heart pounded hot blood through my body. When his hands lifted from my breasts or my shoulders, I cried out for their return.

Gently, almost in inches, he slipped my panties off. Naked, I stood before him, my eyes locked on his.

"Kenneth couldn't come close to portraying your beauty," he said. "Even if he worked every day for the rest of his life."

I smiled and he undressed himself. Moments later, we were in bed, embracing, moving our arms, our legs, turning ourselves to each other, drawing each other deeper and deeper into each other with every kiss, every touch.

"Are you ready, Cary?" I asked, breathing my last bit

of caution before my thundering heart closed down all avenues of thought and left me longing only for him inside me, making us feel like one.

"Yes," he said with a smile. "Protected."

I felt myself being drawn up higher and higher, dangled above the earth, exquisitely tormented by the danger and the sense of abandon. Our moans mingled until each was indistinguishable from the other. I dug my fingers into his shoulders to hold on and to keep him close. We came at each other like the love-starved people we were; desperate for a loving touch, a longing word.

When it was over, we collapsed in a delightful exhaustion, both gasping for breath, neither able to speak. I took his hand and put it over my heart.

"Feel this pounding," I said, shakily. "It's scary, but wonderful."

"Mine's the same way."

"If we died here together, Grandma Olivia would be very upset," I said and he laughed.

"She'd have everyone involved sworn to secrecy and then she'd have us buried at sea."

"But she wouldn't cancel her dinner party that night," I added.

He laughed and turned to embrace me. We lay there, holding each other, whispering sweet promises, dreaming, constructing our wonderful fantasies, weaving a cocoon of dreams tightly around ourselves. After a while, we stopped and dozed, which almost proved fatal, for when my eyes snapped open, it was nearly nine-thirty.

"Cary!"

I sat up, shaking him to wake him.

"Whaa . . ."

"Hurry, get dressed. Raymond will be at Theresa's before you get me back!"

We both leaped off of the bed and threw on our clothes. We got into the truck and for a few frantic beats it wouldn't start. The engine groaned and groaned.

"Cary!"

"It's okay. Just give me a second," he said. He hopped out and opened the hood, fidgeting.

"Hurry, Cary. She'll make so much trouble for you and your mother if she finds out about us."

He jiggled wires near the battery and tried again, and, thankfully, this time the engine started with a sputter. Then we shot off, bouncing so hard over the beach road, my head nearly hit the roof of the truck cab. Once on the street, he burned rubber until we arrived at Theresa's, just minutes before Raymond and the limousine. I didn't even have a chance to kiss Cary good night. Instead, I jumped out and ran to the house, where Theresa was waiting anxiously.

"You're cutting it kind of close, aren't you?" she remarked with a smile.

"We feel asleep," I whispered.

"No calls, at least."

Moments later, we saw the limousine pull up. I thanked her and rushed out, promising to call her in the morning.

Grandma Olivia's dinner party was still going when I arrived. Her guests were in the parlor talking. I was afraid of what I looked like since I hadn't had time to check my hair or straighten my clothes, but I knew if I didn't stop to say hello, she would be furious. I paused in the doorway.

"Good evening, Grandma," I said.

"Well, did you study hard?"

"Yes, Grandma."

"Good. My granddaughter is the prime valedictorian candidate this year."

Everyone nodded with appreciation.

"Melody, you have already met Congressman Dunlap and his wife."

"Yes, how do you do, Congressman, Mrs. Dunlap," I said, stepping forward. They nodded, smiled and Grandma Olivia looked pleased.

"This is Mr. and Mrs. Steiner and Mr. and Mrs.

Becker," she added. I smiled and greeted the other couples. Then I quickly excused myself and hurried up the stairs.

I washed and got into bed, my fatigue now settling into my body firmly. Despite that, I felt wonderful. When I closed my eyes, I saw Cary's loving face before me and imagined his lips on mine again and again. Across the dunes he was most likely in his attic hideaway, thinking about me, gazing out at the same ocean I saw through my window, the water dazzling under the starlight, each whitecap looking like a string of pearls cast back at the shore.

Below me, the voices grew softer until they drifted out of my hearing and I was left with nothing but my own thoughts, whispering promises, counting dreams that took me softly into sleep.

Over the next month, Cary and I were able to meet secretly twice more, each time as wonderful as the time before. His progress with Kenneth's boat continued and it soon began to take shape. Kenneth brought some friends out to see Cary's work and one of them seriously considered hiring him to do a custom sailboat for him as well.

One early spring afternoon after I picked up May and we both peddled out to Kenneth's, I heard a small bark and saw the most beautiful golden retriever puppy poke its head out of the front door of the beach house. May and I ran to pick him up.

"I'm calling him Prometheus," Kenneth announced. "I figure I'll stay with mythological names."

"He's beautiful, Kenneth."

"I thought you'd like him."

May held him and he licked her face, making her laugh.

"She's growing up, too," Kenneth said. "Starting to look like a young lady."

"I know."

"She'll need you around more," Kenneth warned. "Big sister stuff."

"She already has," I said. His eyes widened.

"Oh? Well, um, that's great that she has you to confide in. I have a second surprise for you," he declared, obviously eager to change the subject. "I'm putting *Neptune* on display . . . finally. We're going to have a showing at the gallery and a pretty big party afterward."

"Where?"

"I suppose this is the third surprise," he said. My heart began to thump. "Your grandfather's house."

"Judge Child's house? Really? Kenneth that's wonderful!"

"He volunteered our home when he heard about the opening at the gallery and I decided, why not? He couldn't even begin to pay me what he owes me. If I don't take what I can, my brother and sister will anyway," he said.

I didn't like his cynicism and he saw it in my face.

"I don't have to love him to let him do things for me, do I?"

"Yes, you do, Kenneth. You have to love him. He's your father, no matter what," I lectured.

"My father . . . died a long time ago in the aftermath of a confession. This stranger with the same name and resemblance is just some old, rich man," he insisted. "Anyway, I'm not doing it for myself. I'm doing it for *Neptune's Daughter*. I think that has a certain sense of irony, don't you? Sure you do," he said before I could reply. "You're one of the brightest young women I've known, Melody. You understand much more than you pretend to understand."

"But Kenneth—"

"Let it be, Melody," he said. "Just let it be."

He smiled at May cuddling Prometheus. Then he looked toward the boat and Cary.

"We'll all take a maiden voyage in a month and celebrate the birth of something very beautiful. Right?" he asked me.

"Sure, Kenneth," I said. "Maybe you should invite

Holly to the opening," I suggested. I wanted him to have someone at his side.

"I already did," he said.

"And she's coming? That's wonderful. I can't wait to see her again."

"I'm not saying she's coming. She still has to check her chart first and be sure it's safe," he teased, his eyes sparkling with mischief.

We watched May rush out to show Prometheus to Cary and then Kenneth looked at me in the strangest way. I tilted my head because of the way he was staring and the way a fleeting shaft of sorrow crossed his face.

"What's wrong, Kenneth?"

"Just for a second, with that soft smile on your face, your eyes caught in the sunlight, you reminded me of Haille when she was not much older than you. It was as if . . . as if time had gone backwards, as if nothing terrible had happened yet.

"Hold on to these moments, Melody. Hold on to them desperately for as long as you can.

"Too soon," he said, his eyes darkening, "too soon the winds of jealousy come barreling down and sweep it all out to sea.

"I hope," he concluded gazing at Cary and May, "fate isn't teasing you as she did me."

He turned and went back inside, leaving me shivering with anxiety. Kenneth had made it an awesomely fearsome thing to even think beyond tomorrow. I was filled with so many emotions, I thought I would simply explode and fly off in that wind he warned me might come.

Like a reader terrified of turning the page, I stepped away from the house and walked toward Cary to tell him the news.

# 15
&

# The Unveiling

As the date of Kenneth's opening for *Neptune's Daughter* drew closer, the excitement in Provincetown built. National art magazines sent writers and photographers. Reporters from newspapers in New York City, Boston and even as far away as Washington, D.C., and Chicago arrived to do interviews and get pictures. An invitation to the gala affair following the display at the Mariner's Gallery was highly prized. Kenneth told me that since I was now an expert in etiquette and formalities, I would have to help him with the design and wording for the invitations. The gallery owner provided us with a select list of people to invite, claiming these were the people who had invested in art or who carried influence in the community.

Two days before the opening and party, Kenneth called and asked me to accompany him to the judge's house, where we would meet with the caterers.

"I'm not good at these things," he claimed. "I need the feminine viewpoint."

I knew he was just nervous about going to his father's

home. From what I understood, he hadn't been there for years. The Judge was nervous about it, too. That was something Grandma Olivia revealed.

"This has the makings of a wonderful event," she told me, "but we have to be sure there will be no unpleasantness and certainly nothing that would feed the insatiable appetites of the gossipmongers. I know you've spent an inordinate amount of time at Kenneth's house and although I haven't seen it yet, I know and everyone else will know that you were the model for the work.

"I'm depending on you to play a role in mitigating any difficult feelings. In other words," she said with a sharp smirk, "make sure Kenneth behaves himself. See if you can get him to dress properly and do something with that moss on his face he calls a beard and that mop he calls his hair."

"Artists aren't exactly businesspeople, Grandma Olivia. The public understands Kenneth."

"Not this public," she assured me. "Actually," she revealed in a rather rare soft moment, "I'm more worried about the Judge. He hasn't slept a night since he volunteered to host the gala celebration. I told him it was a foolish gesture, but he insisted."

"Everything will work out just fine," I said.

She nodded, studying me.

"You have grown and matured quite a bit since you've been living here. I will tell you that I have heard only good things about you from the school officials, and people admire the way you look after my handicapped granddaughter. I feel validated for my faith in you and your potential. Don't do anything to diminish that faith," she added in her usual threatening tone.

"Thank you, I think," I replied and she almost smiled.

"You have been to visit my sister and have seen Samuel this week?" she asked.

"Yes." I wondered if she also knew Cary had driven me there. If she did, she didn't mention it. "They're both about the same. No improvement. Grandpa Samuel

267

simply sits and stares most of the time, barely acknowledging I'm there."

"There won't be any improvement," she predicted. "That's not a place to go for improvement. It's where you go to wait. God's waiting room," she muttered. "I imagine you'll have me put there someday, too. If I need to be, don't hesitate," she advised. "Hopefully, that won't be for a while, but when my time comes, it comes," she concluded.

For the gala Grandma Olivia suggested I wear the dress Dorothy Livingston had bought me in Beverly Hills. All these months she never mentioned the two expensive outfits hanging in my closet, but I knew she was aware of them.

"There's no point in letting something like that go to waste. If someone was foolish enough to spend that sort of money, well . . . take advantage of it. I'd like to see you in it first, of course," she added.

I nodded and ran upstairs to put it on. She scrutinized me for a few moments and nodded.

"Suitable," she declared, "for such an occasion. You are someone with position in this community now. You should look the part. There will be a number of young men from quality families attending, too. I hope you make acquaintances with some of these people. Of course, I'll see to it that you are introduced properly. What are you going to do with your hair?"

"My hair?"

"I can have my beautician come over and do something special for you, if you'd like."

"No, I think I'll just wear it down. Maybe just trim my bangs. I can do that myself."

"If you insist," she said. "I have a ruby and sapphire necklace that would go with that dress," she added. "It was my mother's."

"Really? Thank you," I said, truly honored that she would entrust me with such a gift, even for just one night.

I told Kenneth about Grandma Olivia's new and

improved persona when he picked me up to go to Judge Childs's. I thought he would laugh and make his quips about the Queen Lady or something, but he was very distracted by his own thoughts and anxiety. I talked mostly to keep from riding in dead silence.

When we turned up the road that led to the Judge's house, Kenneth almost turned the car around.

"This is a mistake," he muttered. "I shouldn't have agreed to it. All we needed was a reception at the gallery."

"Please, Kenneth. You know everyone is looking forward to a big party. We'll make sure it's fun."

"Fun," he said as if that were a dirty word.

The Judge's house came into view. I remembered the first time I had been here, how much more impressed with it I was than with Grandma Olivia's home. The Judge's three-story Adam Colonial had been restored in a Wedgwood blue cladding and had a semicircular entry porch. What made it even more unique was its large octagonal cupola. There was an elaborately decorated frieze above all the front windows.

The driveway brought us to a circle where there was a whirl of activity. An army of groundspeople were everywhere pruning and trimming, cleaning fountains and walkways, washing windows, planting new flowers in the rock gardens. When we entered the circular drive, I could see the huge party tent, in front of which the caterers were discussing their setup with Judge Childs. Beside him was his butler, Morton. Everyone turned to look our way.

Kenneth just sat in the jeep staring at the front entrance of the house.

"It must have been very nice growing up here, Kenneth."

"Yes, it was," he said and stepped out of the jeep.

Morton approached as quickly as he could to greet us.

"Why hello there, Mr. Kenneth. It's good to see you, good to see you," he said reaching for Kenneth's hand before Kenneth lifted it. He shook it vigorously and

269

gazed at me. His face was bright with happiness. "And you too, Miss Melody. You're looking fine. Isn't this going to be a celebration. The Judge was up an hour earlier than usual this morning. Neither of us could sleep just thinking about all the festivities. It's good you're here, Mr. Kenneth. Oh, it's a fine, beautiful day, isn't it?"

He stood there, hoping for some softening in Kenneth's face, some sign that the war between father and son had ended.

"Hello Morton. It's good to see you, too," Kenneth said finally offering him a smile. "You know, Morton here was just as responsible for my upbringing as my mother and father," Kenneth said.

"Oh go on with you, Mr. Kenneth. I didn't do much."

"No, just carted us kids around everywhere, watched over us, played with us. You taught me how to swing a baseball bat, didn't you, Morton? Morton could have been a pro," he told me.

"Oh no, Miss Melody. That's not true. I wasn't that good."

"He was great."

"He's awful excited, the Judge," Morton said slapping his hands together. "You want me to get you two something? Maybe a lemonade or coffee or—"

"No, nothing, Morton. I want to make this quick," Kenneth said. Morton nodded.

"Well, I'll be around if you need something."

"You always were," Kenneth said. "It's good to see you, Morton," Kenneth added, warming slightly. Morton's eyes watered.

"And good to see you. He talks about you all the time, Mr. Kenneth. There isn't a day that goes by."

"Okay," Kenneth said, turning to me. "Let's do this."

I followed and we crossed the lawn toward the caterers and Judge Childs.

"Hello," the Judge said, his eyes on Kenneth. Kenneth barely acknowledged him with a small nod.

"I haven't got much time for this," he said quickly.

"Oh. Well, let's get right to it, then. James will tell us

270

the menu and how he wants to set up the serving tables. He suggests we have tables inside and outside the tent, but all the food inside. Is that right, James?"

The short, neatly groomed man smiled.

"Yes, Judge Childs. I think that would work. I will have three tables for the entrées: lobster, shrimp, prime roast and duckling, flounder and bass. We will have two long tables for the salads and vegetables and of course, three Viennese desert tables. I suggest we keep the bar outside the tent. It always makes it less complicated when the liquid refreshment is away from the food," he added. "We will, however, have staff bringing glasses of champagne to everyone."

"How's that menu sound?" the Judge asked. Kenneth was staring at the dock, a distracted expression on his face.

"Fine with me," he muttered.

"Now to the decorations," James resumed. "I thought a bouquet of our emperor tulips, jonquils and some daffodils on every table. I would like to suggest a doorway of roses as an entrace to the tent and—"

"This isn't a wedding," Kenneth snapped. He glanced at me for confirmation.

"I think just some flowers on the tables is enough," I said. James nodded with disappointment.

"I didn't know what to do about music," the Judge said. "James here suggested a trio. I thought we could set up a small stage for them over there," he pointed just to the right of the tent. "I'll get one of those portable dance floors and—"

"We don't need people dancing," Kenneth said.

"No? Okay. We'll just have some music. I just thought . . . but if you think that's a bit much."

"The whole thing's a bit much," Kenneth said and walked toward the dock.

Everyone watched him in silence.

"He's just a little nervous about the showing," I explained.

"Of course," the Judge said. "Well then, James can

show us the colors he chose for the tablecloths and napkins."

"They're right in here," he said, gesturing just inside the tent. I followed and looked over his suggestions for interior decorations with crepe paper, balloons and tinsel. I thought it was all spectacular. The Judge was pleased.

"I'll have valet parking, of course. Let's just hope for good weather. Well now, what's left to do?" he questioned, his eyes gazing after Kenneth.

The caterer rattled off a half dozen things, but the Judge had lost interest.

"It might not be a bad idea for you two to talk before all this," I suggested softly. He glanced at me and nodded.

"Yes, I suppose you are right."

He looked tired, old and unsure of himself. Kenneth stood on the dock looking out at the ocean.

"Let me speak with him first," I said. The Judge looked relieved. I hurried over the lawn and joined Kenneth.

"This is stupid," he said. "Half of these people attending think Art's short for Arthur."

I laughed.

"It'll be nice, Kenneth. Let him make a big deal over you. He wants to do it out of pride."

"Out of guilt," he corrected.

"Yes, maybe guilt, too, but at least he cares, feels remorse. My mother shakes off guilt the way you would shake off a fly."

He turned his eyes to me and smiled.

"You feel sorry for him, don't you?"

"Yes," I said.

He shook his head.

"Don't you understand Haille is the way she is because of what he did?"

"No. Look at what she did to me," I replied. "You don't see me turning into my mother."

His smile softened and widened.

"Talk to him, Kenneth. Just make a little peace between you. It will be good for you as well as him."

He grimaced skeptically.

"You said *Neptune's Daughter* was your greatest work, the work you're most proud of. Let it be a happy time then, from beginning to end."

"Melody, Melody, what am I going to do with you? Despite everything, you keep pushing the gray skies away, searching for that rainbow."

"Help me find it, Kenneth," I replied, my eyes meeting his gaze firmly. He nodded, sighed, gazing at the water and then turned back toward the house. "Come on," he said.

"Come on?"

"You're his granddaughter. You belong in every family discussion now. No more false pretenses among us. That's my only demand," he said. I trailed beside him as he walked toward the house, his home, a place he hadn't been for years, but a place that held all his childhood memories and the memories of his mother.

We entered and he gave me a tour.

"He's kept it pretty much as I remembered it," Kenneth said. He laughed. "My mother and her antiques. Some of these things are worth a lot of money though."

We went upstairs and he showed me what used to be his room. He stood there for a long time, a sad smile on his face. When we descended again, the Judge was standing in the doorway of his office.

"Well," he said, looking from Kenneth to me. "This looks like it's going to be the event of the year, huh? I haven't seen your piece, Kenneth, but Laurence Baker told me it's wonderful. Anybody make a preliminary offer yet? If not, I'd like to make an offer."

"It's not for sale," Kenneth said.

"What?"

"I'm thinking of donating it to the museum after the showing."

The Judge's mouth dropped open. "Why, that's a

mighty fine idea, Kenneth. Mighty fine," he said when he'd finally recovered.

"Well, if you *were* going to sell it, I'd buy it myself," I said, wishing Kenneth would accept money for his creation.

They both looked at me and then Kenneth laughed. The Judge's face broke into a smile, too.

"I bet she would," he said.

"She would," Kenneth agreed. At least they were agreeing on something.

"I'm glad we're having the party here, Ken. Your mother would be very proud," the Judge said. "Oh, that reminds me," he added quickly. "I found something the other day and thought you'd want to have it." He turned and went into the office. We followed. He handed Kenneth a leather picture frame in which there was a photo of his mother and him when he was no more than five or six years old.

"He had that serious, artistic look even back then, didn't he?" the Judge asked me.

"He sure looks deep in thought," I replied.

"I remember when Louise bought that frame. She considered it a prime find. That design's all hand-engraved or something," he continued as Kenneth continued to stare at the picture of himself and his mother. The Judge found it necessary to keep talking. "I think it was somewhere down in Buzzard's Bay. She would walk into those tiny stores and dig around like some miner looking for gold and come out with the craziest stuff sometimes. When she found that frame, she said she had just the picture to put in it."

"Thanks," Kenneth said.

"Oh, sure, sure. So, how have things been otherwise?" the Judge asked.

"Otherwise?" Kenneth's mouth turned in at the corners.

"I mean . . ." The Judge looked at me.

"Whatever you have to say, she can hear it, too. She is your granddaughter," Kenneth said.

"Yes, she is," the Judge said nodding, "and I must say I'm proud of her."

"Even though it's a deep, dark secret?" Kenneth taunted. The Judge's eyes grew smaller. He blew some air between his lips and lowered himself slowly to the leather settee, gazing down at the floor like a man who had just received some very bad news.

"There's no sense in my apologizing to you, Kenneth. I've done that a hundred times and you won't hear it. Anyway, I don't expect you to forgive me for something I can't forgive myself. But," he said raising his eyes to Kenneth, "none of it has stopped me from loving you, son. I'm proud of you and what you've done. All I hope is that you can come to hate me a little less. That's all," he concluded with a deep sigh.

Kenneth turned away for a moment.

"You betrayed us, you know, all of us."

"Yes, I did," the Judge confessed. "I was a weak man; she was a beautiful and very desirable woman. It's no excuse; it's just an explanation," he followed quickly.

"You've spent most of your life sitting in judgment on people. Who sat in judgment of you?"

"You did, son, and the price I paid was too much. If I could change things, I would."

Kenneth didn't look convinced.

"Really, I would. I would sooner die than take away your happiness. I wanted only the best for you. None of this has had any meaning to me since your mother's death and . . . since all of you children left." He looked at me. "It's sort of a miracle that Melody has come back to us."

Kenneth glanced at me and then he nodded.

"Yes, it is."

"And it just pleases me to all get out that she and you have taken to each other."

"She's a pest," Kenneth teased.

I smiled through my teary eyes.

"Talented, playing that fiddle, too. You're going to play something for us at the party, aren't you, Melody?"

"What? No, I—"

"Of course she is," Kenneth said eying me. "It's part of our deal."

"It is?" I asked worriedly.

"Well good," the Judge said standing again. He seemed to have trouble getting to his feet, swallowing a groan and forcing a smile. "I guess I'll get back out there and see what that dandified fellow's got planned for me. Wants to string pink roses up the driveway next," he said and Kenneth laughed. Then, as if remembering himself, Kenneth stopped and turned toward the doorway. He paused in it, looked down at the picture of himself and his mother, and gazed back at the Judge.

"Thanks for this."

"Sure."

"We gotta go," he said.

"Yes, it looks like I have some unexpected practicing to do," I quipped and Kenneth laughed.

The Judge followed us to the front door.

"I don't have to say good luck. I know everyone's going to be impressed," he declared. Kenneth nodded, and I could tell he wanted to say "Thank you."

When I looked at the Judge, I saw his eyes were full of tears. He bit down on his lip, smiled at me and went back inside.

"I think he's really sorry, Kenneth."

"Maybe," he relented. We got into the jeep and he sat there for a while, watching his father come out of the house, wave to us and walk slowly toward the caterers.

"He was a very handsome man, always distinguished, gentlemanly. He looked just like a judge. When I was a little boy, I thought he had the power to decide life and death. Don't put your faith completely in anyone, Melody. Reserve some skepticism. It's good insurance. Okay," he said smiling at me. "We'll have a good time. If the Queen will grant you leave, you're invited to dinner tonight. Holly will be here any minute."

"She will? Oh great! Of course I can come. Grandma

Olivia wants me to be a good influence on you, get you to look more like—"

"A businessman, I know. I might put on a clean pair of pants and socks," he said and we both laughed.

Holly, I thought. I couldn't wait to see her again.

Holly came laden with gifts for us: charms and crystals, astrological charts, new earrings for me and a bracelet for Kenneth. After dinner she and I took a long walk alone on the beach and talked about my trip to California.

"Naturally, my sister turned everything around, blamed me for sending such a young, impressionable girl to Los Angeles. Philip said it wasn't surprising," she said with a short laugh.

"Oh I hope I didn't make any trouble for you," I said.

"This isn't a new argument. My sister and her husband formed their opinions of me long ago. Anyway, Billy wanted me to be sure to give you his best wishes and love. He was touched by you."

"And I by him. I thought about him and the things he told me many times while I was in Hollywood."

"Your mother didn't have the slightest—"

"She's like someone under a spell, Holly. If I had known as much before, I would never have gone. I sometimes stop at the graveyard and pretend it's her buried there. She might as well be," I added.

She smiled softly and paused to take a deep breath of the fresh ocean air.

"Cleans out my brain," she said. "Well, I see Cary has won over Kenneth, building that boat." She nodded toward the finished hull. "It looks like it's going to be very impressive."

"He's got his whole heart in it," I said, my own heart swelling with pride.

"Not his whole heart. There's some big part of it here," she said, pointing to my chest. I laughed.

"Tell me about Kenneth," she said after a moment.

"He looks like he's in some state of transition, hovering. His chart indicates he's about to change direction."

I told her about the meeting with his father and the quasi cease-fire.

"They're both getting older. It's time for them to settle things," she said, then turned thoughtful. "Does he talk about me much?"

"Oh you're always in his thoughts," I said. "He often says, 'That's something Holly put in your head,' or 'Holly would have a lot to say about that.'"

"Really?" She smiled. "I like it here. I've been thinking about leaving New York."

"And Billy?"

"I'm thinking about giving him the shop. He'd never leave New York."

"Where will you live?" I asked.

"We'll see," she said flashing a smile at me. "I'm about to discover if I can read my own future," she added. "I've got some strong indications." She beamed and looked back at the house.

"I'd better get home," I said, uncertain if I should question her more. "We all have a big day tomorrow and thanks to Kenneth, I have to play my fiddle."

"That's wonderful. Yes, it will be a big day." She took my hand and we ran over the sand dune in our bare feet, laughing, the stars glittering above us, the ocean smooth and gentle and full of promises. It was good to be happy again, to be full of hope.

The next day, people showed up nearly a half hour early to be the first to get into the gallery. Grandma Olivia put on one of her finest dresses, and wore her string of pearls, her diamond bracelets and gold rings. When she appeared in the foyer, she did indeed look like a queen. Judge Childs came by for us, and in his dark blue suit he looked as handsome as I had ever seen him.

"I tried to get Grant and Lillian to come," he said referring to his other children, "but they were both too busy with their own lives. It's a sad thing when families grow apart," he declared, which was something Grandma Olivia seconded heartedly.

"Once you lose the ties that bind, you drift in the wind," she said. She looked at me after most of her deep pronouncements these days, making sure I took note.

Cary, Aunt Sara and May, all dressed up, were waiting outside the gallery when we drove into the adjoining parking lot. Cary looked very handsome in his suit and tie and May, growing like summer corn, was already over five feet one. Even Aunt Sara had put on something bright and cheery and had dabbed on some makeup and lipstick.

"They're just about to open the doors," Cary said as I got out of the Judge's vehicle. "Those people over there are reporters," he added, nodding toward a small crowd gathered on the sidewalk.

"Ken here yet?" the Judge asked.

"No sir. Haven't seen him."

"Be just like him not to show up," Grandma Olivia muttered under her breath. "Well, Sara, how are you?"

"I'm fair to middling, Olivia. It seems like only yesterday," she said, her pale lips trembling.

"Well it's not only yesterday and we've all got to get on with our lives. This is a very happy, wonderful occasion for the Judge. You shouldn't be here if you're not up to it," she said sharply.

Sara forced a smile.

"Oh, I'm fine. And May's very excited about it," she said, nodding at Grandma Olivia's granddaughter, whom she had yet to acknowledge.

"Tell her hello," she ordered and flashed a smile at May who smiled back and signed. Grandma Olivia didn't wait to find out what she said. She stepped forward with the Judge at her side. The gallery doors were opened and the people began to stream in, most greeting Grandma Olivia and the Judge before allowing them to pass through the crowd. Cary, Aunt Sara, May and I followed.

*Neptune's Daughter* stood in the center of the room,

279

covered with a sheet. The gallery owner, Laurence Baker, was a tall, lean man wearing a somber expression. The way he moved, gliding across the room, and his soft-spoken manner reminded me of an undertaker. His assistants, a man about twenty-four or -five and a woman who looked to be in her mid-thirties greeted people as well. There was some champagne already poured on long tables and some cold hors d'oeuvres alongside them. People went right for the free refreshments and wandered about the gallery looking at the other works of art while waiting for the unveiling.

"Good afternoon, Judge Childs, good afternoon," Laurence Baker said. "And Mrs. Logan. Thank you all for coming."

"Why wouldn't we come?" she snapped back at him.

"Oh, I just meant . . . it's nice to see you," he said and slipped over to another couple.

The gallery was soon full and Kenneth had not yet arrived. I was beginning to get butterflies in my stomach, thinking he might have decided not to appear. What would we do? How would the Judge handle it, and with the big party all set, the food, the music? I looked at Cary.

"When you saw him last, did he say anything about not coming here?" I asked him.

"He didn't say he wasn't, but he did tell me he wasn't happy about all the fuss."

"You don't think . . . was he drinking today?"

"No. Holly was there with him and they were just spending most of the day walking on the beach and talking. Well," he said with a tight smile, "maybe not just talking."

"You didn't spy on them, did you, Cary Logan?"

"No," he said indignantly. "I could just tell from the way they are acting that things are going well between them."

I was about to apologize when we heard the crowd raise the volume of its murmur and turned to see Kenneth and Holly drive up to the front of the gallery in her tie-dyed car. Kenneth had put on a sports jacket, but he wore an old pair of dungarees and a pair of moccasins without socks. His shirt was opened at the collar.

Holly wore one of her long dresses, sandals and beads that reached her waist. She had crystal earrings and a tiara made of crystals and other minerals.

"Artists," Grandma Olivia muttered.

Despite how Kenneth was dressed, he received an ovation when he entered the gallery. He smiled and nodded and escorted Holly to the foot of *Neptune's Daughter*.

"Well," Laurence Baker said stepping up beside Kenneth, "now that the artist is here, we can unveil his creation. As you all know, Mr. Childs has named his work *Neptune's Daughter*. In your program he describes his own work as a view of Neptune's daughter emerging from the sea, metamorphosing into a beautiful woman. The piece attempts to capture that metamorphosis at a climactic point. Without further ado, let's allow Mr. Childs to unveil *Neptune's Daughter*."

Kenneth stood there a moment, his eyes searching the crowd until they settled on me. He looked impishly happy. Everyone held their breath as Kenneth jerked the cord to reveal *Neptune's Daughter*. The sheet fell away from the statue and the audience released a single gasp, followed by loud applause.

Grandma Olivia's eyes widened as her mouth opened, stretching the skin over her cheekbones. Then she turned to me and we both gazed at each other for a long moment. She knew I had been Kenneth's model, but she didn't expect to see a bare-breasted young woman emerging from the water. She turned back to the statue.

"Well . . . well . . . well," Judge Childs muttered. "I told you this was his best work. What do you think of it, Olivia?"

"I think it's shocking," she declared. "I never expected to see such a realistically portrayed female." She stepped forward and studied the face and then looked at the Judge.

"I know," I heard him say.

"I need some more champagne," Grandma Olivia declared and the Judge escorted her to the table.

"What do you think of it, Aunt Sara?" I asked her.

"It looks like Haille," she whispered. "Just like her."

"Yes, it does."

"Jacob wouldn't have approved," she noted and nodded. "No, that he wouldn't."

"Dad didn't know anything about art," Cary said.

Aunt Sara's face brightened.

"No," she said, "he didn't."

I laughed and signed back and forth with May, who was very excited and loved the statue. We listened to other people complimenting it and complimenting Kenneth, who appeared as uncomfortable with adulation as a man standing in shoes two sizes too small.

Cary and I were about to take May outside for some fresh air when Teddy Jackson, his wife Ann, his daughter, Michelle, and son, Adam, entered the gallery. A cold, electric chill shot through my spine. I hadn't seen the man who was my real father since I had returned, terrified of the moment when I would. Michelle, who disliked me intensely, was actually my half-sister. I couldn't help but search her face and Adam's for any resemblances among us.

Fortunately, the Jacksons were quickly approached by the gallery owner and other members of the crowd.

"Let's go," I urged Cary and we slipped outside.

"It was getting hot in there. Mom's not coming to the party," Cary said. "She wants me to take her home first. I'll bring May and meet you up there later."

"Okay, sure," I replied, still stunned by the sight of Teddy Jackson.

"Are you going with Kenneth and Holly?"

"Yes," I said. "I'm sort of assigned to him to make sure she shows," I added and Cary laughed.

Less than an hour later, the invited guests began to leave the gallery to head up to Judge Childs's home. Kenneth and Holly emerged like two people escaping a long school detention and came laughing and hurrying toward me.

"Let's get something to drink and quick," Kenneth cried. I took my fiddle out of the Judge's car and stepped into the jeep. We took off with Kenneth whooping up a storm. The wind played havoc with my hair, but my complaints went unheeded.

"You got me into this," Kenneth shouted. "Grin and bear it."

We were lucky. It was one of the nicest spring days, the wind warm and gentle, the sky almost turquoise with puffy dabs of clouds. When we arrived the trio was playing, valets were parking cars, balloons were bobbing in the wind. Kenneth and Holly headed straight for the outside bar. People converged around him, shaking his hand, patting him on the back. Holly and I helped ourselves to some of the hors d'oeuvres, and wandered about the grounds.

"What a beautiful place," she remarked. I showed her some of the house as well. When we emerged, the Judge and Grandma Olivia had arrived and were well involved in conversations with the guests. I looked about but didn't see Cary or May anywhere. When I spotted the Jackson family again, I felt myself shrivel inside.

The caterers began serving the full meal. I wanted to wait for Cary, but he still hadn't arrived. I couldn't imagine what was keeping him. Finally, I joined Kenneth and Holly and, despite my nervous stomach, had a little to eat. After we'd finished, Teddy Jackson and his wife came to our table to congratulate Kenneth. He shifted his eyes to me, but I looked away. Behind him, Adam grinned, looking as arrogant, but as handsome as ever. Michelle, as usual, looked like she was bored out of her mind.

My eyes went to the tent entrance, hoping for sight of Cary, but he still hadn't arrived. I was about to go into the house and call him when the Judge stopped by and whispered something to Kenneth. Then they both looked at me.

"It's time I was able to step out of the limelight," Kenneth said gleefully. I groaned. They wanted me to perform. An announcement was made to the crowd as I left to get on the small stage where I had earlier left my fiddle. Most of the people drifted out to hear me play. Kenneth and Holly stood toward the back, both smiling from ear to ear. My eyes fell on Teddy Jackson, who wore a soft smile that made my heart pound so hard, I feared I might faint in front of all these people. Finally, I found the strength to lift the bow and begin.

It was a song about a coal miner's wife who refused to accept the fact that he was dead in a mining accident and sat vigil at the mine entrance for days and nights, refusing to eat or drink anything. And then, one night, the miner emerged and there was a great celebration. Once or twice I thought my voice would break, but I kept my eyes closed and envisioned Papa George teaching me the song. When it ended, I received a wonderful ovation and there were shouts for another song. I played two more tunes and then stepped down. Grandma Olivia looked very pleased at the way some of the younger men were vying for my attention. Still, I didn't see Cary in the crowd, so I excused myself and hurried into the house to call him. He picked up after one ring.

"I'm sorry," he said. "I'm just out the door. Ma was crying so hard and was so sad I just couldn't leave her. She kept thinking about Dad. She finally fell asleep. Did you play yet?"

"Yes."

"Oh, damn."

"But I'll play again and again for you, Cary. Just get here as soon as you can."

"On my way," he promised and I cradled the phone. I stood there thinking about poor Aunt Sara. I was so deep in thought I didn't hear Adam come up behind me until he whispered in my ear and dared to kiss the back of my neck. I nearly jumped out of my shoes.

"Easy," he said as if I were a horse he was trying to gentle. "I saw you go into the house and thought we could have a private conversation. You're really getting prettier and prettier, you know. I was hoping," he continued before I could speak, "that you might have realized how good we could be together. I'm a big deal at my college fraternity already and they're are lots of sorority girls to date, but I can't get you out of my mind, Melody. How about giving us another chance?" he asked stepping toward me.

I backed away, shaking my head.

"Get away from me, Adam. I don't know where you get the nerve," I said. He smiled.

"I like that. I like a girl who doesn't give in easily."

"I'll never give into you. Just stay away."

"Now why don't you just try and give us a chance. We're both a little older and—"

"I told you to stay away from me. Stay away!" I screamed at him when he reached for me again. He stopped his hand in mid-air and grimaced.

"What the hell's the matter with you? Who do you think you are, the princess of Provincetown just because you can play the fiddle and sing? I'm not good enough for you now?"

"No, it's not a matter of who's good enough for whom."

"Then what? What?" he demanded. He looked angry enough to hit me.

"Ask your father," I shouted at him. It came out of my mouth before I could swallow it back. He shook his head with confusion.

"What?"

"Just ask him, ask him why you and I could never be," I cried, the tears pouring over my lids. I turned and ran out of the room, leaving him twisting and turning in a whirlpool of confusion.

At first I felt bad about what I had said, but then I felt good about it, actually relieved. It was as if I had passed the curse along, lifted the weight from my shoulders and placed it on the true sinner's.

# 16

❦

# *Our Last Good-byes*

Despite what Kenneth said about losing his enthusiasm for his art, he was busy creating something new only days after the unveiling of *Neptune's Daughter*. The art critics had given it wonderful reviews and he was featured in several magazines and newspapers. *Neptune's Daughter* was delivered to the museum as Kenneth had promised, and later I discovered he had permitted Judge Childs to buy and donate it.

Holly remained after the festivities. I joined them for dinner twice over the following ten days, and once I took May for a bike ride out to the beach and we had lunch with Holly. I saw that Cary was right, she and Kenneth had grown closer. They both seemed very happy.

Cary was working on the detailing of Kenneth's sailboat. The equipment had arrived and he was installing it all himself. A projected maiden voyage was proposed, one that would take the four of us for a day's trip. The boat was in the water now and people from town who had heard about it from Kenneth were coming around to see it. Mr. Longthorpe, a banker, was interested enough in Cary's work to initiate a discussion about his building a boat for him, too. Cary began to design another boat, and we were all very excited for him. I told Grandma Olivia, but she just said it was something only men who ᴀad money and time to waste would find interesting. Nothing that involved recreation was important to her. She considered entertainers, sports figures and the like to be frivolous people who had just not grown up. When I talked further with her about it, I understood these were ideas she had inherited from her rather Puritanical father, but ideas she clung to like a holy rod to help her pass through the trials and tribulations that in her mind were the realities this life bestowed upon us. She believed religiously that the Creator put us on this earth just to be tested, just to suffer and endure. That was the closest she came to any religious affiliations, although she entertained the minister and made contributions to the local church. She never ended a lecture or an explanation without referring to the importance of protecting the family, guarding the reputation. That was the only armor we had to ward off "the slings and arrows of outrageous fortune."

I was beginning to think she might not be all wrong. A mutual respect and kind of truce had developed between us, especially as it looked almost certain now that I would be the class valedictorian. She had arranged for me to have an interview with the head mistress of one of the New England prep schools. In her mind I was following her prescription for the perfect life and she was preparing me to walk in her footsteps.

As the school year moved into its final quarter, plans for the annual variety show were being developed and I was approached by the show's director to perform again. I agreed and we began rehearsals soon afterward. The night of the second rehearsal, I came out of the school, expecting to find Raymond waiting as usual. He wasn't there yet, but it wasn't because he was late. My part had ended earlier than I had expected and I had decided to step out and get some fresh air while I waited.

287

I noticed an automobile across the street and a man sitting behind the steering wheel. For a few moments I stood gazing at the man and the car without fully realizing who it was. When the realization came, I felt as if I had stepped into a pool of ice water. My legs actually turned numb. He rolled his window down and beckoned to me. I didn't move and he beckoned more emphatically. There was no one else around. I hesitated and then crossed the street to the car and Teddy Jackson, my real father, smiled at me and nodded.

"I've been looking for an opportunity to speak to you," he said, "ever since you sent Adam to me. Can we talk for a few minutes?"

I glanced at my watch. Raymond wouldn't be here for at least another fifteen minutes, I thought.

I shrugged.

"Why?"

"We both know you know why," he said, holding his smile. He stopped smiling when I didn't move. "Please."

He leaned over and opened the passenger's door and I went around the car and got in.

"Well," he began, both of us looking forward and not at each other, "I think I rehearsed and replayed this conversation in my mind a thousand times." He turned to me. "How did you finally find out?"

"What difference does it make?" I countered.

"I was under the impression Haille never told anyone. It was a secret she took with her to the grave. Did someone else tell you?"

I looked at him, my eyes burning with the fire in my heart.

"You're afraid someone else in this town may expose you? Is that it?" I shot back at him.

He stared and then he looked through the windshield again.

"I have a family, a wife who doesn't know any of this, a very successful legal practice. I have some reason to be afraid," he admitted. "However, I don't feel good about that. I don't like continuing to be a coward, especially when I see how well you've turned out, how beautiful and talented you are. I'd like to stake claim to you."

"I'm not a piece of property, some acre of land or something to possess," I said. "You don't stake a claim on a daughter."

"I didn't mean for it to sound that way. What I meant was, I'd like to be proud, too. You didn't tell Adam anything, but he was quite upset. He didn't know what to think."

"What did you tell him?"

"I didn't. The coward won out in me again," he said. "I acted just as confused. He's smart though. He didn't buy it and one of these days, he and I are going to have a heart to heart. I guess he won't think it's so wonderful to be a Jackson then," he added a bit mournfully.

"He's spoiled and arrogant," I said. "He needs to be brought down a few pegs, maybe a dozen."

"Yes, he is something of a snob. I will definitely stake claim to that. That's my fault." He paused, gazed at me and then nodded. "I guess I owe you some sort of explanation."

"I don't want anything from you," I said.

"I'd like to tell you some of it. Please."

I said nothing. I just sat there, half wanting to lunge out of the car, and half wanting to lunge at him and demand why he was such a coward all these years. I wanted to pound his chest and pummel his face and scream and scream and scream about the lies, the deceptions, the people who suffered while he built his precious law practice and wonderfully secure family.

"Nearly nineteen years ago, I was a lot less mature than I am now. Not any less than other young men my age," he added, "but I was impulsive and full of myself. My career had begun. I was successful rather quickly, which is not always a good thing; but in my case, I handled it well, invested well, built more and more of a fortune, married a beautiful woman and had my first child.

"Your mother," he continued with a smile, "was the most attractive young woman in this town then, and very seductive. She had a way of directing herself at you that kind of melted your resistance, filled you with fantasies. She was," he said with a laugh, "a terrific flirt."

"I don't want to hear any more about her wild ways," I said. "Every man I've spoken to who has known her talks about her as if she waved a magic wand over them, hypnotized them."

"That's not far from the truth."

"So you don't bear any blame, is that it?" I fired back at him. "It was all her fault. She seduced you and since she seduced you, you felt no obligations?" Tears burned my eyes and my heart thumped like a tiny hammer under my chest.

"No, I'm not going to say that, although I did rationalize it that way for a long, long time," he replied calmly. "I let her blame someone else and cause problems for the Logan family. It was an easy way out for me and I took it."

"Why did she do that?" I asked. "Why didn't she just expose you?"

"I pleaded with her not to, but I think she had other reasons for doing what she did. She didn't do it for me. It had more to do with her relationship with Olivia Logan and the rest of that family. In short, I lucked out and left it that way.

"I don't think you want to know the gritty details," he continued. "Suffice it to say we had a few passionate rendezvous and, well, the rest you know."

"Yes, the rest I know," I said, reaching for the door handle.

"Wait. I didn't just come to see you to tell you all that. I'd like to do something for you," he blurted.

"Oh? Like what?"

"I don't know. Isn't there something you need? Something I can buy you?"

"Buy me a real mother and father," I said. "Buy me a real family with people who love and care about each other."

He shook his head.

"I'm sorry. It wouldn't do anyone any good, least of all the Logans, if I stepped forward and confessed, would it?"

"No. Your confession has to be made to a higher authority." I paused after opening the door and turned back. "There is one thing you can do for me."

"Name it," he said quickly.

"Keep Adam away from me," I said.

"Done. And Melody, I really am sorry," he said.

Just as I stepped out of the car, Raymond appeared with the limousine. I hurried across the street and got in without looking back until we had turned around and were heading back to Grandma Olivia's.

My father was still there, parked, staring ahead at the darkness of his own making.

It took me forever to fall asleep that night. I tossed and turned, my mind fuzzy, full of mists that rolled like the fog. How pathetic my real father had sounded to me. Well all his explanations, his promises and good intentions wouldn't keep the ocean from washing over the deceit. Let it all be swept out to sea where it belongs, I thought. Let me be free of a past that wanted to chain me to despair.

I was exhausted the next day and moved through my classes like a zombie. Theresa kept asking me if I was all right. She thought my mood might have something to do with Cary, because she, herself, had just broken up with her boyfriend. I kept telling her it was nothing like that, but she refused to believe me.

"When you're ready to talk, call me," she said, actually a bit put off.

I had the feeling I was caught in between those webs of confusion that prevented you from doing or saying anything right. It was better to just retreat into a cocoon of silence and wait for it to pass.

When I saw Cary that afternoon, he read my face as quickly as plans for a new yacht.

"More trouble with Grandma Olivia?" he guessed.

"No. We circle each other from a safe distance these days, like two wolves in silent agreement as to each other's territory."

He laughed.

"So?"

I pondered a moment. I had come out with him to Kenneth's dock to keep him company while he completed the finishing touches on the cabin. It was really a magnificent boat and as comfortable inside as he had predicted. He turned from the wiring he was doing on the stove and gazed at me with those green eyes fully focused.

"What is it, Melody? Have you heard from your mother?"

"Hardly," I said with a laugh. "I'd expect to hear from the Queen of England first."

"Then what?" When I wouldn't answer, he turned, putting his tools aside. "If you and I can't trust each other by now with our deepest secrets and feelings, we'll never trust each other," he said and I gazed at him lovingly, appreciatively. I was lucky to have him, to have someone so devoted to me, I thought. Would any of Grandma Olivia's so-called young men of distinguished families have half of Cary's love for me or would they just see me as another part of the puzzle constructed to make them look successful in the eyes of their parents and friends? As if he could read my thoughts, Cary added, "I love you, Melody, and loving you means feeling pain when you feel it, being sad when you're sad and being happy when you're happy."

I nodded. He waited as I took a deep breath.

"Cary, I know who my real father is," I said, "and he lives here in Provincetown."

He stared at me and then slid down against the cabinet to sit on the floor and face me.

"Who?" he asked, holding his breath.

"It's Teddy Jackson," I revealed. For a moment he just sat there stunned, blinking rapidly, his face unchanged.

292

Then, the realizations began to sink in and his mouth opened slightly, his eyes darkening.

"You mean, that skunk, that shark, that ocean scum is your half-brother?" he said. I nodded. "How did you find out?"

"Mommy finally told me before I left Los Angeles," I said.

"And you kept it a secret all this time?"

"I didn't want to believe it or face up to it. I did my best to avoid him and my half-sister Michelle, who, ironically, despises me. I thought I could bury it with the other lies."

"What happened?"

I told him about my meeting my father the night before. He listened, smirked and nodded.

"In character. I'm sorry, but I have to confess something, too," he said. "I have to confess I'm happy."

"Happy? Happy about Teddy Jackson being my real father? Adam and Michelle being my half-brother and half-sister?"

He looked down at the floor.

"There were times . . . because of the things he said, remarks he made, times because of the way he treated you and your mother that I feared . . . suspected . . ." He looked up at me. "I was terrified my father was your father."

"What?" I started to smile and stopped, realizing how horrible it must have been for him to have lived with such an idea.

"I thought that was what he really had confessed to you that day in the hospital when he called you to what he thought was his deathbed."

"But if I knew that, Cary, do you think I would have . . . would have permitted you and me to be lovers?"

"I hoped not, but it was a nightmare of mine."

"Well, I've thought about it too," I said. "We're distant enough cousins so it doesn't matter," I stated firmly.

"You say that now, but Grandma Olivia has your life

293

plotted like a chart for a sea voyage. Don't you think I know why she wants you to be refined and attend those snob schools?"

"It doesn't matter what she wants. I'm tired of worrying about what other people want or expect of me. You were right when you said we should start thinking about the present and ourselves and not drag up the past anymore," I told him.

He smiled, so warmly and lovingly I wanted to rush into his arms. Once again, he sensed my deepest feelings and rose to come to me. We kissed, a long, sweet but demanding kiss, drawing all the pain and darkness out of each other. He lifted me gently to the sofa and we kissed again and again, our lips moving over each other's faces and necks. His hands were inside my blouse and over my breasts. I turned and moaned and he moved beside me. Somewhere, in the back of my mind, a tiny voice was trying to warn me, begging me to think with my brain and not with my heart, but Cary's lips were gliding ever so gently over my breasts, drawing every tingle out of my body and then sending them back tenfold to travel over my stomach, to my legs. I felt myself drifting, sinking, uncaring. I was tired of being reasonable and logical. I pounced at him, hungry for recklessness.

With not a concern in the world, I put up no resistance and in fact helped him take off my skirt. We made love to each other on that sparkling new sofa, the material soothing beneath my naked back. We were both professing our love for each other so passionately and so blindly that neither of us projected the slightest hesitation. He was in me, holding me, rocking me, driving me as far from the places of sadness in my heart as I could go. I thought of nothing but the taste of his lips and the touch of his fingers. We exploded against each other, melding our souls and bodies for an instant during which I was as much a part of him as he was of me.

We were both surprised by our exhaustion and both had to laugh at our desperation to catch our breaths. For a long moment we just clung to each other, still naked, our hearts pounding. Then he rose slowly and sat up, gazing down at me.

"I—"

I lifted my hand to his lips to stop him.

"No, don't apologize. Don't say anything, Cary. I'm not upset."

He smiled.

"It would have been a lie if I said I was sorry anyway," he admitted and we laughed.

Then we heard the sound of a dog barking excitedly.

"What's that?"

"Sounds like Prometheus. We better get dressed, and fast," he said. We scurried about, pulling on our clothes and heard Holly and Kenneth calling. I brushed back my hair quickly and glanced in the wall mirror, but there wasn't time to do much more. They were shouting now.

"What's going on?" Cary wondered as we climbed up the small stairway to the deck of the boat.

Holly and Kenneth were standing on the dock and in Holly's arms was another chestnut-coated retriever puppy. Prometheus was circling and barking.

"He's going to be company for Prometheus," she declared. "We're calling him Neptune in honor of Kenneth's work."

"Oh, he's so sweet," I said hurrying off the boat. She handed him to me and he covered my face with his licking kisses.

"Everything coming along all right down there?" Kenneth asked Cary, his eyes moving from him to me and then back again. Cary blushed.

"Just fine," he said.

"We're still looking at next Saturday then?"

"No problem I can see," Cary replied firmly.

"Okay, then we should do it on Friday, right Holly?"

"You're not getting away that cheaply Kenneth Childs."

"Getting away with what that cheaply?" I asked.

"If he thinks for one moment we're going to consider that a honeymoon—"

"Honeymoon!" Cary and I exclaimed simultaneously.

They both beamed at us.

"Oh, Holly, congratulations," I cried and we hugged, Neptune squeezed between us. He barked his complaint, which caused Prometheus to join in chorus.

"It's just going to be a small wedding at my father's house," Kenneth said.

"Really?"

"It was Holly's idea to let him marry us. I figured I'd save money so . . ."

"That's wonderful, Kenneth," I said, my face flushed with happiness for them both.

"I had a feeling you'd see it that way," he said. "Well, I guess I'd better get back to work. It looks like this piece is going to be interrupted by something called a honeymoon," he declared.

Cary and I watched the two of them walk back to the house.

"I hope that will be us someday," he said. I took his hand.

"It will," I promised.

He put his arm around me.

Maybe it was changing; maybe the storms had really passed over us at last, I thought.

Two days later Cary drove me up to Grandma Belinda's rest home so I could make my weekly visit with her. Cary liked to visit with Grandpa Samuel. He said he at least got him to talk about fishing. I was anxious to tell Grandma Belinda all the good news. It seemed the only baggage I ever brought with me when I visited her were suitcases full of sadness and tragedy. She was still spending lots of time with Mr. Mandel, but this time I found him first in the lobby, playing checkers with another man. He recognized me and smiled.

"Good, you're here," he said. "She needs company. I've been trying to beat Mr. Braxton here at checkers all week, but I never get the time. She doesn't let me out of her sight," he explained with a twinkle in his eyes.

"Just his excuse for being afraid of losing to me," Mr.

Braxton said. "Blaming that poor old lady. You should be ashamed of yourself, Mandel."

"We'll soon see who's going to be ashamed," Mr. Mandel replied and jumped one of Mr. Braxton's checkers.

Cary laughed.

"She's on the bench in the garden," Mr. Mandel told me.

Cary and I split up in the hallway, he going down to Grandpa Samuel's room first. It was a very bright and warm afternoon. The flowers were in full bloom. Lilacs with their dark purple spikes climbed over the walls and gates. Bees hovered over the honey locusts. The yellow tea roses were especially brilliant and there were petunias everywhere. I knew how much Grandma Belinda liked being outside, how much she enjoyed soaking in the sunshine and drinking in the wonderful rainbow colors all around her.

I saw her on her usual bench, a small smile on her lips, her head back with her eyes closed, basking in the sunlight. Her hands were in her lap and she wore one of her prettier print dresses, with a pearl comb in her hair. I couldn't help but wonder if that was the way I would look when I was her age.

"Hello, Grandma," I said as I approached. Lately, she had begun to remember more and more about me, although she still said very little about my mother and asked no questions.

She didn't reply so I sat beside her and took her hand into mine. The moment I did, a shudder of abject terror passed like an electric current up through my arm and into my heart, which stopped and then started to pound again frantically. Her hand was ice cold.

"Grandma?" I shook her. Her body trembled and stopped, but her eyes remained shut. Her lips parted just a little more. "Grandma Belinda!"

I shook her harder and then I turned and shouted to the nearest attendant for help.

"Hurry!" I screamed. He ran over.

"What's wrong?"

"She won't wake up," I said and he knelt at her side, felt for a pulse, opened her eyes, and then shook his head.

"She's gone," he declared as if she had just gotten up and walked away.

"Gone? She can't be gone. She's smiling. She's pleased and happy."

"I'm sorry," he said shaking his head.

"No. Please. Call the doctor. Call someone!"

"Take it easy. I'll get Mrs. Greene right away," he said. Then he leaned toward me. "She doesn't like us to make too much of a deal of it when this happens," he said in a loud whisper. "It disturbs the others and makes it all that much more difficult around here."

"I don't care what she thinks. Get a doctor!"

He stood up.

"I'll be right back," he promised and hurried away.

"Oh, Grandma Belinda, please don't go. Not yet. We're really just getting to know each other and you're all I have. Please, wait," I begged her, babbling stupidly at her side.

I took her cold hand in mine again and sat there beside her, the tears streaming down my cheeks, rocking my body gently back and forth as I muttered my silent prayers and continued to beg her to stay just a little while longer.

Moments later, Mrs. Greene came hurrying down the garden pathway accompanied by two other attendants and a nurse. The nurse charged ahead and examined Grandma Belinda, making the same pronouncements quickly.

"Get the stretcher from the infirmary," Mrs. Greene ordered the attendants. "Bring it out that side door and take her back in that way. I'll call the mortuary."

"No!" I cried and buried my face in my hands.

"You can come to my office, if you wish," she told me curtly. "I'll have to call Mrs. Logan right away. Don't worry. Arrangements have been made. We do that immediately after we accept a patient."

"How convenient for everyone," I replied as I brushed the tears off my cheeks.

She pursed her lips with annoyance and nodded at the attendants who rushed away.

"Stay with her," she ordered the nurse. Then she pivoted and started to march back to the building.

I turned to Grandma Belinda and brushed back her hair. The nurse smiled at me.

"She died happy, thinking of something nice," she said. "And she loved it so much out here," she added.

"I know," I moaned through my tears.

"This is better than her getting sicker and sicker and lingering in the infirmary," the nurse continued, more for my sake than for Grandma Belinda's.

"I have to tell Cary," I realized aloud and rose.

"I'll stay with her," the nurse promised.

I glanced down at her again. Her lips were turning purple and her smile seemed to fade right before my eyes. I reached down to touch her one more time and then, with my chest feeling as if it had turned to stone, I started away.

Cary was sitting in Grandpa Samuel's room and Grandpa Samuel was still in bed, sitting up. He was in his robe and was unshaven.

"He's not talking much," Cary began, but when his eyes settled on me a moment longer, he knew something terrible had happened. "What is it? You look terrible."

"It's Grandma Belinda, Cary," I wailed. "She's dead. She died in the garden just now, just before I arrived!"

He got up quickly to embrace me as I sobbed. Grandpa Samuel seemed to finally notice us and slowly came out of his daze.

"Laura?" he said. Cary turned to him.

"No, Grandpa. It's Melody. She's just come from Belinda. I'm afraid it's bad news, Grandpa. Belinda's gone."

"Gone?" He looked at me, at my tear-streaked face and bloodshot eyes. "I told her not to do it. I told her it was wrong, but she said it was the best, for everyone's best." He stared down at his hands and shook his head. "She always knew what was best, so what could I say?"

"He's just more confused than ever," Cary explained. "What happens now?"

"They are taking her to the infirmary and then calling Grandma Olivia. The arrangements are already made. They were made five minutes after she was brought here," I added bitterly. "Grandma Olivia thinks of everything, plans, plots, never misses a beat for fear of a moment's embarrassment for her precious family."

Cary nodded.

"Yet," he said, "you appreciate all that at times like this."

I hated to admit he was right, to give her any credit.

"Please, take me home," I said.

"Okay. Grandpa, we've got to go now. I'll be back to see you again."

Grandpa Samuel turned back to us, his face full of seriousness, his eyes small and dark as he nodded with tight lips.

"She decided it was for the best," he said. "But I'm not so sure. Go down in the basement. You decide," he added.

"He's just doing a lot of babbling today," Cary explained. He squeezed Grandpa Samuel's hand softly, patted him on the shoulder and then guided me out.

We didn't stop at Mrs. Greene's office nor did we stop at the checker table to tell Mr. Mandel. I thought it was better for him to find out himself. I still felt like I was in a daze anyway.

"I'm sorry," Cary said as we drove off. "I know how much you wanted to get to know her and to get her to know you."

"It was starting to happen, Cary. Each time I visited, she seemed to remember more."

"I'll go right home and tell Ma," he said after we arrived at Grandma Olivia's. "Take it easy. I'll call you later."

"I'll be all right," I said and kissed him.

I found Grandma Olivia in what was Grandpa Samuel's office talking on the phone. She looked up when I appeared, but continued her conversation with the mortuary.

"Yes," she said, "I want the service short, but I'll stay with the deluxe flower arrangements. No," she added firmly, "you can close the coffin immediately. Thank you."

She cradled the phone.

"Actually, I thought she would live longer than I would. She's younger, and nothing bothered her half as much as it bothers me."

"Maybe you just never saw how much things bothered her. You hardly visited her up there," I attacked.

"Don't use that tone of voice with me. I won't be blamed for trying to protect her and take care of her. One day you'll realize all that, especially when you see how most people look after their sick relatives. The country is full of discarded people," she continued. "At least I made sure she died with some dignity and in some comfort with professionals looking after her day and night."

"She didn't belong there. She belonged at home," I wailed. "She wasn't crazy. She was just confused. Grandpa Samuel doesn't belong there either. You have enough money to keep him taken care of right here in his own home, in his own surroundings."

"To do what? Sit around and dribble down his chin, be carried out and left in a chair on the lawn for everyone to see? None of his so-called cronies would come see him. Most of them are worse off or dead. It would just be another family embarrassment, prolonged; and even if I spent a fortune and got him round the clock assistance, I couldn't change his condition. At least he has good medical care, good dietary care and some companionship where he is.

"Don't be so quick to make judgments about things you know very little about," she advised sharply. "You've come late to this family. You have no real idea about the twists and the turns, the ridges and the valleys

301

that were crossed, the storms I've weathered. Belinda was always difficult and always a problem in one way or another, and Samuel was no prize, but I did the best for everyone," she concluded firmly. "I bear no guilt. Her daughter, that's who bears all the guilt."

She took a deep breath and for a moment looked very pale herself. Then she gathered her resolve and stood up.

"There's much more to do, even though I tried to have everything in order." She paused in the doorway and turned to me. "Were you there when it actually happened?" she asked almost in a soft, concerned tone of voice.

"No. She was already gone by the time I found her in the garden. She . . . was smiling," I said.

Grandma Olivia nodded.

"She probably thought of the Grim Reaper as just another gentleman caller asking her for a date," she said wistfully. "She was a pretty little girl. Everyone always remarked about her perfect features. It won't be long before I'll be taking care of her again. You don't lose your burdens just because you leave this world," she muttered and left the office.

I stood there for a while looking around, thinking, feeling such a smorgasbord of emotions: sadness and grief, confusion and sympathy. I went behind the desk and sat.

Mommy should know, I thought. She should be told her own mother had just died. I stared at the phone. I hadn't attempted to contact her once since my return and she hadn't contacted me, yet I hadn't forgotten the phone number. I sucked in my breath, lifted the receiver and dialed. It rang once and then there was an automated voice.

"I'm sorry, but this number is no longer in service," I was told.

"What?"

I dialed again and again received the same automated message. Where was she? I wondered. She always emphasized how important the telephone was to someone

302

trying to get auditions and parts and assignments. I called information and asked the operator if there was a forwarding number. She told me she had nothing listed.

Frustrated, I thought about calling Mel Jensen, but wondered how I would explain not knowing what had happened to the woman who was supposedly my sister. Nevertheless, I finally called and spoke to his roommate because Mel was at an audition.

"Gina Simon?" he said. "I haven't seen her for a while, months. I don't know where she went. Matter of fact, I think Mel said something about her running out on her lease and the landlord being after her," he added.

"Oh. Well thanks, anyway."

"Do you want me to have Mel call you? Where are you?"

"No, it's all right," I said even more embarrassed. "Just say I wish him luck."

"Sure."

I hung up and sat there a while thinking about Mommy. She hadn't been much interested in her mother all these years that her mother was alive as far as I knew. As sad as it was, I didn't think she would be that upset not finding out when her mother had died.

Maybe Grandma Olivia was right: maybe Grandma Belinda was far better off at the home. At least there, no one pretended to be more than he or she was. They took care of you because they were paid to take care of you, and if they liked you and did something extra, it was honest and simple.

Grandma Belinda's funeral was well attended, but not because so many people remembered her. In fact, some people thought she had died long ago. People came because it was Grandma Olivia's sister and Grandma Olivia still commanded great respect in the community. Government officials attended, as did most of the influential businesspeople and professionals. I saw my father and his wife there, but I avoided looking at him as much as possible and he said nothing to me.

Grandma Olivia did not greet the mourners afterward.

303

We all went to the cemetery and then the mourners went their separate ways, except for Judge Childs, Kenneth, Holly, Cary, May and Aunt Sara, who returned to the house with us. Grandma Olivia said wakes and feeding large numbers of people only prolong the final good-bye and delayed getting on with life.

Nevertheless, we had something to eat and afterward, we all sat out in the back and talked. Holly took Aunt Sara for a walk with May along the beach. Holly and Aunt Sara got along well these days. She was actually helping Aunt Sara shed her burden of mourning. Grandma Olivia fell asleep in her chair while Cary talked about the boat with Judge Childs and Kenneth.

Finally, Cary and I went down to the dock and watched the approaching twilight with the gulls gliding gracefully over the silvery water.

"I wonder if Holly is right. I wonder if we all return to some spiritual body full of love and then start again," I said.

Cary was silent for a moment and then he turned to me and smiled.

"I started again. I started when you came here," he said. "So maybe it's true: Maybe love is what makes us alive."

I leaned against his shoulder and he put his arm around me, making me feel secure and safe. The sun continued to dip. Clouds drifted toward the horizon as if they were sinking, too. The gulls called out through the shadows.

And I said a soft good-bye to the grandmother I had hardly known, but whose soft eyes filled me with promises to keep.

# 17
## ❧

# *An End to the Silence*

As Cary had promised, Kenneth's boat was ready for its maiden voyage the following weekend. Of course, Cary took it out on some test runs beforehand and spent the week tuning and perfecting it until he was satisfied. Weatherwise, luck was with us. When Cary came for me early on Saturday morning, it was a nearly perfect day with just a few dabs of clouds over the face of a pale blue sky, and most important, the sea was calm, but with just enough breeze to make for good sailing.

Grandma Olivia said nothing either negative or positive about it at all. She knew where I was going and why, but she ignored my preparations. There was a dramatic change in her demeanor during the week after her sister's death. She was more withdrawn, said less at dinner and spent more time alone in Grandpa Samuel's office reviewing old papers. She dozed a great deal and had fewer visitors.

Judge Childs came around about as frequently as usual, but his visits were shorter and he had dinner with us only once. Toward the end of the week, immediately after he arrived, he and Grandma Olivia went into the office and spent an hour or so behind closed doors going over documents. When he emerged, he looked flustered and tired. He barely spoke to me before he left and after he was gone, Grandma Olivia went directly up to bed, not so much as glancing my way.

She still made daily inquiries as to my progress at school, commented about my appearance, and warned me about not doing anything to ruin the success I had enjoyed and would enjoy, but her words sounded emptier. They were words of duty, automatic words, sentences without passion. Could it be that Grandma Belinda's death really had affected her? I wondered. I was beginning to feel sorry for her, something I thought I would never do.

I didn't mention any of this to Cary, especially the morning of our maiden voyage. He talked excitedly all the way to Kenneth's beach house, giving me little opportunity to get a word in anyway. I had to laugh at his exuberance, but at the same time, I was thrilled by it.

Holly had prepared our cold lobster lunch with salads and Portuguese bread, wine, coffee and carrot cake. She and Kenneth surprised us by buying new matching sailing outfits. It was the first time I had seen her dressed in something reasonably fashionable and I thought she looked fresh and attractive.

"I've got to look the part now, don't I?" Kenneth said, parading about in his captain's hat.

The aura of happiness that settled over all of us was infectious. We fed each other's laughter and joy.

Kenneth and Cary got us underway and we set out to sea, bouncing gently over the waves, the wind stroking our faces, making our hair dance over our foreheads, all of us bathing in the sunlight and the sea spray. The boat was as sleek and as fast as Cary had predicted. It sliced gracefully through the water. Kenneth said it handled with such ease, it could make a novice appear to be a seasoned sailor. He even let me steer to prove it. Cary beamed with pride, strutting over the desk, checking every joint, every mechanical part, just daring something to fail.

After we set the anchor, Cary and Kenneth did some fishing while Holly and I prepared our feast. After we ate I played the fiddle and taught them some of the mountain songs Papa George had taught me. I couldn't recall a time in my life when I felt more contented. All of us sprawled out to rest and actually dozed off a bit before springing back into action and turning the boat toward shore, this time sailing faster, Holly and I shrieking at the waves that splashed over the sides of the boat to soak us. It had been one of the happiest days of my life and I hated to see it come to an end.

Kenneth and Holly had decided to have their wedding the next day at Judge Childs's. It wasn't going to be a very big affair. The Judge would marry them in front of a few friends and there was to be a small dinner party, after which Kenneth and Holly would leave for their week's honeymoon in Montreal. Cary and I had promised to look after the beach house and their puppies, Prometheus and Neptune. Cary said he would take the dogs home with him every night.

We all knew he was going to be busy. Mr. Longthorpe had decided to go ahead and contract with him to build him his yacht. Kenneth offered his home for Cary to use, which meant Cary could utilize the studio and shop. Now there would be reason for him to be at Kenneth's anyway. While he had been working there on Kenneth's boat, the house had become our little paradise, our hideaway from the prying eyes of the world around us. We had only the terns and other birds as witnesses. Now that would continue.

And so as the school year was drawing toward its end, I gradually permitted myself to believe there really was such a thing as a rainbow after the storm. Mommy didn't trouble my thoughts anymore. I accepted that she was gone. I rarely saw my father and never saw or heard from Adam. Michelle avoided me more than I avoided her. It was easy to put it all behind me, to think now of the future, a future that had a place for Cary's and my love.

It was really what I believed as I returned from our day of sailing. Tanned and very contented, I was even eager to share the experience with Grandma Olivia. However, I found the house dark and quiet and discovered Loretta alone in the kitchen. She told me Grandma Olivia had not come down for her dinner.

"It isn't like her to do so, but I brought dinner up to her and she ate in bed," Loretta told me. "That woman isn't right. Something's wrong," she declared, but not with any loving concern. She said it as a matter of fact and went on doing her chores.

All the time I had lived at the house, I always felt uncomfortable going to Grandma Olivia's bedroom while she was in bed. I hesitated to do it now. Although I had developed some level of respect for her, I still wasn't fond of her. I didn't think she was the kind of person who permitted anyone to care for her affectionately anyway. Even the Judge rarely spoke to her tenderly, at least not in front of me. It was as if he thought that if he did, she would either ridicule him or criticize him for it.

Nevertheless, I felt some concern and knocked on her door. There was no response so I knocked harder until I heard, "What is it?"

I opened the door and gazed in at her. She looked like a tiny child in the large bed, her hair loose, her body diminished even more by the oversized pillows.

"I just wondered how you were. Loretta said you didn't come down to dinner and—"

"I'm fine," she said firmly, but then added, "as fine as I can be."

"Is there anything you need?"

She stared at me and then, as if I had asked the silliest question, she uttered a ridiculing groan.

"Need? Yes, I need a new body. I need youth. I need a family with a man as strong as my father was. No," she said, "I don't need anything you can give me." She paused and nearly smiled at me. "You think you've come to where you can start to do things for me?"

"I just meant . . ."

"I'm tired, very tired. The battles wear you down. However, I don't want sympathy and I don't want anyone to feel sorry for me. I'm just stating a fact you will learn yourself one day. You live, you work hard and you die. Don't expect anything more and you won't be disappointed. You can send Loretta up to take my tray. That's what you can do," she said, waving her hand to brush me away.

I started to close the door.

"Just a moment."

"Yes?"

"I don't believe I will be going to the wedding tomorrow. I don't feel up to festivities and parties. It's not much of a wedding anyway."

"Won't the Judge be disappointed?"

This time instead of smiling disdainfully, she laughed mockingly.

"I can't think of anything that means less to me than Nelson Childs's happiness," she said and then, as if her head had suddenly turned to stone, she dropped it quickly to the pillow.

I stared at her. Despite her money and her power, I did feel sorry for her. I had the urge to shout it at her: "I pity you, you and your concern for what's perfectly proper or what's good for the family. Look at what you've become! Look at what you have at the end of your hard, angry life."

The words were teasing my lips, but I swallowed them back and instead I closed the door and went to tell Loretta to pick up her tray. Then I went to bed thinking about Kenneth and Holly's wedding and dreaming of my own, grateful I wouldn't end up like this sad old woman.

Grandma Olivia remained in bed the following morning. She didn't ask for me and I didn't stop by to say good-bye before going to the wedding. Cary, May and

Aunt Sara picked me up and were all surprised to learn that Grandma Olivia wasn't coming.

"Isn't she feeling well?" Aunt Sara asked.

"I don't think so, although I can't imagine the disease or the germ that would have enough nerve to invade her body," I said. Cary laughed, but Aunt Sara looked as if I had blasphemed and had to hide her shock.

The wedding was simple, but very sweet. Judge Childs didn't seem all that surprised at Grandma Olivia's failure to attend. He was too happy about Kenneth's permitting him to perform the ceremony to allow anything to interfere with the joy of the moment. A long table had been set up on the patio. There was champagne and caviar and other assorted hors d'oeuvres first. Then we had a sit-down dinner, catered by the same people who had catered Kenneth's party for *Neptune's Daughter.* That was followed with a beautiful wedding cake.

I met Kenneth's brother and sister and their families, but they were the first to leave. Kenneth and Holly left before any of the other guests because they had to get to Boston to catch an airplane to Montreal.

"Watch Neptune," Holly warned me as I walked with her toward the jeep. "He likes to bury Kenneth's socks in the sand and might just do the same to you and Cary."

We hugged.

"I guess your chart was correct after all," I whispered.

"Yes, yes it was, and if it wasn't, I would have made it right," she declared with a gleeful smile. Then she got into the jeep beside Kenneth. She reached back for me and we joined hands.

"Be careful," she said. "Mercury is not in a harmonious position this month."

"I will," I said and let go of her hand just as Cary stepped beside me. We turned to each other and smiled and thought about the days ahead when we could share the beach house, alone, on a sort of honeymoon of our own.

However, it turned out to be a busy week for both of us. Cary actually began Mr. Longthorpe's boat and I had to start preparing for final exams. Nevertheless, he was there at the end of every school day to pick me up and then to go get May. May had become more friendly with some of her friends and fortunately for Cary and me, wanted to do things with them after school. Aunt Sara let her bring a girlfriend over after school most of the time or allowed her to go to her girlfriend's home so she was occupied.

Usually, I sat on a blanket and studied while Cary worked on the new project. Just before he stopped to take me home, we would go for a walk on the beach or just sit and look at the ocean. Toward the end of the week, it grew unusually hot and on Thursday afternoon, he put down his tools, turned to me and asked if I wanted to go swimming.

"Swimming?"

"Skinny-dipping," he challenged.

Even though we were far from the nearest neighbor and the beach was almost always deserted, the very idea of swimming nude in the daytime frightened me.

"What if someone comes?"

"No one will."

"They might."

"Well, I'm not afraid," he said with that devilish grin and started to take off his shirt. He sat on the sand and pulled off his shoes and socks, looked back at me and then slipped off his pants and underpants. For a moment he just sat there looking at the water. Then he turned back toward me, his eyes so deep, so inviting. "Well?"

My fingers went to my blouse. He rose and walked out to the water to wait. Seconds later, naked, I joined him and he took my hand.

"Ready?"

"No," I said. "It's going to be cold."

"Freezing, but delightful," he promised and we ran into the water, screaming at the tops of our voices, and laughing until the water actually covered us in what felt like icicles. I turned and ran out as fast as I had run in. Cary followed, laughing hysterically at my shrieks. We both collapsed on the warm sand and quickly wrapped our arms around each other.

I was shivering when his lips brushed mine. He rubbed my back vigorously and we kissed again. The sun was warm enough to dry us quickly, but it was the heat of our own passion that drove the chill from our bones. Making love under a daylight sky, out in the open for all the world to see, heightened every tingle, every sensation. The wind was in my hair; there was sand on my face, and my lips were salty from the sea and from his lips. Yet nothing mattered but our great hunger for each other. Before it was over, Neptune came to us and began licking both of us, making us laugh.

"I feel like we're in our own private Eden," Cary said. "Nothing can touch us here. We're blessed, Melody. I'm the luckiest guy in the world."

We pledged our love, wrote our promises in the sand, lay beside each other and gazed up at the blue sky, not thinking about our nakedness.

"I don't know how I will get through each day without you when you go to that snobby prep school," Cary said.

I sat up and braced myself on my elbow, gazing out at the water.

"I'm probably going to hate it," I said. "Maybe I won't go."

"What do you mean? I thought that was settled."

"Grandma Olivia thinks it is, but I'm not sure."

"Really? Well, what will you do?"

I gazed into his face and he smiled.

"Would you just stay here with me?"

"I might," I said and his eyes brightened as if there were tiny candles behind them. Then, they darkened and he shook his head.

"You're the class valedictorian. Everyone will say you've wasted your life."

"I don't live to please everyone, just myself," I said, but he sat up and began to dress. "Cary?"

"Let's not make plans and promises we can't keep, Melody. I'd better get you back to Grandma Olivia's."

312

I dressed quickly and we left.

"I had a wonderful afternoon with you, Cary," I said after we pulled into Grandma Olivia's driveway. "I've been working on our weekend, too. She thinks I'm sleeping over at Theresa's."

"I know how much you hate to lie," he said.

"If it means being with you, it's not a lie. It's a necessity," I said and he smiled.

"See you tomorrow," he promised and drove away. I watched him go and then I turned and went into the big house, a house that had somehow grown more empty and darker every passing day. Almost as soon as I closed the door behind me, Loretta came hurrying down the hallway to greet me.

"I think you better go up and see about your grandmother," she said.

"Why? What's wrong?"

"She don't answer when I talk to her. I was about to call the doctor."

"Doesn't answer?"

I started up the stairs slowly. Loretta watched me a moment and then walked away as if she had washed her hands of the problem. I knocked gently on the bedroom door, waited and then entered. Grandma Olivia was lying there, her head sunk into her large pillow. She didn't turn to see who it was who had entered. I approached the bed.

"Grandma Olivia?"

I gazed down at her. Her eyes moved toward me, but her mouth was twisted grotesquely in the right corner. Suddenly, her tongue jetted out like a small snake and she made a horrible guttural sound that made me step back.

"What's wrong?"

I lifted the corner of the blanket and looked at her small body. Her right arm was bent against her bosom, the fingers of her hand frozen into a claw. I saw where she had scratched her chest and neck.

313

"I'll call the doctor!" I cried and hurried to the telephone. Afterward, I called Judge Childs, too.

Later, I waited downstairs in the living room while the doctor examined her. He and Judge Childs finally appeared.

"Your grandmother has had a stroke," the doctor declared. "I wanted to send for an ambulance and put her in the hospital, but she insists on remaining here under nurse's care. Nearly shook her head off 'No!' I've sent for someone, a Mrs. Grafton, who will be here shortly. She's a fine special duty nurse, but I think it's only a matter of days before we will just have to get your grandmother to the hospital. Her vitals are stable at the moment," he added and turned to the Judge to see if he wanted to add anything.

"I'll see to everything," he said.

"Will she get better?" I asked.

"At her age a complete recovery is unlikely. She might improve with therapy, but for all that, she is just going to have to be in the hospital. For now, I'd rather she be comfortable and happy."

"Happy?" How could anyone be happy like that? I wondered, and besides, I didn't think she was happy before this had happened.

"Well, comfortable, anyway," the doctor said. "For now, she is asleep. The nurse should be here momentarily," he added and then the Judge escorted him, but returned to me.

"It's no fun being old," he said with a small smile. "However, she's an incredibly strong woman. She might make more of a recovery than the doctor thinks. Anyway, after a few days of this, I'm sure she will be taken to the hospital. At that time I'd like it if you came to stay with me. At least until you're off to school," he concluded.

"Thank you," I said, really not sure what I would do.

"Well," he said glancing up toward her room and then at me, "you going to be all right?"

"Oh yes, I'm fine."

"Call me if you need anything or anything changes," he said and left.

Twenty minutes later, Mrs. Grafton, a woman in her mid-fifties, stout and very professional and businesslike, arrived. I showed her Grandma Olivia's room and she went in to examine her. I had Loretta prepare the bedroom next to Grandma Olivia's for her as well. Then I went to the phone and called Cary to tell him and Aunt Sara what had happened.

"I'll come right over," Cary said.

"No, I'm fine. In fact, I'm tired and I want to go to sleep. I have a math exam tomorrow."

"Okay, we'll check on her tomorrow," he said.

"I'd like to go up to see Grandpa Samuel in a day or so, Cary, to tell him."

"He won't even know you," Cary said, "much less understand what you're saying."

"Still, we should tell him. No one else will."

"Okay. You can't break old habits, can you, Melody?"

"What do you mean?" I asked.

"Even now, you can't stop thinking about other people first," he said and then he laughed. "It's all right. I'm just teasing. I can't imagine Grandma Olivia trapped by a stroke."

"She's human, Cary."

"Could have fooled me," he said.

Afterward, before I fell asleep I thought how terrible it was for a woman to have ruled her family so firmly and authoritatively that they felt no love, sympathy or sorrow for her in her time of greatest need. Surely, no matter how vigorously she claimed it, she couldn't be satisfied with herself and what she had accomplished, even in the name of family.

Grandma Olivia did make some improvement over the next thirty-six hours. The doctor returned and declared that she had regained some of her speech ability.

"It will still be difficult to understand her, but there's been more improvement than I expected," he said.

"She's even gotten more control of her hand. We'll see," he added, not as ready to make dire pronouncements now as he had been before. "The nurse will remain another few days and I'll stop by every day," he promised.

Judge Childs was there most of the day as well. Loretta told me. She said it as if she were complaining he made more work for her. I imagined she thought she would have to do less with Grandma Olivia so incapacitated. When I returned from school the next afternoon, Mrs. Grafton told me my grandmother was asking to see me. I went in immediately. I approached the bed slowly. Mrs. Grafton had her sitting up and had her hair brushed. Her mouth was still twisted and her arm lay awkwardly against her body, but when I drew closer, she fixed her eyes on me and reached out with her left hand to take my hand and pull me closer.

"Naia," she uttered.

"Take it easy, Grandma Olivia," I said softly.

"Naaaa . . . thinssssss chaaaa," she continued. I shook my head. I didn't understand. She tried again and again, but the same confusing sounds emerged. Finally, Mrs. Grafton stepped over and took her hand from me.

"Please try to relax, Mrs. Logan."

Grandma shook her head vigorously.

"She has the spirit," Mrs. Grafton said. "Full of vim and vigor."

Grandma Olivia attempted her sounds again. Mrs. Grafton listened and then she smiled.

"What is she trying to say?" I asked.

"She's said, 'Nothing's changed.' Whatever that means," Mrs. Grafton added.

I nodded and looked at Grandma Olivia.

"I know what it means. It means that even now, she wants to run our lives," I muttered. "I'm sure she's going to get better."

I shook my head in amazement and left.

The next day, Cary found the time to take me to see Grandpa Samuel. Since Grandma Belinda's death, I

316

hadn't been there to visit and neither had Cary. Now, with Grandma Olivia's illness, I felt even more guilty about neither of us going to see him. There was no one to be sure he was being well looked after, no one except us, I thought.

Returning to the rest home was sad for me. I had to remind myself Grandma Belinda was gone. When we entered the lobby, we saw Mr. Mandel sitting alone on a sofa just gazing down at the floor. He looked up and immediately smiled at the sight of us.

"How are you, Mr. Mandel?" I asked.

"Oh, I'm fine, dear. Fine. It's nice to see you again. Very nice." His eyes seemed to go in and out of focus as he tried to understand why we were there. Had Belinda died or not? I could almost hear him wonder.

"We're here to see my grandfather," I explained.

"Oh. Oh yes, yes. What's his name?"

"Samuel Logan," I said.

"Oh yes. I don't think I know him," he said and nodded. Then he gazed down at the floor and grew silent. We said good-bye and went through the lobby to Grandpa Samuel's room, where we found him sitting by the window, staring out, a blanket over his lap.

"Hi, Grandpa," Cary said first. He didn't turn from the window until Cary took his hand. "How are you doing, Grandpa?"

Grandpa Samuel stared at him and then his eyes went to me.

"Yes, Melody's here, too, Grandpa."

He looked at Cary and then at me.

"You got her. Good, good," he said before looking out the window again.

Cary shook his head and shrugged. I stepped forward to take Grandpa Samuel's hand from him.

"Grandpa Samuel, we came to visit you to tell you Grandma Olivia's sick. She has a nurse at the house," I said. "The doctor didn't think she would get much better, but she already has."

He looked at me.

"I told her no, but she said it has to be. Tell your mother I'm sorry," he said. "I told her no."

"It's no use," Cary said. "I told you. We're wasting our time. He doesn't even know where he is anymore. He won't remember us being here afterward, Melody."

"I guess you're right," I said.

Suddenly, Grandpa Samuel turned to us again, this time his eyes more vibrant.

"You go look and you'll see it wasn't me. I didn't sign anything."

"Look where?" I turned to Cary. "Why does he keep saying these things?"

"You know he's confused. It probably doesn't mean anything," Cary reminded me.

"I told her no," Grandpa Samuel repeated. "I told her it was a sin."

We spent another fifteen minutes or so trying to get Grandpa Samuel to understand who we were and why we were there, but he never seemed to grasp the present. He was lost in his memories, drowning in them.

On the way out, I complained to Mrs. Greene about Grandpa being stuck in his room on such a beautiful day.

"For your information," she replied, "he was out all morning and was just recently brought in. Unless you plan on being here twenty-four hours, I would advise you not to criticize," she snapped and walked off.

"I'd rather die in my bed than be brought here," I said. "Grandma Olivia is not wrong in being stubborn about it."

"It's just lucky she can afford to have a nurse around the clock," Cary reminded me. "Otherwise, she would be someplace like this by now."

He took me home and went back to work on the boat. I still had a slew of finals for which to prepare, but as I sat in my room studying, my mind kept wandering back to Grandpa Samuel's eyes and his great fear of being blamed. Why was he so adamant now, at this time in his life? Was it because he thought he was soon to meet his Maker?

How had they arranged for my grandmother to be stuffed away at so young an age? I wondered. What sort of diagnosis had the doctors made? What had Grandma Olivia said about her? Curiosity drew me away from my work and I went downstairs and out the back to go around the house to the basement. It was in there that I had found Mommy's pictures and learned about the secrets this family buried in its closets. I thought maybe Grandpa Samuel was right. Maybe I should go back and see what I could find again.

On the north side of the house there was a metal cellar door. I didn't think anyone had been in it since Cary had brought me last year.

I hesitated in the doorway. What did I really expect to find? Did I want to find it? Did I want to read all the horrible things? I paused and thought about the twisted and sick old woman now trapped in her own body upstairs. Perhaps justice had been done. Perhaps it was time to forget.

And yet, I couldn't turn away. Maybe it was morbid curiosity; maybe it was a need to understand. I continued down the stairs and opened the next door, stepping in to pull a cord that turned on a swinging, naked bulb to illuminate the basement. I stood there for a moment, recalling the boxes on the metal shelves where we had found the photographs. I went back to them and began to sift through the cartons, their sides, tops and bottoms, limp from the dampness. There were so many photographs, old school papers, old bills, delivery slips, a trail of purchases and events that were unremarkable, the same sort of trail every family left, I thought.

All the boxes were the same. Grandpa Samuel's declining mind was filled with corridors of distortions, I thought. It was all just part of his garbled imagination now. I started to rise to leave when I saw what looked like a metal box buried under some wooden boards on the other side of the basement. I went to it, lifted off the boards and pulled out the box. It was locked and there were no keys in sight.

Why had this been left buried here and why was it the only thing locked? I brushed it off and took it with me when I left the basement. I didn't go back into the house. I went around to the garage where I knew there were tools and found a screwdriver. It took a while, but I worked one between the lid and the box and gradually, after some effort, got the lock to snap open. Then I lifted the lid and looked inside.

There was a small pile of documents in business envelopes. I took one out, opened it and removed the paper. Then I sat and read.

Of course, I always thought it was just an exaggeration to say 'my heart turned to stone' or 'my blood ran cold.' How could a human heart stop, shudder, crumble and regain itself? How could your body freeze and return to warm?

Yet all of that happened to me and I thought I would never stand, never breathe, never be able to utter a sound. My eyes wanted to sink from the words they read.

However, there was no retreat, no denial, no shaking of the head that would change the reality before me.

I caught my breath and sorted through the remaining papers in the box, reading, growing more and more shocked. Finally, trembling so badly I was sure I would stumble before I stepped outside, I put all the papers back, closed the box, and got to my feet.

No hurricane, no tornado, no earthquake would rock this family as much as what I carried in my hands.

# 18

## At Long Last, Love

*I* climbed the stairway slowly, each step more ponderous, heavier than the one before. My body was trying to resist as if I were carrying myself toward fire. I did feel like someone approaching the doorway to hell behind which I would surely find the devil herself. Under my arm, the metal box and its horrible information burned.

The late afternoon sun had fallen behind dark clouds. Shadows appeared to grow right before my eyes as I started down the second floor hallway toward Grandma Olivia's bedroom. My heart thumped with each step. I felt drugged, dazed, moving through the corridors of a nightmare. I wasn't even sure I could speak. I thought that when I opened my mouth, all I would do is hiss.

Just before I reached the bedroom door, it opened and Mrs. Grafton stepped out. At first she didn't see me in the shadows. Then I stepped forward into the dim hall light. My appearance gave her a start and she gasped, putting her hand to her heart.

"Oh, I didn't see you standing there," she said. She

321

paused, blinking rapidly as she studied me. "Are you all right?"

"I have to talk to my grandmother," I said in a dreary, dark tone.

"She's going in and out," she said.

"Nevertheless, I have to talk to her," I said. Mrs. Grafton shrugged.

"Suit yourself. I'm going down to get something to eat and then I'll be bringing her dinner."

I nodded and she walked away. I hesitated, my hand frozen in the air between the knob and myself. I was hoping that at any moment this really would prove to be only a nightmare. Perhaps when I touched that doorknob, I would wake with a shudder and find myself in bed.

I didn't.

I turned the knob and entered the bedroom.

Grandma Olivia was propped up somewhat on double pillows. Her hair lay in loose strands around her cheeks. Her mouth, twisted and puffy, was slightly open and her eyes were closed. Crippled, felled by this illness, she would have resembled any one of thousands of elderly people stored in old age infirmaries waiting for the clock to make its final tick. However, her diamond rings and bracelets, her rich satin sheets and her linen nightgown loudly declared that this was still a woman of power and prestige. She could issue orders from beyond the grave.

I stood by the bedside glaring down at her, watching her small bosom rise and fall. Her nose twitched and her lips trembled and parted showing some gray teeth. Her forehead formed folds, as painful ugly thoughts traveled with lightning speed behind her eyes and reverberated in that darkness closed up within her.

I waited and then I put the metal box down on the bed beside her and opened it. Her eyelids fluttered, opened and then closed before opening again. She gazed up at me, her eyes gathering light as she became more and more aware of where she was and who I was. Her mouth opened and she uttered some sound. Surely, I thought, some command.

"I've come to ask you some questions," I said, "and I want you to know right from the start that your illness won't stop me from demanding answers."

Her eyes widened, both with surprise and indignation. She started to protest when I lifted the metal box and held it up high enough for her to see. Her eyes shifted, studied the box and then returned to my face, her face grimacing with new anxiety.

"Yes, Grandma, I found it. Grandpa Samuel talked about it enough to catch my curiosity and I went down to the basement where you had buried all your sins and I found it and what was inside," I said, plucking the first document and holding it for a moment. Then I put the box down and unfolded the document.

She started to shake her head, but I continued.

"I know you are well aware of what is on this and the other papers, but I want you to look at it again. I'm sure you buried everything downstairs so you wouldn't have to look at it again, but now you do."

I thrust the paper out, holding it in front of her. Her eyes moved over it and then she tried to turn away, but I reached out quickly and put my hand on her forehead, easily bringing her head back so she had to look at me and the paper.

"Who did you think you were? Did you think you were God? What gave you the right to do such a thing, to control everyone else's pain and suffering, to determine someone's whole life and the lives of those who loved her and she loved? From where did you get this arrogance of power?"

She began to struggle with speech.

"Fa . . . mmmm . . ."

"How did you get this?" I asked, pulling another document from the box. "How did you get him to do it? It has something to do with all the rest of it, doesn't it? I'm going to find out, Grandma. I'm going to learn every

323

nitty-gritty detail and I'm going to expose all of it," I declared.

Her eyes went as wide as they could and for the first time since I had known her, I saw real fear burning in them. She shook her head vigorously.

"Naaaaa."

"Yes, Grandma, yes. The precious Logan name will be dragged down into the gutter where it belongs. You may have wealth and property, but you're no better than the most common criminal and neither are those who assisted you in this."

"Fammmmmm."

"Oh, you're trying to tell me you did this for the family again, is that it?"

She nodded.

"You were just protecting all the others?" I asked with a cold smile. Once again, she nodded vigorously. My smile evaporated. "That's the biggest lie of all, Grandma Olivia. Whatever you've done, you've done for yourself, to keep your precious high and mighty position in the community, or your precious reputation. Or you did things to get revenge or hurt those who didn't give you the love and respect you thought you deserved. Don't throw the word 'family' at me. Family is just your excuse for evil. I know that now."

She stopped shaking her head and stared. I put the documents back into the metal box.

"I don't know the end of the story, of course, but I will get to the end," I promised.

I closed the box and put it under my arm again.

"As I look at you now, I realize you are only just beginning to get what you deserve, Grandma. I almost pitied you. I almost did what you hate: I almost felt sorry for you, but you don't have to worry about that anymore. I can't find enough forgiveness to sympathize one iota with you. You're home free there, Grandma," I said.

"When I finish this, I'm going to tell the doctor to put you in the infirmary where you belong. You told me not to hesitate when the time came, didn't you? You were so brave then. Well, Aunt Sara, Cary and I will see to it and even Judge Childs will not resist."

I paused.

"I assume he knew about this too, didn't he?" I asked, holding up the box. She stared a moment, closed her eyes and then opened them and shook her head. "He didn't? Why not? You mean there was something he would have denied you after all? Were you afraid of that?"

She nodded and then started to shake her head and reach out for me, but I stepped back.

"There is nothing you could say, nothing, no words, no thoughts, nothing that would justify what you have done and the pain you have caused."

I turned and she cried out in her distorted way, uttering a guttural scream that reverberated through my body. With all her remaining strength, she propped herself up and then cried out again, but I turned my back on her and marched out of the room, the echo of her horrible sound shut away behind me.

As soon as I left her, I went downstairs to the office and called Cary.

"I want you to come and get me, Cary," I said. "I need you to take me someplace."

"When?"

"Right now," I said.

"What's going on? You sound so strange," he said.

"Will you do it?" I replied.

"Sure, but—"

"Thank you. Just be patient with me and I'll explain everything in time, okay? Please," I added.

"Okay, Melody," he said. "I'll come."

After I finished talking to him, I took a deep breath, went to the telephone book, looked up the number and called my father. His wife answered.

"May I please speak with Mr. Jackson?" I said.

"Whom may I say is calling?"

"Melody Logan," I said curtly.

"One moment please."

Seconds later, he was on the phone.

"This is Teddy Jackson," he said formally.

"Meet me in your office in a half hour," I said.

"Pardon?"

"Meet me in your office. I have something to show you and something to ask. Actually, a lot to ask."

"I'm not sure I understand," he said weakly.

"You will," I promised. "Be there," I said and hung up, my heart pounding so hard, I had to pause to take a deep breath and calm myself.

I saw Mrs. Grafton walk by with my grandmother's dinner tray. She glanced in at me, but continued toward the stairway.

Grandma Olivia won't have much of an appetite tonight, I thought.

Twenty minutes later, Cary pulled up in front of the house and I ran out to get into his truck.

"What's going on? Something more with Grandma Olivia? Did they take her to the hospital?"

"Not yet," I said. "Take me downtown, Cary."

"To where?"

"My father's office," I said.

"What?"

"Please."

He stared at me a moment.

"What's in that box?"

"I promise I'll explain everything as soon as I can," I said. "Trust me."

"Sure." He shrugged, started the engine again and drove us away.

"Whatever it is, I hope you'll tell me about it soon," he said as headed toward Commercial Street. He glanced at me. "I don't remember you ever acting this strange, Melody."

I took a deep breath but said nothing. He shook his head and drove faster. When we arrived in front of the law offices of Teddy Jackson, we saw the lights were on inside and his car was in its reserved parking space. Cary started to get out of the truck.

"Please wait for me in the truck, Cary," I said.

"Why?"

"This is something I have to do myself first. Please."

"I don't like this, Melody. You're in some kind of trouble. I should know more about it and I should be able to help you."

"I'm not in trouble, Cary. It's not that. Please, be a little more patient," I said.

Reluctantly, he got back into the truck and closed the door.

"Thank you," I said and stepped out.

My father's offices were plush, richly carpeted with real leather waiting room sofas, paneled walls and oil paintings. There was a large legal library and his own office was oversized with a set of back windows giving a full view of the harbor. He was standing by the window with his hands in his pockets gazing out when I entered.

"What's this all about?" he asked, obviously a little annoyed at the way I had ordered his appearance.

"It's about all this," I said, putting the metal box on his large, dark mahogany desk. He stared at it a moment and then walked over.

"What's this?" He opened the box and took out one of the documents. As he read it, his face took on more of a crimson tint. He glanced at me, put the paper down and read another. "She gave you this?"

"No. She had it hidden in the basement," I said.

He nodded, blew some air through his lips and then sat at his desk.

"Who else knows about it?"

"Just me for now," I said. "Cary is waiting outside in the truck, but I haven't told him anything yet. I want to know everything first, every dirty detail."

"I don't know every dirty detail," he replied sharply. I glared down at him and he shifted his eyes guiltily away. "I didn't want to do it, but she blackmailed me," he began and turned back to me.

I sat in front of the desk.

"Go on," I said.

"I didn't think she knew the truth about Haille and

me. I'm still not positive about how she found out. I suspect Haille told her, taunted her with it maybe. I don't know."

He pulled himself up in his chair.

"She came in here that night, calling me to this office almost the same way you did," he added with a small smile, "and she told me what had happened and what she wanted and what I had to do.

"I started to resist and she told me she would not hesitate to expose me, to bring Haille back, to destroy me just when I was getting a wonderful start.

"So I did what she wanted. I took care of all the legal issues," he confessed. "I wasn't happy about it and I couldn't look Jacob and Sara in the face anymore, but in time she had me believing it was for the best."

"Oh, I'm sure you were concerned," I said disdainfully.

"Well, I . . . look, it was her decision," he protested.

"She wasn't the mother; she wasn't the father. It wasn't her decision. You let her play God!" I shouted.

He seemed to shrivel in the chair. His eyes went down.

"What happened to her?" I asked. I didn't want to say anything to Cary before I knew every possible detail and before I knew her final fate.

He looked up.

"Olivia didn't tell you anything?"

"Grandma Olivia had a stroke. I thought everyone in Provincetown knew by now. She can't talk."

"Oh."

"Well?"

"I know only what I was told, Melody. Laura and Robert Royce went sailing. They got caught in a storm and Robert drowned. Olivia told me Karl Hansen picked her up in his fishing trawler and brought Laura directly to her. She was a raving lunatic, suffering from traumatic amnesia. She was naked when he found her at sea and Olivia, well, Olivia thought the worst of that, of course. Anyway, Karl had worked for Samuel and knew who Laura was. Olivia took control after that. She made sure

Karl told no one and then she decided to have Laura secretly institutionalized. I think the whole affair embarrassed her. Legal guardianship was established and Laura was left there where she remains to this day, as far as I know. I never . . .'"

"Never cared to find out?"

"It was out of my hands by then," he protested. "I just assumed, as the years went by, that she never . . . that it was for the best."

"Which eased your own conscience," I accused. I stood up. "I expect you will give us any help we need now," I said. He nodded.

"After I had discovered that the man I believed was my father was really my stepfather, I used to dream about the man who was my real father. I used to imagine he was a wonderful person, someone who might not even have known he had me as a daughter, but once he found out, he would come running to me, wanting to love me, to do things for me. I used to dream we would finally have a daughter–father relationship."

"Melody—"

"Now," I quickly continued, "I am grateful that you chose to be a coward. I don't want anyone ever to know that you are my real father," I said. "I couldn't get over the shame."

He stared at me, his face bright red, while I gathered up the papers and put them back into the metal box.

"You're just like her, actually," I said. "No wonder fate brought you together."

"Melody . . ."

I turned and walked away from him, hopefully forever.

Cary read the documents ravenously and then put the papers down and looked at me, his eyes wide, his mouth pulled so tightly in the corners, his lips looked like they would snap.

"I don't understand," he said. He shook his head, refusing to believe in such a betrayal and such deception.

We were sitting in the truck in front of his home. Dark

clouds had accompanied the twilight and now there was a steady, hard rain. I told him all that my father had told me.

"All this time we've been thinking Grandpa Samuel was babbling about what had been done to Grandma Belinda," I concluded.

"How could this be? Why?"

Tears spilled over his lids and trickled down his cheeks as if they were tiny watery creatures escaping. He didn't seem to realize it, even as they dripped from his chin.

"Her own grandmother," he said. "My father's mother . . ."

"In her distorted way of thinking, she somehow believed she was protecting the family from disgrace and hardship. There is no way to justify what she did and I condemn her for it as much as you will," I said, "but after living with her and learning who she is and some other things she believes and has done, I understand how this could have happened."

"I don't. I never will."

He closed his eyes and held his head back as if to swallow down some pain.

"My father . . . my father suffered great guilt about Laura."

"I know."

"And Grandma Olivia knew it, too. She must have known it," he said quickly.

"Maybe. Maybe she saw only her own guilt, her own pain, her own fears, Cary."

"She doesn't have an ounce of love in her," he muttered through his teeth. "I hate her more than I have ever hated anyone. I'm glad she had a stroke. I hope she dies tonight," he said.

"Don't become like her, Cary. You only end up so full of hate you can't love."

He stared a moment.

"What do we do? Do I tell Ma now?"

"No. Let's go there first," I said. "Perhaps . . . we can bring her home."

He nodded, smiling.

"Maybe so." He reached for the key in the ignition.

"We'll go in the morning, Cary. It's too late now," I said.

"No. I don't want to think of her being there five minutes more," he said. "We have to go now," he insisted. He looked at the papers. "I know where this is. It's a four, four-and-a-half hour drive."

"But it will be the middle of the night," I reminded him.

"Who cares about that?" he said and started the engine. "I can drop you off, if you want."

"Cary Logan, do you think I would let you do this yourself?"

He shook his head.

"Okay, let's go," I said. "We probably couldn't sleep anyway. Shouldn't you tell your mother something?"

"No, I don't want to utter one more lie, even a white one," he said.

I smiled.

"Okay, but we've got to be prepared for anything, Cary."

"I'm prepared," he said. He started away. "As prepared as I could ever be."

It was a long, hard ride. Cary talked more about Laura than he had ever talked, recalling things they had done together, things she used to say. I sensed these were thoughts he had forbidden himself to have these past few years. He was afraid of what reviving such memories might do to him.

A few times during the journey, he sat there silently, crying, tears streaming down his cheeks as he relived the tragedy and everyone's sorrow.

How could Grandma Olivia attend those services knowing what she knew? I wondered. How could she be so confident she was doing the right thing for the family, so positive that she could bury her feelings, watch her son suffer and not say a word? Instead of a heart in that chest, she surely had a cube of ice, I thought. How horrible her own parents must have been to her to shape her into the woman she had become.

I shouldn't have been surprised. She put her sister away without a single regret and did the same to her husband. Individuals meant nothing in the face of her fanatical faith in the family name. Love was merely a minor inconvenience. Correct behavior, prestige, respect, wealth and power were the five points of her star, and that star was embedded on the face of her soul.

I lay back and closed my eyes and dozed for a while. When I woke, we were near a town. I saw the lights of an all-night restaurant.

"You want some hot coffee or something?" Cary asked,

"Yes, please," I said and we pulled in and ordered coffee and doughnuts.

Cary drank and ate in a deadly silence, his eyes fixed on his anger, brightening with the stream of furious thoughts behind them. I didn't speak. I reached for his hand and smiled at him. He snapped out of his daze and nodded.

"I'm all right," he said. "We'll be all right."

"Yes, we will, Cary. We will," I agreed.

We had another hour's ride before we found the entrance to the institution. It was a tall, gray stone building with a parking lot on its left. It was too dark to see clearly, but we could make out some nice grounds around it. We saw the high fences and then woods.

The outside lights in front of the building were bright. We parked and after Cary shut off the engine, we just sat there, both trying to gather strength.

"Ready?" he asked me finally. I nodded and we got out and walked to the entrance. The door was locked, but there was a buzzer beside it with a little sign that read USE ONLY AFTER TEN P.M. Cary pushed the buzzer and we waited. Because of the reflection of the outside lights on the glass of the doorway, we couldn't see very much of the inside. It looked like a small entryway before a set of double doors. No one came so Cary pushed the buzzer again, holding it longer.

"It's pretty late, Cary."

"Someone's got to be here," he said undaunted.

Finally, the double doors were opened and a redheaded man in a pair of white pants and a light blue shirt stepped out. He looked no more than thirty, thin and slim-waisted, at least six feet tall with freckles over his forehead and cheeks. He peered through the glass before opening the door, scowled and then opened it quickly.

"What'dya want?" he demanded.

"We're here to get someone," Cary said firmly.

"Huh?"

"My sister," Cary said.

"What the hell are you talking about? It's almost three o'clock in the morning," the redheaded man said.

"I don't care what time it is. She's not supposed to be here," Cary said and stepped between the man and the door. The redheaded man recoiled as if he thought Cary would strike him.

"You can't come in here now. Visiting hours begin at ten A.M.," he said.

"We're here and we're coming in. Get whoever is in charge," Cary ordered.

The redheaded man looked from him to me and then stepped toward the double doors. Cary put his hand out to keep the double doors from closing.

"You're going to get into big trouble for this," the redheaded man threatened.

"Good," Cary said. "Now go get a supervisor or someone. Do it!" Cary ordered, so fiercely, the man rushed off. Cary and I followed and entered the lobby. There was a counter with a glass window ahead of us. To the right were sofas and chairs, small tables, magazine racks and a television set. The door directly in front of us most probably led into the institution, I thought.

We waited and finally heard footsteps on the other side

of the door. It was opened and a very heavy woman in a nurse's uniform came charging out, her dark brown hair chopped rather crudely at the nape of her neck and ear lobes, her hips rubbing against the stiff material of the uniform, producing a loud swish.

"What's this all about?" she demanded, directing her beady black eyes at Cary. She folded her arms over her heavy bosom like a battering ram and walked within inches of him.

"My sister was illegally brought here," Cary said. "We've come to take her home."

She stared at him a moment, grimaced with confusion and then glanced at the redheaded man.

"Should I call the police?" he asked.

"Not quite yet," she said. Her curiosity was piqued.

"Who are you and who is this sister you are looking for?" she asked.

"I'm Cary Logan. This is Melody Logan. My sister's name is Laura. Show her," Cary said and I produced some of the documents taken from the metal box. She eyed me suspiciously and then took them and began to read. When she was finished, I saw that her face softened a bit.

"You just found out about all this?" she asked.

"Yes, today," Cary said. "Those papers are incorrect. My sister did have parents and not a legal guardian," he said.

"Where are your parents? Why didn't they come here, too, if this is so?"

"My father recently died and my mother . . . my mother is not able to make this journey. In fact, she doesn't know the truth yet," Cary explained.

The nurse handed the documents back to me.

"This is a legal matter," she said. "It has to be handled in a proper way."

"Look—"

"But as for your coming for your sister," she continued, "I'm afraid you're too late."

"What?"

334

My heart stopped. I stepped forward and took Cary's hand quickly.

"This young lady unfortunately died a short time after she was admitted," she said.

"Died? How?" I asked.

"She drowned. We informed the grandmother about it. She was listed as next of kin."

"How could she drown?"

"It was deliberate, self-induced," the nurse confessed after a moment. "I'm not permitted to discuss the details. There are always legal issues when something like this occurs. It wasn't our fault, however," she added quickly. "I really don't understand who you are and why you're here," she continued.

Cary just stared at her, refusing to believe her.

"I want to see my sister now," he said.

The nurse looked at me to see if she had heard right.

"Don't you understand what I'm saying?" she said.

"Cary, come on," I said.

"No. I want to see her right now. I'm not leaving until I do," he insisted.

"Call the police," the nurse told the redheaded man. He spun around and disappeared inside.

"Cary, it's no use," I urged. He shook his head.

"You're lying," he told the nurse. "She got to you. You were told to say this in case I ever arrived, weren't you?"

"Absolutely not. I don't know anything about you," the nurse said. "And I don't lie about my patients."

Another attendant arrived, an older, bigger man.

"You having some sort of trouble, Mrs. Kleckner?" he asked.

"Yes," she said. "The police have been called, Morris. No one is permitted into the hospital," she said, her eyes fixed on Cary.

"Cary, let's go," I pleaded, but he was as stiff and unmovable as one of Kenneth's statues. It was like trying to uproot a tree.

The larger attendant took his position in the doorway. Mrs. Kleckner turned to me.

"I'm not lying about this. You have to go through proper channels and you will learn I've told you the truth. You're just making things harder for yourselves."

"I'm sorry," I said, "but you have to understand we just learned about all this and it really was done illegally. I'm sure you can imagine the shock. That's why he's so upset. He doesn't mean to make trouble for you. Please understand," I begged.

She considered and then nodded.

"Wait here. I have something that might help you accept what I'm saying," she declared and left us. The attendant was joined by the redheaded man and they both blocked the doorway.

"Cops are on their way," he said gleefully.

"Cary, we're only getting ourselves into deeper trouble," I whispered. He didn't hear me. He glared at the two attendants. Moments later, the nurse reappeared, carrying a small cloth bag.

"These were her personal things. Among them," she said, "is this," she said, lifting a thick notebook out of the bag. "It was her diary. Her doctors encouraged her to keep it, hoping recollections, thoughts would help her revive her identity. Apparently, no one ever came for it. If she wasn't gone," the nurse added in a harder tone, "I wouldn't be giving it to you, now would I?"

I took the bag and the notebook and tugged on Cary's hand.

"Please, Cary. She's right."

He wilted, accepting what he was told.

"Where is she buried?" he asked softly.

"I don't know. You'll have to contact Mr. Crowley tomorrow and ask him for whatever details he has. He's the administrator here. He will be in his office at nine a.m. I'm asking you now to leave these premises. The police are on their way and you will be placed under arrest if you don't go," she threatened.

"Cary—"

"We're too late," he said more to himself than to me.

"I'm sorry," Mrs. Kleckner said, "but I have told you

the truth. I've done more than I have to do and more than Mr. Crowley will approve of, I'm sure."

"Thank you," I said, pulling Cary harder.

He stepped back with me.

"Laura," he said shaking his head. "I'm sorry we were too late."

We reached the truck just as the police car arrived. The officers spoke to Mrs. Kleckner and then questioned us. When I promised we would leave, they let us go.

Cary drove back on the strength of his anger and hate. We hardly said a word to each other. All that mattered to him now was to find out where Laura had been buried. It was mid-morning by the time we drove into Grandma Olivia's driveway. Both of us were physically exhausted, but our emotions gave us the strength to continue.

Loretta came rushing down the hallway when we entered the house.

"Where have you been?" she asked.

"What is it?"

"Your grandmother turned worse last night and was rushed to the hospital," she said.

"She's not going to die," Cary said, shaking his head at me. "She's not getting away that easily."

Loretta's eyes nearly bulged out of her head.

"What?"

"Nothing. We're on our way to the hospital," I told her and we left.

We found Judge Childs in the lobby talking with the doctor when we arrived.

"Melody! Where have you two been?" he asked. "Everyone's been worried sick."

"Never mind where we've been," Cary said. "How is she? Can she talk?"

"I'm afraid not," the doctor said. "She's fallen into a coma."

Cary's shoulders sank. Then he brightened with a thought.

"Do you know about Laura?" he asked the Judge.

"What? What about Laura?"

337

"He doesn't know, Cary," I said. "She did tell me that."

"What's he talking about, Melody?" the Judge asked.

We went to the hospital cafeteria to get something to eat and I told my grandfather the story. He listened with horror.

"I guess I really never knew her," he said. "To keep all that from me. She was a very determined, private woman who literally needed no one. I'm sorry," he said to Cary. "I'll find out what you want to know. I promise," he said. "You two go home and get some rest. Let me take care of this."

"Thank you, Grandpa," I said and he smiled.

I went home with Cary to help him with Aunt Sara and May, after which we went up to his attic hideaway and fell asleep in each other's arms.

At the moment it seemed to be the safest place in the whole world.

# *Epilogue*
### ❧

Grandma Olivia died two days later, having never regained consciousness. Her doctor said it was a blessing because if she would have come out of the coma, she would have been far worse and Olivia Logan was not the sort of woman who could live under institutionalized care.

Cary didn't want to attend the funeral, but a strange thing happened to me. I suddenly saw things from Grandma Olivia's prospective. Why air our dirty laundry in public? Why embarrass the family?

"After all," I explained, "you still want to live and build a life here, Cary."

He listened and then shook his head with a smile.

"You were probably the right choice for Grandma Olivia's throne, Melody. I'll give the devil her credit there, but that's about all," he added firmly. "Okay, I'll put on the proper face. I see I'm going to need you to make sure I do the right things from now on," he kidded.

Kenneth and Holly had returned from their honeymoon and we had all spent a night together going over the recent events.

"She was a cold, hard woman, and so intimidating, most men didn't challenge her, especially the men in her family," Kenneth remarked. "I remember how afraid I was of her when I was younger and used to visit with Haille, Chester and Jacob. When she told us something, we did it and did it fast. I never thought of her as happy though."

"She didn't want anyone else to be happy either," Cary muttered.

None of us spoke. It was better to let the thunder and lightning play itself out and look forward to brighter skies.

The funeral was as large as expected. We decided not to have Grandpa Samuel brought along. He didn't understand what was happening and we all agreed it would be just more confusing and troublesome for him.

I don't know how I got through my final exams, but I did and my grades were as good as I had hoped. I stayed at Aunt Sara's and shut myself up in what had been Laura's room, spending almost two days writing and rewriting my valedictorian speech.

Since Grandma Olivia's hospitalization and death, I had moved in with Cary, Aunt Sara and May again. I hated the thought of being in that grand empty mansion, full of darkness, shadows and family secrets.

The Judge began to go over all the estate documents for us and one day, we all went to his home to listen to what would be. Grandma Olivia had done what she had promised . . . she had left instructions for my taking eventual control of most of the family fortune. In the meantime it was held in a trust supervised by her bankers and brokers and the Judge was appointed executor.

"You will have to decide about the house," he said. "You can put it up for sale or you can move into it."

"Let's put it up for sale," I said quickly. "I don't think it holds enough happy memories for the family."

"I understand," the Judge said.

With such a fortune in our hands, Cary could be confidant that his boat building business would be a reality. He could build on his small beginnings and establish his own company. Kenneth gave him advice and the two of them went searching the area for a good site to put up a factory.

The night before graduation, Cary and I took a walk on the beach. I was too nervous to sleep anyway. So much attention was on me and our family since Grandma Olivia's passing. I was nervous and sure the audience would hang on every word of my valedictorian address.

"Have you given thought to what you want to do, Melody?" Cary asked me. We stopped at the edge of the water and stared out at the moonwalk that led to the edge of the world.

"I'm not going to the prep school, Cary. The kind of life Grandma Olivia was designing for me is not the life I want for myself," I said. "I don't want to strive to get my name in the society columns."

"I know you're very smart and should probably go to college, but—"

"I don't want to go to college just to say I'm in college, Cary. Maybe I'll go next year. But somewhere close. I think I have a clear view of what I want now."

"What's that?" he asked turning to me.

"I want something simpler but more substantial. I want what I never had, Cary. I want a real family, real love."

"Could you have it with me? Now?" he asked timidly. "We could build this new business together and we could build our own house and we—"

I put my fingers on his lips.

"I was wondering when you would have the nerve to ask," I said and he laughed.

We kissed and held each other. The ocean seemed to glitter even more and the stars, the stars were never ever as bright.

The next day was magnificent. Without a cloud in the sky, with the wind warm and gentle, we were able to have an outdoor graduation ceremony. I began my speech with the first lines of a mountain song Papa George had taught me years and years ago.

> "I have come a long way from home with just
>   a hope and a prayer,
> But I got a suitcase full of memories to keep
>   me warm on lonely nights."

I turned to my fellow graduates and talked about graduation as a kind of pulling up on the anchor and setting sail—of being captains of our own destiny. We were leaving our parents, our friends and our teachers back on the shore and setting out on a course of our own making. I talked about courage and opportunity and thanked our families and teachers for giving it to us. I ended by singing the first line of *This Land Is Your Land* and an amazing thing happened: the whole audience joined me and sang the whole song.

I was overwhelmed by the applause and the congratulations afterward. People who didn't know me well told me how proud Grandma Olivia would have been. Cary's eyes grew dark and angry, but he kept his rage contained when I gave him a look of reprimand.

Afterward, we had a party at Aunt Sara's. Kenneth, Holly and Judge Childs were there, as well as Roy Patterson and Theresa. Cary made a clam bake and I played the fiddle. Judge Childs said he would take a piece of the graduation cake up to Grandpa Samuel the next day.

Cary and I set a date for our wedding soon afterward. In the meantime, I spent my summer days with May and Aunt Sara while Cary worked on the new boat and began to build the factory on the site he and Kenneth had found.

One morning May came in with the mail and waved something at me, all excited. It was a postcard. It had been sent from Palm Springs, California. There wasn't much written.

> Hi,
>     I just thought I'd drop you a line to tell you I'm no longer with Richard. I'm with a real agent this time. He's even taken me to Palm Springs for a holiday and he says I have a good chance of making it.
>     Wish me luck.
>
> Gina Simon

"Who's Gina Simon?" May signed and then pronounced as best she could.

"Just someone I once knew," I said. "No one, really."

I tossed the card into the garbage can, but later, I went back and retrieved it.

I couldn't help it. I was like someone lost on the desert who had been given a drop of water to cherish. What else could I do?

I went upstairs and put the letter with my other mementos.

And then I looked at Laura's bag of possessions, the only things left from her strange and tragic existence. Neither Cary nor I could get ourselves to do anything about them.

I couldn't just ignore them anymore, however. I reached in and took out the thick notebook which had been her diary. Then I went downstairs and sat behind the house in the big wooden chair that faced the ocean and I began to read.

*A long time ago, I lived a fairy tale life,* it began. My eyes lifted from the page as I took a deep breath.

Off in the distance a sailboat looked caught in the calm and remained painted against the blue horizon while above it, puffy white clouds waited for the same wind.

All the world was standing still, holding its breath. Even the terns froze on the beach and looked my way.

When the wind began again, it carried a song it wished I would sing for Laura, for Cary, for all of us.

I would sing it, I thought.

Now, finally, I would sing it.

POCKET
BOOKS

# The Logan Family Series
## THE NEW VIRGINIA ANDREWS®

# MELODY

### Book 1

Growing up in a small West Virginia mining town,
Melody Logan feels secure in her father's unwavering
love, despite her gorgeous mother's obvious
unhappiness. Then he is killed, and Melody's mother
wastes no time in dumping her at Cape Cod with her
father's family. Marooned among virtual strangers,
Melody is utterly alone. Her cousin Cary resents her for
using his dead twin sister's room and clothes, yet he
defends her when she is taunted at school.

And it is Cary who finally begins to reveal the truth
about Melody's parents – a sad, shocking story of defiant
love that only deepens her confusion. Yet Melody knew
nothing of the dark deceptions that would soon surface
. . . or of the devastating betrayals she would face before
she glimpsed the faint, beckoning lights of a safe
harbour.

**0 7434 9513 6**

**£6.99**

POCKET
BOOKS

## The Logan Family Series
### THE NEW VIRGINIA ANDREWS®

# HEART SONG

### Book 2

Left by her mother with her stepfather's relatives on Cape
Cod following his sudden death, Melody feels utterly
marooned. The wealthy, tight-lipped Logans harbour dark
secrets, and no one but their good-hearted son, Cary, will
breathe a word about them. Then her mother dies in a car
accident and Melody is left feeling more alone that ever.

Forced to live in a room and wear the clothes that
belonged to Cary's dead twin sister, Melody sometimes
feels she has no identity at all. She manages to escape
from the family by taking a summer job with Kenneth
Childs, whom she believes might be her real father. And
from the moment she learns that she and Cary aren't real
cousins, the tender affection she feels for him matures
into something much stronger. But although Cary has
pledged his love for her, she knows she cannot echo his
words until she discovers the buried truth about her past.

0 7434 9514 4

£6.99

POCKET
BOOKS

## The Logan Family Series
### THE NEW VIRGINIA ANDREWS®

# MUSIC IN THE NIGHT

### Book 4

For Laura Logan, life on Cape Cod with her beloved
twin brother, Cary, has been nearly perfect. Until the
vicious rumours begin at school – cruel voices saying
unspeakable things about the Logans. Not until
handsome, gentle Robert Royce moves to town does
Laura feel truly carefree and happy again. But while his
smile is driving the shadows from Laura's heart, she still
worries about Cary, whose gloomy moods drift in like
the coastal fog.

When the dark thunderclouds that have been gathering
on the horizon suddenly burst with tragedy, they howl
a name from the Logan's shameful past that plunges
Laura into a silent, terrible agony. Now Laura can only
dream of the warm, sun-filled life she so desperately
desires . . .

0 7434 9510 1

£6.99

POCKET
BOOKS

This book and other **Virginia Andrews** titles are available from your book shop or can be ordered direct from the publisher.

|  |  | **The Logan Family Series** |  |
|---|---|---|---|
| ☐ | 0 7434 9513 6 | Melody | £6.99 |
| ☐ | 0 7434 9514 4 | Heart Song | £6.99 |
| ☐ | 0 7434 9512 8 | Unfinished Symphony | £6.99 |
| ☐ | 0 7434 9510 1 | Music in the Night | £6.99 |
| ☐ | 0 7434 9511 X | Olivia | £6.99 |
|  |  | **The Hudson Family Series** |  |
| ☐ | 0 671 02964 9 | Rain | £6.99 |
| ☐ | 0 7434 0914 0 | Lightning Strikes | £6.99 |
| ☐ | 0 7434 0915 9 | Eye of the Storm | £6.99 |
| ☐ | 0 7434 0916 7 | End of the Rainbow | £6.99 |
|  |  | **The Wildflowers Series** |  |
| ☐ | 0 7434 4034 X | Wildflowers | £6.99 |
| ☐ | 0 7434 0444 0 | Into The Garden | £6.99 |

Please send cheque or postal order for the value of the book, free postage and packing within the UK; OVERSEAS including Republic of Ireland £1 per book.

**OR: Please debit this amount from my:**

VISA/ACCESS/MASTERCARD ..........................................

CARD NO .............................................. EXPIRY DATE ..............

AMOUNT £ ....................................................................

NAME.............................................................................

ADDRESS........................................................................

........................................................................................

SIGNATURE ...................................................................

Send Orders to SIMON & SCHUSTER CASH SALES
PO Box 29, Douglas Isle of Man, IM99 1BQ
www.bookpost.co.uk
Please allow 14 days for delivery.
Prices and availability subject to change without notice